Parlatheas Press Titles:

Mask of the Vampire

Chronicles of Damage, Inc.
Book 2

Stormy McDonald
Jason McDonald

Parlatheas Press, LLC
Hollywood, SC

Mask of the Vampire
    Copyright 2022 by Jason McDonald & Melanie McDonald

Characters and Setting:
    Property of Alan Isom, Jason McDonald, & Melanie McDonald

Parlatheas Press, LLC
P.O. Box 963
Hollywood, SC 29449-0963
https://mcdonald-isom.com

Note: This is a work of fiction. Names, characters, places, and incidents are either a product of the authors' imaginations or are used fictitiously. All situations and events in this publication are fictitious and any resemblance to actual persons, living or dead, or to businesses, companies, events, institutions, or locales is purely coincidental.

Cover & Interior Design: MJ Youmans-McDonald
Cover image from www.pixabay.com with some modifications
Title page border by user 3209107 from www.pixabay.com

ISBN: 978-1-7368235-1-4 (paperback)
ISBN: 978-1-958315-04-0 (hardback)

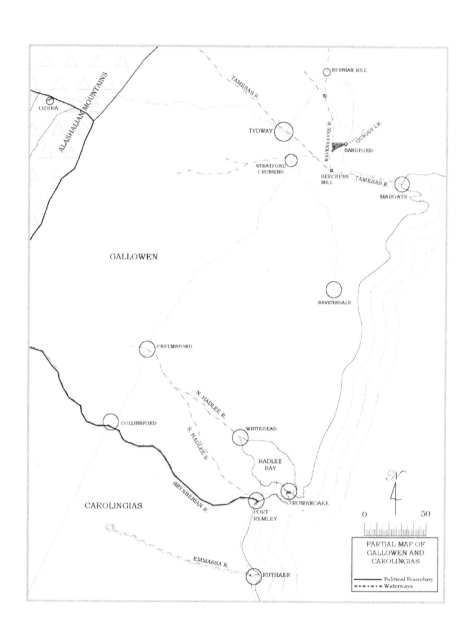

PARTIAL MAP OF
GALLOWEN AND
CAROLINGIAS

CAST OF CHARACTERS

(In Order of Appearance)

Hector de los Santos: An Espian bounty hunter and leader of Damage, Inc. Only a select few know he is from the world of Terra, rather than Gaia.

Aislinn Yves: A half-elven ranger. Damage, Inc.'s tracker and healer. Killed by a clockwork monster in the quarry outside Ruthaer. Hector sent her to the healers of Ozera, in the hope she could be resurrected.

Hummingbird: A young, empathic elf from the continent of Altaira and Dave's student. After she was injured by a clockwork monster, Hector sent her to the healers of Ozera.

Dave Blood: Damage, Inc.'s archer. A kinsman of Robert Stone. Like Hector, Dave is from the world of Terra, rather than Gaia.

Tealaucan Rathaera: Last Xemmassian flight-master on the continent of Parlatheas. Due to events in <u>Phantoms of Ruthaer</u>, his ghost possesses the body of Allyrian Carmichael.

Lady Lahar Aneirin: Countess Devon of Carolingias and Countess Colliford of Gallowen. Owner of the ship *Lady Luck*, and business partner of Lord Vaughn.

Lord Roger Vaughn: Earl Wolverton of Gallowen and Viscount Snowdon of Carolingias. Owner of the ships *Trinity* and *Phosphorus*, and business partner of Lady Aneirin.

Count Dodz: A Rhodinan nobleman and employee of "The Collectors," the power behind the government in the city of Erinskaya, Vologda.

Ymara Dapniš: A vampire slain by Damage, Inc. two and a half years ago on the continent of Altaira. Through means unknown, her essence was bound to a bone mask made from her skull.

Eidan Yves: The alter-ego of Brand, the bronze dragon who shares a soul-bond with Aislinn Yves. As Eidan, Brand takes on the form of an adult elven male with coppery hair and dark bronze eyes.

Xandor ap Kynan: Born into Clan Tanjara of the Alashalian Mountains, Gallowen's Iron Tower Corp trained him to be a ranger and forward scout. He is a childhood friend of Aislinn Yves and Brand.

Robert Stone: A swordsman and founding member of Damage, Inc., he is Dave Blood's kinsman. Robert arrived on Gaia from the world of Terra with Dave and Hector. He spent two years as a prisoner of Sha'iry priests before his friends managed to rescue him.

Jasper Thredd: A portly human mage who originally hailed from Tydway, capital of Gallowen. One of the founding members of Damage, Inc.

August Sabe: An exiled knight from Michurinsk, rumored to have fled his family in disgrace. He is a friend of Xandor and Damage, Inc.

Mi'dnirr: A dærganfae vampire of unknown age. Reputed to inhabit the Haunted Hills and rule the dærganfae there. He is credited with killing Evan Courtenay just outside Ruthaer.

Sister Inez: One of the senior clerics and Medicus Prima of Ozera. She is in charge of the hospital.

Phaedrus: The half-elf founder and leader of Ozera, referred to as "El Patrón" by the villagers.

Brother Simon: One of the senior clerics and Aerarium Praefectus of Ozera. He is in charge of the Aerarium and training clerics who catalogue and study dangerous artifacts.

Shayla Yves: Aislinn's mother. She lives in Ozera and serves as a midwife.

Anauriel: A one-eyed dærganfae from the Haunted Hills currently lurking in Ozera.

Gideon Maccabeus: a Francescan battle-cleric of l'Ordiné Fratres Maqebet who helped Damage, Inc. rescue Robert Stone from the Sha'iry.

Sister Georgiana: One of the senior clerics and Librarius of Ozera. In charge of the library and Simon's second-in-command of the Aerarium.

Sister Lorena: Armarius of Ozera, in charge of the scriptorium and gatekeeper of the library entrance to the Aerarium.

Sahmaht: A Parlathean lioness who befriended Xandor in the no-man's land between Trakya and the White River. (See The Cayn Trilogy, book 1: Son of Cayn)

In memory of Momma Chris, for whom nothing was more important than family. Although she left the mortal realm too soon, she remains a shining example of the love we should share with our family — both that of blood and of choice. She lives on in our hearts.

– Stormy & Jason

The hardest thing in life is to learn which bridge to cross and which to burn.

– David Russell

CHAPTER 1
LADY LUCK

August 12, 4237 K.E.

5:00am

Weak light from a single glow-stone did little to illuminate the roughhewn passage stretching before Hector, transforming the granite tunnel into a monstrous throat. Darkness clawed at the edges of his vision as he crept forward, scimitar held before him. A sinister metallic scrape pierced the silence, and his heart leapt into his throat. Raising his light higher, he sought the source of the sound, but it eluded him in the skittering shadows.

A dozen gangly-bodied gnomes with bulbous red eyes sprang from the gloom, wielding miniature crossbows covered in an array of silver wire and brass gears. A rain of dart-like quarrels filled the air. Hector put his back to a stalagmite, letting the bolts whiz past. Taking a deep breath, he charged, flashing his light into the grotto, but the diminutive attackers melted away like so many phantoms.

Behind him, Aislinn whispered, "What now, fearless leader?"

Hector glanced over his shoulder. Aislinn's almond-shaped eyes shone eerily in the darkness. The trust reflected there was a dagger in his heart. Beside her, Hummingbird peeked out from behind a chunk of pale feldspar. Her elven features were sharper than Aislinn's, tempered by her youth and fear. Guarding the rear, Dave hunkered down with a hawk's-head arrow nocked on his bowstring.

With every step inside the massive granite pluton, he grew more certain that they had walked into a trap. Someone once said, 'retreat is the better part of valor' — or perhaps it was 'discretion' — but he couldn't remember who. He half turned, intending to flee the cavern and tunnels, when a child's cry pierced the shadows.

Aislinn laid a hand on Hector's shoulder and said, "Lead the way." Her soft words echoed weirdly, answered by another scrape of metal on stone.

Swallowing against the dryness in his throat, he gave Aislinn a curt nod and pursued the fleeing gnomes. The lightless heart of the granite dome shivered and shifted around them, suddenly revealing the lip of a yawning chasm. Off to one side, the floor sloped under the far ledge, leading down into a stygian chamber. As Hector descended, his fingernails bit into his palm around the hilt of his scimitar.

Shadows surged, and small arms clutched at Hector's legs and waist. He looked down into the milky white eyes of gnome children. Their hungry mouths gaped open, revealing jagged yellow teeth and blackened tongues. Bloody tears streaked their dirty faces.

From behind him, Dave yelled, "NO!"

Hector spun around. Easily twelve feet high, the freakish offspring of a spider and a praying mantis loomed above them. Joints in its chitinous armor gave off a dull orange glow, as if coals burned within its matte black body. Its faceted black diamond eyes shimmered with an inner light.

Impaled on the end of its articulated foreleg, Aislinn hung like a ragdoll. The creature drew her closer to its dripping mandibles. Malevolent fire within its eyes blazed brighter, and Aislinn's sword slipped from nerveless fingers.

Time slowed.

Hummingbird's scream tore through the air as one of the creature's spear-like legs pierced her shoulder.

Dave's black arrow slammed into the creature's mouth.

The clockwork insect's foreleg uncurled, and Aislinn's lifeless body slid to the cavern floor.

Bolting upright, Hector drew in a ragged breath. Sweat plastered his black hair to his forehead and neck. Sounds from the memory-fueled nightmare echoed in his head. He smelled the metallic tang of blood.

Yanking the bedsheet from his legs, he rolled off the cot into a shaft of moonlight from the ship cabin's tiny round porthole. Adrenaline pounded in his veins. He needed something to break. Instead, he screamed at the world, giving it all his loss, rage, and hatred as he drove his fist against the hull. The prickling sting of the mysterious magic in his blood healing his busted knuckles amplified the discord in his soul. He pounded his fists against the boards again and again, until both hands were swollen and bleeding.

His rage slaked, Hector dropped onto his bunk and rested his forehead in his palm. The pain of losing Aislinn filled his chest with a heaviness that made it hard to breathe.

Trembling fingers clutched his gold and silver crucifix — the last remnant of his former life on Terra. Everything else had been taken away or lost during his six years in Gaia.

"Santa María, Madre de Dios, ruega por nosotros pecadores, ahora y en la hora de nuestra muerte," he prayed. "Hail, Mary, full of grace, I stand before you, sinful and sorrowful; despise not my petitions, but in thy clemency hear me. Please watch over Tallinn and Brand. Help them reach Ozera in time to save Hummingbird. Holy Mother, I beg you: beseech the Eternal Father to show mercy. Please... *Please,* restore Aislinn to life and health." Crossing himself, he whispered "Amén" and kissed the crucifix to seal the prayer.

It had been a week since Aislinn's death. After the dust settled in Ruthaer, Hector, Dave, and Teal had been "politely transferred" to Countess Devon's ship, *Lady Luck.* Sailing north, they'd left the Carolingian coastal village far behind them. He hadn't looked back.

The past three days they'd traveled the open sea with no sight of land. During that time, the bounty hunter had volunteered for every task the ship's bosun would give him, hoping exhaustion would numb him into a stupor. However, his subconscious wasn't so easily tricked, and each time he slept, the memory filled his nightmares. There were so many things they... HE... could have done differently that day. So many things had been left unsaid. Hector held on to the fragile hope Aislinn would return when Phaedrus called her. He sighed and rubbed the grit from his eyes with the damp sheet.

Faint grey light of false dawn cautiously entered the cabin. The caravel rocked gently in the ocean's swells, bringing him back to the present.

Ahead lay the Tamesas River, which led to Tydway, the capital city of Gallowen. There, he intended to collect their friend, Jasper Thredd, from the Academia de Artes Magicae before continuing into the mountains to Ozera.

His thoughts turned to Lord Vaughn, Earl Wolverton of Gallowen and Viscount Snowdon of Carolingias. Hector wondered why the nobleman had agreed to help them. True, Damage, Inc. had stopped the ghūl, Evan Courtenay, from using an ancient relic called the Orbuculum to turn Ruthaer into a permanent gate to the aethereal world, but there was more to it. Repeatedly over the past few days, he had caught Lord Vaughn watching them.

Hector's gaze settled on the other side of the narrow cabin. Dave Blood sprawled across a second cot, sleeping with his unstrung longbow nestled against his side like a lover. One hand clutched his ever-present flask. Bandages covered a deep cut on his left forearm and ugly bite wounds on his shoulder and side, inflicted by Evan's undead revenants. Along his chest and arms, a rainbow of bruises warred with the archer's tattoos for dominance. His body glistened under the salve the ship's chirurgeon had administered after pronouncing it a miracle the archer still lived. It made the whole cabin smell like menthol and camphor.

Incongruous with his tattoo and bruise covered torso and arms, Dave wore a gold necklace loaned to him by Aislinn the night before their ill-fated excursion to Ruthaer's quarry. Its Elven-crafted links, fashioned in the shape of oak leaves joined tip to stem, bore a silver brooch inlaid with a balas-ruby the size of a grape. A black hairline fracture marred the gem's heart. As unreliable as it was, it was the only protection the archer had against the mind-controlling influence of the vampire they dubbed Lady D — a creature Hector thought destroyed over two years ago. Somehow, Lady D had continued to influence Dave, giving him mental nudges, and driving him deeper and deeper into the bottle. It had come to a head in Ruthaer when the sorceress, Consuelo, had used Lady D's powers against them while wearing a rune-marked bone mask.

Ghost-white scars glared at Hector from Dave's neck, shoulders, and upper arms. The thick whirls and loops of Elven tribal markings and Gaelic knotwork tattoos had once hidden the scars, but Lady D's power had revealed them.

The events at Ruthaer still baffled Hector. True, he was no expert, but it just didn't add up. Vampires were undead — soulless, animated corpses like ghūls or zombies — which could be destroyed by decapitation or fire. Yet Lady D was different. As near as he could gather from Dave, her essence inhabited the bone mask currently hidden aboard their skiff, cradled in a sling above the *Lady Luck's* starboard rail.

Hector doubted he'd ever learn how the sorceress had obtained Lady D's skull.

Dave slept on, left arm flung over his eyes, and a foot resting on the floor to ward off dizziness. The previous night, Hector had left Dave on deck, teaching Teal to sing "Blow the Man Down" while they passed his flask between them. Dave's ability to sleep — both without apparent nightmares and through Hector's venting — meant he'd managed to get well-and-truly tanked before crawling into bed.

A sharp rap sounded at their cabin door. Hector pulled on a semi-clean tunic and ran his hands through his shoulder length hair, tying it back in a queue before padding to the door on bare feet.

"¿Sí?" Hector opened the door a crack. A bald marine waited outside. Over his dark red tunic, the guard wore a wide baldric that wrapped around his barrel chest and fed into a leather frog, where a gleaming cutlass hung at his side. Behind him stood Taddy, a lad of no more than fourteen summers and the *Lady Luck*'s youngest crewman, holding a covered tray. The smell of kahve and warm toast drifted into the cabin.

"Everything alright in there?" asked the marine, trying to catch a glimpse of the room behind Hector.

"Sí," Hector replied. "¿Qué pasa?"

"Sorry to disturb you, sir. We heard shouting."

"That was me. No hay ningún problema." Turning to the boy, Hector said, "Muchacho, is that our breakfast?"

"Yes, sir," Taddy said, nudging past the marine, "and a message from the captain."

"What time is it?"

"Third watch, sir," the marine replied. "It's just past two bells. Sun will be up shortly. You sure there's nothing going on in there?"

Hector grimaced, opening the door enough to take the tray. He noted the sailor's scrutiny of his hands, but all that remained of the damage he'd done to them were fading bruises. "Thank you, we're fine. I stubbed my toe, that's all."

"Sure," said the marine. "Let us know if you need a leech."

Hector cut a glance toward the sailor, wondering if he was joking. After handing off the tray, Taddy saluted and scurried away with his escort in tow. Hector elbowed the door closed and sat the tray atop a narrow table with an upturned lip around its perimeter.

A shuttered lantern hung from a ring in the central beam, its polished brass fittings reflecting the porthole's meager light. He slid open a single panel, revealing a glowing milky quartz crystal, which spilled soft light across the floor and table. Munching on a triangle of toast and jam, Hector read the captain's note.

"Dave." He nudged the tall, lanky archer, but received no response. He called the archer's name again, louder, with the same result. A kick to his foot set Dave to snoring, and the sound rattled the cabin. Hector's mouth compressed in a grim line. He knew one sure way to wake the archer, but he'd rather return to Fangpoint Lighthouse and steal food from one of the brown bears who shared the island with the sea ranger, Tallinn. At least the bear would kill him quickly.

Bracing himself, Hector reached across the narrow bunk and pinched the neck of Dave's flask. He breathed in and out, then snatched the container and lunged away in one motion.

He almost made it.

Dave's red-rimmed eyes snapped open as his free hand caught Hector's wrist in a vice-like grip.

"Amigo, it's me."

The archer blinked hard a few times. His grip relaxed, and he struggled upright. "Dammit, Hector. What the hell?" One elbow on his knee and forehead in hand, he groped blindly for the flask.

"The captain sent for us."

"What the fuck does he want?"

"We're in Mersea Bay. If the wind holds, we'll reach the port at Margate within the hour and stop for supplies before heading upriver to Tydway. Lady Aneirin wants to speak to us beforehand." Hector pulled on his boots. "I'm going to find Teal. Meet us on deck." He stepped out into the passageway, then leaned back through the door and fixed Dave with a piercing stare. "We have toast and kahve for breakfast. Be sure you put something in your belly besides that rotgut you've been drinking."

CRSO

5:25am

On deck, Hector surveyed the triple-masted cargo ship. At the prow, the ship's busty figurehead held aloft a tall copper lantern. Inside its glass panes, a coil of fine silver wire tethered a thick spike of quartz to the lantern's cap and base. Similar lanterns hung from the lowest yardarms and a final pair capped lamp posts sprouting from the corners of the aft deck. Sails in varying shades of grey gave the impression of storm clouds hovering just overhead.

Above the sails, at the tip of the mainmast, a triple barred flag fluttered in the morning breeze. When they set sail from Ruthaer, the *Lady Luck* had displayed the Carolingian flag with its silver dogwood and green hill, all on a blue field. This morning, the ship flew Gallowen's standard. The Highlord's personal crest of a rampant gold dragon occupied the central field of white, flanked on the halyard side by an argent tower on a black field to represent the order of the Iron Tower, and on the fly end by a golden owl on a green field to represent the order of the Horned Owls.

On the mizzenmast flew a solid black flag with a stylized ship's compass in white and the motto, "Ante Ferit Quam Flamma Micet," the standard of the ship's owner, Lady Lahar Aneirin, Countess Devon of Carolingias and Countess Colliford of Gallowen.

Their first day aboard, Teal had translated the motto for Hector: "Strike Before the Flame Glimmers." To Hector, the flag and its motto seemed more appropriate for a pirate than a noblewoman. Still, he had to concede there was an air of menace about the half-elven countess.

Hector spotted Tealaucan Rathaera, last Xemmassian flight-master in Parlatheas, leaning against the starboard rail where it met the forecastle, watching the eastern sky change colors. Bits of twine and scraps of ribbon fluttered at the ends of several dozen braids binding the teen's long golden locks in cornrows. Teal turned at his approach, and he had to do a double take. Soft lips, lustrous amethyst eyes, and wondrous curves graced a body most men would kill to touch. However, Hector had seen glimpses of the male half-dragon ghost who currently possessed the body once belonging to Allyrian Carmichael of Ruthaer, and it was difficult to reconcile the two.

Today, she — no, *HE*, Hector reminded himself — he wore a tunic and breeches donated by Jared, one of Ruthaer's guardsmen, after Teal refused to wear a dress. Even so, many of the sailors on deck took notice of Teal's figure limned in the predawn light. If only they knew what Hector knew.

"I like the braids," Hector said by way of greeting.

Teal nodded and gestured toward a group of ebony-skinned sailors mending ropes. "Yon women from the south Karukera Sea took pity 'pon me and bound my hair whilst sharing songs and drink with Dave." He frowned. "'Twas wondrous strange. Crewmen proffered colorful bits of ribbon as though expecting praise for the gesture."

Hector grinned. "Don't tell me you don't recognize tokens of affection when they're offered." He laughed at the shocked dismay on Teal's face. "They see a pretty young woman when they look at you, remember?"

"Would that I could change mine appearance to match my true self."

Hector studied the young woman, wondering how people would react to a seven-foot tall, bronze-scaled man with reptilian facial features.

The sky brightened. Any moment now, the sun would breach the horizon. Joining Teal at the railing, Hector drew a lungful of salty air, and let it out slowly. "You ever see the green flash?"

"Aye, once. 'Tis an evil omen."

Hector cocked his head to one side. "I heard it was good luck."

"I saw it the day mine brother led an army 'gainst our home."

"The brother you killed?"

Teal nodded. "Aye, the very same. On that day, the Dark One's foul hordes did destroy all I loved, and I was doomed to relive the battle countless times o'er the endless centuries." He fell silent, searching the horizon while a gentle breeze teased his braids. The fiery rim of the sun broke the ocean's surface, and the tension drained from his feminine shoulders. "I must needs ask thee something."

Hector raised an eyebrow and waited.

Teal turned his back on the sunrise, and scanned the deck, noting the position of each person there. "What was Allyrian Carmichael?"

Hector's brow furrowed. "Ruthaer's constable said she was a spoiled chit, but you saw the eviscerated hearts on her mantlepiece, and the blood-caked tub in her bedroom. I found bare, bloody footprints that looked an awful lot like hers at the monastery where the monks were slaughtered, and the gnome children from the quarry insisted she murdered their parents."

"An thou didst believe me to be this evil wench when you pursued me from Ruthaer's chapel, wherefore didst thou not seek retribution?"

Hector leaned on the railing, watching the waves roll by. That day on the riverfront, he had held his dagger to her throat, but when she spoke in the language of dragons, a spark of hope stayed his hand. That single moment of restraint had saved his and Dave's lives the next day. They never would have escaped the so-called authorities from Rowanoake without Teal's knowledge of the secret doors and passages within Ruthaer's barrier islands. "At the time, I meant to but, in hindsight, I'm glad I didn't," he answered. "We needed your help."

Teal remained quiet. The sun rose higher, silhouetting a flight of pelicans skimming the water.

"Why did you ask about Allyrian?"

"I dreamt of her yestereve," said Teal. "Perhaps I did imbibe overmuch from Dave's wondrous flask, but 'twas not the first time I did see her in my sleep." He paused, gathering his thoughts. "The last time I endured the fall of mine people, fog did enshroud the Praesidium and the sea. Ne'er before was I aware we did replay a battle already lost three millennia past. On that day, I realized we were but phantoms, yet I could do naught to change mine actions. After I slew my traitorous brother, we fell from the skies above the Praesidium. Green light flared from the horizon as I entered the fog. Rather than strike the sea as I had countless times before, I woke in the forest. The sound of coursing hounds rang through the trees..." He gestured at his slender form. "I found this child lying in a grove, bloodied and all but dead, horror etched 'pon her countenance."

All expression dropped from Hector's face, leaving a blank mask. "She was wounded?"

"Aye. Upon either side of her spine, the skin was rent, exposing hollow wing sockets."

"Was she a demon?" Hector's voice was soft, but it held a dangerous edge. Visions of the demoness who served Consuelo, the sorceress who escaped Damage, Inc. five months earlier, came to mind. Through a twisted turn of events, Consuelo died helping Hector and Dave save Ruthaer, but they never found her demon. Up to this moment, Hector had assumed the succubus had fled.

Teal shrugged. "I cannot say for certain, but the air did carry a hint of brimstone. At the time, I thought it came from the beast which did attack her."

"It may be nothing, but you weren't wounded when the village guards found you. Not even a bump on your head."

"I only know what I saw," Teal replied.

"Was there anything else? Did the girl have horns or a tail?"

Teal started to answer, but the forecastle hatch banged open, and Dave stalked out on deck.

His back to the approaching archer, Hector warned, "Don't mention these dreams to anyone else — especially not Dave. He has enough on his plate. We'll talk more when we reach Tydway. I know someone who may be able to offer some insight on how to get you back into your own form. In the meantime, if you feel the urge to do anything you normally wouldn't, you let me know."

Dave joined them and leaned against the rail. Shielding his eyes with his hand, he peered out over the horizon. "It's too fucking bright out here."

"You drink too much," Hector said.

"Go to hell."

"I'm already there," Hector grumbled.

A sharp whistle pierced the air, eliciting a flinch from both Dave and Teal. "All hands fall to!" shouted the bosun. Men and women poured from companionways and scrambled down the rigging to form orderly ranks on deck. Only the helmsman and the lookout in the crow's nest remained at their posts.

Captain Smeyth strode across the deck, sporting a brilliant turquoise calico jacket with bright gold buttons.

Thick bunches of snowy lace spilled from his collar and sleeve cuffs. Blousy black breeches, white hose, and shiny leather shoes with gold buckles completed his ensemble. He tugged at one sleeve, eyed the ranks of sailors, and bellowed, "Stand ready for inspection! Admiral on deck!"

The door to the aft cabins opened, and Lady Lahar Aneirin stepped forth. Just shy of six feet tall, she stood eye-to-eye with the captain. Despite being announced as the ship's Admiral, she was not in Naval uniform. Instead, she wore a long crimson shirt, cinched at the waist by a wide weapon belt, over sturdy brown canvas pants and polished boots. A broad brimmed cavalier hat with a huge black ostrich plume perched atop lustrous mahogany hair, leaving the pointed tips of her ears exposed. Dark, almond shaped eyes seemed to drink in the morning light as they swept over the crew and their passengers. She walked among the sailors, speaking softly to each in turn.

Dave muttered a curse.

Hector pulled his attention from the countess and her crew to find the latest source of ire for the archer. Lord Roger Vaughn sauntered over to join Hector, Dave, and Teal. Although he'd dressed casually over the past three days in simple tunics and cotton breeches, today he wore a pale silk shirt and a black-on-black brocade vest. Despite the finery of the shirt and vest, his leather pants and boots were more practical work and travel attire.

A glint of light drew Hector's eye to the nobleman's chest, where a platinum chain supported an ornate medallion with a sparkling blue sapphire. Inset in the gem's surface, silver filigree formed a stylized mountain-top rising above waves.

Dave's gaze fixed upon the necklace. Cold tension emanated from the archer, and his hands curled into fists.

Hector shifted a half-step toward a section of pinrail. He didn't know what upset Dave, but he feared things were about to turn ugly.

"Good morning," Lord Vaughn greeted the trio at the rail. When only Hector nodded in return, the older gentleman quirked an eyebrow at Dave and Teal. "Too much revelry last night?"

"Whatever it takes to lay our personal demons to rest for a few hours, Milord," Hector replied. "Otherwise, we'd never get any sleep."

"Perhaps," the nobleman said, locking eyes with Dave, "but alcohol is a demon, too. Believe me, I know its treachery all too well."

"It's the lesser of evils, for the time being, señor," replied Hector. "I prefer to deal with one catastrophe at a time, when I can. Reaching Ozera with the Orbuculum from Ruthaer is near the top of my list." Neither Lord Vaughn nor Dave seemed to hear the bounty hunter.

Dave advanced toward the nobleman and demanded, "Where did you get that locket?"

Roger reached up and touched the medallion's surface. "This belonged to my wife."

"No, it didn't, asshole," Dave said loudly, drawing the attention of everyone on deck. "Where did you steal it?"

Lord Vaughn and the archer glared at one another, their expressions identical. Realization swept over Hector, and he suddenly knew why the nobleman had joined them on their journey from Ruthaer to Tydway.

Out of the corner of his eye, Hector saw the captain throw a questioning glance toward Lady Aneirin. Her face pinched, she gave him a quick shake of her head.

Dave took another step closer to the nobleman, raising his fists.

Keeping his arms by his side, Lord Vaughn seemed relaxed, but his gaze never left Dave's.

Quick as a snake, Dave pivoted at the hip and swung a powerful right cross.

Lord Vaughn was quicker. Knees bent, Roger shifted his weight back and to the left, letting Dave's fist slip past. Shifting side to side, he backed away. "This locket was my wedding present to Bryony. Fighting me won't change the truth, Clement."

"Oh, *no*," Hector muttered.

With a snarl, Dave leapt forward.

Lord Vaughn spun, letting him go by. Off balance, Dave stumbled and went down in a sloppy roll. Roger waited for the archer to recover.

Dave jumped to his feet, turned, and threw a left jab, followed by a right hook. Each time, his target slipped and rolled out of the way with the barest of movements. Dave settled into a fighting stance and probed with a series of left jabs.

"Dave, are you sure you want to do this?" Hector asked. "*Él es tu padre.*"

"Shut up," Dave snapped. Sweat beaded on the archer's forehead, and it was apparent three days of solid drinking had taken their toll.

"We should talk about this when you're sober," Roger said.

With a huff, Dave gave Lord Vaughn a final scowl, then stalked away to his cabin.

Hector said, "Teal, go after him. Make sure he doesn't set anything on fire."

"Aye, sir," he replied before dashing off.

Roger leaned against the rail beside Hector. "How long have you known?"

"That you're Dave's father? I was certain about thirty seconds before he took his first swing, although I suspected the two of you might be related during our dinner aboard the *Trinity*."

Behind them, Captain Smeyth bellowed, "Alright, ye dogs, back to work!"

Roger let out a low sigh. "I wish that had gone better."

Turning to Roger, Hector said, "Señor, you provoked him. He hates being called Clement and hasn't used that name since we arrived in Rowanoake six years ago."

Lady Aneirin seemed to materialize from Lord Vaughn's shadow. "He's right, Roger," she said.

"I don't see how this is my fault," Roger protested.

Giving Lord Vaughn a stern look, Lady Aneirin said, "Try harder. You shouldn't have worn Brie's medallion where everyone could see it."

"I had to be sure who he really is, Lahar."

"Phaedrus tried to tell you. Besides the fact that he looks like you and Brie, how many Terran boys named Clement Tyler could there possibly be?"

"I have a lot of enemies, Lahar. Someone claiming to be Clement after all these years... I expected a trap."

"Roger, you can't treat your son like an enemy spy and expect positive results. If you two can't resolve this, I'll confine you both to your cabins. Do not disrupt this ship again."

Roger gave her a quick, apologetic nod.

His eyes still focused on the forward cabins, Hector asked, "How far is it from Margate to Tydway?"

"That depends on the wind and the tide," Lord Vaughn replied, "but if all goes well, we'll reach Tydway in two days. My home is just west of the city. We can spend the night there, gather our gear, and make an early start the next day for Ozera."

"Two days," Hector mused. He shook his head and said, "Milady, you might as well confine Dave. He won't be sober, much less rational, for at least a week."

"I think it's ill advised to take him to Blaiðwyn Hall, Roger. Not now," said Lady Aneirin.

"Lahar, I've already lost fifteen years. I need him to understand what happened, why I wasn't there to protect him and his mother."

"Señor, Lady Aneirin is right. To be honest, you shouldn't plan on riding with us to Ozera, either. It will only make Dave more belligerent."

"It's my duty to see that the Orbuculum reaches Ozera without incident," replied Lord Vaughn. "Us traveling together is the safest option. Having an opportunity to get to know my son is a bonus."

Hector shook his head. "Dave is stubborn. You aren't going to win him over by yourself. You'll need help from a friend of ours, Robert Stone. He's the only one Dave listens to when he gets like this."

"If I let Clem... *Dave* ride away when we reach Tydway, will I ever see him again? Will he ever give us the chance to get to know one another?"

"I don't know, señor. Dave tends to avoid everything about his past, and you won't win him over by pushing him."

"Damned if I do, damned if I don't," muttered Roger.

An uneasy silence settled over the trio.

"When we reach Tydway, I'll need to visit the Academia Magicae," said Hector, thinking of Teal and the vampire's mask.

"We heard you had a mage on your team of hunters," said Lady Aneirin.

Hector nodded. "Jasper Thredd. He's been teaching for the past year or so. I need to let him know what happened in Ruthaer. He'll want to travel with us to Ozera."

"What about Robert Stone?" asked Lord Vaughn. "Where is he?"

Hector rubbed his thumb over the platinum signet ring on his right hand, embossed with a dagger-pierced globe — the emblem of Damage, Inc. The ring's magic blossomed, allowing Hector to discern the direction of its five mates. He ignored Dave's ring. The next closest was Jasper in Tydway, then two more, belonging to Aislinn and her dragon-brother, Brand, clustered to the west in Ozera. The final ring, Robert's, was farther west, somewhere in the Detchian territories.

A cloud swept in front of the sun, stealing the morning's warmth. "I can't say for certain where Robert will be at any given time. He's constantly on the move. Two years as a prisoner of the Dark One's Sha'iry changed him, and he's still trying to sort it out. If you want Robert's help with Dave, we should be able to get a message to him through the church."

"Have faith," Lady Aneirin replied. "The Eternal Father works in his own time, according to his greater plan, though we can only see it in retrospect." Her Elven accent lent the words a musical lilt. "What about the other member of your team, Eidan Yves?" she asked.

"He should already be in Ozera waiting for us." Hector avoided mentioning Brand. As far as he knew, only Damage, Inc., Aislinn's mother, Shayla, and the half-elven priest, Phaedrus, knew the dragon's inherent magic allowed him to shapeshift into an elf. To the rest of the world, the copper-haired elf called Eidan was Aislinn's brother.

Lahar gave the bounty hunter a shark's smile — all teeth and no warmth. "Before we make port, I want you and your friends down in the hold. That surly beast you call a horse broke free of its stall again, released your other horses, and bit a crewman. While you're down there, the stalls need mucking. When you're done with that, you can go ashore to purchase grain."

"Aye, aye, Almirante," Hector replied with a jaunty salute.

CHAPTER 2
MARGATE

August 12, 4237 K.E.

7:15am

Teal worked a currycomb through the tangled mane of Dave's strawberry roan gelding. Behind him in the next stall, a dapple grey of similar size and build munched contentedly on its portion of grain. This was the flight-master's first time dealing with horses, and he found the experience of grooming the creatures soothing.

Across the aisle, the third horse, a buckskin stallion whose coat shimmered like spun gold, impatiently eyed his human. Hector dumped a shovelful of wet straw and manure in a narrow wheelbarrow and shook a finger at the horse. "Caballo, stay in your stall. Two more days and you get out of jail, but if I hear about you biting anyone else, I'll let the ship's cook serve you to the crew for supper."

"How long hast thou known Caballo?" Teal asked.

"Feels like forever," Hector muttered. Straightening, he rested his hands on the end of his shovel. "He and I have put up with each other for four years now — four long, cursed years."

"You sound like bond-mates."

With shocked expressions on their faces, Hector and Caballo backed away from one another despite the cramped quarters, and Teal had to fight to keep from laughing.

"We should get the hell off this ship," Dave growled from the aisle.

"Be patient," Hector said. "We'll be in Tydway tomorrow night. Besides, it would take longer if we rode." He sighed and scraped the last of the muck from the hold floor. "Come with Teal and me into Margate to buy grain. We can visit a fletcher for arrow parts."

Dave shook his head. "Can't leave the skiff unattended in port."

"You're being paranoid, Dave. No one's going to steal Lady D's mask."

"Says you. Dodz is still out there."

Teal stopped brushing the gelding's mane and asked, "Is the spirit in the mask named Lady D or Ymara? Thou hath called it both."

Dave hissed and made a sign against evil.

"We call her Lady D after a Terran prince who sold his soul for the power to destroy his enemies," Hector replied. "Legends claim the Dark One turned him into a vampire. The other name, which Dave and I will thank you to not repeat, is a title. It means 'princess' in Deshretan, and it's what *she* wants to be called — which is why we don't. No need to draw her attention by using a name or title she associates with herself."

"I see," Teal replied, but his confused expression belied his words. "Perhaps 'twould be best to keep the mask close at hand where this Count Dodz cannot steal it."

"No one touches the mask." Dave reached to the gold necklace at his throat and rubbed a dirty thumb over its balas-ruby brooch. "It's too dangerous."

"I agree," Hector said. "We'll keep the vampire's mask hidden on the skiff until we can buy a warded lockbox in Tydway." He turned to Dave. "Come with us today and take a break from the *Lady Luck* and Señor Vaughn. Hovering over the skiff will attract attention to it. Do you want Lady Aneirin or her crew wondering what we're hiding?"

Dave stiffened and growled something incoherent.

"What was that?" Hector asked.

"Nothing."

"If you do stay aboard, at least offer Lord Vaughn a truce. Trust me, he wants you two to be friends."

"Bullshit," Dave coughed into his fist.

"Amigo, take the time to get to know him. He's a good man. When William Howard and his band of pirates kidnapped you, Lord Vaughn didn't hesitate to rouse his troops to rescue you and Teal. Lady Aneirin wouldn't be helping us if it weren't for him. Plus, they're both excellent contacts for us to have in Gallowen and Carolingias. Between the two of them, we might finally have an end to our troubles with Rowanoake."

"Keep dreaming," Dave grumbled. He gripped the wheelbarrow handles and made his way to the center of the hold, where a block and tackle system waited to raise a cargo platform to the main deck.

❧❧

9:30am

Hector and Teal made their way along Margate's waterfront. Overhead, the cries of gulls played tumultuous counterpoint to the stevedores' work songs. Crates and barrels lined the docks, ready to be loaded onto ships or carried to warehouses via flatbed wagons. Here and there, ragged children begged for coins and ran errands. The scent of food drifted from pubs, competing with brine and the reek of ordure.

"How do humans live midst this foulness?" Teal demanded.

"The same way rats and gulls do — by snatching a meal where they can," answered Hector.

A filthy old man with a dirty bandage over his eyes crouched in the shadow of a building, a tin cup in his hands. "Alms!" he called out as they drew near.

Ahead of Teal and Hector, Lady Aneirin and the two sailors flanking her ignored the beggar and entered the customs house.

Teal slowed. "Why does this blind man beg? Whence are his kinsmen to care for him?"

"Keep walking," Hector murmured, gripping Teal's elbow and propelling him down the street. "That's neither an old man, nor is he blind. He makes his trade gathering information. The local thieves' master and at least one member of the city council will know Lady Aneirin's every move while she's in town, along with everything they can learn about us."

Teal cast a furtive glance over his shoulder. A scruffy street urchin darted away from the beggar into an alley.

"Beggars and thieves are nothing new," Hector commented. "How is it you've never seen either?"

"Amongst my people, everyone worked and contributed in some way," said Teal. "Families cared for the orphaned and infirm. As for humans, I had no cause to go amongst the villagers of Eibhir, where Ruthaer now lies, nor to the larger settlements. Mine and Tarnillis' task was to guard the Praesidium and the coast against predators from the sea."

"Tell me about Tarnillis. Was she your dragon?"

"I did love her from my youth," Teal said softly, and his gaze grew distant. "She was most beauteous, with lustrous scales and graceful form. None could match her fierce spirit or wondrous wit. The day she did assent to bond with me, I thought my heart should burst from happiness, but 'twas naught compared to the day she chose me for her mate."

Hector blinked in surprise. "Was... was that a common occurrence among dragons and riders?"

"Nay. 'Twas forbidden, but we were young and foolish and in love." Teal glanced at the bounty hunter. "I can see in thy face thou dost wonder how our love could be."

"Maybe a little, but Tarnillis could alter her form, right? Why was your relationship forbidden?"

"Aye, she could, but how did you know this? Dost thou know of a living dragon who can?"

Hector nodded. "I know one. Is it uncommon?"

"It was in my time," replied Teal. "Only the Tenné — those you call bronze dragons — who were faithful to the god Xardus were gifted with the ability to alter their form. Long before my birth, the Council of Elders in Revakhun Toaglen, the birthplace of the first dragons, judged my people to be abominations. The Tenné were sundered into two factions — those bound to the Xemmassians by Xardus' will, and those who rejected Xardus. The Council of Elders cast out the Xemmassians and the Tenné who were our kith and kin."

Following directions he received from the *Lady Luck*'s bosun, Hector turned left onto a broad thoroughfare lined with shops. Two blocks ahead, shoppers thronged the entrance to the market. "Let me guess," he said. "The ones who rejected Xardus were allowed to stay in Revakhun Toaglen."

"Yes. We believed 'twas jealousy at the root of our exile. You see, none of the other races of dragons nor the Tenné who rejected Xardus received the gift of shape changing. 'Twas a source of great friction.

"The Tenné who served Xardus sought to mend the rift with their distant brethren but faced obstacles at every turn. The Council imposed strictures upon us, our interactions with other races, and our very purpose for being. They forbade the mating of dragon and Xemmassian, on pain of death, when my sire was but a hatchling. They even attempted to forbid our bonds to one another.

"When war erupted betwixt Xardus and Sutekh, the Council refused to defend us against the Dark One's followers. They would not even broker a truce betwixt Tenné and Obsianus. Gules and Glacies joined the cause of Obsianus, and, with mine brother's betrayal, the Xemmassians and our dragon kindred were annihilated."

Teal fell silent, and Hector thought of the ghosts he'd seen in the aether while in Ruthaer. Dragons, the half-dragon Xemmassians, humanoids, and other things for which he had no name battled in the ghostly fog. Until Teal revealed hidden doorways in the cliffs, Hector would never have guessed there had ever been a settlement of any kind atop or within those barrier islands.

In the market, Hector was occupied with purchasing grain for his horses, treating Teal to meat pastries, and helping the flight-master purchase a change of clothes. After a considerable amount of searching, Hector found a fletcher willing to sell him arrow shafts and two dozen brilliant red pinions from a Pandarian fire swan for fletching. The bounty hunter had given up hope of finding Dave any black vulture feathers when he and Teal happened past a shop with elaborate masquerade costumes on display. Several minutes of haggling later, the shopkeeper consented to sell Hector nine black quills at twice the price he paid for the exotic swan feathers.

On the street and headed back to the harbour, his thoughts returned to Aislinn, Brand, and the bond they shared. "Teal, tell me about the soul-bond."

"What dost thou wish to know?"

"How does it work? I mean, could a dragon bond with anyone? What happened if the bonded pair decided to go their separate ways — could they sever the bond?"

Teal smiled. "Thou art most inquisitive today. Very well. There was a rite, sacred among my people, called the zhii'gron. Its closest translation is soul-bond. This ritual was reserved for mated pairs who entered their twilight years together. Their spirits became one in every sense, and they passed together into the realm of the dead. Few mated pairs ever chose this bond.

"The more common pairing betwixt Tenné and Xemmassian was called vaatzheymah, or brother-bond. This was a working partnership, severable if necessary. The pair were a strong team, able to share thoughts and sense one another's emotions, but they remained separate — still individuals. Their bond lent power to the dragon's innate abilities and strength to the Xemmassian. We underwent rigorous training, both mental and physical, to ensure we each possessed the strength and control necessary."

"What do you mean?"

"The deeper and stronger a bond, the harder it became for the individuals to separate themselves from one another, even for privacy's sake. Can thou imagine ne'er being alone, even in thy most private thoughts and actions, or attempting to make love to one who has another being within their mind, sharing the experience? For this reason and others more pertinent to our survival, mine ancestors learned to keep the bond... soft, or mayhap shallow is a better word.

"Those who entered the vaatzheymah unprepared, without the needed control, found their bond growing, their minds and spirits entangled as firmly as in the zhii'gron. More oft than not, it ended in tragedy."

Hector jerked to a stop. His normally swarthy complexion paled, and he stared at his companion in horror for several long seconds before finding his voice. "You mean the death of one killed the other?"

"Aye. The survivor's spirit dwindled within until despair did claim him."

"And there was no way to save the survivor?"

"What ails thee, hunter? Thy countenance is of one who hath been given a death sentence."

"Brand..." Hector worried his signet ring until he could feel the pulse of the other five rings, wishing he could tell if everyone was alive and well.

"Brand is the dragon you sent Ruthaer's lightkeeper to find?"

Hector nodded and ran shaking hands through his hair. "Twenty-five years ago, in a sea cave near Ruthaer, a dying dragon named Aleuria entrusted an egg to a fisherman named Alaric Yves. His daughter, Aislinn, raised the hatchling, Brand, in Ozera."

"Aislinn is thy elf-woman who was slain?"

Hector struggled to swallow the sudden lump in his throat and nodded.

"Twenty-five years..." Teal mused. "Your Brand is still but a child, scarcely more than a hatchling. What of his sire?"

"In Revakhun Toaglen, from what I was told. Aleuria left him, but I don't know why. Aislinn told Dave and me that Brand planned to visit the islands and wanted her to go with him."

"What art thou not saying? Why dost thou fear for the dragonling's life?"

"Brand and Aislinn... She was a child when Aleuria died, but she helped care for the egg. Aislinn said they bonded before Brand even hatched. They could feel each other's heartbeat, emotions, and share thoughts — even see through each other's eyes."

"By Xardus' great horned head! It should not be possible. Only the children of Xardus could form such a bond."

"Aislinn and Brand are unique," said Hector. "She was... is only half elf. Everyone believed Alaric, her father, was human, but Aleuria chose him for a reason. What if he had a Xemmassian ancestor?"

"If his daughter and the hatchling formed a spontaneous bond as thou say, then 'tis a certainty."

Hector's expression grew more intense. "Do you think you can help Brand?"

"I shall do aught I can, but the loss of a bond-mate is traumatic, even for the trained. The deeper the bond, the greater the wound to the survivor's mind and spirit." As the bounty hunter started to walk away, Teal stopped him. "Hector, it doth occur to me that Brand may be the last of my people and my kinfolk. Your Aislinn, too, had she lived."

"Miracles happen," replied Hector. "The healers and clerics in Ozera have saved lives where all hope was lost. They will save Aislinn. Brand needs her." He started down the cobblestone street to the waterfront, but his whispered words carried back to Teal. "I need her."

CRESO

9:40am

Dave glared at the jumbled disarray in the skiff's port-side locker. He and Hector had been putting it off, but with Tydway so close, it was time to organize. Piece by piece, he removed and sorted Hector's spare tunics and breeches from Hummingbird's and Aislinn's clothes, packing them into saddlebags. As he found bottles and jars from Aislinn's first aid satchel, he returned them to their hardened leather case. When done, he closed the storage compartment. Made to look like part of the skiff, the lid disappeared seamlessly into the bulkhead when he locked it.

The storm that welcomed them to Ruthaer had ruined their food stores and everything had been thrown to the fish. Now, the empty starboard-side locker lay open to air out. He glanced past it toward the bow and away, resolutely turning his back on the vampiric mask and Evan Courtenay's pilfered dærganfae dagger hidden within that cubby.

Making his way aft, he opened his locker. Two quivers stared at him like empty eye sockets. He lifted a snarl of tangled line, and arrowheads spilled around his feet. "Sarding hell."

A cloud passed in front of the sun. As its shadow fell over him, a cool hand caressed his shoulder. Dave flinched and spun, snatching a dagger from his belt. The skiff rocked and swayed in its cradle, forcing him to crouch and grab the gunwale. He was alone.

'Something troubles you, my archer.'

The air shimmered. Hate and desire burst through him. Closing his eyes, Dave made a sign against evil and grasped the brooch at the base of his throat. "Work, dammit."

'I only wish to speak with you.'

Lady D appeared in his mind, dressed like a Deshretan princess in a bone colored, sleeveless tunic over matching blousy sherwal trousers. Twisting blood-red sigils crawled across her clothes and skin, just like the one etched on the vampire mask's forehead. Combs studded with garnets like glistening drops of blood bound up her wavy black hair. Her onyx eyes burned with amber fire. She brushed a hand over his shoulder and across his chest, sending burning tongues of lust licking from his scars into his core.

Dave's willpower buckled. His chin tipped up, offering her his throat. *'Soon,'* she whispered. *'I offer you a warning, my archer. Dodz is coming.'*

"Where is he now?"

"Your pardon, Bayim, are you unwell?"

Dave's eyes snapped open to find the ship's Turkestani quartermaster, Salizar, gripping the skiff's rail. The archer drank deeply from his flask before answering. "I'm fine. Pirate bastards in Ruthaer rifled my lockers and made a mess of things."

"You looked as though you saw an 'ifrītah."

"I said I'm fine."

"As you wish, Bayim." He touched a fingertip to a bright blue khamsah charm dangling from a gold hoop through his right earlobe. "If you wish for a charm against evil, you have but to speak. Zola and Sakina are skilled at piercings and charm making."

Dave rubbed a thumb over the balas-ruby. "Thanks, but no thanks. I don't do piercings."

Salizar touched his forehead and dipped a short bow in the archer's direction. "Let me know if you change your mind, Bayim. One can never have too much protection, or too many allies."

CHAPTER 3
CAVERNS

August 12, 4237 K.E.

9:05am

Count Zhevon Dodz crouched beside a narrow crevice and strained to catch any telltale sounds of movement in the stygian darkness. With Carolingian troops crawling over Ruthaer's barrier islands, he'd spent the last three days exploring the caverns and tunnels within the quarry's plutonic dome north of the village, hoping to find a secret passage into the ghūl's lair.

A relic had given the creature power over the Luminiferous Aether, the realm of the dead. Although the Orbuculum was lost to Dodz for the moment, he felt certain there were other treasures to be found for which his mysterious employers, the Collectors, would pay handsomely. Unfortunately, he'd been forced to fight his way through a half-dozen feral gnomes intent on devouring the flesh from his bones. By his reckoning, one still lurked in the shadows, biding its time.

Today, he'd found the first bit of red wax wedged in a crack. The bounty hunter's trail-markers led steadily downward, through a twisting maze of passages marked by scrapes and chips he'd come to recognize as tracks of the monstrous clockwork bug the sorceress, Consuelo, called Akkilettū.

He silently cursed the sorceress and the demon who served her. He should have refused this der'mo job. His mistake was thinking the task of tracking down and killing the bounty hunter, Hector de los Santos, would be simple. The sorceress had boarded the *Inquisitor* at Gräfendorf, in the Detchian country of Essen, with four servants: a woman and three filthy guttersnipes. She handed him a letter from Boyar Zinovii Tretyakov of Erinskaya, informing Dodz he was to accept her *assistance*. What the devka didn't know was the letter contained a hidden message instructing Dodz to dispose of her, as well.

They were in the Karukera Sea when the sorceress sacrificed one of the slave-urchins to her abyssal master. The next night, the battle scarred Akkilettū climbed out of the sea and into the ship's hold, clutching a blackened skull in its mandibles. For three days and nights, the sorceress remained in the hold with that clockwork creature, chanting and screeching. Another slave-child was sacrificed. The fourth night, somewhere off the coast of Peninsular Espia, Consuelo emerged carrying a glowing, rune-marked ivory mask.

The woman's exultant cry as she donned the mask turned to screams of agony. Dodz, along with the captain and crew, watched her writhe on deck. Her screams grew weaker with each passing minute, until she lay still as a corpse. Dodz stepped forward to remove the mask, when it suddenly transformed the sorceress into the beautiful and exotic vampire, Ymara Dapniš.

Burning pain erupted in the scars on his left forearm at the thought of the vampire — scars where she punctured his flesh, leaving her mark on his body and psyche. His jaw clenched against the urge to scream, and he sagged against a rough rock wall as her voice lanced through his mind.

'Köle, you waste time in sub-Gaian halls while the archer slips ever farther away with my mask.'

"I refuse to be your thrall, worthless shlyukha. Leave me be," he whispered.

'You are mine, köle, now and forever, and you will address me by my title!" Her voice thundered in his mind before dropping into a seductive purr. "You have a choice: pain or pleasure. Serve willingly, and I will reward you with the power for which your heart lusts. Defy me, and I shall see just how much pain it takes to break you.'

A hiss escaped the count's lips. "What do you want from me, Ymara?"

'A willing host.'

"Please, take the archer. He is yours, da?"

'I prefer a female host. Besides, the archer is imperfect and lacks your... ambition.'

Dodz cursed and railed against the compulsion building in his veins. "Stop!" he begged. "I will come to you, but I wish something in return."

Ymara's rich, sinister laugh filled his mind, and the pain softened into something more akin to pleasure. *'What is it, köle? What do you desire?'*

"To destroy both the bounty hunter and his archer." Silent stillness washed through Dodz. Just as he dared to hope the vampire had retreated, her voice drifted through him like tendrils of smoke.

'Find Akkilettū. Use it against them.'

Her presence faded, but Dodz knew she wasn't gone. She lurked in the depths of his mind like rot hidden within perfect-seeming fruit. Dodz cursed the loss of his ruby brooch aboard the storm-wrecked *Inquisitor*. It looked like a woman's bauble but, thanks to the enchantments provided by his patron among the Collectors, it had protected him from all forms of mind control, even the vampire's. With the brooch's loss, Count Dodz had become Ymara's unwilling servant.

Dodz intended to kill Dave Blood, retrieve the brooch, and restore his own freedom. Afterward, he would complete his original job and deliver the bounty hunter's head to his employers in Erinskaya. With the mask, he should receive a nice bonus.

For now, he considered Ymara's instruction to find Akkilettū. The thing hadn't attacked him so far, which likely meant the bounty hunter and his archer had destroyed the clockwork monster. It left Dodz wondering how he could use it against the two men.

Extracting a glass vial from an inner pocket of his dusty leather jacket, he gave the viscous green liquid a vigorous shake to rekindle its glow. He scanned the area above and around him, searching for danger, before entering a narrow, rubble lined crevice. Inch by inch, he worked his way through, emerging into a chamber with a domed hollow where part of its ceiling had collapsed. A black metal leg-tip protruded from a glassy puddle of basalt.

"So much for Akkilettū," he muttered to himself in Rhodinan.

He raised his light higher. Smooth obsidian stripes and basalt mounds interspersed shattered chunks of granite, as if intense fire had melted part of the room. Dodz considered the destruction, the broken leg-tip, and what little he'd been able to learn about Hector de los Santos and Dave Blood. Perhaps the ceiling *had* melted.

A starburst of light twinkled within the debris.

Dodz wedged the end of his light in a crack above the passageway and set to work shifting rock. Slowly, the mangled and crushed remains of the clockwork creature's mantis-like head and thorax came to light, partially embedded in a mass of dark stone. Of its original six black diamond eyes, only one the size of an owl's egg remained undamaged. The rest were cracked and cloudy.

He gripped the eyestone in one gloved hand and pulled, but it would not come free. Pursing his lips in frustration, he drew his dagger and pried away bits of carapace around the eye socket. The black diamond still wouldn't budge. He glared at the stone.

Its facets winked back, as if taunting him.

He took up a chunk of granite and smashed it against the glassy basalt trapping the head and thorax. A thin web of cracks raced outward from the point of impact. He smashed the small boulder down again, harder. Sharp chips flew in all directions, and a sliver of basalt pierced his hand. Grimacing, he removed the splinter.

Blood dripped onto the diamond.

CR&SO

Icy darkness pressed in from every side. Glossy stone stretched under Aislinn's cheek and her prone body. Smooth as glass, it had the cold feel of a polished gem.

Silence.

'Brand, what happened?'

More silence. Fear set her pulse racing, but it seemed... weak. She couldn't feel her brother's heartbeat. She reached for Brand through their soul-bond, but he wasn't there. She was alone.

A ragged memory surfaced. Danger and death were coming for her, the Tanjaran seer had warned. The old clanswoman had been right, but it was her mentor, Edge Garrett, that death claimed in the Haunted Hills. Before they left Ozera, Aislinn's mother had begged the ranger to stay out of dærganfae controlled lands south of the Alashalian clans, but the fae had committed one atrocity more than the old man could bear, slaughtering an entire village to steal its children.

She wondered how she could possibly tell her mother the awful truth of what happened to Edge — that her moment of indecision between fighting and following Edge's orders to run had cost the man his life. In her mind's eye, she saw Edge with an ivory dærganfae dagger in his heart. His heterochromatic blue-grey eyes stared sightlessly in her direction. A sob escaped Aislinn, though she tried to stifle it.

She reached for Brand again, like a wound she couldn't stop picking. His absence was a searing pain in her heart and mind that turned into a knot of rage. If the dærganfae had hurt him, she would see them all dead.

A sudden pinpoint of light beckoned like a distant star.

Aislinn climbed to her feet, hands outstretched above and to the side in search of obstacles. Two steps to the left, she found a wall as glassy smooth as the floor.

She struggled to understand what happened and where she was, but she couldn't remember anything after burying her hatchet between the quicksilver eyes of the dærganfae who'd slain Edge. Aislinn wondered if she'd hit her head, but a quick search of her scalp revealed no bumps or bruises. Fingertips on the cold, smooth stone, Aislinn started walking toward the distant light.

The feeling of something watching made her pause and try, once more, to access the bond with her dragon-brother. "Brand, where are you?" she whispered.

CR80

9:30am

Angry, Dodz struck the clockwork creature's head again. The carapace gave way, and the black diamond moved. Twisting and pulling, Dodz worked the gemstone free, along with a twelve-inch rod. Flattened and curved like a scythe on one end, oily fluid oozed along its length. Dodz' mouth contorted into a moue of distaste. He pulled a handkerchief from his sleeve, wiped the viscous liquid from the rod, then dropped the soiled cloth amid the debris at his feet.

Dodz held the octagonal cut diamond close to his light, searching for a means to remove it from the blade-like metal without damaging it. Unable to see anything obvious, he pulled off one glove and ran his fingertips over the seam where gem and metal met.

"Brand, where are you?" The vaguely familiar female voice sounded close.

Dodz dropped into a crouch. Ears straining to catch any sounds of nearby movement, he searched the rocks and debris. Silence greeted him. He couldn't be certain, but the voice sounded like that of the bounty hunter's elf-woman — except she was dead.

Ymara instructed him to use Akkilettū against Hector and Dave.

His look became calculating. Aboard the *Inquisitor*, he'd seen Akkilettū spear a sailor and raise him up to its face as if to devour him. Instead, the creature's eyes took on a fiery glow. The man stared into those hellfire diamonds for only a moment before he slumped, lifeless, and the creature dropped the corpse to the ship's deck. Afterwards, the clockwork arachnid grew stronger, its damaged parts less of a hinderance, as if powered by the sailor's death.

If the dead monster's eyestone held the spirit of the bounty hunter's woman, it would prove an invaluable weapon, but who was this Brand she called to? He raised the stone higher. For a moment, light flared within the gem, competing with Dodz' glowing vial, giving him the impression something within the stone gazed back.

Dodz placed a tentative fingertip on the black diamond. Immediately, the sound of footsteps filled the air. He lifted his finger from the stone, and the sound died. Satisfied, he closed his fist around the black diamond.

The sound of footfalls returned. After several minutes, he grew impatient, wondering if the spirit was really Aislinn Yves, and who the mysterious Brand might be. A wave of dizziness swept over Dodz. The light grew dim and shifted to pale green.

The broken rocks of the cavern faded, replaced by a circle of stones partially filled with sand and rotting seaweed. A creamy egg striated with veins of bright copper rocked and shifted in the odd nest. A small hole gave birth to branching cracks over the shell's surface.

His heart thudded in his chest, as if the organ was twice its normal size.

'*Hungry.*' The growling voice was inside his head.

"I'm here, Brand," a girl child's voice responded. "I brought you smoked fish." Dodz looked down, expecting the child to be at his side, and found *he* was the child, as if he'd fallen into a strange dream.

A short talon pierced the shell. '*Aislinn, help me out,*' the disembodied voice demanded.

"I can't. You have to do this on your own, like a baby bird, so you'll always remember your strength."

The creature in the egg emitted a wordless growl, and another hole appeared in the eggshell, followed by a scaly hand-like appendage.

Dodz realized he was seeing a dragon hatch. His gaze darted from the nest and around the cavern. Dark, briny water covered half the room. Outside the nest, the desiccated remains of a huge dragon sprawled on the stone floor. Somehow, he knew it was the hatchling's mother.

Movement stopped for several minutes while the dragonling rested, then the egg resumed rocking. It rolled and crashed against a rock. The girl cried out and took a step forward before forcing herself to be still.

A fist-sized metallic eye appeared at one of the many holes riddling the eggshell. His vision wavered, and suddenly Dodz could see both the hatching egg and the watching elfchild. She was small, probably no more than eight or nine summers in human terms. In the odd green lighting, her long braids were the color of verdigris, but he knew that, under the sun, they would be the color of a campfire, striated gold and orange.

'*Aislinn.*'

"Come out, little brother," she replied.

The dragonling gave one more tremendous shove against the shell encasing him, and it burst, spilling his glistening wet body into the sand. He struggled up onto four legs and spread his leathery wings for balance. He swayed for a moment, then stumbled forward.

Aislinn laughed and rushed to him, throwing her thin arms around the dragonling's warm, scaly neck.

For a terrifying moment, Dodz felt himself trapped in the girl and dragon's combined psyche. Fighting back the rising panic, he focused his willpower and forced open his clenched fist. The black diamond and its metal rod clattered to the rocky floor. Cold sweat beaded his forehead, and his breath came in ragged gasps.

The vision felt real, as if he'd lived it himself. The girl and the dragon had shared a powerful bond. It suddenly occurred to him that if the dragon was alive, it might be able to sense her spirit in the eyestone.

His bare fingertips stretched toward the stone once again before he caught himself. He needed information about spirits trapped in gems to fully utilize the gift Ymara had given him. Like everything else Ymara offered, this gift came with a price. His mind worked furiously. The Academia de Artes Magicae in Tydway was closest, and it was one of the three largest in Parlatheas, alongside the mages' guilds in Erinskaya and Pazard'zhik.

Dodz pulled his glove back on and studied the curved, blade-like rod. It would be a simple thing to hone it to a razor's edge. For the first time, Dodz thought of the archer and smiled.

He gave the chamber one last searching look before producing a platinum bracelet bearing four charms: a treasure chest, a book, a compass, and a corked bottle. The enchantment on the bottle faded as he removed it from the chain, and it grew to fill his palm. Carefully removing the cork, he poured out a circle of white sand, then returned the bottle to the bracelet, where it shrank to the size of a charm once again.

Light in one hand and diamond-tipped rod in the other, Dodz stepped into the circle, spoke a single word, and vanished in a blaze of light.

CHAPTER 4
OZERA

August 12, 4237 K.E.

10:00am

Facing east and south, snow-white cliffs plunged fifteen hundred feet from the summit of Ozera's Lumikivi Mountain to the sprawling expanse of Grimshaw Valley. Long before Phaedrus made the mountain his home and his followers established their village, the Alashalian clans and the elves before them considered the white mountain a sacred place of healing.

At its summit, Phaedrus and his followers had taken the once barren overlook and worked over the course of years to smooth the stone and carve out contours for seating. At its center, they transformed a small spring into a serene reflecting pool, letting it feed into a narrow, rippling stream where those who came to meditate could rearrange the rocks and pebbles to achieve differing levels of sound. Cultivated trees and shrubs surrounded Sunrise Chapel, providing shade and the sounds of leaf and twig in counterpoint to that of the stream. Around the rear of the chapel, nearest the trees, vine-covered timber columns supported a thatched roof where pilgrims could shelter from sun or rain.

Humans and elves were not the only ones to make pilgrimages to Lumikivi. Each spring, peregrine falcons returned from their winter homes along the coast to raise their young in the rocky heights. From the day he and Aislinn first saw them, Brand loved to fly with the falcons. Despite the difference in their size, the adult raptors had not feared the dragonling. Instead, they tolerated his early attempts to imitate their graceful flight and heart-pounding dives to catch prey on the wing. The following year, the returning fledglings seemed to take it upon themselves to teach their odd cousin the proper way to fly, demonstrating dive after dive and circling in the updrafts until Brand mastered their skills.

Now, as the copper-haired half-elf Eidan, he sat on Aislinn's favorite perch, his feet dangling over the sharp edge.

Deep inside his heart and mind, Brand coiled and writhed in grief-stricken rage.

Behind him, Xandor cleared his throat. "Your mother asked me to find you."

Eidan didn't turn to look at the Iron Tower ranger. "I came up here to watch the sunrise, hoping a few falcons might still be here, but they've all gone."

"One of the Sisters of Mercy brought word that they'll have everything ready tomorrow afternoon." Xandor paused, then sighed. "Eidan, are you sure you and your mother don't want to wait a few more days?"

"Emä and I have already been through this with Phaedrus, Xandor. We'd rather not have a funeral at all, but she and I need closure. Brand refuses to let Aislinn go. That's why he gave Jasper all those pearls and that diamond and ebony jewel box. He requested Kemetan preservation oils and asked Jasper to have the Academy mage-artisans enlarge the jewel box to be Aislinn's casket — he wants to be able to see her. He's adding her to his treasure hoard."

Xandor crouched by Eidan and lowered his voice. "You and I are the only ones here. Why are you talking as if you and Brand aren't one and the same?"

"I don't think we are, Xandor. Brand and I have been at odds ever since the resurrection ritual failed, each of us struggling for dominance. It's all I can do to hold Brand inside. To be honest, if it weren't for the fact that Emä needs me, I wouldn't bother fighting him. He's so *angry*. I don't know what will happen after Aislinn's funeral."

"It's only been two days, Eidan. You and your mother should wait. Aislinn would want Hector, Dave, Hummingbird, and Robert to be here."

"*Only two days*? It's been a week since Brand burst out of his cave and flew east when Aislinn and Hummingbird were wounded. I'm sorry to exclude Hummingbird and Robert, but we have no way of knowing when he'll arrive or when Hummingbird will wake again, much less be strong enough to leave the hospital. As for Hector and Dave, Brand and I don't want them here. It's the only thing we agree on." Eidan plucked a loose rock from the ground at his side and sent it sailing over the valley fifteen hundred feet below. "Brand says it's their fault she's dead."

"The lighthouse keeper from Ruthaer said it was an ambush. Blame the creature or its master, not your friends."

"Hector and Dave aren't my friends," Eidan snapped. "Brand and I should have gone with Aislinn to Ruthaer to help Tallinn, but she wanted to go with *them*. There was a time when I thought it would be impossible, but they've driven Aislinn and Brand apart. He and Aislinn... Xandor, they *fought*, and that's never happened before. Not even once in the twenty-five years since Brand hatched. Now, the grief and rage are driving him mad. Driving *us* mad."

"Surely something can be done."

"I don't know. Brand felt everything that happened to Aislinn, including the moment her heart stopped. He thought he was dying, too. Hope that Phaedrus could save her was all that kept him going. Now, it's revenge on Hector and Dave that drives him."

"Revenge?"

"He means to kill them both."

Xandor rested a hand on Eidan's shoulder. "We'll think of a way to stop Brand from doing anything we'll all regret."

"I don't want to stop him," Eidan replied.

"What! Why not?" Xandor demanded.

"You were there when the healers brought Hummingbird back from the brink of death, Xandor. I know you saw her vision of what happened and felt her pain — her *fear* — filling the hospital halls. Hector led them into that cavern, and Dave obviously wasn't watching their backs."

"Even the best of us gets ambushed, Eidan. Accidents happen."

"It wasn't an accident. It was recklessness," Eidan argued. He climbed to his feet and faced the ranger. The man's mismatched eyes — one the color of spring leaves, the other the frozen grey of a winter sky — echoed Eidan's grief. Aislinn and Brand had known Xandor since she was in the early years of her apprenticeship with the Iron Tower ranger, Edge Garrett. When they first met, the man before him had been a boy of ten summers. Eidan surmised it was Xandor's admiration of Edge that led him to join the ranger corps. "You're a good friend, Xandor. Will you help us protect Hummingbird?"

"That's up to her. Aislinn told me about Hummingbird, that she's the last of her tribe, and how Hector and Dave found her in a Flainnian slave market, abused and broken. Eidan, she chose Dave — most likely because he is the scariest, hard-hearted bastard in existence. It's her decision to continue with him or not. You and I don't have the right to take away her choice."

Eidan didn't understand Xandor's reluctance to help. The young elf needed protection — most of all from people like Dave.

"Come on," Xandor said. "There's enough food for an army laid out in your mother's kitchen. I know you don't feel like it, but you should try to eat something and help us convince Shayla to do the same."

Eidan let the ranger lead him down the mountain. He had the disheartening feeling these would be the longest two days of his life.

CXEO

10:15am

In the hospital's critical care ward, Hummingbird lay under soft cotton sheets. Except for the slow rise and fall of her breathing, she could have been an exotic wax figure with short crimson hair framing a dark amber face adorned with red whorls and white dots. Behind closed lids, her eyes darted rapidly.

A circle of telgid — huts made of woven grass mats — surrounded the hollow, grass covered mound of the sacred lodge housing winter food stores, medicinal herbs, and the shaman's story blankets. The afternoon sun warmed the girl's skin and her long, crimson braids. Seed heads on golden prairie grass tickled her arms. One more step, and she would enter the village clearing, perhaps see her little sister and one of their cousins making grass dolls.

Part of her knew this wasn't real. She walked the Dreaming Grounds, the place each elf of Altaira's Vaimurahvas — the Spirit Nation — carried within their heart and mind. It was their connection to Dioth Cyela — their creator — to Altaira, and to each other. Here, they saw and communed with friends and family across the grasslands as easily as walking from one telgid to another. The Dreaming Grounds were a place of sharing and emotional healing — but that was before slave traders from Tirna Flainn and their allies decimated her people.

A shadow passed over the sun, and a distant voice whispered her name. Not her true name, but the name she wore now like armor against her past.

Hummingbird closed her eyes and shivered as she turned away from the village. Sadness welled up and spilled down her cheeks. She wasn't home. This was all an illusion.

When she dared look again, a dark smudge of storm clouds lay on the distant horizon, and tiny flickers of lightning streaked the sky. Against the slow-moving thunderhead, a pair of winged shadows circled. As they rolled and twisted, Hummingbird could make out a ragged crown of feathers and sharp beak on one of the figures. It was the eagle she'd seen near Ruthaer's quarry, only twenty times larger. The other, equally enormous shadow sported a long, sinuous neck, and tail. A single word whispered through the grass: Dragon.

Ahead of her, wilted waist-high grass stretched as far as the eye could see. There were no signs of life. No bison, no birds, just an endless sea of death. Slowly she turned, knowing what she would find.

A barren, hollow mound of sod came into view — all that remained of her people's sacred lodge. The telgid which should have surrounded it had burned to ash. Hummingbird wanted to climb atop the mound and scream to the sky, but scorched earth and the charred bones of her people surrounded it, blocking her path.

Grief hit like a fist in her belly, driving the air from her lungs, and she fell to her knees. A rumble of thunder reached her, so muted by distance she could barely hear what it said.

Its voice told her Death was coming.

CHAPTER 5
STORM WARNING

August 12, 4237 K.E.

6:00pm

Late in the day, when the shadows were long and the sun perched between the overcast sky and the horizon, Hector found Dave on the forecastle deck, watching the shoreline glide past. It was largely open farmland as far as the eye could see, dotted here and there by cottages, barns, small herds of cattle, and thin lines of dark trees marking streambeds.

"Dodz is coming," Dave said.

Hector glanced to the lower deck, his hand near his scimitar. Teal worked among the sailors mending rope, seeming at ease with their idle banter. Sailors up in the rigging shortened the sails in anticipation of the rain that had been threatening all afternoon. Nothing appeared to be amiss. "What makes you say that?"

Dave touched the broach in the hollow below his throat. "She warned me." He pushed away from the rail and started pacing, punctuating each turn with a drink from his flask.

Hector watched Dave and wished, for the thousandth time, that the enchantment which kept the archer's flask full would fade. Dave lowered his flask, and Hector noticed him brush Aislinn's oak-leaf chain and the balas-ruby brooch with his thumb.

"Amigo, you can't trust Lady D."

"I don't."

Hector searched Dave's eyes. "Is the brooch not working? How did she warn you?"

Dave glanced up into the rigging and across the deck. He didn't look at Hector when he spoke. "Back in Ruthaer, when I was down in that cistern with William Howard's pirates, one of them grabbed the brooch. He had his fist around it, trying to snap Aislinn's necklace. Lady D warned me that Dodz would take the mask. We already know he has a magic item that lets him teleport. He could appear anywhere he wants — even here on this deck in the middle of the night — and steal the mask. We need to get off this ship."

Hector knew Dave well enough to know the archer wasn't telling him everything, but he didn't press the issue. "Dave, Jasper has always said teleportation magic requires a precise location. We're on a *moving* ship. Logically, Dodz can't reach us here even if he can sense the mask the same way you can. Instead of fretting and leaving the *Lady Luck*, let's use the time between here and Tydway to plan."

A derisive snort escaped the archer as he shook his head. "Even the best laid plans go pear-shaped, Hector."

¡Maldición, Dave!" He crossed into the archer's path, forcing him to stop pacing. "Do you even hear yourself? How do you know Lady D doesn't *want* Dodz to find us? If we go ashore now, that's exactly what will happen. Here, we have Lord Vaughn and Lady Aneirin's resources, and in Tydway we'll have Jasper."

"Don't let that fat bastard use magic on me."

"Dave, I know magic freaks you out, but Jasper has been our friend since day one in Gaia."

"No spells," Dave argued.

"Jasper is a lot more powerful than he lets on. First thing when we get to Tydway, we'll tell him everything that's happened and let him look at that brooch of yours. Maybe he can boost its power."

Dave glared at the passing countryside for a time, then finally nodded. "You realize I'm royally screwed if the priests in Ozera can't destroy the mask, right? I'm already a danger to you and everyone else on this ship."

"Don't think like that. If Phaedrus and his priests can't destroy it, maybe Jasper or one of his colleagues at the Academy can. Worst case, we have them come up with something stronger than that brooch to keep her out of your head."

"And Dodz?"

"You can burn that bridge when we get there. Besides, I'd like to have a rather pointed conversation with him regarding his dealings with a certain sorceress and with the Howard family."

"You better talk fast, because I promised to cut out his heart and eat it."

Hector's face twisted with disgust. Footsteps on the portside ladder saved him from having to respond to Dave's statement. The captain's cabin boy, Taddy, appeared. "The admiral requires your presence at dinner this evening, sirs." He gave Dave a curt nod. "Proper dress is required at the admiral's table. You'll find a shirt in your quarters."

Dave scowled and gave the cabin boy a growling curse. "I'll eat in my cabin, or not at all."

Taddy's eyebrows disappeared into his hairline. "No one refuses dinner with the Admiral," he gasped.

"Thank you, Taddy, we'll be there" Hector replied.

"Not me," Dave insisted. "Especially not if Vaughn is going to be there."

"Dave and I will be there," Hector reiterated with a warning glare at Dave. "What time does the admiral dine?"

"Sunset, sir. I'll fetch the two of you in about an hour."

"What about Teal?"

"Milady made no mention of her, sir. She's free to eat with the crew or in her cabin, whichever she likes."

CRSO

7:00pm

'*Where are they, little brother?*' Brand's voice echoed within Eidan's head, drowning out what August Sabe was telling him. Visitors milled in and out of the kitchen, bringing food and condolences to Eidan and his mother.

Eidan winced. He clenched his fist, activating the magic in his signet ring, embossed with Damage, Inc.'s dagger-pierced globe. To the west, the pulse from Robert's signet ring moved steadily toward Ozera. To the east, Jasper was in Tydway, while Hector and Dave were still well beyond the city.

The dragon writhed inside his elven form but could not break free. '*Let me out, Eidan. They are close enough. We can have our revenge tonight.*'

'*No,*' Eidan silently replied. '*Emä needs me.*' He wrestled with the dragon inside, forcing it to be still. When he opened his eyes again, August stared at him, his steel grey eyes filled with compassion.

"I'm sorry," Eidan said. "What were you saying?"

"Only that I wish there was something I could say or do to ease your and Lady Shayla's suffering," August replied.

Filled with heartfelt concern, his deep voice seemed more suited for the stage than actual life.

"I appreciate that, August, and I'm sure Emä does, too. Do me a favor, though. Don't write any poetry for her."

The Rhodinan warrior-poet's hand flew to his heart. "Whyever not?"

"I've seen how women respond to your poetry, August. I could name a dozen or more towns from here to Orleans where fathers and husbands curse your name, and I imagine Xandor could do the same with towns in Michurinsk and Vologda."

August's broad shoulders slumped, and he assumed a hurt expression. "What is poetry, if not a means to express our innermost feelings? I cannot help what others feel or how they choose to express themselves."

"Exactly," replied Eidan, pointing his finger at the bard's chest. "No poetry for my mother. Please, August."

"As you wish, tovarishch," August relented. He gripped the young man's shoulder and took up a pensive pose. "Eidan, you take good care of your mother, but she still worries about you."

"I know, but there isn't much I can do about that. She has always worried about Aislinn and me, but, then again, we wandered off the path of peace and safety a long time ago."

His eyes taking on a fierce light, August smiled and shook his head. "Such a life would not suit either of you."

"What about Hummingbird? Do you think she would choose Ozera over the dangers of bounty hunting?"

August placed his hands on his hips, and Eidan could practically see the wheel turning inside the bard's head as he stared off into the distance. "I don't know." August frowned, and his eyes brimmed with tears as he said, "She seemed broken in body and spirit when Hector and Dave bought her freedom, but there is adamantium in that girl's spine. I think..."

'Let me out!'

Brand's roar drowned out August's words, and Eidan felt the first tingles of static electricity on his skin. He rubbed at the fine hairs on his forearms, trying to force them to lie down. His eyes darted to the clusters of people scattered around the kitchen.

"Eidan, what's wrong?" asked August.

"I need some air." He could only hope the electricity gathering around him remained unnoticeable as he hurried from the kitchen and past the parlor on his way out the door. His mother called his name, but he didn't stop.

Outside, the last rays of sunset filtered through the trees. Neither he nor his mother wanted a wake, but their friends and neighbors kept coming, bringing food, and offering help.

Eidan stumbled off the porch and around the side of the house, where a narrow strip of moss-covered ground separated the house from the closest trees and led to their root cellar doors. Down a short flight of stairs and through a secret door, he hurried along the tunnel toward the series of caverns where Brand kept his treasures.

A burst of pain dropped Eidan to his knees. He crawled to the shore of a crystalline lake lit by dozens of softly glowing crystals. Rather than his own face, he saw Brand reflected in the water's surface.

'I've had enough of this game, little brother. Your time here is done,' Brand's voice hissed.

"Not tonight," he replied through clenched teeth. A haze of ozone surrounded him. "Tomorrow. After the funeral, I'll let you out."

Brand's angry growl vibrated through Eidan and sent ripples over the lake. *'I will hold you to your promise, little brother.'*

CHAPTER 6
DINNER

August 12, 4237 K.E.

7:10pm

Thunder rumbled in the distance. Sinister bruise-colored clouds pushed toward them from the west, and the smell of rain carried on the breeze. The boards creaked and groaned as the ship strained against its anchor near the southern riverbank.

Taddy knocked on the louvered aftcastle hatch and waited. From within, a second, softer knock sounded, followed by the murmur of voices. Finally, a woman's voice called out permission to enter. The boy announced Hector and Dave, saluted smartly, and retreated.

Blue-white light from the ship's crystal lanterns hanging on the deck above obscured the darkness beyond the room's bank of lead-paned windows, turning the glass into sheets of molten silver. Lady Aneirin lounged in a throne-like chair at the head of the table. Lord Vaughn stood at the table's foot wearing a tentative smile. A pair of empty chairs waited on each side. In the center, a round wooden stand held two bottles of wine and six crystal glasses.

"Gentlemen, welcome to my table." Lady Aneirin gestured to the vacant chairs, offering them their choice. Hector rounded the table and took the place on Lord Vaughn's right, facing the door, while Dave moved to sit near Lady Aneirin, facing the windows. "Roger, if you would be so kind as to ring Cook, perhaps Dave would do the honor of pouring the wine."

Dave turned to their host and gave her a small nod. He reached for the closest bottle, studied the label, replaced it, and picked up the other. Not satisfied, he returned it and looked about the cabin for other bottles.

Lahar's eyebrows rose and she straightened in her chair. "Is something wrong, Mister Tyler?"

"That isn't my name — not anymore. As far as I'm concerned, Clem Tyler died a long time ago. I'd appreciate it if you'd call me Dave Blood."

She inclined her head. "Very well, Mister Blood. Would you care to tell me why you disapprove of my wine?"

"You have a two-year-old bottle of Pueblo Cadrete Garnacha from Zaragoza, which is a young and fruity red. On the other hand, you have a bottle of old vine Ordóñez Godello from Oviedo, a more acidic, woody flavored white. What's on the menu for tonight, fruit and cheese or fish?"

Lady Aneirin smiled. "Very impressive. There may be fruit for dessert. However, for the main dish, the ship's cook promised beef tenderloin with rosemary gravy and roasted potatoes."

Dave eyed the bottles of wine and shook his head. "Milady, for beef, I recommend an Alicante Monastrell or an Aged Tempranillo from Cadiz if you want Espian wine. However, I'm partial to Francescan Duréza, bottled in Amienes." He reached to his belt and withdrew his flask.

"Dave, what are you doing?" Hector hissed.

The archer arranged four glasses, then used the wine towel to wipe the mouth of his flask before pouring a small measure of deep red wine into each one. He gave them a minute to breathe before passing a glass to Lady Aneirin, then Lord Vaughn and Hector. Dave raised his glass and took a swallow. Having poured from his own flask, he made sure he followed proper court etiquette by drinking from his first to prove the wine wasn't poisoned.

Lady Aneirin never took her eyes off the young archer as she lifted her glass and let the wine roll across her tongue. "Dry, without being uncomfortably so. A hint of fruit, but stronger spice. I approve. However, unless you have a bottle hidden in your cabin or sailing skiff, we'll have to make do with the wine Captain Smeyth has in the cabinet there." She pointed to a line of paired doors under the windows.

Dave held out his hand for her glass. The lady tilted her head and arched an eyebrow as she handed it to him. He filled it from his flask and handed it back, then proceeded to fill his own and Hector's.

Lord Vaughn held his glass forward. "Only a half-measure for me, please."

His jaw clenched, Dave avoided looking at the nobleman as he poured the wine.

A door in the corner opened, admitting the rich aroma of gravy followed by four sailors bearing covered silver trays.

Behind them came a plump woman with smokey-blue hair. She carried a tray containing salt and pepper mills, four pewter mugs, and a pitcher of water. With carefully timed choreography, the sailors lifted the tray covers, revealing the cook's masterpiece.

"It looks and smells delicious, Belinda, thank you."

The older woman smiled at Lady Aneirin. "My pleasure, Admiral. Ring when you're ready for us to clear the table and bring dessert."

When the cook and her staff were gone, Lady Aneirin offered up a brief prayer of thanksgiving. For several minutes, they ate in silence.

Hector cleared his throat. "Excuse me, Milady, but are you an admiral in the navy of Carolingias or Gallowen?"

"Oh, I assure you, I've never been deemed fit for military life — it was the whole bit about unquestioningly following orders I didn't agree with. I did, however, serve as a privateer for the Confederation of Nations."

Hector's fork clattered on his plate as it slipped from his fingers. "You're a pirate?"

"My husband is the former Queen's Champion of Carolingias and currently serves as Queen Ambrose's chief military advisor. It would be ill-advised, to say the least, for you to accuse me of piracy. What I am is a respectable merchant who owns a fleet of ships and fifty percent of an import/export business. Being that I started out as captain of a single ship and gradually added to my fleet, promoting captains from among my bosuns and quartermasters, it pleases them to refer to me as their admiral."

Lord Vaughn burst into laughter. "Come down off your high-horse, Lahar. You were a rogue and a pirate before Cerdic made an honest woman of you." The glare Lady Aneirin cast at him only made him laugh more.

"I seem to recall you weren't much better, *thief,* even though you worked directly for the Highlord," she responded. "Bryony changed you from a vagabond into a semi-respectable spy master."

Lord Vaughn's mirth evaporated. With a doleful sigh, he scooped up the wine glass by his plate and drained it.

"Roger, I'm sorry."

He held up a hand, fingers splayed. "It's alright, Lahar. I've just been missing Brie more these past few days. I wish..."

"So do I, but we can't change what happened. Her death was not your fault."

"The hell it wasn't." Three pairs of wide eyes locked on Dave. He, in turn, cast a hate-filled glare at Lord Vaughn. "If you gave a damn about my mother, she wouldn't have been alone with hunters chasing her — chasing us — halfway across America. Where the fucking hell were you when dærganfae attacked and butchered her?"

Lady Aneirin's soft voice drifted through the room. "Moving heaven and earth to reach Terra, but fate and the Dark One were against us."

"Dave." Hector pinned his friend with a stern look. "No fighting."

Dave glowered at Lord Vaughn then stood as he shifted his gaze toward the admiral. "Milady, this was a mistake." He tossed his napkin on the table and turned to leave.

"Mr. Blood, sit down," Lady Aneirin ordered.

"But —" Dave started.

"Sit," she repeated.

Resuming his place at the table, Dave stared at his plate.

"Your mother was Bryony Tyler?" Hector asked Dave. When the archer didn't respond, he turned to Lord Vaughn. "She was your wife?"

Roger nodded.

"If you don't mind my asking, señor, what happened?"

"I was too late. By the time we reached Terra, the dærganfae had already found Brie. Lahar's ship mage tracked them using the locket." Roger scrubbed one hand over his face and through his silver-flecked brown hair, then faced Dave. He swallowed hard and emotion made his voice tremble. "We made it to Cam and Nate's home as the fae made their exit. Some of the crew went inside to find Nate and Cam while the rest of us fought the fae. I saw Clement on the porch, right before the house exploded."

Dave refused to look at Lord Vaughn. Instead, he met Lady Aneirin's dark gaze. "Were you there?"

She nodded. "I lost four good crewmen that night."

"Clem —"

"Don't call me that!" Dave shouted, rounding on Roger. "Don't *ever* call me that again."

"I'm sorry," Roger replied. "It wasn't — and still isn't — my intention to hurt you or make you angry."

"Yeah? Well then, you shouldn't have worn her locket. You have no right to it, not after you abandoned her. We lived like tramps, drifting from place to place, never stopping more than a few days at a time."

"I swear to you, I didn't abandon Brie. The Archer — the dærganfae assassin who killed the Carolingian royal family during the Plague War — had a vendetta against us for foiling his attempts against Queen Ambrose and the Highlord. The Archer murdered my father, my brother, his wife, and their son on the king's highway, less than a mile outside Tydway. He left behind a vulture-fletched arrow, making sure I would know it was him.

"Brie and I were in Carolingias when the news reached us. Your mother and Queen Ambrose were close friends. Brie... Brie had only just realized she was with child the week before. We debated on the best course of action and finally decided you and she would be safe on Terra with her sister, Camellia. I stayed here on Gaia to hunt down that dærganfae."

"Safe? We weren't safe!" Dave bellowed. "We fled Charleston when I was three and were on the run for *four years*, old man! If we were lucky, we saw Aunt Cam, Uncle Nate, and Robert once a year — maybe. We lived like gypsies, barely scraping by. Mom read tarot cards to the gullible, sold magic charms, and sometimes she even sold herself."

Lord Vaughn's face paled, then flushed deep crimson. His eyes flashed with rage as he shoved up from the table and stalked toward Dave.

Fists clenched, Dave met him halfway, ready for another fight. Hector and Lady Aneirin scrambled to their feet, prepared to separate the two men.

"You're wrong. My wife, *your mother*, would never sell herself!"

"How would you know? You weren't there! I was seven when she was murdered! The police, the people who ran the orphanage — hell, even Robert's uncle Daniel — said she was a whore."

' "They didn't know her," Lady Aneirin said, her elven voice cutting through the tension. "They made up a story to fit events they couldn't explain. Tell me, Mr. Blood, how did you know it was dærganfae who killed her?"

"I saw them," Dave replied simply. "At the time, I thought they were elves, like in a book she'd been reading to me. I told the police and anyone else who would listen. Aunt Cam and Uncle Nate were the only ones who believed me, and then the dærganfae killed them, too, the very night they brought me home. Those fuckers made Robert and me orphans." Without another glance at Lord Vaughn, Dave stalked out, slamming the door behind him.

CRSO

8:00pm

"Please excuse me," Roger murmured and retreated through a small side door, locking it behind him.

Hector remained standing at the foot of the table, uncertain if he should remain or follow Dave.

Lady Aneirin sighed and resumed her seat. "How long has Dave known Roger is his father?"

"I don't think he did until today," Hector replied. He gathered his plate and glass, then moved down the table to sit beside Lady Aneirin. "I confess that, after seeing them side by side and how Lord Vaughn reacted when William Howard and his crew kidnapped Dave, I suspected — but I thought, perhaps, he had come here from Terra, like Dave, Robert, and me.

"The thing is, Rowanoake issued its warrants with our real names four and a half years ago. Phaedrus knows who we are and where we're from. You should have seen the padre's face when Robert and I went to him for confession, our first time in Ozera." A nostalgic smile stole across his face, then he sobered. "If Lord Vaughn knew, why hasn't he tried to contact Dave or Damage, Inc.?"

"Fear. He was afraid of exactly what happened tonight," Lady Aneirin replied.

"I can understand that, I guess. Dave has had a difficult life, to say the least. Like Dave said, he and Robert were orphans. Robert had his father's family, but Dave only had Robert. Circumstances kept them apart most of their childhood. Once they found each other again, they became as close as any two brothers ever were. Most people assume they are brothers."

"Phaedrus did say they looked similar, which is odd."

"Why? Their mothers were sisters. It isn't that uncommon for cousins to look alike."

"It is when one of them is adopted."

"¿Qué? What are you talking about, Milady?"

"If they had a son, Roger and Brie had planned to name him after their fathers — Robert Brynmor. But when the time came, Brie told Roger she named their son Clement, after her mother's family, because her sister had already adopted a baby boy and named him Robert."

"That must be a mistake," Hector said. "Robert can't possibly be adopted."

"I only know what I was told. Brie found a way to communicate with Roger from Terra. From what my husband and I understood at the time, she couldn't do it often, and only under specific circumstances. It's how Roger learned the dærganfae were after her and Clem."

"Without Terran science to test their blood, there's no way to know anything for certain," Hector conceded, "but their resemblance is uncanny if they aren't related. Maybe you can explain something else to me. How is it that Lord Vaughn had a Terran wife? After Dave, Robert, and I found ourselves in Rowanoake six years ago, Jasper consulted his instructors at the Academia de Artes Magicae, trying to find us a way home. Every mage and mystic who knew anything about interplanar travel told him it wasn't possible to open a portal to Terra."

"I won't pretend to understand how the magic works, but it's difficult and dangerous. The last time a mage managed to travel directly to Terra, he nearly died — I should know, because I was there.

"As for Roger and Bryony, I'll leave it for Roger to share what details he wishes."

"Did Lord Vaughn remarry?"

"No. There were offers, of course. Lords and knights from Gallowen and Carolingias, even a few from Francesca, proffered their daughters like prized cows." Lady Aneirin made a disgusted noise. "I don't know what Roger said to them, but the offers stopped rather abruptly.

"He loved Bryony more than life itself — he still does," Lady Aneirin continued. "When The Archer killed her and took the locket, it gave us a way to track his movements. Roger was a man obsessed. My crew and I helped him hunt that assassin across multiple worlds until we finally caught up to him, and Roger got his revenge. I will say this, though. That locket is Roger's most prized possession. It holds an image of him and Bryony, and one of her with their son."

"Dave recognized the locket as hers, but wouldn't she have shown him a picture of his father, or told him the man's name?" Hector asked.

"If they were on the run, information like that would be dangerous for a little boy to know," Lady Aneirin said.

"You're probably right." A boom of thunder vibrated through the ship, rattling the window glass against its metal lathes. Hector drained his glass. "Thank you for dinner, Milady. I should check on Dave."

He was halfway to the door when Lady Aneirin spoke. "Señor de los Santos, if Damage, Inc. finds itself in need of work, I could always use a team with your *reputation* for getting a job done. Pay a visit to Universal Exports — we have offices in most major cities in Parlatheas, and a few in southern Altaira, should you find yourself on that side of the world again. The office managers know how to reach me quickly."

Surprised by both the job offer and the Terran business name, Hector swept a low bow to the countess. "Thank you, señora. Out of curiosity, how did you choose the name for your company?"

Lady Aneirin smiled. "Bryony chose it. She said it was from a series of popular spy stories by a Terran bard named Fleming."

Hector laughed and gave Lady Aneirin another short bow. He was still grinning when he walked out the door.

CHAPTER 7
CLOUDBURST

August 12, 4237 K.E.

8:30pm

Lightning streaked across the sky. The slap of rain driving across the river's surface toward the ship was like the sound of ten-thousand pairs of hands clapping out of rhythm. Hector raced across the deserted deck toward the forecastle cabins, but the downpour swallowed the ship before he reached the door.

Drenched, he peeled off his homespun shirt, wrung it out, and mopped his face and hair before entering the cabin. Darkness and the scent of grain alcohol greeted him.

"Dave?" A surly grunt followed by the gurgle of liquid through a narrow spout answered him. Hector drew a thin bone tube from his belt, thumbed off the cap, and shined the ensuing beam of light around the room. The archer was shirtless and barefoot on his cot, back pressed into the corner where the cotton ticking met the wall. On the floor, almost directly underneath the shuttered lantern on its ceiling hook, the silk shirt Dave wore to dinner lay in a crumpled heap.

"You should have hung up the shirt," Hector said. "Silk is expensive."

"Damned thing feels like eel slime," the archer replied. "Slick and sticky at the same time. Makes my fucking skin crawl."

Hector shook his head. He opened the lamp shutter, toed off his boots, then proceeded to hang up Dave's shirt and his own wet clothes. Rain drummed on the deck overhead, and gusts of wind moaned in the rigging. Dressed in the cotton trousers he wore for sleeping, he sat on the edge of his bed and looked over at Dave.

"So... dinner was awkward."

"I don't want to talk about it."

"How long have you known Lord Vaughn es su padre?"

"What part of *I don't want to talk about it* did you not understand, Hector?"

"¿Cuánto tiempo?"

"That man may have slept with my mother, but he isn't my father. I don't have a father. I spent two-thirds of my life hearing I was the bastard son of a whore."

"¡Dios Mío! ¿Estás ciego?"

"Dammit, Hector, speak English."

"You have to admit, you look like Lord Vaughn."

"Whatever." Dave raised his flask. "Both of us being tall and dark-haired doesn't mean anything."

The bounty hunter shook his head. "It isn't just that. Your eyes are the same shape and color. The way you both squint and pinch your mouth closed when you're angry is identical. Robert is the only other person who can match that look, and I've always thought you two looked more like brothers than cousins."

"Why the hell won't you leave it alone?"

"I can't."

"Fuckin' asshole." Dave turned up his flask and chugged the contents, only stopping when he finally had to take a breath. "Fine," he growled. "Robert's mother and mine were more than just sisters, they were identical twins. Their mother named them after damned flowers. Camellia and Bryony." His voice cracked when he said his mother's name, and he tilted up his flask once again.

"Lay off the booze."

The archer ignored Hector.

"Dammit, Dave. Why do you do this to yourself?"

"It's the only thing that drowns the memories," he said. Dave stared down at the flask clutched in his fist. His greasy hair hid most of his face.

Hector leaned forward. "You think you're the only one with bad memories? We all have things we regret, amigo."

"Leave me alone, Hector."

"Dave, Aislinn and Hummingbird are waiting in Ozera, and you're drowning yourself in rotgut whiskey. Whatever it is you're trying to forget is eating you from the inside out, just like Evan Courtenay's ghūl rot."

Dave gripped the flask tighter. "We don't know that the clerics were able to save them."

"Brand and Aislinn's rings stopped moving the same day we left Ruthaer, so I *know* he reached Ozera with her. Tallinn and his winged horse were successful. It's up to Phaedrus now, and I trust he will do everything he can. More than that, I have faith. You said it yourself in Ruthaer: we've seen real miracles here in Gaia, and, if anyone deserves one, it's Aislinn."

Light flared through the porthole over Hector's head, and thunder crashed against the boards, setting the ship atremble and the lantern overhead swinging. When the noise subsided, Hector asked the question that had been on his mind during dinner, "What happened to you and Bryony?"

"I'm not nearly drunk enough," Dave grumbled.

"Any more drunk and you'll pass out," Hector replied.

As answer, Dave took a long swallow. The cabin became still with only the sound of his breathing to fill it.

Hector sat quietly, waiting.

Dave tipped up the flask again.

Interrogations were a nasty business, and Hector had become adept at reading people, knowing when to push and when not to. Sure, he had a reputation for torturing the information out of people. How could he not? That reputation had served him better than any hot poker. With it came the body language he projected every day, such as the hard stare he was using on his friend right now.

Dave swiped the back of his hand across his mouth. Slowly at first, he began to speak, punctuating his words with more shots of whiskey.

"For a few years after I was born, we lived with Cam and Nate, my mother's sister and brother-in-law. I have vague memories of it, just bits and pieces — feelings mostly. Looking back, the whole situation was fucking fishy. Robert and I called both women 'Momma.'

"Something happened, though. I was three when Bryony put me in the car and drove away. That's one of the few things I remember clearly, because I didn't want to go.

"First place we stopped, she dyed her hair dark, changed her clothes, and her make-up. The only thing she didn't change, never changed, was her locket. It had pictures in it...

"Keep in mind, I was just three at the time. I think she stole a car and acquired one of those pull behind campers. I remember the thing seemed huge. After that, we lived like gypsies, skulking from one campground to the next. When you're little, you don't think about money, or what your parents do to get it. I spent my days outside, exploring, sometimes playing with whatever kids I found, but didn't give a thought to the people I saw around our place.

"We never stayed anywhere long, and always, *always* left in the middle of the night. Sometimes the camp owner chased us away; other times, we moved for no apparent reason at all."

Dave scrubbed a hand through his hair almost exactly like Lord Vaughn had earlier. It was a gesture Hector had seen Robert make dozens of times, but rarely Dave.

"I was six when we hooked up with one of those carnival fairs. Bryony told fortunes, sold a few charms and potions. She was in to voodoo or hoodoo or some shit at the time. One night, a man followed us from the fairgrounds to our camper. Said he wanted to talk to her. I remember thinking he had a weird accent. Next thing I knew, she jumped the bastard. Knocked him flat on his ass and slit his throat before he had a chance to scream. There was blood everywhere...

"She didn't wait for the police — just shoved me in the car and drove away. Later, she said the man was going to rob us, maybe kill us. We stopped staying in campgrounds after that, and she started teaching me to fight." Dave took another swallow as he stared out the black porthole. "Imagine me, fuckin' six years old, and learning to fight. She did it right, too. She taught me to kill. That was when I realized people were after us. Maybe I never noticed them before, or maybe the attacks were getting more frequent, but we were leaving a trail of bodies.

"The first person I ever killed was some bastard who got the jump on her in an all-night grocery parking lot. It was my seventh birthday, and she'd stopped to get me a cupcake."

Hector's eyes narrowed as the pieces of his friend's life fell into place. The source of Dave's general disdain for humanity was coming clear for the first time, and he wondered what Lord Vaughn would think if he heard this story.

"A week later, she pulled off onto this narrow dirt road in the middle of the woods and parked in a clearing. She took a couple of backpacks out of the trunk, set the car and camper on fire, and we walked away.

"We lived off the land for days, maybe weeks, I don't know. Nights were getting cold when we came across an empty cabin and moved in.

"She wouldn't let me go outside alone. Kept saying it was dangerous. Then, late one night I heard her talking to someone. When I asked her about it, she said my father was coming for us. Can you even imagine? To be a kid with no father, and then to be told he's coming for you?

"A few nights later, there was a knock on the door. I opened it before she could stop me. There was a bright flash, and I was thrown across the room. Then my mother was there, with a wand in one hand and fire in the other. She fought the man at the door — he had pale skin, ink-black hair, and pointy ears. He looked like a fucking *elf*. Can you believe that shit?"

Taking another swig, Dave continued, "I ran down the hall to the backdoor, planning to go around and come at the bastard from behind, but there was another elf waiting for me. Tall and thin, with the same jet-black hair and creepy silver eyes, he held a recurve longbow in his hand. I dodged into the bedroom and locked the door, then climbed through a trapdoor into the crawlspace under the cabin.

"Light flickered and flashed through gaps in the wood floor over my head. It was like watching a lightning storm through an inferno — hypnotic and terrifying at the same time. The cabin was burning down around them, but Bryony was every bit as fast and ruthless as the elf she fought. She almost had him when she stumbled and fell to her hands and knees. It wasn't until she tried to get up that I saw the arrow in her back." His eyes flicked up and met Hector's briefly before falling back to his flask. "It had black feathers. The elf who came in the backdoor shot her again. She fell hard, and I..."

Dave jumped to his feet and paced across the floor. Clenching his fist, he punched the hull.

"I sat there under the floor like a frightened rabbit while they butchered her. I don't know how, but she found me. She wedged her fingertips between two floorboards. I touched them while her blood dripped down on me, and the light died from her eyes."

"Madre de Dios," Hector breathed, horror and sadness warring on his face.

"Things get murky after that. I wandered in the dark until I stumbled across another cabin and hid in the shed. Come morning, someone opened the door. Hell, I thought they had found me. I grabbed a pair of garden shears and skewered the fucker. Turned out to be a park ranger. The police came, of course. They put me in a hospital, handcuffed me to a bed, and set a guard on my door. I was fuckin' seven!"

Dave gripped his flask. His hand trembled, and Hector wondered if there'd be more.

After he calmed enough to speak, Dave continued, "Robert's parents came. I told them everything, even described the men who killed my mother. The doctors said I was delusional — making shit up — but Uncle Nate believed me. I remember there was a lot of shouting. Eventually, he and Aunt Cam won their argument with the police and doctors, and I was released.

"On the trip home, Uncle Nate told me we had been attacked by dærganfae, not elves. Apparently, he and Bryony had faced them before. Uncle Nate and Aunt Cam assured me the police would keep us safe, but they didn't. The same night we reached Charleston, the fae bastards came for us. Must have been following me the whole time."

Dave took a long swallow. "They forced their way in, tied up Nate and Cam, and hauled me outside. Someone else was there... I vaguely remember a fight. I bit the guy carrying me — took out a chunk of his arm — and ran for the house when he dropped me. About the time I climbed up on the porch, the whole fucking house exploded.

"I woke up in an ambulance, sirens blaring, and an IV in my arm, with no clue what happened to the dærganfae who tried to steal me or the men they were fighting." Dave took another long drink. "I'm cursed, Hector. Robert's parents died because they took me in. My mom died because of me. And now Aislinn, maybe even Hummingbird." The last few words had come out a low whisper, leaving Hector to wonder if he had really heard them.

"Lo siento, amigo. You have to believe me when I say none of it was your fault. You know that, right?"

"I opened the door at the cabin. The dærganfae couldn't have gotten inside otherwise. They were following *me* when they killed Aunt Cam and Uncle Nate."

"None of that makes it your fault," said Hector. "The dærganfae assassins bear that responsibility."

Dave growled low in his throat. "They aren't the only ones who died because of me."

"People you killed to save your own life don't count, Dave."

"I'm not talking about that. When Robert's uncle refused to take me in, the state put me in foster care with an Irish woman who had all her fosters call her Móraí. I'd been with her almost a year, just long enough to start to settle in, when she died. Seafood poisoning, they said, but she never had any kind of fish in the house. When I was twelve, there was a girl who lived next door to the group home I was in. Tilly wasn't afraid of me like the other kids. She died in a hit-and-run late one night, roaming the streets with me. I was holding her hand..."

Hector shook his head. "Dave —"

"Don't you get it? I'm cursed! I kill the people I love." Under his breath he murmured, "Just like Tilly; just like Aislinn."

The way Dave spoke Aislinn's name caused Hector's jaw to drop. He'd long suspected the archer's feelings for Aislinn ran as deep as his own, but he couldn't believe Dave had actually admitted it to himself, much less out loud. Reaching out, he said, "Let me have some of that."

Dave handed over his flask but kept his head down.

After taking a pull of the fiery liquid and handing back the container, Hector said, "You aren't cursed, and you didn't kill Aislinn or Hummingbird. That damned bug tried, but we have not lost them. You'll see when we reach Ozera."

CHAPTER 8
ESCAPE

AUGUST 13, 4237 K.E.

1:53am

Rain pounded on the deck overhead. Dave shifted fitfully in his bunk. The elven chain across his throat kept him pinned down and made it hard to breathe. It burned his skin. The darkness shifted, and he became aware of Ymara's presence. A shadow among shadows, he couldn't see her, but he felt her nearness.

'Poor, tormented archer,' she whispered. 'So much pain.'

"Leave me alone, Ymara," he grumbled.

'How did it come to this? Captured and chained here like some common cur when you were born to be a wolf among the sheep.'

His blood surged in response to her voice, a rising tide of savage fire. It sang to him of freedom and revenge. Nothing would be forbidden with her at his side, every hunger sated.

'I can take away this terrible pain in your heart and free you from your bondage,' she breathed in his ear, 'but you must do something for me in return.'

"Yes," he managed to gasp.

'Swear, archer.'

"Swear?"

'Swear you will help me be free.'

"Anything," he rasped.

'Give me your hands. Together, we will break this chain and be gone before your captors know you are free.'

He reached to his throat and the chain there. Her hands slid over his, guiding him to an ill-made link he hadn't noticed before, helping him manipulate the ring and toggle-like pieces in the darkness.

The chain dropped away, and he sat up. Lightning flashed, showing him the room. The Espian in the other bunk scowled in his sleep, his fists clenched.

'Quietly, now,' Ymara murmured. 'We mustn't wake the hunter, or he will try to stop us. Your weapons are in the corner by the door.'

Dave nodded. Although the room now seemed clear as day, he still couldn't see Ymara. He strapped on his belt and scabbard, then drew a heavy-bladed hunting knife and stepped toward the sleeping man.

A boom of thunder rattled the cabin. The man muttered in his sleep and rolled onto his side. Dave scowled as he stared at the stranger in the cot. Something seemed familiar about the Espian, but he couldn't quite place it. Sheathing his weapon, he withdrew, instinctively sliding into the room's inky shadows. When the man's breathing deepened, Dave gathered his bow, arrows, and boots, donned a seal-grey cloak, and slipped out to the narrow corridor, where he finished dressing.

Rain lashed the ship, and wind moaned among the shrouds. Lanterns fore, aft, and midships cast radiant starbursts through the driving storm, but he didn't need their light. At the starboard rail, a sailing skiff hung in its cradle, ready for launch.

Through the wind and rain, he heard a distant shout. Dave raced across the deck, his cloak billowing around him. He grabbed the line securing the skiff's cradle with one hand, while the other tugged loose the mooring hitch and belaying pin. The ship shifted, and the skiff swung toward the pinrail, where it struck a sailor with a resounding thud. A figure raced from the aft deck, golden braids streaming behind like tentacles.

Dave reached for his sword.

The young woman slid to a stop at the rail, caught the skiff's transom, and shoved the small boat aside. A thin, swarthy sailor collapsed to the deck.

A powerful gust shoved the skiff free and beyond the rail, and Dave let the line play out through the launch pulley.

"Thou canst not save thy sailboat!" shouted the woman.

For a moment, Dave thought he knew her and the unconscious man on the deck. Cloudy images and the beginnings of names danced just out of reach, then Ymara called to him. In a swirl of grey oilskin and driving rain, he leapt to the rail and rode the line down to the skiff where his princess waited.

CR80

4:30am

Hector lurched awake, still trapped in the vestiges of his nightmare. The glaring blaze of the clockwork monster's black diamond eye filled his vision. Floundering for his weapons, Hector fell out of bed. The jarring impact knocked the wind from him. Overhead, a pinprick of light leaked from the shuttered lantern.

The ship swayed in the river current, no longer buffeted by gusty winds. The muffled sound of crewmen moving about and calling to one another carried through the bulkhead. Hector released the breath he hadn't realized he was holding and yawned as he climbed back into bed. He considered trying for a few more minutes sleep, but his mind latched onto the stillness in the room.

Dave wasn't snoring. He wasn't even breathing.

The bounty hunter squinted at the opposite bunk. A distant flicker of lightning split the darkness, revealing an empty cot. A sense of unease snaked through Hector.

A sharp knock rattled his cabin door. "Bayim, are you awake?" a baritone voice called out. Heavy-handed knocking shook the door again. "Bayim! The captain wishes to see you!

The bounty hunter stumbled to the door. He snatched it open as the Turkestani quartermaster, Salizar, made to knock again. "¿Qué pasa?" he demanded. "¿Qué hora es?"

"Apologies, Bayim, but we had trouble during the storm. Captain Smeyth wishes to see you." The mountainous quartermaster quirked an eyebrow at the shorter man. "Though, for propriety's sake, I recommend you wear more than your small clothes."

Hector knuckled the sleep from his eyes. "Is Dave already on deck somewhere? What happened?"

"Don't ask questions!" the quartermaster shouted. "Jump to! Get dressed and report to the captain!"

Startled, Hector leapt back, his hand instinctively looking for a weapon he wasn't wearing. With a sharp nod, the ship's officer departed.

The bounty hunter slammed the door. After opening the overhead lantern's shutter, he dressed in his still-damp clothes while puzzling over the odd summons. His gaze settled on the corner where they stowed their saddlebags and gear. Only his half remained. His adrenaline spiked.

Hector snatched the blanket from Dave's cot, revealing Aislinn's sparkling necklace of golden oak leaves and the sigil-etched back of the silver brooch. He suddenly viewed Dave's behavior the previous afternoon in a new light. Suspicion that the archer had not told him the entire truth about Lady D crystalized into certainty.

"¡Carajo! ¡Esa perra! ¡Voy a matarla de nuevo!"

Still swearing in Espian, Hector scooped up the necklace and brooch, then raced from the room. He burst through the forecastle hatch to the main deck, searching for the skiff, but the lines and pullies which cradled it yesterday held one of the ship's longboats. "Ugh! ¡Yo soy estúpido!" He twisted his signet ring around his finger and closed his fist around the embossment. The magic in the platinum flared to life. The closest of its five mates lay upriver, moving west at a steady pace. That was Dave in their sailing skiff.

Pulse pounding, Hector ran across the deck, snatched open the aftcastle hatch, and entered without knocking. "Señor Vaughn!"

The sharp tip of a sword pricked his back. "Someone better be dying, Señor de los Santos, for you to burst into this cabin unannounced," Lady Aneirin said.

"Señora. Almirante, perdóname por favor. Es una emergencia."

"Habla Glaxon, cazador," she replied. Her sword tip didn't waver.

Hector drew in a deep breath and counted to ten before exhaling. "Admiral, Dave and our skiff are missing." The sword at his back disappeared, allowing him to turn and face Lady Aneirin.

"I'm aware," she nodded. "He and the skiff went overboard at the height of the storm. Tell me, can Dave swim?"

"Yes, but —"

"Then there's a chance he made it to shore. I'll let Captain Smeyth know. We have one longboat away and a second ready for launch. Roger is waiting for you to go with him and lead the search."

Hector shook his head. "Dave didn't swim ashore. He's headed upriver, toward Tydway."

"How do you know?"

Hector showed her his platinum signet ring. "Each of the six original members of Damage, Inc. has one — Aislinn, Eidan, Jasper, Robert, Dave, and me. After we rescued Robert from the Sha'iry, I asked Jasper to enchant our rings with a tracking spell."

"You know where each of your team members are at any given moment?"

Hector waggled his hand side-to-side. "It gives me a direction along with a general sense of distance. The closer we get, the better I'll be able to pinpoint Dave's location — I just hope he keeps wearing it."

"How far upriver is he now?"

Hector clenched his fist around the signet ring and compared the signature of Dave's ring to Jasper's. "Not quite a third of the way between us and Tydway."

"Wait here." She left the room, and he heard her shouting orders on deck. The smell of strong tea laced with chicory and bergamot drew his attention to a carafe on a silver tray, flanked by a short pitcher of cream and a jar of honey. A heavy clay mug stood at the end of the table near the admiral's throne-like chair.

Hector paced to the windows and back, mulling over Dave's abandonment of the brooch and his escape. Hector didn't believe in coincidences. From the sorceress' last second escape that spring, to Consuelo turning up in Ruthaer ahead of Damage, Inc., in possession of a mask that transformed her into Lady D, to the mask's continued ability to speak to Dave after its host's death — the chain of events smacked of a sinister hand at work behind the scenes.

The door opened, admitting Lady Aneirin, Lord Vaughn, and Teal. Lady Aneirin took her seat at the table and drained her clay mug. A moment later, Belinda appeared from below with a carafe of fresh kahve and three more mugs. The rustle of sails, the creak of the windlass raising the anchor, and sailor's shouts as they prepared to make way filled the silent cabin.

The admiral fixed Hector with a dark and dangerous glare that reminded him of his mother's expression when she'd caught him skipping school. Once the cook departed, Lady Aneirin said, "Señor de los Santos, you've been withholding information."

Hector heaved a sigh and massaged his temples. "Sí, señora, but not with malicious intent. There are things in Dave's and my past that we simply can't afford for our enemies to learn. Events we rarely speak of, even with those who were there to witness them. If you don't mind me asking, how did Dave get off the ship with our skiff?"

"They were blown over," replied Teal. "I remained 'pon the rear deck midst the storm, watching the lightning. Haidar, the lad who walked the watch, saw the skiff buffeted and in danger of breaking free. Whilst he did race to it from one direction, I espied Dave closing from the bow. The skiff caught Haidar 'gainst the pinrail. Dave did help me free him by pulling upon the mooring line whilst I pushed the skiff. No sooner than the sailor fell free, a new gust did strike the little craft, sending it o'er the rail. Dave did try to save it but was pulled over after it." Teal bowed his head. "I am sorry that I could not save him."

"Had you tried to stop him, he would have killed you, Teal. He isn't in control of his own mind anymore."

"Hector, what are you talking about? What's happened to my son?" Lord Vaughn asked. Even though he tried to control it, the emotion of finding his son and then losing him again made his voice crack.

Hector swallowed against the lump in his throat and laid Aislinn's gold necklace and the balas-ruby brooch on the table. "I'm sure you each saw Dave wearing this and probably noticed the scars among his tattoos. This brooch, flawed as it is, protected him from Lady D, a vampire who bit him two years ago."

"When you recounted events to me in Ruthaer, you said the sorceress, Consuelo, impersonated this Lady D," said Lord Vaughn. "Are you telling us there really was a vampire in the area?"

"Consuelo had a skull mask. It made her look and act like Lady D, and it allowed her to control Dave before we discovered the power in this brooch." He closed his eyes for a moment, and saw the bloody, skinless mess of the sorceress' face after the mask ripped free. An involuntary shudder of disgust coursed through the bounty hunter. "Dave brought the mask out of the cistern with us..." His jaw clenched around a curse. "Soy un idiota. I've had it wrong from the beginning."

Lady Aneirin gave Hector a quizzical look and asked, "What are you talking about?"

"I thought Consuelo controlled the mask, but it's the other way around. The mask controlled her." Hector paced across the room, head down, brow furrowed in thought. As impossible as it seemed, he feared Lady D herself had set these events in motion nearly two years ago.

Roger blinked, then his eyes widened. "Where is this mask now?"

"Hidden on our skiff."

"The one Dave's taking to Tydway?" Lady Aneirin asked with a flash in her eyes.

"Sí, señora," Hector replied.

"Perhaps, whilst we have time to kill, thou shouldst start at the beginning," Teal suggested.

"I agree," said Lord Vaughn. "The more we know, the better able we'll be to free Dave from this vampire."

"The beginning..." Hector muttered and paced the length of the table before his audience. Outside the stern windows, the countryside slipped past with increasing speed. "About three years ago, Dave, Eidan, and I were in Vologda. We'd tracked a group of slavers from Francesca to the city of Erinskaya and were gathering evidence for King Edmund to present to the Confederation of Nations council. That's where we learned about the Sha'iry's search for an artifact called the Akshan, and their plan to force our friend, Robert Stone, to help them."

"The Akshan?" Lord Vaughn asked, confusion clear in his eyes.

"It's a sentient artifact with a predilection for cats. Akshan is also the title of the lycanthrope who is the alpha, more or less, of every feline on Gaia, from the smallest housecat to the strongest lycanthropes. They — the lycanthrope and the sentient artifact — guard the slumber of Ka'Sehkuur, an insane entity some worship as a god, and others call the destroyer of worlds.

"Someone killed the Akshan, and the artifact disappeared. Ka'Sehkuur started to wake up. The Dark One sent his Sha'iry to recover the artifact and enthrone a new feline lycanthrope to stop Ka'Sehkuur."

Hector shook his head. "That part really isn't relevant, now. What you need to know is the Sha'iry took Robert, thinking he had a magic item that would help them find the Akshan artifact. Seven of us — me, Aislinn, Dave, and Jasper, plus an Iron Tower ranger named Xandor, August Sabe from Rhodina, and a Francescan warrior-priest called Gideon — chased Robert and the Sha'iry from Francesca to Trakya, where we lost them. Jasper and Aislinn combed the local church and mages' libraries trying to discover their destination and came across an ancient Korellan journal that pointed us to the Väkivartija elves in the mountains of Altaira on the other side of the world."

Hector dropped into a chair, propped his elbows on the table, and leaned his forehead against his palms. "Leaving Xandor and Jasper behind in Trakya to foil a Sha'iry coup, the rest of us travelled to Altaira. What we found was the beginning of a trail of clues. We hired a pair of locals, Cinaed and Shona, to be our guides. They led us to the caverns of Bloodstone Peak, a dormant volcano with a hot spring lake in its caldera acidic enough to melt flesh. Traps, both magical and mundane, riddled the caverns and passages. Less than twelve hours in, Dave became separated from the group.

"The third day, we stumbled across a lavish apartment. Lady D was there, in red lacquered plate and chain armor that glistened in the lantern light like fresh blood. I didn't see Dave, only the hawk-head arrow that punched through Gideon's arm. Dave had become her thrall.

"Aislinn and Shona went for Dave while Gideon, Cinaed, and I faced the vampire. She held Cinaed with a single look, as if he was a living statue, then turned her black-eyed gaze on me. I could hear her in my head, but I wasn't affected like Cinaed.

"As we crossed blades, Lady D told me, 'The archer is *mine*, now and forever.' Sword-to-sword I was outmatched, but she didn't kill me — not even when Aislinn's scream drew my attention from the fight." His haunted eyes met Roger's. "Dave had her pinned to the floor. He was snarling and growling at her like a rabid wolf.

"Lady D meant to enslave the rest of us as well. We'd all be like Dave. It took Gideon and me fighting together to cut off the vampire's head. As soon as we did, her hold on Cinaed and Dave broke. We burned her corpse to ashes, but not her head. I pulled out Lady D's fangs and flung the head, along with her broken sword, out into the acidic lake. Even now, I wonder if the vampire tricked me into doing what she wanted."

"Lady D is an odd name for a vampire," Lord Vaughn mused.

"Sí, señor, it is. Dave talked about the vampire in his sleep, called her Ymara Dapniš. The things he said... they were terrifying. Dave has always been superstitious, and hearing her name made things worse for him. So, to lessen her power over him, we called her Lady D — if we spoke about her at all. It seemed to work. He stopped having nightmares.

"However, not long after Consuelo and her pet demon escaped us this past spring, Dave's nightmares returned. Like before, he had trouble differentiating the dreams from reality. Then, Lady D turned up in Ruthaer, working with that ghūl, Evan Courtenay. Somehow, Consuelo retrieved her skull from that lake of acid in Altaira and fashioned it into a mask. She *became* Lady D." He stopped suddenly, and a look of shocked horror covered his face. "Madre de Dios... the bug."

"What bug?" Teal asked.

"The clockwork bug that attacked us in Ruthaer's quarry. It was like a vile cross between a giant spider and a praying mantis, made of black metal and chitin, with black diamond eyes and hellfire leaking from its joints. It was damaged, half its face melted, and parts of its armor plating replaced with hardened leather. Why didn't I see it before?" Hector lurched back to his feet and resumed pacing. "I should have asked Aislinn if acid could cause the damage we saw on the pieces in the gnomes' workshop."

"Focus, Hector," Lord Vaughn commanded. "What about my son?"

"Dave still hears Lady D in his head. This brooch," Hector said holding up the gold necklace and balas-ruby, "helped him resist her but it wasn't enough. I thought he would be safe on this ship with us here to protect him. She must have been biding her time."

"Upon the ship whence we first met Lord Vaughn, I did hear Dave speaking to someone when I sought to convey Lord Vaughn's dinner summons," Teal said. "Someone he wanted to stay out of his head."

"Lady D," Hector groaned. "Somehow, she convinced him to remove Aislinn's necklace and leave the brooch."

"So, where will he go?" asked Lord Vaughn.

"Tydway? It's the closest city," Hector said with an uncertain shrug. "If Lady D is in control, I imagine she'll make him find someone to wear the mask, to become its new host. If that happens..." his voice trailed off. "Sir, I'd rather Dave not have that burden added to his conscience."

Lord Vaughn nodded. "We'll find him."

"Lady D is both unpredictable and cunning. Worse, she has access to Dave's thoughts." Hector turned to Lady Aneirin. "Admiral, do you think we can catch him?"

"We carry more canvas, so we're faster than the skiff, but he'll have more maneuverability in this river. With three more ships, we could form a blockade and run him down with longboats."

Hector shook his head. "That would get someone killed."

"Pray tell, how is having him ashore better?" asked Teal.

"We can ambush him. Catch him before he has a chance to kill someone, and then fasten that necklace and brooch back on him. Once we get Dave to Tydway, maybe Jasper or one of the other mages at the academy can find a better way to block Lady D's influence."

"Our first priority should be to destroy that mask." Lord Vaughn punctuated his words by banging his fist on the table. "Not containing it."

"Señor, Dave tried to smash it in the cistern. He couldn't even scratch it," Hector replied.

"Phaedrus and his librarians should be able to break its power," Lord Vaughn said.

Lady Aneirin clasped Lord Vaughn's wrist and waited for him to meet her gaze before saying, "You're putting a lot of faith in Phaedrus and his followers."

"We need their help, Lahar."

"We'll send a message to Ozera the moment we reach Tydway but, as my husband would say, we cannot misplace our faith in the Eternal Father. It is *His* help we need."

CHAPTER 9
TYDWAY

AUGUST 13, 4237 K.E.

8:00am

The home of Radren Witt crouched behind a fence of brick and wrought iron. A poorly maintained privet hedge straggled along the inside of the knee-high brick, leaving the house visible through patches of leafless gaps and dull grey twigs. A cobblestone path led from the gate to the front door. The house itself appeared to have started out as a single-story clapboard building under a thatched roof, but it had been added onto in the half-timber and brick style common in the newer sections of Tydway.

Dodz, once more impeccably dressed in the finery of a nobleman, minced up the walk, careful to avoid the disreputable tangle of weeds crowding either side of the pavement. On the doorstep, he removed a small wooden compact from his pocket and examined his disguise one last time: blackened hair, the best theater beard and mustache money could buy, and cosmetically aged skin. The only thing he hadn't changed was the frost-blue of his eyes. Satisfied, he put away the mirror, adjusted the mink collar of his short cape, and rapped on the door with the foot of his walking cane. Silence answered. Scowling, he banged on the door again.

He stepped back and studied the door stoop. A brass ring hung from a length of braided wire threaded through a small hole in the wall to the door's right. He hooked the ring with the nighthawk shaped head of his cane and gave it a sharp tug. Beyond the door, a bell clanged.

Moments later, a dour-faced hag in a threadbare servant's dress opened the door. She neither greeted him nor offered to let him inside.

"Guten morgen, frau. I have an appointment with Herr Witt," Dodz announced in flawless Detchian.

The woman looked him up and down as if he were a filthy beggar before stepping back and gesturing for him to enter. He found himself in a spare room that served as a bedroom, kitchen, and sewing room all in one. The silent woman marched across the room and down a short hallway to an ironwood door, which she opened without knocking. Beyond lay a broad, well-lit room. A wide chandelier hung from the ceiling over a long table covered in alchemical flasks and strange apparatus for which Dodz could only guess their uses. Shelves bearing leather tomes stood in a corner near the fireplace, flanked by two heavy chairs and a small side table.

There, a rail-thin man of middle years swiped at the last of his breakfast with a hunk of bread. Hastily licking his fingers clean of every last crumb, he drained his flagon and rose from his seat to study the visitor to his domain.

"Herr Tarnistan, I presume?"

"Magier Witt, thank you for seeing me so early," Dodz replied with a brief nod and a sharp-eyed look at the servant cleaning away the man's breakfast dishes.

"Ja, your message left me most intrigued. Come, show me this gem."

Dodz waited for the serving woman to retreat into the hallway and close the heavy door. He gave the barrier a glare, suspicious that the servant stood beyond, spying on his business with her master.

"Ignore Marda. She is deaf," the Detchian mage stated, leading his guest toward the worktable.

Dodz produced a leather-wrapped bundle. "I am told you are the Academia's authority on soul gems — both their creation and their uses." When the mage smiled and gave him a slight bow, Dodz unwrapped the bundle to reveal his newly sharpened prize. "I recently acquired this blade."

"Wunderbar!" The mage's soft exclamation was little more than a whisper.

"You can sense the spirit?" Dodz asked.

"Nein. Not without touching the stone."

"What about another mage or a cleric?"

"Such a thing could only happen if someone sought this particular spirit at the exact moment you or I were communicating with it, und the likelihood of that... Well, to say the odds are infinitesimal would still be too great a coincidence. Now, may I examine the stone?"

The moment Dodz acquiesced, Witt snatched up the blade by its wire-wrapped hilt and walked to the window, where he let the morning sun play across the diamond's black facets. "Where did you come by such a treasure?"

Dodz waved a hand vaguely west toward the Alashalian mountains. "Half buried in an old ruin."

The mage inhaled and exhaled slowly, then touched the gem's flat top with a single, bony fingertip.

CRSO

A distant pinprick of light pulsed, then flared. Aislinn flinched away from the glare. The sudden motion with her eyes closed made her world spin. She stumbled, expecting to crash against the glossy black wall, but met no resistance.

Surrounded by the smell of earth and trees, she felt sunlight warm her face, and nearby, wrens chirped.

"Well, wha' do we have here, lads?" a voice said.

Aislinn's eyes snapped open. The lush, rounded peaks of the Alashalian mountains rose around her, guarding a broad valley. She stood beside an earthen cart path that led to the Tanjaran village of Ogham. On her left, a wooden stile split a thick swath of blackberry brambles, providing access over a stacked-stone wall into an apple orchard.

She turned to find three young men leering at her. The eldest, no more than fifteen summers, stood a head taller than Aislinn, and was a step closer than his companions. Small pig-like eyes peered out from a round, ruddy face topped by an unruly mop of flaxen hair.

"Looks like a wild fae, Årgeir," one of the other boys answered. His carrot-colored hair was drawn tight into a topknot with the underneath shaved. Stepping to the side of the cart path, he moved to flank their prey.

With her back angled toward the blackberries, Aislinn half turned so she could see all three bullies. "What do you want? I'm busy."

"Oh, aye, we saw how busy you were, standin' there wi' yer eyes closed," the smallest of the three snickered.

"Ye've been about our village four days now, doin' chores for tha' orchard keeper's boy. It's time ye did some work for me," the leader said.

"And if I don't?" she asked.

"Oh, ye will. 'Tis only a matter of whether I beat ye before or after."

"Ha!" she laughed. "I'll tell you what, if you leave now, I won't embarrass you in front of your dogs by kicking your ugly ass."

Årgeir's heavy brow drew down into a scowl, and he bared his teeth. "Bitch, when we're done with you, you'll beg to lick my boots."

Brand's angry cry echoed through the valley, and his vision overwhelmed Aislinn's. She could feel the wind whip past his face as he dove off the mountain peak and skimmed the treetops. She pushed back against their bond, struggling to separate herself. A fist slammed into her gut, stealing her breath.

Aislinn doubled over, gasping. She heard the three young men laughing, and anger boiled through her veins. Tears blurred her vision, and she squeezed her eyes tight. She gulped a shuddering breath and looked up as the red-haired boy came at her again. He drew back to kick her in the ribs, and she plowed into him, shoulder first, sending him staggering back across the path.

Her hand found the leather-bound handle of her hatchet and snatched it from her belt as she rounded on the other two.

"Watch out, Årgeir!"

"I can see, Colm," Årgeir snapped. "Ulfrað! Get back over here. She can't hit all three of us at once."

Murder flashing in his eyes, Ulfrað staggered back toward them, his face as red as his hair. A bright green orb streaked through the air and smacked the center of his forehead, laying him out flat.

Aislinn had just enough time to register the apple bouncing into the grass before Årgeir and Colm were on her. She elbowed the smaller boy in the gut and swung the hatchet backhanded, driving the axe-head's poll against Årgeir's ribs like a hammer. The larger boy grunted, but his fist didn't slow as it crashed against her cheek. She flew back into the blackberry bramble, darkness pulsing at the edges of her vision. A thousand points of pain erupted across her back, neck, and arms.

'*Zu'fen svadrisis kornarii*,' Brand hissed.

'*Niid*,' Aislinn growled back. '*No killing*.' The dragon hissed again. Her pain leaked through the bond, fueling his rage.

Ignoring the thorns, Árgeir grabbed a fistful of Aislinn's shirt and drug her back to her feet, shaking her until her teeth rattled. "Ready to do what you're told, fae?"

From the corner of her eye, she recognized Xandor trading blows with Colm. She'd been helping the fourteen-year-old youth with his chores while she waited for Edge to arrive in Ogham.

Árgeir backhanded her, and she tasted blood. "Go to hell," she spat.

Wind roared in her ears. Brand was drawing closer by the second. If she didn't end this quickly, he would likely maim or kill one of these stupid boys. She drew back and kicked Árgeir in the crotch as hard as she could. His eyes crossed, and he fell to the ground, gasping and cradling his injured manhood.

Seeing his leader down, Colm broke free from Xandor and raced back toward the village. The towheaded boy grinned at Aislinn. His left eye was already swollen, but his right sparkled with excitement.

"This lot's been in need of a good thrashing for years." He studied her face for a moment, then said, "Come on. My mum and gramma will fix that shiner and your busted lip."

"I doubt mine's as bright as yours," Aislinn said, smiling as best she could. "Did you see where my axe went?"

"Aye, but we'll need a trained rabbit to get it out o' those bushes. Leave it for now."

With a rush of wings, Brand dropped to the cart path. He barely fit between the trees and the orchard wall. Growling low in his throat, he slithered toward Ulfrað and Árgeir.

Aislinn stepped in front of the young dragon, blocking his way. "Everything's alright," she soothed, wrapping her arms around his long neck. "The fight's over."

"They hurt you," Brand grated. Electricity crackled over his scales and around Aislinn. He drew in a deep breath, preparing to spit a burning ball of plasma at the offending scoundrels.

"Don't!" Aislinn said, stroking his scales. "It's over now. Besides, we'll get in trouble with Edge if we hurt them."

"I don't care!" the dragon roared. Electricity gathered in his scales during his dive from the mountain streaked from his snout and burst overhead with a deafening boom.

The two remaining bullies scrambled to their feet and staggered away, casting fearful glances back at the dragon and the girl standing between it and them.

Aislinn turned to Xandor. "Where's my axe?"

Awestruck, Xandor pointed, and Brand reached through the bramble with a long-taloned foreclaw. The briars scraped impotently over his bronze scales.

"Thank you," she said, standing forehead to forehead with the dragon. "Why don't you find a big lake, and get some supper? I'm safe." She looked over her shoulder at the young man waiting by the stile. "Where's the closest lake inside Tanjara borders?"

He thought for a moment, then pointed west over the peaks. "Next valley over will be best. Big lake, big fish."

"No," Brand rumbled, "I want to stay with you. Those three might come back with reinforcements."

Aislinn considered Brand's fear. "Xandor, do you think those three are stupid enough to come after us again if Brand leaves?"

"They're mean, but not dumb. More like than not, Årgeir will go to his da and make us out to be the villains. Breac already hates you for bein' an elf."

She turned and faced Xandor, eyebrows high. "That's *his* son? Oh, great. I'll be lucky if Breac doesn't try to have me burnt at the stake. What's he got against elves, anyway?"

"You... well, elves... look a bit like the dærganfae." He spat in the dirt, as if the word tasted bad in his mouth. His fists clenched and unclenched, over and over. "Bastards have stolen bairns and young folks from villages all over the place," he snarled. "Breac lost his wife and eldest son ta the fae... Årgeir was only three or four summers, Rhun was maybe five. My da told me about it after they stole my sister." He hung his head. "If I hadn't already met you before... I don't know if I could believe you're not fae, either, despite your red hair and green eyes."

Aislinn leaned back against Brand's chest. To her eye, Xandor looked like he felt the same about dærganfae as she did about pirates.

'*Distract him*,' Brand urged through their bond, '*or he's going to be looking for another fight — just like you.*'

"Will your parents get mad if Brand stays with me?"

Xandor closed his good eye and breathed heavily for several long seconds. The tension faded from his shoulders, and he shook his head. "Not so long as he stays by the orchard. Apples don't get scared. Mum's chickens and the cow, on the other hand..." He grinned. "Come on then. Your cheek's turning purple."

Aislinn and Brand followed Xandor along the road beside the orchard to his family's home. His mother was crossing the barnyard, her apron full of eggs, when they arrived. She took in their battered appearance, mouth open in an "O" of surprise.

"Xandor Baendra ap Kynan o'r Perllan! What ondskap have ye been up to now?"

"Wasn't me, Mum!" he protested. "Årgeir, Ulfrað, and Colm caught Aislinn on the far side o' the orchard. She stood up to them, and they tried to thrash her. I had to help."

Her mouth turned down in displeasure. "I suppose ye did, lad, but I'll not have the two o' ye drippin' blood in my house. Draw a bucket o' water and go round to the kitchen door."

Xandor's grandmother *tsked* at the sight of them, and soon had each of them sitting on the kitchen steps, cold wet rags pressed to their bruises. She sat on a milking stool before them, rummaging through an apothecary's case on her lap. Like most people of the Alashalian Clans, she had heterochromatic eyes. Hers were bright spring green with an inner ring of snow-cloud grey. The boy at Aislinn's side was unique in having one eye of each color.

"Alright ye two, pay attention. Bein' that the two o' ye have many a bruise in your future, ye'd best be learning how to tend them."

"Gramma..." Xandor protested.

"Hush, lad. It doesn't take the sight to know the two o' ye are scrappers, bound for many a fight. It's the sight that tells me great and terrible things lie in your twined futures." She lifted a small jar from her box. "This is for your faces. It's made mostly of daisy juice for the swelling, with a little arnica and willow for the pain and bruising, in rendered beeswax with sunflower and walnut oils." The old woman dipped a finger in the jar and rubbed a thin layer below and around Xandor's swollen eye. When she was done, she held out the jar to Aislinn. "You'll need to put this on twice a day for the next few days."

"Thank you." Aislinn wrapped her fingers around the small jar, the side of her hand brushing the elder's palm.

Xandor's grandmother grabbed Aislinn's hand, and her two-toned eyes grew distant. "Beware, child," she rasped. "Thy future is plagued by Darkness. Danger and Death move inexorably toward you. They will be both your undoing and your salvation."

The girl's eyes darted from the old woman, to Xandor, and back again. She tried to pull away, but the aged fingers only gripped tighter. "Ow! Let go."

'*What's wrong?*' Brand's voice was loud in Aislinn's head.

'*Xandor's grandmother is weird,*' Aislinn replied, '*and strong.*'

Xandor leapt to his feet and leaned into the kitchen. "Mum! Gramma's taken by the sight!"

Brand's roar echoed off the mountainside as he dropped into the barnyard. He tried to wedge his head between Aislinn and the old woman, but Xandor's grandmother thrust out a gnarled hand and pinched the tender septum at the end of his snout. The dragon froze, his huge eyes crossed in an effort to meet the old woman's gaze.

"First and last of your kind, two halves of a greater whole, key the Súmairefola longs to find; it shall strive to own your souls," the woman chanted. "One slain by rage in mountain naos, one slain by hate midst sacred trees, spirit caught in the eye of chaos, the kiss o' Death shall set you free..."

"Mum!" Xandor's mother burst from the house and jerked to a stop. Her eyes went wide as she stammered, "D... d... dragon!"

Dizziness swept over Aislinn, and shadows closed in from every side, consuming her sight. When her vision finally cleared, she found herself alone on her knees, arm outstretched toward the distant pinpoint of light.

'*Brand?*' she stretched and strained to reach the dragon through their soul-bond but met only emptiness. She was still in the glassy tunnel, her bond with Brand blocked or broken. Aislinn fought the tears threatening to overwhelm her. Despite the events being long past, the vision had been so real. Even now, the throb of bruises lingered. She raised trembling fingers to her mouth, then across her forehead, through her hair, and over the back of her neck, expecting to find a wound or bruise but found neither.

Aislinn leaned against the cold wall and wondered if she'd lost her grip on sanity. Perhaps she should have listened to her mother and never left Ozera.

She glanced over her shoulder. An impenetrable wall of darkness blocked her path back. Something niggled at the edges of her consciousness, but it slipped away each time she tried to grasp it. Something about the darkness... A sense of unease slithered over her skin, leaving goosebumps in its wake, as if someone was watching her.

CRSO

8:25am

Magier Witt turned to Dodz with a lascivious grin. "Der geist is fresh und new. She is not yet aware she no longer lives."

"I wish to learn more about the spirit in the gem," Dodz said. "Can I do this without harm to myself?"

"Oh, ja, if you have strong enough will. If not..." The mage shrugged and his lips curled in a calculating smile. "If not, you may find yourself trapped in the stone, und der geist in control of your body. Perhaps you will sell the stone to me? I have use for it in my research."

Dodz shook his head. "Nein. The stone does not come free from the blade, und I am fond of both."

"Come, Herr Tarnistan, I make you a generous offer."

"Nein. I will pay you for knowledge I can use." He untied his coin purse from his belt and held it up for his host to see its contents. "I have brought fine gems for your payment, sir." A rainbow cascade poured forth into the mage's waiting palm, and Dodz observed the hunger in the other man's gaze. "Do we have an accord?"

"Ja, diese is good. Perhaps is best we should sit." He gave his guest a polite bow and gestured to the sitting area. "Dizziness is common when using soul gems. We would not wish you harm."

Dodz settled in the chair, the wire wrapped hilt clutched in his fist and the curved, scythe-like blade along his forearm. "Very well, Herr Witt, how do I question the spirit? Can it be done without revealing myself to her?"

"Ja, ja, is simple to understand. You only must think of question, hold it firm in your mind when you touch the stone. A simple question yields a simple answer. It is all in how you ask. For example, asking 'What is your name' has a simple answer. Asking 'Who are you' is much more complex."

"So?"

"Simple questions are answered with words. Complex questions with memories. For the unprepared, the experience is... disorienting. However, you must keep emotion in check. Be an impartial observer. The moment you let emotion into the picture, you open yourself to the spirit, Herr Tarnistan, to its influence. Come. You give it a try. Ask her name."

Mimicking the mage, Dodz laid a fingertip on the black diamond. Nothing happened. He raised an eyebrow at Magier Witt.

"You must remove your glove. Communication requires direct contact."

Rather than remove his glove, Dodz pulled up the cuff of his sleeve and pressed the stone to his exposed wrist. Although his accidental communication with the spirit in the stone the previous morning had revealed her name, he asked again. As promised, his simple question yielded a simple word answer: Aislinn Yves. Dodz looked up at the mage hovering nearby. "How do I know the spirit speaks true?"

"The spirit cannot lie, Herr Tarnistan. However, it is the nature of these spirits to guard their secrets. Once she understands she is a prisoner, you may expect her to omit details if you are not strong enough to compel her full answer. Now, perhaps you would like to ask her a complex question here in the safety of mein laboratory?"

Dodz nodded, noting the ill-hidden eagerness in the mage's expression. He shifted the black diamond to within a hair's breadth of his wrist and let his eyelids fall, watching through his lashes. The moment Witt began to cast, Dodz launched himself from the chair and slit the mage's throat with the razor sharp Akkilettū blade.

His movement was so swift, the Detchian mage did not realize he'd been struck. His lack of voice was the only indication something was wrong. He raised a hand to his throat, confusion clouding his features. At his touch, blood gushed forth.

Fascinated, Dodz studied the edge of his blade and discovered there was no blood. The black stalk remained as smooth and oily looking as when he had pulled it from the creature's head. He sneered at Herr Witt. His faux Detchian accent fell away. "You should have been satisfied with the gems, comrade. At least then, you would have enjoyed a few more days of life."

Dodz returned the scythe-like blade to its newly crafted sheath and rewrapped it in leather. When finished, he crept to the front of the house and found the servant sitting near a window mending a hem. She remained unaware of Dodz' presence until the garrote wire cinched around her throat.

Ten minutes later, Dodz let himself out the way he entered Magier Witt's home. He felt more confident in his ability to question Aislinn Yves' spirit about Hector de los Santos and Dave Blood and achieve his goals. With a spring in his step, Dodz disappeared into the morning foot traffic. Behind him, an explosion shook the home of Radren Witt and engulfed the house in flames.

CHAPTER 10
A WATERY TRAIL

AUGUST 13, 4237 K.E.

8:30am

The tide and a strong breeze carried the *Lady Luck* steadily up the River Tamesas throughout the morning. With each passing hour they didn't spot the skiff, Hector grew more worried. While Teal spent his time in the crow's nest atop the mainmast, Hector remained on the aft deck, continuously checking the tracking spell in his signet ring.

"Señor Greene, does the river turn north?"

At the helm, the bosun shook his head. "She bends and twists like a snake but mainly heads northwest. A couple of smaller rivers come in from the north though."

Hector swore under his breath. Nothing was ever easy. He hurried down the ladder and knocked at the officers' quarters. Inside, Lord Vaughn, Lady Aneirin, and the captain gathered around a detailed map of Gallowen spread across the central table.

"Dave turned north," he announced. "He must know we're getting close."

"How close?" Lady Aneirin asked.

Hector pointed through the forward starboard bulwark. "I can't say exactly, but less than a quarter the distance we were behind him when we weighed anchor this morning."

Lord Vaughn glanced out the bank of windows at the landscape falling behind. "The Raveneffre joins the Tamesas in the next mile, maybe less. He could reach Herian Hill by midnight tomorrow if he went without sleep."

"I'll have the lads prepare a longboat, admiral." Captain Smeyth gave a short bow to his boss and started shouting orders as he stepped out on deck.

Fifteen minutes later, the anchors splashed into the river upstream of the confluence of the Tamesas and its smaller tributary. In the distance, a tall, tower-like building straddled the Raveneffre's bank. A wooden wheel half the height of the building, its axle cradled in a thick stone wall rising from the riverbed, turned with the current and emanated a low rumbling like distant thunder.

Four crewmen rowed Hector, Teal, and Lord Vaughn upstream to the mill. When questioned, no one there had noticed a sailing skiff, but the people they asked were more focused on carrying grain into the mill or sacks of flour out to waiting wagons. Back in the longboat, Lord Vaughn spotted a pair of boys on the far bank fishing in the willow shade and directed the crewmen closer.

"Much luck today?" Lord Vaughn called as they glided past.

"Nah so much, yer lor'ship," the older boy replied. "Few bites 'ere an' there's all."

Hector shook his head. Fishermen everywhere seemed to be protective of their favorite fishing holes. The boy's answer would be the same whether he had caught a hundred fish that morning or none at all. He pulled a silver coin from his pouch and held it up to catch the sun and the boys' attention. "We're looking for a man in a sailing skiff. Dark hair, beard, no shirt, lots of tattoos. You happen to see anyone like that this morning?"

The boys glanced at each other before nodding to the bounty hunter. The older boy pointed upriver. "Right barmy lookin', that one. 'E were talkin' to some'un, but twernt nobody in the boat with 'im what we could see."

Hector thanked the boy and pitched the silver coin to him. The child caught it from the air and touched the brim of his cap as he bobbed his head. The bounty hunter checked the tracking spell once again. Dave's ring hadn't gotten any farther away since they anchored a half-hour earlier. He turned to Lord Vaughn. "He's stopped. Either he's gone ashore, or he's waiting to ambush us."

Lord Vaughn's sharp gaze turned upriver, calculating. "The west bank rises into a bluff over the next few miles and stays well above the river until it reaches the lock at Catwrath Falls. On the east, a road connects Beecher's Mill and the surrounding farms to Sandford. It's the only solid place to cross Quaggy Creek for miles — a cypress bog lies between here and there. Beyond the bog, the river's east bank turns steep."

"Dave isn't familiar with this area — almost all of our bounty work has been west and south of the mountains —

he shouldn't know about the road. Abandoning the skiff before he reaches a town or bridge doesn't make sense. Could he take the skiff through the bog?"

"The trees and underbrush are too thick for sail. He could drop the mast and row, but that will leave him pinned in the main channel, same as the river. On foot, there are lots of places for a man to hide, but that won't get him into a city, and you said this vampire's mask may be looking for someone to wear it."

Hector pondered the best course of action. Dave knew he'd make better time in the skiff than over land to reach a town of any size, yet he'd pushed to go ashore and ride for the city. In hindsight, he recognized Lady D's influence behind the archer's plan.

Dave was smart. Lady D was cunning. If they worked together, Hector suspected they could easily outfox him. What he didn't know was if Lady D had Dave's full cooperation.

"Yesterday afternoon, Dave was worried about Dodz coming after the mask," Hector said. "He wanted to leave the ship and ride for Tydway. I have to wonder if that was Lady D talking."

"Then we need to go upriver and find where he's stopped," Lord Vaughn replied. "If he did abandon the skiff, we can always go back to the *Lady Luck* for your horses. We'll travel faster on the road than he will through Quaggy Creek bog."

The top three feet of the skiff's mast protruded from the dark, cloudy water of a tree-shrouded cove. Hector eased over the longboat's gunnel. Fear gripped his heart as he drew a deep breath and dove down to the river's bottom. Dave's signet ring lay somewhere below.

Hector followed the angle of the mast down. Light emitted by the thin bone tube in his right hand only gave him a few short feet of visibility, but it didn't take long to find the jagged hole in the skiff's hull and the open lockers. Small fish darted out and away when the light hit them. A swirl of current, and a ghost of movement passed in his peripheral vision, sending him into a jerking roll in the opposite direction in time to see a pale, soft shelled turtle dart through the roots of a cypress.   In a tangle of sail and rigging, he found Dave's ring.

He pushed off and kicked to the surface. "He scuttled it. There's a big hole in the bottom."

"Perchance he happened upon another craft," Teal offered.

"Why would he steal another boat?"

Teal shrugged. "If the mask is self-aware, as thou doth suspect, will it not know thou dost hunt thy friend and seek to hinder thee?"

"She would," he said, leaning his forehead against the hull. The weight of responsibility carried in his voice when he spoke again. "He left his ring so I can't follow him."

"Hector." Teal gripped the bounty hunter's shoulder until he looked up. "When first I espied thee in Ruthaer, I knew thee for a hunter. 'Twas evident in thy movements and the way thou didst follow the traces my feet left in the dust and dirt. Thou did not need magic for that."

The bounty hunter nodded, a spark of hope igniting in his gaze. "The skiff's lockers are open. Whatever he left in them is scattered, but I want to see what I can salvage before we leave it," he said. "I wish I had a sack."

One of the crewmen reached under his seat, pulled out a burlap bag, and tossed it to him. Hector smiled. He had forgotten about the admiral's crew being 'privateers.'

Hector knifed down into the river depths again. Holding his light in his teeth, he cut a length of the rigging line to tie the sack to his belt, then set about searching the wreck from stern to bow. The anchor still lay in the aft locker, but all of Dave's gear and their money was gone. One of Hummingbird's knives was wedged against the gunnel wall with Aislinn's first aid bag. Aislinn's empty saddlebags and a few stray items of clothing that hadn't drifted away in the current lay scattered in the muck around the boat. All this went in Hector's sack.

His lungs began to burn, but he needed to check one more locker. Hector gripped the upper edge of the bow and allowed some of his air to escape. His feet floated toward the surface.   Shining his light into every dark corner, he searched for predators.   A fat catfish as long as his arm stared back at him, its mouth opening and closing as though it wanted to speak. Watching the fish, Hector reached in and freed Evan Courtenay's box from the straps that held it against the bow platform.

He slid the lid open just enough to see the tip of the ivory dagger within, then buried it in his sack while offering a silent prayer of thanks that Dave hadn't pitched it in the River Tamesas or taken it with him. Whatever its provenance, the blade was important enough for Evan Courtenay to send his minions to attack Ruthaer's shrievalty, and Hector suspected it was equally important to the dærganfae vampire, Mi'dnirr. However, it must not have meant much to Lady D. It was the small things that buttressed his faith.

Unable to stay any longer, he half-swam, half-pulled himself up the mast to the surface.

"We're going to have to put ashore and find which way he went," Hector said, as he held the longboat rail with one hand and passed the sodden sack to Teal. "He'll be looking for a horse."

"We're still south of the main channel of Quaggy Creek," said Lord Vaughn. "With any luck, he won't try to cross the bog. It's riddled with quicksand, and I've heard rumors of sinkholes. However, if he makes it to the road, he could follow it to Herian Hill or back to Margate. Which do you think more likely?"

Hector's brow furrowed, and he studied the muddy bank and rivulets winding among the trees. "I don't know," he finally replied. "Abandoning the skiff to travel on foot doesn't make sense. I'm going to check the shore, see if I can find any tracks." He pushed off the side of the boat and frog-kicked his way to the shallows.

The temperature was sweltering, and the sun crossed the sky too quickly. Eyes on the ground, Hector stalked the bank until he found Dave's tracks and followed them into the swamp. A twinge of guilt stabbed his conscience as he thought about the horror story Dave told him the night before. Perhaps he'd pushed his friend too hard, and the memories made the oblivion Lady D offered seem appealing. He kept searching, unaware that Teal and Lord Vaughn followed close behind, until a hand grabbed his arm and pulled him to a stop.

"¿Qué? ¿No ves que estoy ocupado?" he snapped.

"Aye, I see that thou art too occupied to espy the rather large mereyeht sunning upon the bank yonder," Teal replied.

Not recognizing the Kemetan-sounding word, Hector looked over his shoulder and spotted four alligators. A suspicious glint in his dark eyes, he turned back at Teal. "You understand Espian, now?"

"One does not need to speak thy tongue to glean the meaning of words of a similar sound," Teal replied. "Thou shalt do thy friend no good by being eaten."

Hector shuddered at the imagery evoked by Teal's words. He ranged farther along the shore. Neither Dave nor Lady D would have left the river without another means of travel. A dozen yards farther along the bank, he found the churned earth and deep tracks left behind by a drove of hogs. In the distance, he heard snorting and grunting punctuated by a sudden squeal.

Motioning to his companions, he followed the swath of destruction into the forest. The noises grew louder, more frenzied. Cold dread swept over the bounty hunter, and he broke into a run.

The trio burst through a thicket to find a roiling mass of wild hogs and piglets vying for access to a carcass. The ruined remains of a bedroll lay trampled into the churned earth.

"Hi-yah!" Hector shouted, waving his arms at the animals. "Get out of here!"

Pigs scattered into the trees, revealing the grisly remains of a heavy boned man. Swallowing back his gorge, Hector bent over the body, only to realize there was too much damage to identify the man or how he died. The only thing he could say for certain was the bone structure didn't match Dave's.

Lord Vaughn picked his way around the edge of the clearing. "Here," he said pointing to tracks leading into the trees. "He took the dead man's horse."

"How far are the nearest towns?"

"By road, it's eight leagues from Beecher's Mill to Sandford, then about twenty-three to Herian Hill. In the other direction, it's only twenty leagues back to Margate."

"Alright," Hector said. "Let me follow his trail a little way to get a feel for his direction."

"What dost thou wish to do about the corpse?" Teal asked.

"Leave it," Hector replied, calculating distances and time in his head. At a reasonable speed, they had two days to catch Dave before he reached a town of any size, but he doubted Lady D would be so kind to Dave or his stolen horse.

Teal scowled but said nothing as the two men followed the hoofprints through the trees. As soon as they were out of sight, he ran for the longboat and its waiting crew.

By the time Hector and Roger returned, Teal and the mariners had retrieved the sail from the sunken boat and wrapped the body for transport to the mill village.

"Let's get back to the ship. We'll have a hard ride to reach Sandford before dark," Lord Vaughn said as they settled into the longboat.

CR&O

11:45am

The *Lady Luck's* crew unloaded Hector's horses and gear at Beecher's Mill. Dressed in worn leathers, Lord Vaughn helped him saddle the animals and secure saddlebags under the curious scrutiny of the locals.

"When we reach Tydway, I'll alert the city guard to be on the lookout for Dave," Lady Aneirin said.

"Do me a favor, and stop at Blaiðwyn Hall," Lord Vaughn responded. "Tell Syon and Aunt Ivy what's happened and to expect us later this week. Have the guard watch for Dave in Tydway, but not approach him."

"What do you plan to do when you catch him?" she asked.

"Take him to Ozera," Hector replied. "The faster the better, but I also need to contact Jasper Thredd in Tydway. We need him to work on a container for the mask."

Lady Aneirin handed a small box to Lord Vaughn. "Stay in contact. Alert me the moment you have him. I'll have transport to Ozera ready and waiting."

"Will you tell Phaedrus to expect us?" Lord Vaughn asked. He opened the box and removed an ornate piece of twisted and whorled silver, which fit over his left ear as if custom made. He removed a small brooch from the box before handing it back to Lady Aneirin. The second piece of jewelry bore the symbol from her flag.

Lady Aneirin gave him a curt nod. "I spoke to Phaedrus earlier. He promised to have Brother Simon start researching similar artifacts and how to counteract them. He recommended I speak to Master Meuricel at the Academia's library as well." She glanced up at the midday sun. "You three best be on the road. You've a long ride ahead of you."

Teal eyed the horses, a look of consternation clouding his features. "Art thou certain these beasts are the best way to travel?" he asked Hector.

The Espian pinched the bridge of his nose. "You never rode one, did you?"

"Nay. E'en had I been small enough to ride such a creature, Tarnillis was my bond-mate, and would have me upon none but her."

Hector's hand spread over his mouth, and he stared at the teen through wide eyes, fighting to hold back the bawdy comment on the tip of his tongue.

"You'll have to learn on the road or stay on the ship," Lord Vaughn said as he swung into the saddle. "We don't have time to coddle you."

"Quick lesson," Hector said. "Always mount from the horse's left side. Don't ask me why, just do it. Left foot in the stirrup, step up and swing your leg over." He helped Teal up onto Aislinn's dapple grey gelding, then handed him the reins. "Pull the reins left or right to turn his head, pull straight back to stop. Remember you're in charge, and don't let Feldspar graze while he walks.

"Walking and galloping are smooth enough to sit. Anything between, stand in the stirrups and bend your knees to absorb the shock."

Teal opened his mouth to comment, but Hector turned away and swung up onto Caballo. Without looking back, he kicked his horse into a canter and headed northeast away from the mill.

Two hours later, the road met another. Hector slid from his saddle, searching the dirt and dust for the odd, scallop-edged horseshoe prints they found in Quaggy Creek bog. After several fruitless minutes, he climbed back into the saddle and looked out across the farmland around them. "Milord, Dave didn't pass here on the road."

"If we're going to be traveling together like this, you should both call me Roger."

"Roger," Hector repeated and pointed to a distant farmhouse, "should we ask if anyone saw him?"

"Hector, you know Dave best, so I'll follow your lead, at least until we catch him."

The bounty hunter pursed his lips and tried to imagine himself in Dave's situation, to anticipate the vampire's demands.   Finally, he turned Caballo north, toward the closer towns, and clicked his tongue to get the horses moving.

CHAPTER 11
GATHERING COURAGE

August 13, 4237 K.E.

Aislinn

The tunnel ahead seemed unending, and the distant light grew neither closer nor brighter. Aislinn continued to push forward, occasionally trying to reach Brand through their bond. Lost in thought, she failed to notice the whisper of voices until she found herself standing in the mouth of a firelit cavern, faced with five young men. For a moment, the sight felt wrong, as if there was something important that she was forgetting.

"Who are you?" she demanded.

"Hector de los Santos," the Espian said with a smile. He crossed the uneven floor and held out his empty hand. "What's your name?"

She grasped the waiting Espian's hand. "I'm Aislinn," she said, but her attention was on the tall, scowling figure on the far side of the cave with his bow drawn and aimed at her chest. The thick-shafted arrow would easily shatter her ribs and pierce her heart at such close range. The other three young men — a swordsman who looked enough like the archer to be his kinsman, a husky mage with a thick beard and a pipe clenched in his teeth, and a red-faced knight in plate armor, whose cold eyes marred his angelic features — watched the exchange, poised to attack. "How did you smuggle weapons in here? More important, do you know how to get out?"

"Be on your way, wench," the knight snapped. "We aren't here for you."

"Shut up, Killian. Nobody asked you," Hector retorted. To Aislinn, he said, "Our exit strategy is a bit fluid at the moment. If you can help us find a young nobleman named Thomas Odell, I don't see why we can't help you escape in exchange. He's short, mud-brown hair, acts like his crap doesn't stink."

"I think I know the one you mean. Whiny brat, thinks everyone is his personal servant?"

The swordsman stifled a snort of laughter. "That sounds like the councilman's son."

'*Danger and Death move inexorably toward you,*' the Tanjaran seer's voice whispered. The scene before her wavered and vanished, taking Hector, Dave, Robert, Jasper, and Killian with it like so many ghosts. The distant light she'd been following died, leaving her alone in the smooth, dark tunnel once more. The loss was bitter.

Memories assailed her in a sudden torrent. Images flickered in and out of existence faster than her mind could register, and the old woman's foretelling resonated in Aislinn's mind. The words 'Darkness,' 'Danger,' and 'Death' pounded in her ears like the beating of a drum, until they were all she could hear. She'd puzzled over the foretelling ever since leaving the Tanjaran village of Ogham, and never came to any conclusions, expecting it to only be understood in hindsight.

Darkness could mean any number of things, from her current predicament to the Dark One's minions, or the entity himself. *Danger and Death...* She'd thought those words meant the dærganfae and the death of her mentor, Edge Garrett, but they could reference any of dozens of situations she'd found herself in over the years.

From the time she could walk, Aislinn was drawn to trouble. She was the first in the water, swimming amongst the alligators and daring the older children to follow. She climbed the tallest trees and braved the dangerous currents in Shark Hole Creek for the chance to meet a dragon. A few months after her mother settled them in Ozera, Phaedrus caught Aislinn wandering the passages and caverns beneath the cathedral, even though the underground entrance was supposed to be a closely guarded secret.

Of course, the words 'Danger and Death' could just as easily mean Hector and Dave.

Hector's daredevil attitude and rakish charm had drawn her like a moth to a candle. He had an insatiable curiosity which led him into places and situations a more cautious person would have fled. Break into a foreign prison run by half-dragons to rescue a councilman's son? Sure! Explore creepy caves in search of pirate treasure? Where do we start! Invade the capital of a foreign country to rescue a kidnapped queen? No problem! If it weren't for Hector's inordinately good luck, they'd all be dead several dozen times over.

Dave, on the other hand, was only happy when he was shooting something. Surly and irascible, the archer seldom spoke to anyone other than Hector or his cousin, Robert, in the early days of her acquaintance with him. Despite Hector's reassurances, Aislinn felt certain the archer would have killed her without a second thought if given the slightest provocation. Looking back, she wasn't' certain if it was Hector's influence or the threat of being burnt to a cinder by Brand which stayed Dave's arrows. It wasn't until she helped Dave bully Robert, Jasper, and Brand into helping them break Hector out of Rowanoake's prison that Dave finally conceded to speak with her.

Shaking off the memories, Aislinn tried to understand where she was. It felt as though she'd been walking forever, and the monotony wore on her nerves as it had in the never-ending tunnels under Pazard'zhik. She'd lost all sense of time there, too.

A new barrage of memories struck her like a bolt of lightning: following the Dark One's Sha'iry across Parlatheas from Francesca to Trakya after the priests kidnapped Robert; the seemingly endless halls and chambers beneath Trakya's capital city; her unexpected separation from Brand. Without Dave and Hector, she would have gone mad.

Back against the cold glassy wall, Aislinn slid into a crouch, vaguely aware something was wrong with her memory. Dave, Hector, Jasper, and Robert rescued her from the Seldaehne prison four... no, five years past. Two of those years had been spent chasing the Dark One's minions across three continents to recover Robert. They'd returned home to Ozera with Robert and an orphaned Plains Elf called Hummingbird.

Unfortunately, none of that told her where she was now. She took a steadying breath and tried to assess her situation logically. First, what did she know? She'd woken alone in a dark tunnel, with no memory of how she got there. She was hallucinating, reliving random fragments of her past. Her bond with Brand was somehow blocked or severed, leaving a gaping hole in her soul.

Aislinn searched her scalp again for evidence of a head injury, probing inch by inch, and felt nothing more serious than a vague soreness behind her left ear, like a bruise nearly healed.

Perhaps the answer wasn't an injury to herself... or maybe it was, and she was actually lying unconscious in Ozera's critical care ward. Aislinn pinched herself on the arm. The resulting pain convinced her she really was awake, and it left her with only one possible answer to her puzzle: she'd fallen victim to some sort of magical trap. She had to escape. She'd give almost anything to hear one of Hector's bawdy jokes or even one of Dave's strange Terran curses, but silence pressed in, stifling even the sound of her breath.

"Dave. Hector? Hummingbird! Where are you?" Her voice fell from her lips in a choked whisper, swallowed by the inky blackness. She ran trembling fingers over her belt and fumbled loose her wheel-cross. A short prayer set the leaves and knotwork on the hand-carved oak aglow with deep purple light. It pushed the darkness back a few feet, revealing a faceted tunnel, like a hall of mirrors. The bruise-like color of her light was wrong. It was supposed to be blue — bright and soothing, like a summer sky.

"Alright, then," she whispered, "weirdness or not, it's time to get out of here and find my friends." She raised her light higher, seeking a clue to which direction led out. One way looked as unfamiliar as the other. Aislinn murmured another prayer and pushed onward.

CRSO

11:00am

Ozera's carillon filled the air with music, drawing Hummingbird from the Dreaming Grounds. Drifting between sleep and wakefulness, she sensed a cloud of grief hovering nearby.

"Regenia, how is she?"

Sadness and optimism grappled.

"Still sleeping, Shayla. Sister Inez and Brother Giovanus say she could come back to us at any moment, but El Patrón says we must guard her spirit from despair. He instructed us to keep a window open at all times so sunlight and fresh air can reach her, and that we should talk to her."

"May I sit with her for a while?" Aislinn's mother asked.

"Of course, Shayla. I think she'd like that. Perhaps you could tell her about one of the new babes born this week."

Retreating footsteps preceded the scraping of wood on tile and the rustle of fabric, followed by a soft sigh.

"Come home, Hummingbird," Shayla whispered. Strong, warm fingers grasped Hummingbird's hand, and her sense of Shayla's grief grew sharper.

"My daughter gave her life for you. Do not squander her gift."

Rumbling from the distant storm at the borders of the Dreaming Grounds seemed to underscore Shayla's words.

"While you and I grieve our loss, the world carries on as it always has. In the four days since Brand and Tallinn brought you and Aislinn back to Ozera, I've lost my daughter, suffered through the ritual at Brodgar Tor, and helped three women deliver new babes into the world. People have come to Ozera for healing while others have journeyed home — some to a distant city, some to the eternal kingdom." Shayla drew closer, her breath teasing Hummingbird's cheek. "Listen to me. It is not yet time for you to leave this world."

Hummingbird considered Shayla's words. There was more to her plea than she said.

"Come back, Hummingbird. I need your help."

Here it was.

"I need you to help me save my son."

Of the things Shayla could have said, this was not one Hummingbird expected. She hardly knew Aislinn's brother. In the few weeks they'd both been in Ozera before she went to Orleans with Dave and Hector, she'd only seen Eidan a handful of times. If something happened to him, his mother would do better to ask Hector and Dave for help. What did she expect Hummingbird to do?

Desperation.

"Please, Hummingbird. He's keeping something from me. I... I fear he may kill himself. "

Hummingbird owed Aislinn a life-debt. Saving Eidan might be the only way to repay it. Drawing upon the meager strength sleeping inside her, she closed her hand around Shayla's.

CHAPTER 12
SAYING GOODBYE

August 13, 4237 K.E.

6:00pm

Robert Stone dipped his hands into a shallow basin and splashed cold water over his face and hair before using a rough cotton towel to remove the worst of the road dust. Outside the window of his one-room cabin, the last golden rays of sunlight shimmered over Ozera's autumn leaves. He and Gideon Maccabeus, the Francescan battle-cleric who'd been his traveling companion over the past few months, had arrived in the village to discover they barely had an hour to get their horses stabled and themselves cleaned up before Aislinn's funeral.

He couldn't believe she was gone.

The message he'd received three days ago was cryptic, only telling him he was needed in Ozera posthaste. Robert twisted his signet ring and closed his fist around the embossed emblem. Jasper, Eidan, and Aislinn's rings pulsed nearby. Hector and Dave were too far east to arrive in time.

Robert rinsed his towel and gave his boots and rapier hilt a quick dusting before dressing in black and running a comb through his sandy-blonde hair. He wished he had time for a shave and haircut. His beard was as wild and unkempt as Dave's. With one last look out the window, he buckled on his sword belt and donned a plain cavalier hat before hurrying out the door.

He strode behind the adjacent cabin and took the forest path leading to the Yves residence. After a quick walk, he emerged in a small grass-covered yard behind a throng of villagers. Murmuring apologies as he pushed his way through the crowd, he made eye contact with a portly figure in a dark blue and silver mage's robe on the front porch.

"Robert! I'm so glad you made it," said Jasper Thredd, meeting him at the steps and pulling him into a hug. When he stepped back, he kept a hand on Robert's shoulder. "I've missed you. How've you been?"

Robert shrugged. "Taking things one day at a time, my friend. You?"

"Between teaching and research, the Academy has been keeping me busy." He half turned to the two other men beside him. "You remember August and Xandor?"

More poet than warrior, August's youthful face lit up as he tipped his head toward Robert. Rumored to be the exiled son of a Rhodinan nobleman, he had a statuesque physique and wore a silver and azure surcoat over his black shirt and pants, a wide sword belt, and freshly polished boots. Not a single black hair on his head was out of place.

In contrast, the Iron Tower ranger looked ready for battle with two swords strapped across his back. Tall and lean with intelligent, heterochromatic eyes, he wore a black leather doublet with a stiff collar and a silver tower with three horizontal arrows emblazoned over his heart. His square jaw was clean-shaven, and his pale blonde hair cropped short in standard military fashion.

Off to one side, an old man with cloudy eyes rose from a chair. His formal white sash, with two diagonal tridents over a black tower, contrasted starkly with his night-blue tunic.

"This is Tallinn," Jasper said, helping the old man face Robert. "He's a sea ranger from Ruthaer and a friend of Aislinn's father."

"Sir," Robert said, "I'm sorry to meet you under such circumstances. I wish our meeting could have been happier."

"As do I," Tallinn replied.

A middle-aged Espian joined them on the porch. "Buenas tardes, are you the other pallbearers?" Each man nodded in response. "I'm Eliezer, a friend of Shayla's. She and I work together at the hospital. El Patrón sent me to tell you he is ready for us."

August turned and gently knocked on the front door. When it opened, he murmured to the woman inside, who nodded in turn before closing the door.

As the others followed Eliezer from the porch, Robert held Jasper back so that a gap formed between them and the others. "What's going on, Jasper? Phaedrus doesn't normally hold funerals in Sunrise Chapel, and why in the world is the funeral today? What's the rush?"

"I don't know," Jasper replied. "Eidan and Shayla insisted, and Phaedrus didn't argue. Ever since the resurrection ritual failed, they've all been acting strange." He paused, considered his words, then amended, "Well, stranger than normal. Eidan and Shayla both have pushed for the funeral to be over and done with. There wasn't even a formal wake."

"I guess they didn't really need one, did they? I mean, the healers would know if Aislinn was in a coma or something, right?" Robert said, scratching his chin. "Shouldn't we at least wait for Hector and Dave?"

Jasper shrugged, twisting his ring. "Something's delayed them. There's no telling when they'll make it."

"We should still hold off a few days. You and I both know they'd move the world to be here if they could."

"Look, all I know is Shayla and Eidan want to have the funeral today."

Robert frowned. "Why didn't Hector and Dave return to Ozera with Aislinn?"

"You know Hector. No job left unfinished, no matter what," Jasper replied. "Tallinn said Hector, Dave, and someone called Teal were hunting a ghūl when he set out for Ozera with Aislinn and Hummingbird." He stopped and pulled Robert aside. "As terrible as this is going to sound, it's probably better this way. I get the feeling Aislinn's family doesn't want Hector or Dave here." Jasper looked around to make sure no one overheard as he said, "Brand's kept himself hidden, but Aislinn's mother says he blames them. If they were here, there's no telling what would happen. He might even try to kill them in Sunrise Chapel."

CRSO

6:30pm

As Ozera's leader and high priest, Phaedrus welcomed those gathered for the funeral procession. A shaft of sunlight pierced the foliage overhead to shimmer on the half-elf's pale hair and highlight the somber expression in his green eyes. After a short prayer, he signaled the pallbearers and led the way up Lumikivi Mountain toward Sunrise Chapel.

Eidan held his mother's hand as they walked behind the diamond-and-ebony casket, followed by dozens of Ozera's residents. At each prayer garden along the meditation trail, a pair of trestles waited to support the casket while Phaedrus offered up a brief prayer.

By the time they reached the summit, the setting sun had transformed the sky into a canvas of fiery oranges, reds, and purples. The pallbearers placed the casket on an intricately carved catafalque near the edge of the overlook before taking their places on either side of the seated family.

Eidan stared through the casket's crystalline side panel, oblivious to the words Phaedrus spoke. The Sisters of Mercy had dressed Aislinn in the soft, dark leathers and homespun she preferred in life, choosing a shirt of mossy green that would have matched the color of her eyes. Her autumn-gold hair covered the small pillow beneath her head and trailed down around her shoulders. A woven crown of thornless roses from a vine planted by Aislinn's mentor, Edge Garrett, rested on her brow. The snowy flowers gave her skin the illusion of color, making her appear as though she were only sleeping.

Tears filled his eyes and slid, unheeded, down his cheeks. Once again, he found himself reliving Aislinn and Brand's argument about leaving Ozera to live with Brand's father. The dragon homeland, Revakhun Toaglen, lay far to the east in Tethys Oceanus. It was far enough away they likely would not see any of their friends again for many years, if ever. Eidan wished he could go back to the last night they were together and prevent the awful things Brand and Aislinn said to one another.

Thunder pealed, and Eidan snapped back to the present during Phaedrus' benediction. Inside him, Brand roared. Invisible talons pierced his heart and lungs as the dragon clawed his way toward the surface. Eidan ground his teeth and refused to relinquish his place at their mother's side.

Eidan remained seated with his fists clenched in his lap while the villagers filed out of Sunrise Chapel. When all that remained were himself and Emä, Phaedrus, and his four friends, Eidan slid to his knees before his mother and bowed his head.

"I love you, Emä. No matter what happens tonight, please remember that."

"Eidan, what are you talking about? What's going to happen?"

"I don't know," he groaned. "Brand is coming. I need you, all of you, to go now."

"Brand is my friend," Jasper replied. "I'd prefer to stay."

"We swore an oath to always be here for each other," Robert added. "I have no intention of breaking that promise."

"*Please go.*" Eidan pushed to his feet and backed away, trembling with the effort of holding Brand in. The fine hairs on his arms and neck stood on end.

"Be at peace," Phaedrus said, offering Eidan his hand.

Panic marring his features, Eidan gripped his coppery hair with both hands. Electricity popped and fizzed around him, building into a hazy cloud. Once again thunder rolled overhead.

"Eidan, what's happening?" Shayla asked. She started toward him, her arms open to take him in a hug.

"Emä! Stay away from me!"

Lightning streaked from the heavens, striking the bare rock between Eidan and his mother. Shayla cried out and stumbled back, terror twisting her features, even as August swept her up and retreated down the mountain path. Lightning struck again, blackening another patch of rock. Phaedrus led the others back beneath the twilight shadowed trees at the chapel's edge.

Electricity arcing from his body, Eidan staggered to the central pool and fell to his knees.

Brand's bronze dragonhead reflected in the water's surface, his face haloed by a vast hurricane. He gazed up at the clouds. '*Do you think this is the* eye of chaos *Xandor's grandmother meant all those years ago?*'

"We aren't trapped," Eidan replied. "I think she meant something a bit more literal, considering death is the only way to escape."

'*We* are *dying,*' the dragon's voice rumbled. '*Our death knell has already begun. Can't you hear it?*'

Eidan glanced at the high priest. "Phaedrus says it's only our grief."

'*No! It's more than that. It's a shadow that haunts my dreams and speaks of our doom.*'

"Brand, you have to calm down."

The lightning storm intensified. '*Aislinn's Terrans must suffer for taking her away from us. There is not much time. We must go now!*'

"What about Aislinn?" Eidan asked the beast in the pool. "She's here." He pointed to the diamond casket. "You wanted her with us, but if we are dying, why go to the trouble?"

'*She calls to me,*' Brand replied. '*She wants me to come to her. This way she will be with us, forever.*'

Eidan drew a deep breath, then let it out in a shuddering sigh and reached toward the pool. Brand mirrored his motion. Electricity sparked and danced over his bronze scales.

"Don't forget Emä," Eidan rasped. "She needs us."

'*Shayla suffers as we suffer, little brother. The sooner we die, the sooner she can restart her life.*'

"But I want —"

Talons met fingertips at the water's surface, and a crackling ball of lightning enveloped them both. Moments later, the sixty-foot-long dragon leapt off the cliff from Sunrise Chapel, bearing Aislinn and her casket with him. In the distance, thunder echoed from the mountains to the stars.

CRSO

8:00pm

Wings spread in a slight curve just above horizontal, Brand caught a column of warm air rising from Grimshaw Valley and let it carry him and Aislinn upward in a tight spiral. Years of practice told him when he'd reached sufficient altitude to tilt into a downward glide. He flew along the face of Lumikivi Mountain's white cliff and aimed for the mouth of his cave five hundred feet below the mountain's summit.

His muscles quivered with exertion, reminding him he had not completed his oonveytik ssifruen, a period of self-induced hibernation while his body underwent rapid, painful growth. Canting left then back to the right, he executed a wide turn to approach the dark opening head-on. Muscle memory took over and he pulled up, pushing his hind legs forward. The casket shifted, throwing off his center of balance, and his tail slapped against the cliff face below the cave's exterior ledge. For several heart pounding seconds, his wings beat furiously to keep him from tipping backward.

Brand landed hard inside the cave mouth with a grunt. Crushing pressure seized his chest, and Aislinn's casket hit the stone floor with a sickening thud. Her body shifted, and the bedding around her became jumbled. Heart pounding, he sucked in great gulps of air as he stared at the disarray inside the diamond and ebony casket.

"Aislinn, I'm so sorry," he gasped.

Fighting spasms of pain, he grabbed hold of the nearest huckle and made his slow, staggering way down the short tunnel to his cavern and his hoard. There, he swung his long tail over a stacked stone plinth he and Aislinn built many long years ago, scattering its contents. With a heave, he placed Aislinn and the casket on top, where it filled the surface with bare inches to spare.

In a shallow niche on the opposite side of the cavern's entrance, a cluster of dark yellow citrine crystals gave off a warm, buttery glow that caught and refracted in patches of quartz on the walls and ceiling like so many stars. He took the chunk of crystal from its home, replacing it with Eidan and Aislinn's signet rings.

The citrine's radiance filled the casket with a glow resembling early morning sunlight. Inside, Aislinn looked like a broken doll, her face pressed against the casket's crystalline side. The crown of roses was crushed and flung near her feet.

The glowing crystal dropped to the floor. Brand reached out, but then pulled back his foreclaw. He couldn't bring himself to open the casket.

"If not for Hector and Dave, none of this would have happened," he grumbled as another wave of fatigue washed over him. Visions of the two Terrans mocked him. Even as his hate solidified, a chill rolled over him and left him shivering. The crushing pressure in his chest returned, worse than before, and he collapsed onto the sandy floor.

"You'll suffer for this," he vowed, tasting grit.

Wings folded, Brand coiled into a ball atop the scattered coins, gems, and trinkets from the plinth, pressing them into the sand. His last sight and thoughts before his eyes drifted closed were of Aislinn, locked inside her diamond jewelry box.

CHAPTER 13
PURSUIT

August 14, 4237 K.E.

1:20pm

Leaving Caballo at the water trough, Hector stepped onto the wooden porch and paused in the wayside inn's doorway. Sunlight spilled around him, throwing the tiny dining room into shadow.

"Oiy know what uh saw, Bill!" an old man sitting at the bar exclaimed. Behind the long counter, the barkeep rolled his eyes. "Carl, let it go. Your eyes were playing tricks on you."

The old man shook his head and hit the bar top with the heel of his hand. "Oiy weren't 'mag'nin' it!"

Hector crossed the straw covered floor, produced a coin, and slid it across the counter in front of the old man. "Bring the man a drink, and one for me."

Carl turned bloodshot eyes on the hunter at his right, squinting at his young, swarthy face. The tapster sat two full mugs on the bar. The old man wrapped shaking hands around the heavy clay and nodded to his new companion. "Thank ye kindly." He downed half his mug and wiped his mouth on his stained sleeve.

"I'd like to hear about what you saw," Hector said softly.

Carl's eyes grew suspicious. "Why? You don't know me."

Hector shrugged. "I'm searching for a tattooed desperado. Tall, dark hair and beard, has a bow as long as he is tall. I hoped maybe you saw him."

The innkeeper laughed. "Carl's the wrong man to ask. He only sees the demons in his drink."

"What about you?" Hector asked. "He come in here?"

The man behind the counter shook his head and rounded the bar to check on a pair of customers finishing up a meal in the room's far corner.

The old man guzzled the last of his drink, letting some dribble down his chin. He stared off into the distance before saying, "Oiy saw Death last night, lad. 'E stared right at ole

Carl and froze me like a statue. Oiy thought he were goin' ta take me straight ta hell."

"¿Perdoné, señor?

Carl shivered. "'E galloped through town in the wee hours, cloak billowin' around 'im and his horse like it were alive."

"How do you know it was Death?"

"His face was naught but a skull, boy, and his eyes... Thcy burned like a wolf's."

Color drained from Hector's face. He pulled out two more coins and laid them on the counter while signaling the innkeeper. "Bring this man a meal and more ale," he said, and left the inn.

Out in the mid-day sun, Hector joined Roger, who stood with the horses, watching the villagers go about their lives, while Teal leaned against the porch rail, trying to stretch his aching back and leg muscles.

"We're going to have to push harder," Hector said. "He's got more than six hours on us, at a gallop."

"He can't maintain that pace," Roger replied. "He's going to ride this horse into the ground just like the first one."

"He doesn't care." Hector stared up the road, not seeing the tiny hamlet or its people. "Based on the description I was just given, Dave's wearing Lady D's mask."

"*What?*"

"Did thou not say the vampire was a woman when ye first slew it?" Teal asked. The freckles dusting his pert nose stood out against skin pallid with pain.

Hector nodded. A vision of Consuelo's skinless, bloody face swam in his mind's eye, and his jaw clenched. He climbed back on his horse and waited for Roger and Teal to do the same, but Teal didn't move. A passerby leered at the strange, tall girl who stretched first one leg, then the other. "Teal, sube a ese maldito caballo y vámonos," Hector growled.

"Forgive me, Hector, but I cannot apprehend thy meaning."

"He said it's time to go," Roger translated.

Teal turned a pleading look on both Hector and Roger. "Prithee, let me stretch a bit more. 'Tis nearing a full day since we rode forth. I ache in places I would rather that I ne'er knew I possess."

"And you're going to hurt a whole lot more before we're done," Hector snapped.

"This body is too soft," Teal muttered as he limped the few steps to the grey gelding and glared at the horse. "Forsooth, now I doth understand wherefore he calls thee Feldspar, for thou art as unyielding and uncomfortable as the stone for which thou art named." His face contorted with pain as he raised his foot to the stirrup and pulled himself astride, but he made no further complaint.

"It's ten miles to Herian Hill," Roger said. "I'll check in with my people when we arrive, see if anyone has seen Dave. He'd have to pass through town if he wants to cross the river. At this pace, he'll be in Tydway before midnight."

Hector nodded. Worry etched his features as he studied the road ahead. "We have to catch him."

"We will," Roger replied.

The three snapped their reins and galloped out of town.

CR&O

8:00pm

Back to the wall, Hector sat at a corner table and watched the tavern while nursing his mug of ale. Clusters of patrons talked casually about the weather or how much they had lost at the gambling house. No one mentioned a stranger wearing a skull mask. Hector wanted to take comfort in the lack of news, to allow himself to believe they'd gotten ahead of Dave, but his sense of unease grew.

Still dusty from travelling, Roger pushed through the main door and across the firelit room. He slid into the seat beside Hector and motioned for the bar wench.

"None of my people have seen him," Roger said in a low voice. "They're checking with their informants and contacts among the local thieves and beggars."

Hector gave his mug a mirthless smile. "Nada es fácil."

The bar wench sat a frothy mug on the table. "Anything else?"

Roger shook his head. When she left, he asked, "Any word here?"

"No."

Roger took a long swallow, then asked, "How did the two of you get here?"

Hector raised an eyebrow, wondering what the man was seeking. "That's a broad question. Care to specify?"

"You and Dave. How did you come to Gaia?"

Hector took a long swig before answering. "We don't know. I mean, I can tell you what we did that day, but not how it actually happened. You see, it was Robert's birthday, and as a surprise, Dave and I took him to an abandoned lighthouse. The three of us were in a fencing club. It had gotten boring, so we went beyond the strict forms and rules — we'd started writing our own choreography and doing stage fights.

"That night, we took turns fighting each other up the circular stairs. When we reached the top and went out on the gallery, a thick fog had set in. It wasn't until Jasper found us there that we learned we weren't in Kansas anymore, so to speak. We were at the top of Rowanoake's lighthouse, with no way back to Terra." Hector raised his mug to his lips and watched Lord Vaughn over the rim, trying to gauge the man's reaction. "Do you mind if I ask how you ended up with a Terran wife?"

Roger stared off through the crowd, but Hector knew he wasn't seeing these people or the tavern. He probably wasn't even seeing Gaia.

"You already know about The Archer's attempt to assassinate Queen Ambrose. What I didn't tell you and Dave was that the queen escaped him using Terran talismans that took her to Charleston. Bryony Tyler was with Ambrose when we finally found her. She was the most beautiful woman I'd ever seen..." Roger smiled. "I made a spur of the moment decision and ended up staying in Charleston for a while. One thing led to another, and Brie came to Gaia with me to get married." He sighed. "She loved it, and never wanted to leave. She was a natural with magic. The only thing she ever regretted was not having her family at our wedding."

"Why couldn't you?" Hector asked.

Roger stared at the mug in his hands. "Well, for one thing, her parents didn't approve of me. They never got past the fact that I was from a different world.

"Brie and I discussed it. We probably could have convinced them, but in the end, we didn't want to risk it. As you know, Gaia and Terra are but two of infinite worlds, like the endless stars in the night sky. Sages theorize that the two worlds shift and move in an endless cycle, making portals between here and Terra unreliable. You can get there from here, if you're willing to world-hop, but it requires a specialized mage, and the route is dangerous."

"Is that how you sent Dave's mother back to Terra?"

Roger nodded and drank deeply before speaking again. "Looking back, I realize sending her away was a mistake. I've spent all these years thinking The Archer murdered both my wife and our son... that I didn't get there in time to save them. I won't make the same mistake again."

CRΧΘ

8:00pm

Darkness came early under a heavy pall of black clouds. Avoiding the glistening pools of lamplight, Dave Blood hid inside the folds of his oilskin cloak as he stalked the shadows. Behind the vampire mask, his dark eyes searched the cobbled streets of Herian Hill. To either side, stone buildings stood shoulder to shoulder, each with a wrought iron balcony.

Mist swirled in the air, thick as fog, yet heavier, more wet. Droplets clung to the hair and skin of two doxies at the corner, sparkling like stars in the diffused light, lending them a veil of beauty to cover their shabby clothing and careworn faces. He studied each in turn with eyes that burned amber within the depths of his hooded cloak. He dismissed them — neither of them *felt* right.

On silent feet, Dave drifted down a lightless alley, the skull mask lending him strength, stealth, and the ability to see in the dark. On the next street, he watched a young woman exit an apothecary's shop and start his direction, her gait distorted by a limp. Through the mist, there seemed to be something familiar about her.

He turned away.

'*Archer, wait. She's the one.*'

"No, she isn't, Ymara. Look at how she walks," he replied.

'*Ignore the flaw, it can be corrected, with time. Hurry, I tire of this half-existence.*'

Ignorant of the danger, the girl passed under a lamp, and hair the fiery golden-red of autumn leaves shimmered in the swirling mist. An aching pain seared his heart, and he closed his eyes as he turned away. For the briefest of moments, the memory of another girl with hair that color and eyes of moss green flecked with bronze filled his inner sight, and a name surfaced: Aislinn.

Ymara Dapniš' ghostly image suddenly loomed over him and the image shattered. A warrior-queen who would not be denied, she sent a spike of hunger and lust into Dave's brain. *'You will think of no woman but me!'* Ymara's voice thundered inside his head. *'The memory of that half-elf is a festering weakness. You are greater than this, stronger. Forget your past. Let me be your world. Give me this girl.'*

"She's not right for you. We should go somewhere else," he replied.

'No, she's the one. Take her. Take her now.'

The young woman passed the alley mouth, a short cloak wrapped tight around her shoulders. His hand rose under Ymara's command, fingers almost brushing the ends of the girl's hair, and he could feel the warmth rising from her. The ache of longing tugged at him. He could hear the beat of her heart, the flow of blood through her veins. She was prey, and he the predator.

Dave clenched his hand into a fist, allowing the girl to continue on her way. "No," he said, a spark of defiance kindling in his soul. "Not that one."

An ethereal hand clamped around his throat. Pain flashed through his body, seizing his muscles, and sent him crashing to his knees. His lungs refused to draw air and vent the scream echoing in his head.

Interminable seconds passed before Ymara released him. Chest heaving, he struggled to his feet. Muscles quivering, he leaned against the cold wall. The girl Ymara wanted was long gone.

'Do not defy me again,' the ghost snarled.

Dave dashed across the street and into another alley. He worked his way to the main thoroughfare where the busy inns and gambling houses dominated the crossroads market. The street lanterns grew more numerous, making it harder to stay hidden. He climbed up the side of a stable, and lay prone near the peak, watching people pass below. Couples, small groups, the occasional lone man entered his vision and disappeared again.

There were so many people. Deep down inside, he wished they would all go away. His tiny bit of resistance had kept the women they'd met safe so far, but he didn't know how long he could keep it up. The vampire inside his head would not tolerate another missed opportunity.

As if reading his thoughts, Ymara said, '*Anyone you choose will be me, with time. Pick one, my archer. I hunger for you.*' Aethereal hands caressed his back, and he shivered.

He remained silent, staring down into the street. A tall, tawny haired young woman with freckles dusting her pert nose stepped down off the porch of the inn across the way, turned, and headed north up the center of the street. She had the walk of someone too long in the saddle, but the bearing of a warrior.

A warrior.

"No, Ymara, let me find someone better," he murmured.

'*Enough of these delays, archer. I want her.*'

CHAPTER 14
CHASING TEAL

August 14, 4237 K.E.

8:20pm

Teal limped toward the crossroads that marked the center of town. Even after a hot bath, his muscles protested with each step. He longed to fall into bed and sleep, but he knew it would only make matters worse. He needed to stretch the parts of him cramped from too long in the saddle but sensed running through town and climbing the sides of buildings would be frowned upon.

Men and women crowded the thoroughfare, some heading home for the night, others just arriving. Most congregated in front of the two lantern-lit warehouses that faced each other from across the street. Flanking the garish doors, doe-eyed women, wearing kohl eyeliner and little else, smiled and beckoned men to enter their gambling house with a smile or crooked finger. Spontaneous bouts of laughter from inside joined the constant chatter outside, giving Herian Hill a festive air at odds with its shabby appearance.

Teal studied the passing humans, trying to make sense of their society. They all seemed so... soft. He wondered how many of them had ever had to fight for anything in their lives and decided that the answer was very few.

Apparently lost in his own thoughts, Lord Vaughn pushed his way out of a tavern and passed by without acknowledging Teal. The expression on his face made Teal think the man had received grave news. Glancing through the tavern window, he spotted Hector at a corner table. The Espian looked little better than the nobleman.

The flight-master pulled in a deep breath, and held it for a moment, steeling himself to deal with whatever new catastrophe was upon them. He wound his way through the tavern and stood before Hector.

"What art thou doing?" he asked.

Hector drained his mug. "Thinking."

"Dost thou plan to sit here and think all night?" Teal asked.

Hector blinked and looked up at the tawny-haired teen. He slowly shook his head.

"Then get thyself up and let us be about our business! Yon nobleman wanders the street. I can only assume the two of you have discovered some ill news."

"That's just it. We haven't heard anything," Hector replied and stood, "but you're right, I need to get out of here. Which way did Roger go?"

"He headed toward our inn, but I do not know if he shall stop thither. 'Tis of more import to find the archer. What will Dave do without that beast he rode to death this afternoon?"

"He'll steal another," Hector said.

"Then pray, let us find him afore that dread event doth occur," Teal said. "I've no desire to be upon another horse e'er again."

"Ozera's in the mountains," Hector said. "You're going to have to ride something, and I'm fresh out of dragons." Hector pushed Roger's half-finished mug toward Teal. "Finish this. It'll help take the edge off the pain."

"I would sooner return to the caves of my people and the quiet of death's embrace than journey on a horse into the mountains," Teal said. He downed the dark ale in one long pull.

"You're not going anywhere that I can't keep an eye on you. Allyrian Carmichael has a lot to answer for, and you're possessing her body. Eventually, she'll want it back."

"Perhaps," Teal replied, "but that is trouble for another day."

They walked out of the tavern together and turned back toward their inn. "Let's find Roger, and watch the road out of town," Hector said.

"How dost thou know which road he's like to take? He may leave the road altogether," Teal said.

The buzz of feather fletching split the air a half-second before the arrow slammed into Hector's side and sent him sprawling. A woman screamed, and the crowd seethed as people tried to escape the sudden violence while others shouted for the city guard.

"¡Maldito hijo de puta!" Hector grated through clenched teeth. "¡Él jodido me disparó!" Blood soaked his shirt and welled around the hand clutching his ribs. "Qué color..." he coughed, "...feathers?"

Teal crouched beside him and squinted at the fletching in the dim light. "Red, I think."

"Pull it out... try not... to break..." he panted.

"Thou art mad!" Teal replied.

"Do it," Hector growled.

Teal nodded, gripped the arrow shaft close to the hunter's body, and jerked it straight back. Hector gasped as the arrowhead tore the flesh between his broken ribs, and his eyes rolled back in his head. Teal pressed a palm against the wound, then jerked his hand away as something sharp pricked his skin.

Vaguely aware of the knot of onlookers, he stared at Hector's blood shimmering and sparking as if filled with stars. It was only then that he remembered the aftermath of the fight with Evan Courtenay, and Dave's odd comment about Hector being unable to die.

Hector pushed his signet ring into Teal's palm. "Run," he coughed, and blood sprayed from his mouth.

"What?" Teal demanded. "I am no coward, Hector. I'll not run and leave thee undefended."

"Run, damn it!" Hector gasped. He dropped flat on the cobblestone pavement, eyes closed. His chest rose, fell, and did not rise again.

Teal glanced over his shoulder and saw a tall, cloaked figure across the street, bow in hand. A man wearing the red and white striped surcoat of the city guard ran toward the bowman, blade out. The archer was a blur as he slapped the heavy yew limb against the guard's head, felling him.

For a moment, a streetlamp penetrated the shadows within his hood, and Teal saw the death-head mask. The mask's maker had found a way to retain the lower mandible, completely covering the man's face. Twisted red lines formed an ungodly sigil on the mask's forehead. Sharp fangs — two pair flanking the central incisors on the upper row, and one pair rising from the lower — glistened like pearls.

"Xardus, be with us this night," Teal prayed, slipped Hector's ring on his finger, and ran.

CR8D

8:35pm

Boots pounding on wet stone pavers, the lithe woman raced into a pool of light. With inhuman strength of her own, she jumped, wrapped her hands around a lamppost, and swung around in a complete circle.

Her boots struck Dave square in the chest. He hit the pavement, rolled back over one shoulder, and skidded to a halt on one knee. Lunging forward, he was after her again, dark cloak billowing around him. He carried his longbow in one hand but didn't dare shoot the fleeing figure. Instead, he ran harder, his slightly longer legs gaining on her by inches with each step.

Tawny braids flowed behind his prey as she darted into a narrow alley, planting her foot against the far wall, and kicking off to make the turn.

Dave rounded the corner, trying to imitate the move, but crashed into the wall. He hissed as pain exploded in his shoulder.

'*Faster!*' Ymara urged. '*Do not let her escape!*'

The predator in him surged after the girl, adrenaline rushing with the thrill of the chase. Within the mask, his eyes shone with abyssal fire.

The girl leaped up, caught the bottom edge of a balcony, and swung onto the railing. She hopped across the corner to the other handrail.

In a single swift motion, Dave slung his bow across his back and followed. He was fast, but she was faster. He crossed the railing as her feet disappeared over the edge of the roof. Growling low in his throat, he climbed after her.

Scampering on all fours, the girl raced to the peak of the roof and slid down the other side. Momentum propelled her to the next roof, where she rolled on its flat surface and came up running.

Dave had fallen behind in the climb, but she had nowhere to go. He jumped to the flat roof. The girl was at the parapet on the far side, searching for a way down. He charged, confident he would catch her here.

She turned at the sound of his pounding steps, and her eyes grew wide. She rolled up onto the narrow ledge, and right over the side.

Dave hit the edge with both hands and leaned out, glowing eyes searching the darkness below. The heavy mist turned into a light rain.

At his side, Ymara's ghost pointed. *'She climbs down the wall.'*

At the opposite corner, he spotted a clay pipe attached to the side of the building, leading down to a rain barrel. He slid down its length and leapt past the barrel. Creeping along the base of the wall, he was within easy reach when the girl jumped the last few feet to the ground. His fingers grasped her arm, jerking her against him.

Even as his other arm reached around her waist, the girl grasped his wrist and used it to swing herself onto his back. Now, her arm was around his throat. Her other hand wormed between her body and his back, reaching for the dagger he could feel pressed between them.

His free hand caught a fistful of braids, and he lurched forward, dragging the girl over his head to the ground. The archer didn't let go. He jerked the girl up and bashed her head on the paving stones again and again.

'Do not kill her!' Ymara's will clamped around him, stopping him.

"Let me go, Ymara!" he grated between clenched teeth.

That moment of stillness was all the girl needed. She twisted free and rolled to her knees, then lunged upward and drove her fist into his solar plexus. His breath whooshed out, and he could do nothing to defend himself against the rain of blows battering his torso. In the blink of an eye, she swept Dave's feet out from under him. When he toppled to the ground, she stomped him hard in the ribs before running away.

"Damn it!" Dave snarled. Suddenly free of the force locking his muscles, the archer rolled to his feet.

He burst onto the next street in time to see his target dive into a passing wagon, then flip out the other side. He dodged around, spotting her as she disappeared into an alley. He dashed into the darkness a few seconds later and smiled. It wasn't an alley. It was a tiny courtyard with solid clapboard walls on all three sides.

His quarry didn't slow. At the far corner, she jumped up, planting her hands and feet against the walls, looking for leverage to monkey up to the roof again, only to slip on the damp wood. She twisted in mid-slide and landed in a crouch, facing him.

"Enough!" she demanded. Her chest heaved from exertion. "Dave, thou must throw off thy shackles. Remove thy mask."

The archer slipped his bow from his back and leaned it against the wall, out of the way. He took off the mask, but instead of dropping it, he held it out to the young woman. "Put this on."

৫৪৪১

8:45pm

Slowly, Teal opened his left hand and extended it to the archer. Rather than taking the proffered mask, he grabbed the hand holding it, his right fist already in motion, but so was Dave's. They struck simultaneously. His blow glanced across Dave's beard, but the archer's reach was longer, and his fist plowed into Teal's cheek.

Dave slipped free of Teal's grip and swept his feet from under him. The flight-master hit the ground hard, flat on his back. Between the punch in the face and his head striking the cobbled street, he lay there stunned with rain dripping into his eyes.

Dave planted one boot on Teal's hair, fanned out across the muck and grime. He studied Teal as if he couldn't recall his captive's name. His gaze darted to one side.

"No," he growled.

"Who art thou speaking to?" Teal asked.

Dave didn't answer. Instead, he seemed to experience some sort of internal struggle before dropping down to place his knees on Teal's shoulders, his thighs trapping Teal's head.

Teal bucked, and his lower body curled up until his legs wrapped around Dave's upper arms and chest with his ankles locked behind the man's back. He continued to roll, pulling his shoulders free, followed by his head, and pushed up on his hands.

Even as Teal twisted, Dave dug his fingertips into Teal's saddle-sore thighs. Teal screamed, a sound of equal parts pain and rage. He jerked one knee forward and kicked the archer. They were too close for the blow to have full force, but it was enough to escape. He rolled and turned.

Dave bared his teeth in a savage grin and lunged. The rain-slick walls around them echoed with the dull thud of traded blows and grunts of pain.

CRSO

8:55pm

Blood trickled from busted lips and knuckles.

'She tires. I see it in her eyes.'

Dave growled low in his throat and rushed his lithe opponent. Her defense grew sloppy as her reaction time slowed. One eye was swollen shut, and her cheek was purple. He, on the other hand, felt no pain. Ymara's strength buoyed him. His shoulder struck her chest, sending the girl flying back against the wall.

She managed two staggering steps before her knees gave out. She struck the dirty pavement with a wet splat.

Dave retrieved the mask where it had fallen during their struggle, then pinned the girl down again, sitting on her pelvis with his lower legs across her thighs, and one hand firmly pressed to her sternum. She writhed beneath him and cursed in a harsh, sibilant language.

Dave froze, listening. In the corner of his mind, memory stirred. Although he didn't understand the words, he recognized the language. The shadowy figures of a woman and a dragon formed in his mind's eye. Before the image came clear, Ymara was there, filling his senses, reminding him what they would do together when she had a new body.

He reached up to fit the mask over the girl's scraped and bloodied face, but her knuckles bashed against his cheekbone. The ring on her middle finger bit into his skin, drawing blood. She followed this attack with another which sent the mask clattering to the ground.

Dave jerked the girl forward by a wad of shirt, then slammed her against the cobbles, once, twice, then a third time, until she went limp. He reached for the mask.

Pain exploded in the back of his head, sending him sprawling over the girl's body. Dave managed to push himself up, and the world exploded again, sending him spiraling into black oblivion.

CRSO

9:00pm

Hector's lungs heaved with the exertion of chasing the two across town. His ribs protested the abuse, but he ignored them. He knelt and hog-tied Dave before rolling the man off Teal onto the rain slick cobbles. Fresh contusions and weeping lacerations covered his face and torso. The bounty hunter turned to Teal, and realized he looked just as rough as Dave. The two had beaten the living hell out of one another.

"You, there! Put your hands up where I can see them!" a voice called from the courtyard entrance.

Hector sighed and raised his hands before climbing to his feet and facing the narrow access. Two deputies waited with weapons drawn and a gaggle of onlookers at their backs. "My name is Hector de los Santos," he announced. "I'm a bounty hunter, working for Lord Roger Vaughn."

"You have papers to prove that?" the guard on Hector's left asked. He seemed a bit older than his companion, more wary.

"Not on me," Hector replied.

The senior guard reached to his belt pouch and produced a pair of manacles as he edged closer. He held his sword at the ready, eyes roving, not becoming too focused on Hector or the two figures lying behind him. "Turn around."

"Lord Vaughn has rooms at The Kestrel on Derby Street. Please send someone to fetch him and bring a healer. The young lady is injured."

"You can tell it to the duty officer at the gaol. Now, turn around."

"What's this?" asked the second guardsman as he lifted the bone mask from the cobblestones.

"It's a cursed artifact," Hector replied. "Put it down."

But the guard wasn't listening. The tip of his tongue slid over his lips, and his mouth fell slightly open. He turned the mask in his hands to stare at the strange face and ran his thumb over the fangs. A flicker of pain darted over his face and vanished as his thumb continued its journey up and along the mask's cheekbone.

"Officer, please give me the mask," Hector repeated.

The guardsman's expression turned to one of wondering adoration as he gazed at something only he could see. "Anything you command, Ymara Dapniš," he whispered.

"Deputy!" Hector shouted, but it was too late. Brandishing his short sword, the younger guard turned on his partner and attacked. The senior guard raised his weapon to fend off the blow, but he was off balance and unprepared for the force behind the strike. He went over backwards and sprawled on the wet stones.

A feral light ignited in the younger guard's eyes as he clutched the mask to his chest with his left hand and raised his sword, this time to deliver a killing blow.

Dodging the prone guard, Hector dove at the possessed man's legs and received a pommel-strike between his shoulder blades for his effort, but the man went down. His elbow struck stone, and the mask flew from his grip a scant second before his head struck the ground. The bounty hunter took the stunned man's weapon and tossed it to his partner, then scrambled after the mask on his hands and knees.

The moment his fingers touched the mask, Hector felt the compulsion batter his will, demanding he claim the mask, run his fingers over its surfaces, touch the over-sharp fangs. A voice whispered to him, growing clearer with each word, until he recognized the rich contralto of Lady D, the vampire who called herself Ymara Dapniš.

'Surrender yourself to me,' she said. 'I can give you anything you desire.'

The ghostly figure of a Deshretan woman in plate and chain armor shimmered into view. The woman's image came clearer. Red lacquer flowed over the armor like fresh blood. Her skin turned the deep tan of a desert-dweller, and her full lips flushed crimson. Eyes black as night bored into his, a carnal promise of violence to come.

Hector returned her gaze with a glare. "Puta, vete al infierno. The only thing I want is for you to leave my friends alone."

The vampire ghost snarled. Her will beat against his, but she could not compel him. Hector dropped the mask onto Dave's cloak and tied the fabric into a bundle.

Even as the ghost vanished, her response echoed in Hector's ears. 'The archer is mine, hunter.'

CHAPTER 15
BLAIÐWYN HALL

August 15, 4237 K.E.

7:00am

The dull throb of aching muscles and abused skin drew Teal up from the darkness. Soft voices and the touch of gentle hands seeped through the pain. He allowed his eyes to drift open to mere slits — enough to see through his lashes — and made out shadowy shapes on either side. He opened his eyes farther, and sharp pain lanced through his skull. His eyelids clenched shut. Nausea twisted his gut. Teal's muscles constricted, which only served to spread the agony. He groaned.

"Welcome back to the land of the living, chérie." The female voice was warm and motherly, with a musical accent Teal didn't recognize. A strong arm slid under Teal's shoulders and lifted him while someone stuffed pillows behind his back and head. "I've something for the pain, if you think you can drink it."

"Sick," Teal croaked.

"That's from the crack in your skull," a young male voice responded. His voice sounded slightly nasal, with overly rounded vowels. "Sip the tea. It will help."

A cup pressed to Teal's lips, and he smelled mint, along with something woody, and some type of flower. He took a tentative sip. Mint and a generous portion of honey almost covered the bitter tang, but not quite. It left a thick film in its wake that soothed his dry throat and settled his churning belly. A few swallows later, Teal managed to open his eyes and look around.

The painted faces of strangers peered back at him out of shadows housed in gilded frames sprouting from deep green walls like' exotic fungi. Overhead, the ceiling bore an uncanny resemblance to snow clouds. Heavy velvet drapes flanked the single, rain-washed window like sentinels, ready to stop unwelcome sunlight at a moment's notice. An ornate chifforobe stood near a dressing table, where a mirror reflected the light from a lamp set atop a low, wide chest of drawers. There, a man in cream-colored robes packed bandages and bottles into a leather satchel.

At the bedside, an old woman with silver hair framing her golden-brown face set aside the cup in her hand before examining Teal with intense amber eyes. There was something familiar about her, but in his groggy and pain-wracked state Teal couldn't place what. Apparently satisfied, the old woman smiled. "You gave us quite the scare, chérie. Between the beating you took and that crack in your skull, we didn't know if you'd ever wake, even with what healing Jacob and I could offer."

"Gentle lady, where am I?"

"You may call me Madame Ivy, and this is Blaiðwyn Hall. My nephew — Lord Vaughn — and your young man brought you here late last night."

"My young man?"

"He hardly left your side for a moment," Madame Ivy replied, and shifted aside.

Hector dozed in an overstuffed wing-back chair that matched the walls. Mud speckled his pants, and he still wore his torn, blood-caked shirt. His shoulder length black hair partially concealed his face, and Teal realized how young the bounty hunter looked — no more than twenty summers, if he had to guess — despite the constant danger and strain the man lived under. Then again, he'd recovered from wounds that should have killed him, at least twice to the flight-master's knowledge. Teal, himself, had seen the magic in the bounty hunter's blood, so perhaps he aged more slowly as well. Teal turned back to the woman.

"What of the man we did pursue? Did Hector apprehend him?"

Madame Ivy's smile slipped away, replaced by such aching sadness, Teal feared she might weep. "They've two men chained to the wall in the donjon tower. Moon mad, les deux, raving about some Deshretan princess no one sees save them. One threatens all manner of horrible violence when he's free, and the other says things to make une putain blush."

Teal reached for the woman's hand. "Thou art sad, Madame Ivy. What troubles thee?"

The old woman patted Teal's hand. "I recognized one of the lads, chérie. I'm afraid this latest turn may be more than his father can bear."

Across the room, Hector twitched. A frown tugged at the corners of his mouth, and he groaned. Another twitch, and he jerked upright, chest heaving. Hector gave the room a wild-eyed search before flopping back in the chair with a shuddering sigh. Seconds passed while his breathing calmed, then he shoved his hair back from his face and rubbed the sleep from his eyes. Finally, he stood and ambled over to the bed. "Morning. Señora, do you mind if I take your place for a few minutes?"

"Not at all. I understand we're to have another guest join us, so I need to set the maids to airing a bedroom and check on things in the kitchen." She bustled toward the door, spry despite her apparent age, catching the young healer by the elbow on her way past. "Come along, Jacob. You need breakfast, and those two need some time to themselves." She turned back and pointed to the cup on the side table. "See that Teal drinks the rest of her tea."

Hector gave Ivy a short bow and waited for the door to close before turning to Teal. "I need to ask you some questions."

"I shall do my best to answer thee well and true."

"Do you remember your name?"

"Aye. 'Tis Tealaucan Rathaera, same as yestereve when we parted, after thy erstwhile friend shot thee down in the street."

"Three days ago, you told me about a girl you helped, and I asked you a question about her that you never had a chance to answer. Do you remember what I asked you?"

"I do, and thou told me not to speak of it to anyone else. The answer to thy question is yes, she bore wounds upon her scalp and at the base of her spine, as if horns and a tail were ripped from her body, along with her wings. Art thou now satisfied I am still myself?"

Hector blew out a noisy breath and pulled his hair back into a queue at the base of his neck. "Fine. Tell me what happened. Dave is in almost as bad a shape as you."

"I ran as thou did command, and Dave pursued me through the streets as a predator does its prey. 'Twas naught more than much needed exercise, until he managed to catch me. Only then did it come clear the deadly danger he posed. I did attempt to capture him for thee, but he is a fierce brawler."

"Sorry about that. I expected to catch up with you before things got out of hand."

Teal reached up and touched the bandage stretching around his skull. "Strange and terrible magic binds the archer, Hector. His eyes glowed in the darkness, even when the mask was not upon his face. He spoke to the empty air and listened as though hearing a response. Worse, he did attempt to place the mask upon my face. Tell me: had he succeeded, would I have ended up enspelled like him, or would the mask have devoured me like the sorceress under Evan Courtenay's dominion?"

Hector picked at the quilt covering the narrow bed, refusing to meet Teal's gaze. "Like the sorceress, most likely, but things are worse than I thought," he muttered. "Even without a host, the mask is able to enslave men's minds."

"I beg thy pardon. How is that possible?"

The bounty hunter shrugged. "A city guard picked up the mask last night... pricked his finger on one of the fangs... now Lady D has him under her spell, too."

"What of the charm the archer left behind on the *Lady Luck*, the necklace and brooch?"

"It didn't help either one of them. Roger and I think the mask's influence is stronger, but it's possible the brooch's magic is spent. We've sent for help, but I'm worried Dave may be too far gone."

CRSO

8:30am

A carriage clattered and jounced along the long drive leading to Blaiðwyn Hall, the ancestral home of Earl Wolverton, Lord Roger Vaughn. A half-mile back, they'd passed through the estate's main gatehouse, its gloomy grey stones surmounted by a pair of wolf statues. Although visually appropriate for the Wolverton estate, the statues — larger than life and poised as if to leap down on attackers with gaping maws of sharp fangs — elicited a visceral fear in the viewer.

Within the walls, a brief sward gave way to a dense park of old-growth trees, no doubt home to the earl's personal stock of game. The forest, in turn, yielded to shaped hedges and swaths of manicured lawn. A glowing white gazebo gathered roses around its feet like a hen with chicks.

Jasper Thredd peered through mist-laden air beyond the carriage window at the imposing edifice crouching at the end of the drive. Its dark grey stone facade and ancient tower exceeded the gatehouse in dour gloominess despite the beauty of the grounds. He fidgeted with the rings adorning each of his fingers, chafing at the carriage horses' pace and the mysterious message he'd received from Hector, delivered by Lady Lahar Aneirin, Countess Colliford, no less. Until the previous day, Lady Aneirin and Lord Vaughn were nothing more than names on a list of Academy Library benefactors. He wondered how Hector had managed to gain their favor, and why the message's hinted trouble prompted the countess to act as a messenger.

The mist turned into a drizzle as the vehicle rumbled to a stop before a low porch and imposing door bound in iron and bronze. Footmen and grooms descended on the coach and unloaded the parcels and crates tied to its rear footboard and roof. Jasper climbed out to oversee their work, careful not to jounce the carriage as he shifted his bulk. Many of the things he brought were fragile, but there were also volatile elements among his things which would react poorly to rough treatment. As an afterthought, he reached back into the conveyance, retrieved his official robe, and slipped it on over his tunic. The silver sigils along the hem of the midnight blue fabric brushed the tops of his worn boots, keeping the rain from his clothes, but the robe did nothing to keep it from his hair and beard.

"Jasper!"

The mage turned, spotted Hector emerging from the stables, and bustled forward to catch the bounty hunter in a bear hug. When he finally released his friend, he asked, "How bad is it?"

"Ha!" Hector's bark of laughter held a bitter edge. Dark circles underscored his eyes, and he had the haggard look of too many sleepless nights. "The usual."

"That bad?"

"Maybe worse. I won't know until you see what you can do for Dave. We can't transport him to Ozera in the state he's in. Not with any degree of safety, anyway. Did you happen to get the list of supplies?"

"I did. Are you taking up sculpting?"

"After a fashion."

Jasper glanced at the servants carrying the last of the crates into the main hall. "I was summoned to Ozera six days ago. August and Xandor were there, helping Eidan keep his mother in check — she meant to murder a blind man. Apparently, Mrs. Yves blamed him for what happened to Aislinn. The sad thing is, I think the old man agreed with her."

"Did you see Aislinn and Hummingbird?"

"Hummingbird was in the critical care ward. She was poisoned, and they almost lost her. The healer I spoke to said it may be a while before she's strong enough to go home." He fiddled with the rings adorning his left hand and shifted from one foot to the other. He swallowed audibly, licked his lips, and said, "Aislinn... Hector, they couldn't save her."

"No." Hector stumbled back and shook his head as if trying to dislodge the words from his ears.

"There was nothing they could do. Father Phaedrus tried to call her back to this side of the veil, but her spirit didn't answer."

"NO! You're wrong!" Hector's shout echoed through the yard. "She can't be gone!"

"Hector, there's more," Jasper said, trying to calm his friend, ready to stop him from doing anything foolish. Aware of the coachman at his back tending the horses, he kept his voice low. "Brand has lost his ever-loving mind. Eidan gave me enough pearls to fill a cauldron so I could acquire Kemetan preservation oils and have a jewelry box enlarged to serve as her casket. It's beautiful, by the way, fit for a princess. All carved ebony at the seams and diamond panes for the panels. But Aislinn, lying in that box wearing riding leathers and flowers in her hair, was the creepiest thing I've ever seen, Hector. Who ever heard of a dragon adding a corpse to his hoard?" Jasper scratched at his beard, contemplating the wisdom of what he was about to say. He had no idea if it would do more harm than good. Deciding forewarned was forearmed, he said, "Brand means to kill you and Dave."

Rain streamed down Hector's face. He opened and closed his mouth several times before he managed to ask, "When's the funeral?"

"I'm sorry, Hector, Eidan and Shayla refused to wait. They held it the day before yesterday at sunset, atop the cliffs at Sunrise Chapel so Brand could attend. Afterward, he flew away with Aislinn, casket and all."

"Where?"

"His cave, I assume. Leaving Sunrise Chapel was the last I saw of him."

Hector hung his head. "Dave and I should have been there. Did anyone contact Robert?"

"He and that Francescan battle-cleric, Gideon, arrived in Ozera about an hour before the funeral procession started. One of the villagers stepped aside to let Robert be a pallbearer. He looked grim and... unkempt, like Dave. He said he'd wait in Ozera for the two of you."

"What about Tallinn?"

"I heard him tell Xandor he planned to go home the next morning." Jasper looked up into the rain. "This is going to get worse before it gets better. Let's get out of the weather. You can tell me why we're at this manor house, and what I can do to help Dave."

CR&EO

8:45am

The estate's seneschal waited in the foyer with a bevy of servants and boxes between the curves of double stairs. Behind him, a pair of glass paneled Francescan doors in the gallery let out into a courtyard surrounding the ancient donjon. "Welcome to Blaiðwyn Hall, Magus Thredd. My name is Syon, the estate steward. I've taken the liberty of having the maids prepare the Blue Suite for you near Master Hector and Miss Teal. Shall I have your things moved there?"

"Thank you, no," Jasper replied. "We need a workroom. Something with a large table, a locking door, and nothing valuable, if possible. Do you have an outbuilding no one is using? I need to set up some alchemy equipment, and there's always a danger of fire."

"More like explosions," Hector muttered. Jasper turned to him with a glare, but Syon remained impassive and unruffled.

"I have just the thing, sir. His Lordship has an interest in alchemy, himself, and has a laboratory on the grounds. If you gentlemen would like to wait in the drawing room while the lads move your things, I'll have refreshments brought in."

Hector cleared his throat and asked, "Will we see Lord Vaughn today?"

"At dinner this evening, sir," Syon replied. "He rode to Tydway early this morning but left instructions for you to be given anything you need. He did ask that you not leave the estate before he returns."

"Did he happen to say why?"

"Yes, sir. His lordship said I should inform you that a certain councilman of your acquaintance from the city of Rowanoake is currently seeking audience with the Highlord. Lord Vaughn has gone to speak on your behalf."

"Rowanoake?" Jasper demanded. "Hector what have you done now?"

"Nothing. William Howard showed up in Ruthaer and interfered with our job. Lord Vaughn arrested him for piracy."

"Are you going to end up in jail?"

Hector made a face and shrugged. "It depends on the Highlord. Let's hope Lord Vaughn is in favor at court."

The drawing room turned out to be a combination library and music room. Shelves filled with leather tomes and scroll cases lined half the walls from floor to ceiling. A variety of chairs and settees had been artfully arranged across the floor. The other half of the room sported a sideboard with cut crystal decanters and glasses, plush seating, and a rosewood harpsichord. Family portraits hung between the windows, but none showed the current Earl Wolverton as an adult.

In place of pride above the mantle hung a life-size oil painting of a woman in pale grey silk under a rose arbor. Ornate combs held her honey-colored locks away from her smiling face to trail across her shoulders in a cascade of soft waves. A blue and silver locket and a matching wedding band were her only jewelry. The combination of the pale gown and vibrant flowers seemed to intensify the blue of her eyes, as if the artist had used actual sapphires, yet there was a hint of mischief in her expression. The image was so lifelike, Hector half expected the woman to leap from the gilded frame. He frowned — he could see more of Robert in that look than Dave.

"Wow, she's a beauty," said Jasper. "I wonder who she is."

"Our host's late wife, Lady Bryony Vaughn, Viscountess Snowdon of Carolingias," Hector answered.

"She looks familiar. I wonder if I've seen her out and about in Tydway."

"Not unless you're a lot older than you let on," said Hector. "She was murdered fifteen years ago."

Behind him, a quick knock preceded the door sliding open to admit a maid bearing a tray laden with a tea service and a selection of muffins and scones. After she left, the two men settled across from one another. Hector told Jasper about Dave's encounter with the vampire in Altaira, her surprise return in Ruthaer, and everything he knew about the mask. He'd barely finished his tale when another knock heralded the arrival of Syon, come to show them to the alchemy building across the back lawn.

CHAPTER 16
ALCHEMY AND MAGIC

August 15, 4237 K.E.

9:45am

The interior of the alchemy laboratory proved to be a single large room with cabinets and a work counter on either side, and a single steel-plated door flanked by shelves of equipment at its far end. A long worktable occupied the center of the room. Behind the far door, they found a narrow, book lined space with a smaller table.

After Jasper pronounced the windowless building perfect, he set about unpacking his supplies, which included a number of rare oils and unguents, thin laths of various materials, and a plethora of powders. In a pair of crates marked with his initials, Hector found bags of sculptor's clay, gypsum powder, a jar of turpentine, delicate sculpting tools, two mold frames, and a selection of inks and dyes.

"You never told me why you need all the sculpting material and two arcaloxós," said Jasper, handing Hector one of two identical silver boxes.

"Dave is convinced that Rhodinan Count we met in Ruthaer is going to try and steal the mask. I need a second box for a decoy, just in case. As for the clay, you and the clerics are going to need a model of the mask's markings to study."

"You understand I need to examine the real mask, don't you?" Jasper asked.

"No, you don't." Hector's brow furrowed as he studied the silver box. Even though he held it in his hand and felt its weight, it was impossible to focus upon and could only be seen in his peripheral vision. He ran a fingertip around the hair-line seam where lid met base. He extracted the gold skeleton key from its inset lock. An intricate array of wards and cuts lined the key's bit, the work of a master locksmith. The second box yielded a different, yet equally complex key. "Can you enchant these boxes so no one can see inside with magic, and no psychotic energy can leak out? They need to be completely sealed off."

"I think you mean psychic energy," Jasper said, taking back the silver box. "The arcaloxós already carry intense wards. The academy always has a few on hand for storing dangerous or volatile objects, but if this mask is as powerful as you say, I'll need to add customized spells. There's no guarantee what I put together will be strong enough if I don't know what I'm warding against. Even then, we may need to go to the academy and ask the Council of Archmages for help."

"No. We don't know we can trust them. *You* have to do this, Jasper. For Dave."

"Then let me examine the mask."

Hector rummaged in his pocket and held out the balas ruby brooch. "Can you use this? It kept Lady D out of Dave's head, sort of."

Jasper raised an eyebrow. "What do you mean, sort of?"

"All I can tell you is that it kept Lady D from controlling Dave in Ruthaer. I don't know if the power faded, or if the mask is getting stronger. Now... now it doesn't help at all."

Holding the brooch up to the lantern hanging above the worktable, Jasper studied the arcane engravings on its front and back. The spinel's facets winked at him, with the exception of one bearing a black hairline fracture in its heart. "There isn't enough magic in this gem to light a firefly's butt, much less power the spells on this beauty. Where did you get it?"

"Found it on a shipwreck. I think it belonged to that Rhodinan calling himself Count Dodz."

"Hmm... I recognize some of these spells, but not all. I can take it back to the academy and have our head librarian, Master Meuricel, look it over."

"Can't. The brooch goes back on its chain around Dave's neck the moment we're done here."

"Even if it has no power?"

"Power of suggestion, amigo. It's his magic feather. A placebo for his mental state."

"His what?"

"Never mind, it's a Terran thing."

"If you say so." Jasper reached into his sporran and extracted a small book and quill. "Let me make a sketch of the brooch and copy down these symbols. It may come in handy when I examine that mask," Jasper said, giving Hector a pointed look.

"Fine," Hector huffed. "Can you do it without actually touching it? I'd hate to have to chain you up in the donjon alongside Dave and the deputy."

"I'd hate to go to prison," Jasper replied. "In all seriousness, though, mind control is tricky to overcome. It's a good thing I've spent the last couple of years researching counter-spells and wards against it."

"You have? Why?"

Jasper shivered. "I had a bad experience."

Hector wanted to ask what happened, but Jasper's expression made him hold his tongue. Instead, he asked, "Would the brooch work if we replace the gem?"

"If we found one that could hold enough power. Now stop stalling, Hector. Show me the mask. I have strong mental defenses against mind control. Plus, I have an amulet of my own. It isn't as elaborate as yours, but it should serve its purpose. If it turns out that isn't enough, you're going to prep the mask with this." He held out a tiny glass bottle from his collection on the worktable. Wax sealed the stopper in place.

"What is it?"

"A potion. It paralyzes on contact."

"Really? What made you bring that?"

"Each arcaloxós has a thief-ward in its lock, in this case a spring-loaded needle. I planned to use the potion on them, but after what you told me about the deputy, I think it would be better to use it on the mask's fangs. If I lose control and try to prick my finger, one touch of that stuff will immobilize me for about fifteen minutes. More than enough time for you to take the mask and clap me in irons."

"That plan is loco, amigo."

"Do you have a better one?" Jasper asked.

"You already said my plan wouldn't work, so no, I suppose not. Wait here."

"You left the mask unattended?"

"Of course not. Caballo's guarding it," Hector replied.

As the door closed, Jasper muttered, "Now who's plan is loco?"

CR80

10:00am

Hector returned a quarter-hour later carrying a cloth bundle. Jasper watched from the far end of the room as the bounty hunter thumped his burden on the table and undid the knots, all the while swearing in Espian and grumbling about selling willful horses who took themselves too seriously to something called a gravy train. The knots finally came loose, revealing the bundled fabric to be Dave's cloak. In the lantern-light, the bone mask gleamed, and the blood red etching on its forehead twisted and writhed like living fire. In addition to painting the fangs with paralytic potion, Hector encased the fang-tips in balls of red wax.

"Let's start with it inside an arcaloxós," Jasper said. "I need to see how much, if any, power escapes." Once Hector locked away the mask, Jasper murmured a spell. Gold flashed in his pupils, revealing the magic in the laboratory as colors. Dave's cloak glowed deep azure with an enchantment for protection, as did the locks on several cabinets. The tracking spells in his and Hector's signet rings pulsed gold, and Dave's brooch gave off no aura at all.

Deep reddish-purple magic seeped from the silver box, like blood through a bandage, and spread across the tabletop. Hands behind his back, Jasper took a half step forward. "Alright, open it."

The moment the lid began to rise, magic spilled forth and flowed up Hector's arms, seeking a crack in his defenses. The magic surged and formed sphere, its color thinning as the spell spread through the room. In most spells, that fade would mean the power weakened at the edges, but Jasper couldn't be certain about this one.

He steeled his resolve. The oncoming magic collided with his personal protections. Like thick slime, the foreign magic slid across Jasper's magic and forced its way between the overlapping layers. He watched it come, waiting to see what would happen.

It started as a distant whisper, barely loud enough to classify as a sound, the language undecipherable. Next came a craving for something indefinable. It nagged at him, growing stronger second by second. Given enough time, he knew the craving would become all-consuming.

The whispering grew clearer until a woman's voice called to him, her silken tones promising him pleasure, power, anything his heart desired. It was like thick, soft fur caressing his psyche. Jasper stepped toward the voice. Another step, and his belly pressed against the worktable. He passed his hand through the energy surrounding the mask, feeling the power at its source.

Gently, he turned the mask over. His fingertip brushed the sigil pulsing on the concave surface. The inner and outer markings were mirrors of one another — or they passed completely through the bone. Only then did he understand that the markings weren't carved. Somehow, someone had fused demonic magic into the bone.

This was not some cursed item created by the sorceress, Consuelo, over a few months' time. It felt more like an evil intelligence possessed the mask, held in an imperfect prison. A working like this would have taken more energy than a single human practitioner could possibly wield. It would have taken a powerful entity — or a group of humans working in tandem — a year or more to complete.

The call grew stronger, more seductive. Warmth curled through his body. He could see the shadow of a woman in his peripheral vision. She promised to be his, and his alone, if he would help her escape her prison.

Jasper turned over the mask. Perfect, pearly teeth grinned back at him. He felt the sudden need to study the fangs closer. As if they belonged to someone else, his fingers picked at the wax.

Magic flared, binding him more effectively than any rope or manacle. The siren's song transformed into a scream of frustrated rage. His vision narrowed as he struggled.

Another hand appeared, and the mask slipped away, carried by the thief. The voice cursed and railed as it receded, and the shadow disappeared. Ever so slowly, the spell woven by the vampire's voice slipped from Jasper's mind, yet he could not move. Sweat dripping from his face and soaking his tunic, he took in ragged gasps as he tried to catch his breath.

Time passed. Hector appeared at the table, clamped iron manacles on Jasper's wrists, and retreated. Finally, the binding spell dissipated, and Jasper was able to inspect his hands and fingertips. Relieved to find no evidence of wounds or blood, he turned from the table to find Hector watching him, his scimitar in one hand and a bludgeon in the other.

"Are you alright, amigo?"

"Fine," Jasper answered. His voice sounded weak. He cleared his throat and tried again. "I'm alright — still my own man. I've never seen a compulsion spell so strong. Why doesn't it affect you?"

"No sé, amigo. Maybe it's an unexpected benefit of whatever it is that makes me heal faster than normal. I hear Lady D's voice, but that's all it is: a voice."

"Hmm. I wish you'd let me have some of your blood to study. Think of the good we could do just in the area of healing."

Hector shook his head. "No. I used my blood to heal Hummingbird so she wouldn't bleed to death in Ruthaer, and it poisoned her."

"Hector, it may have poisoned her, but it saved her, too. She's alive. You shouldn't feel bad about what happened."

The bounty hunter waved away the mage's response. "Let's focus on helping Dave."

Jasper stroked his beard as he studied the sketch of the brooch and the notes he had made. "Good news first. Lady D's compulsion can be blocked. As you said, the brooch did it, and I can modify the magic of the arcaloxós to do the same. The bad news is, it's only temporary. There's an intelligence inside the mask that wants to get out. That red sigil on the mask's forehead is demonic in origin, which probably means the mask and whatever's inside is abyssal.

"Destroying the mask is a possibility, but it may only release Lady D. We need it exorcised, which means we need a priest — a powerful one. We'll have to hope they can do it in Ozera. Otherwise, we may have to seek help from the Archbishop of Zaragoza."

"I expected as much," replied Hector. "How long will the silver box hold her?"

"There's no way to tell," Jasper replied. "Now that I know what I'm up against, I'll put everything into it I can. I'll need the brooch, my cookbook, plus some of Lord Vaughn's supplies, to create the containment spells. However, no matter what I do, Lady D will get free. It's a reality that we need to prepare for." He searched the room. "Where is the mask?"

Hector removed the manacles from Jasper's wrists, then pointed to the steel door. "Locked in one of your boxes in the office. It's as far as I could get it from you without leaving the building."

"Does the door lock?"

"I can bar it, if necessary, but there isn't a keyed lock."

"Good enough. I hope his Lordship doesn't mind me raiding his cabinets."

"He won't," Hector replied. "You can trust me on that."

"Does that mean there are things I *can't* trust you about?" Jasper grinned.

Hector laughed and shook his head before closing the door between them.

CHAPTER 17
A MEETING OF MINDS

August 15, 4237 K.E.

3:00pm

'Time grows short, köle.' Ymara's disembodied voice ripped through Count Dodz' mind. Keeping his features calm, he set his fork on his plate and glanced at the nearest diners. No one seemed to notice him.

'The hunter plans to imprison me. If he does, I will be unable to guide you. You must come to me now.'

The image of gates surmounted by snarling wolves flashed in his mind's eye. Dodz pressed fingers to his forehead. A sledgehammer beat against the inside of his skull, threatening to burst through at any moment. His unspoken reply increased the pain. *'I do not recognize the place, Ymara. It could be an estate or a prison. Either way, it will take time to locate.'*

'Köle, I require your presence now!' Ymara's voice thundered.

Dodz clenched a fistful of tablecloth and bit the inside of his cheek against the agony she sent lancing through him. *'Pospeshnost' budet moyey smert'yu.'* Lips pressed in a cold smile, he forced a thought through the miasma of pain. *'I sense your desperation, Ymara. You fear this hunter.'* He tensed, half-expecting the vampire to render him unconscious. *'Give me time. I know the bounty hunter's destination, and I have a plan.'*

The pain receded to a dull throb, a token of Ymara's lingering displeasure. Dodz dabbed the sweat from his brow and raised his wine glass with a trembling hand. What had been an expensive Francescan vintage now tasted of blood and ashes. His appetite gone, Dodz dropped a few coins on the table and left the trattoria without a backward glance.

A steady drizzle slicked the thoroughfare. Although cart traffic remained as busy as ever, few pedestrians ventured along the flagstone sidewalks. He turned up his collar and contemplated purchasing a hat.

As he trudged up the street, he noticed a figure in the mouth of a narrow alley. Swathed in black rags from head to toe, only his silvery almond-shaped eyes were visible. Their gazes met, sending a jolt of unease through the count. Quickening his pace, he retreated back the way he came. Two blocks later, the same figure stared at him from a shadow-filled doorway.

For the better part of an hour, Dodz wound his way through the city, entering random shops and slipping out through their back doors. Each time he returned to the street, the watcher was there on the opposite sidewalk. Oblivious passersby ignored the mysterious figure as if he did not exist.

Fighting the urge to run, Dodz entered a residential district where bourgeois homes surrounded a tree lined park. He came to a stop beneath the drooping boughs of a hemlock and turned to face his stalker, knife in hand. The park and surrounding streets lay empty. Silence settled around him. Even the plop of rain dripping from the trees stilled.

A shadow fell over him. The scars on Dodz' left arm from Ymara's fangs ignited with molten fire. He sucked in a hissing breath and clutched at the phantom wound.

When he looked up, solid quicksilver orbs stared back at him from a scar-covered dærganfae face. His instincts screamed for him to run, to do anything, but he remained rooted in place like the tree at his back.

Mi'dnirr's long, bone-white fingers grasped either side of Dodz' head, and he felt something *other* enter his consciousness. It rifled through his memories until images of Ymara and Aislinn came to the forefront.

The world around Dodz faded, leaving his consciousness suspended in an agonizing maelstrom of blood-tinged mist and infinitesimal motes of dancing fire. Beside him, armored in blood red plate and chain, Ymara's ghostly image coalesced in his mind's eye. Her skin held the deep tan of a desert-dweller, and her full lips flushed crimson, sending carnal desires through his body.

Across the maelstrom, Mi'dnirr's silver eyes locked on Ymara.

"Mi'dnirr, who was once called Bēl Šibṭu, bringer of plagues, I give you greetings," Ymara said with a courtly bow.

"Nin Dapniš, inducer of conflict," Mi'dnirr responded in a voice like an endless swarm of stinging insects. "Is this creature yours?"

"It is bound to my will, brother, and serves my purpose."

Their words echoed inside Dodz' mind, overwhelming his senses and threatening his sanity. The truth of Ymara and Mi'dnirr was beyond his understanding, yet they had sheathed themselves in corporeal forms and used his head as a place to parlay as if it were a room at an inn.

"It has taken something from me," said Mi'dnirr. "I want it back."

"The female half-elf?"

"Yes."

"I have need of her," Ymara said. "Allow me this gift for a time."

"What is it you seek?"

"Freedom for myself and our siblings."

The silver eyes seemed to contemplate the words and drain the very meaning from them. "Ymara... I do not recall that being one of your many names."

"I chose it in remembrance of the Deshretan princess who traded her flesh to me in exchange for power."

"The wind speaks true then. You sold yourself to a mortal."

"I sought a way to end our imprisonment!" Ymara snapped. "Who are you to question me, in your dærganfae vessel?"

"Unlike you, I was summoned from the abyss," Mi'dnirr replied. "I did not choose to be trapped in this wretched flesh."

Visions of death and ruin seared Dodz' brain. He realized that, unlike his sister, Mi'dnirr didn't want to control the world, he wanted to destroy it.

"Brother, be at ease," Ymara said. "Our time has nearly come."

"Has it?" demanded Mi'dnirr. "Where have you been? You left our company more than three millennia past."

"Servants of the sephiroth trapped my vessel deep within sub-Gaian halls behind wards and spells I could not break. Such was their curse that only a human not born of Gaia could carry me to freedom."

"You found such a creature?"

"He found me, but my escape required the sacrifice of my flesh."

"How did you do it?" asked Mi'dnirr. His quicksilver eyes burned fever bright. "Tell me. Even now the descendants of my vessel's kinsmen hold me blood-bound to their territory, using talismans carved from the very bones of my summoner."

"You obviously did not allow them to remove your head."

"No, they would never do that," he replied. "I am their king."

"A king imprisoned in his own kingdom?" she mocked.

"Who are you to speak?" Mi'dnirr hissed. "You, like me, have little freedom, if you must resort to servants to do your bidding."

"For now, you speak true," Ymara conceded. "Blood and magic etched my essence into my former vessel's skull. I helped a power-hungry fool transform it into a mask, but Sutekh's ghūl captured her before I completed the transference to my new vessel. Now, I abide until I can claim another."

"Why haven't you?" Mi'dnirr asked.

"The Terran hunter I tricked into releasing me from my imprisonment stands in the way."

"Hector de los Santos," Mi'dnirr rasped. "He proved useful against Evan Courtenay."

"He is a festering thorn in a lion's paw," Ymara spat, "and immune to our direct influence. He has touched the void between worlds and bears a spark of Creation's Fire within his blood, rendering him nearly immortal."

Between the two vampires, the sparks of fire paused in their swirling dance, suspended in the blood vapor trapping Dodz' consciousness. For one blessed moment, the barrage on his senses receded. Then, Ymara spoke again.

"One good did come of my sojourn with the ghūl, Evan Courtenay. I learned the ancient race of Xemmassians are no more, and their ancient knowledge lost. Together, you and I can undo what their gal'bâru wrought upon our brethren. We nine shall be free to wreak havoc upon Gaia's mortals once again."

"The Xemmassians are not destroyed, Ymara. I recently discovered a soul-bound pair."

"Impossible."

"I snatched the female half-elf in your servant's possession from the clutches of Evan Courtenay's revenants a fortnight past and claimed her for myself. She and the young Tenné she calls brother are of that ancient race. I sent her to destroy the ghūl and acquire the dærganfae blade he stole, but Akkilettū captured her spirit."

"A dead half-elf and an ignorant dragonling are no threat to us."

"I did not say she perished."

"Without a spirit, her body will die, brother."

"Nay, Ymara. The bounty hunter did spill his own blood into her wound. Ever since, her body has lain suspended, neither dead nor alive. Were her spirit to be freed from Akkilettū's eye, she would be restored to life. Together, she and the Tenné *are* a threat to us."

"Wise brother, I have missed your counsel, but there is no need to fear the Xemmassian scion."

"Perhaps, but rebellion starts with the tortured dreams of a slave."

"I will not allow the girl to escape." Ymara fell silent, then sinister laughter erupted from her lips.

The sound filled Dodz' head, and he felt the seams of his skull pulling apart.

"A Tenné, here within our grasp after all these years. We shall use it to free our siblings and be revenged upon Xardus."

"How?"

"By making the celestial's last child serve as Šar Naspantu's vessel. Through the dragon, the first of our imprisoned siblings shall be set free and given form."

"Again I ask you: how?" Mi'dnirr demanded.

"See for yourself." Ymara's fiery sparks coalesced into seven twisted sigils. Mortal beings appeared, no two the same race or species, within the abyssal signs. Then, the blood-mist surrounding Dodz' psyche separated itself into horrific figures. Each stepped into a sigil and took up its trapped sacrifice. Rather than devour the mortals, the demons flowed *into* them, and the fiery sigils slithered over their new skin to become abyssal tattoos. The figures of Mi'dnirr and Ymara joined them, bringing their company of demonic siblings to nine.

Dodz felt the weight of millennia in the demons' gazes, and with it, the insatiable hunger. Consumed by horror, his consciousness fled.

CHAPTER 18
FLIGHT

August 15, 4237 K.E.

7:30pm

Sweat-soaked and coated in a generous amount of both clay and plaster, Hector emerged from his ad hoc workspace to find Jasper sprawled on his worktable, sound asleep. Of the various oils, powders, and bric-a-brac he spread across the space that morning, only two things remained: the silver box — newly inscribed with arcane signs and sigils — and the ruby and silver brooch.

He studied the room in bemused wonder. Glass vials and containers gleamed upon their shelves. Not a speck of dust remained anywhere; even the floor and ceiling looked freshly washed. The space was cleaner than when they'd entered that morning.

Jasper stretched and yawned before sitting up. "All finished?"

"No. The gypsum needs a few hours to set. I'll need another day. You?"

"Hopefully. We need to test this arcaloxós and make sure it works." Jasper pointed to the ornate box. "Let's see how I did."

Hector picked it up and studied the markings. Jasper's spellwork covered every surface, inside and out.

"No one will be able to find the mask using magic once I lock it inside?"

"That was one of the goals," Jasper replied.

Taking the box, Hector carried it into the other room and pushed the door closed. It was a moment's work to fit the mask inside, engage the lock, and pocket the key. Back in the main workspace, he placed it on the table and took a step back.

Jasper murmured an incantation, and his eyes glowed. The sight sent an involuntary shiver up Hector's spine. The mage made a series of complex gestures and spouted a series of words that sounded like gibberish to the bounty hunter. Nothing happened.

"We won't know for sure until we let someone older and wiser than me have a crack at it," Jasper said with a grin, "but I can't detect the mask."

Hector pocketed the brooch and scooped up the box. "Better yet, let's go up to the donjon and see how Dave and the deputy are feeling."

Fading twilight greeted them. At some point, the clouds had blown away. Now, early stars dotted the sky, and lanterns marked the path to the manor door.

Jasper's stomach rumbled, and he patted his paunch. "Do you think we missed dinner?"

"Hard to say." Hector looked down at his filthy tunic. "I doubt they'd let me near the kitchen in this state, much less the dining room. How is it you're fresh as a spring daisy?"

The mage grinned and waved his hand. Magic rippled over Hector, pulling out the day's sweat and grime in passing, leaving him clean and his clothes fresh.

Hector looked down at himself and frowned. The glossy polish on his boots reflected the lantern light, offending his natural inclination to pass unseen. He was thankful he wasn't wearing anything metallic other than his signet ring and matte-black belt buckle. "That's a useful trick. Can you put it in a charm or something I can use on Dave?"

"Are you mad? He'd kill us both!"

"Nah, he's too superstitious about killing mages. Bad luck and all. Besides, he owns and uses enchanted items."

"Items he chose, with ambient effects he manages to ignore. A charm like that would require conscious intent to use."

"He *intentionally* used exploding arrows in Ruthaer, and they were anything but unnoticeable," Hector groused.

"He used them?" Jasper exclaimed. "I wish I'd been there to see it. How big were the fireballs? Did he like them?"

"They combined archery and fire. Of course Dave liked them! He damn near dropped a mountain on our heads, and then he managed to set me on fire."

Jasper laughed. "That's Dave for you, but back to the cleanliness charm. What could you possibly say to convince him to use one?"

"He wouldn't need to take a bath or pay the laundress anymore."

"Well, there is that, I suppose. The man has a serious aversion to soap, but I can't say I blame him. You never know what some people will put in the stuff."

The front door opened as Hector reached for the latch, and Syon appeared on the threshold. "Master Hector! I'm glad you're here."

"What's happened?"

"Lord Vaughn has arranged for your immediate transport to Ozera. You need to gather your things and be ready to depart from the pier within the half-hour."

"A pier? I don't recall seeing a river near the estate," said Jasper.

"No, sir," Syon replied. "We have a lake."

Jasper waited, but the seneschal offered no explanation as to how they would travel.

"What about Dave and the deputy?" asked Hector.

"Lord Vaughn is with them now. They fell unconscious."

"I see. Syon, please have someone assist Teal and bring down my saddlebags," Hector said. "We'll collect the horses and ask the stableboys for help with our things from the alchemy building."

"I'll meet you in Ozera tomorrow after I finish the other arcaloxós," Jasper said as they led the horses across the lawn. "In the meantime, I'll ask Master Meuricel to research the symbols on that brooch and see what he can dig up in the library about artifacts like the mask."

"Lady Aneirin was supposed to ask the Academy's librarian to pull information together for us," responded Hector. "With any luck, he'll have something useful ready for you. I'd like you to be part of whatever team Padre Phaedrus assigns to the mask."

The mage gave him a solemn nod, but said, "I'm not sure how you plan to convince Father Phaedrus. He has strict rules about who's allowed in the Aerarium. Ozera takes in some rather strange and dangerous items."

"Your help is going to be one of the conditions of me turning over the mask to them. Dave and I need someone we know and trust to ensure Lady D is gone, once and for all."

"Phaedrus is the most famous holy man east of the White River, possibly west of it, too. If he tells you the mask — or any other evil artifact — is no longer a threat, you can trust him. To be honest, I don't think they need my help. There are rumors that he's asked for and received aid from the Eternal Father's celestial children in the past. Given the circumstances, they may be willing to help him again."

"I've seen a celestial or two, myself," Hector responded. "They aren't all as holy and pure as one would expect."

CR80

11:59pm

Dave woke lying against a curved plank wall, his wrists in shackles. Aislinn's gold chain around his neck and the now familiar weight of the balas-ruby brooch elicited a sigh of relief. Heavy bolts secured thick iron bars to dark wood beams and floor planks stretching into the darkness beyond a thin spill of lantern light.

Somewhere in that darkness, heavy breathing hinted at the presence of another prisoner. Other than that, silence reigned. In every other jail he'd ever had the displeasure of visiting, there was always noise — the mutter of other prisoners, guards on patrol, rats in bedding straw. For a moment, he wondered if he'd gone deaf and imagined the breathing, but the clink of chains and his involuntary groan when he sat up dispelled that fear.

"You gave us quite the run." Hector emerged from the shadows and waited at the edge of the light.

Dave climbed to his feet and staggered to the cage door, his body protesting each movement. He gripped the bars with bruised fists. "Where the hell are we?"

"The *Lady Luck*'s brig. We'll be in Ozera in a few hours."

"Don't bullshit me. This doesn't feel like a ship, and you sure as hell can't get to Ozera on one," Dave said.

"Amigo, Lady Aneirin and your father were keeping secrets from us."

"I don't have a damned father," Dave snarled. "Now, where the fuck are we?"

"I told you, we're on the *Lady Luck*. Es una aeronave."

"A flying ship? If that's true, why the hell did we spend all that time fucking sailing to Tydway? They could've taken us straight to Ozera."

"I could make a few guesses, but I'd rather not."

Dave grimaced and rested his forehead against the bars. His head pounded, and his stomach churned. "What day is it?"

"The fifteenth, I think. You missed Blaiðwyn Hall, your great-aunt Ivy, and Jasper — you were a raving lunatic at the time, " Hector replied. "Now, I'm not telling you anything else until you've answered some of my questions."

Dave's scowl deepened.

"What do you remember about the last three days?"

"I remember being chained down, and Ymara —" Dave made a sign against evil. "*Lady D* helped me get free."

"The only chain was Aislinn's necklace, amigo. What else do you remember?"

Dave mulled over the images in his mind. He couldn't be sure how much was real versus the vampire showing him what she wanted him to see. He shook his head. "I don't know. That bitch twists everything to suit herself. Did I steal a horse?"

"More than one," Hector said. "Do you remember wearing the mask?"

The bowman swallowed hard. "No," he lied. He had no intention of ever telling anyone the things he'd dreamed or done with Ymara, or the power the mask lent him. "Where is she?"

"*It*, amigo, not she. It's locked up."

"I could see her, Hector. She was there, like a ghost."

"The mask is haunted, amigo. It's a good thing Blaiðwyn Hall was close to Tydway."

"Did you let Jasper use magic on me?"

"No. He enchanted a box for the mask so none of its power leaks out."

"How do you know it works?"

"Because we're having a conversation."

Dave looked around his cell. "Any particular reason I'm wearing chains and in the brig?"

"I insisted. Do you remember trying to kill me and Teal?"

Dave's brow furrowed and his grip on the bars tightened. "I swear, I tried not to, but I couldn't stop."

"I believe you, Dave. I knew you were resisting Lady D when I heard the fletching buzz, and Teal said it was red rather than black. Why did she make you shoot me?"

"You keep getting in her way. Lady D wants someone to wear the mask, someone to *become* her. Is the ghost lizard still alive?"

"Yeah, but he's pretty beat up — cracked ribs, fractured skull, and a concussion."

Dave winced. "She gave as good as she got. I hurt worse now than when William's pirates worked me over. Where's my flask?"

"Confiscated, for now, along with your weapons and anything else you might use to hurt yourself or someone else."

"Damn it, Hector. I need a drink."

"Too bad," a new voice said, "because you aren't getting anything other than water." Lord Vaughn entered the pool of light surrounding their portion of the lower deck, steely determination on his face. "When you leave this ship, you're going directly to the hospital to be cured of your addiction and see what can be done about the vampire."

"The hell I am," Dave growled.

"Call this an intervention. You need help, even if you refuse to acknowledge it," Lord Vaughn replied. His voice softened. "I want to help you, son."

"I'm not your son! I'm no one's son!"

"You *are* my son."

"Stay the fuck away from me."

"I can't. I won't lose you again."

"You can't lose what you never had," Dave snarled. He turned to Hector. "Give me my damned flask."

The bounty hunter shook his head. "Not yet, amigo. It's best if you're sober when we reach Ozera. Phaedrus and the healers need to see the worst of what the mask does to you if they're going to help."

Dave drew in a sharp breath and backed away from the bars. "No. Please, Hector. Don't let her take me again."

"We have to do this, if you're ever going to be free."

Dave retreated to the far corner, slid down the hull into a crouch, and bowed his head. "There's only one way I'll ever be free, Hector. You know it as well as I do."

"Don't give up hope," Roger pleaded softly.

"Hummingbird needs you, Dave, now more than ever," Hector added.

The archer's head jerked up, and he met Hector's bleak stare. In that moment, he knew Aislinn was gone. With a roar, he slammed his fists against the boards.

Roger pulled a key from his pocket and reached for the door.

"Don't, señor."

"We have to stop him. He'll break his hands."

"Lord Vaughn," Hector said, "I hate to say it, but you need to leave him alone. I'll stay down here until we land in Ozera. If her ladyship would send Salizar to unlock the door once we arrive, and perhaps spare me a few sailors to escort Dave and Teal to the hospital, I'd appreciate it."

A long minute passed, punctuated by the clink of Dave's chains and a torrent of curses. Finally, Lord Vaughn turned to Hector. "I'll go, but I want your assurance none of you will leave Ozera without seeing me first."

"Of course, señor," Hector replied a little too quickly.

"I mean this, Hector. It's important."

Hector sighed and said, "No promises, but you have my word we'll at least try."

"Fair enough. I'll be staying at the Oak Grove Inn."

CHAPTER 19
ARRIVAL

August 16, 4237 K.E.

2:30am

The moon rested on the western horizon when the *Lady Luck* descended onto Lake Silfravatn outside Ozera. Electricity sparked and danced from the ship's odd lanterns to her sails and over a web of silver and platinum set in the hull. The lightshow diminished as they neared the water's surface. Within minutes, Captain Smeyth and his crew had the ship tied aft-first to a broad pier lit by multicolored glow-stones. They lowered a drawbridge-like panel in the ship's stern and off-loaded their cargo and passengers.

Hector led his horses from the hold and joined the landing party. Finding neither Lord Vaughn nor Lady Aneirin on the pier, the bounty hunter was relieved the nobleman had honored Hector's request to give Dave space. He cast a worried glance at his friend. Dave swayed on his feet, and sweat dripped from his face, despite the cool mountain air. There was an obvious tremor in the man's hands. Teal leaned against a pier post, his eyes still glassy and pain filled.

"I think the two of you should ride," Hector said.

"I shall not climb upon that beast's back again, though I be forced to crawl from hither to yon," Teal replied.

Dave staggered several steps from the pier, dropped to his knees, and retched. Fortunately, his stomach was empty.

Hector let go the horses' reins and crouched by Dave. "Come on, let's get you up on Chili."

"Sick," Dave mumbled.

"I know, amigo. Do you think you can stay in the saddle?"

The archer's stomach heaved again, and he collapsed, his muscles trembling.

"¡Santa Maria! Help me get him on his horse," Hector ordered the sailors.

The crewmen assigned to escort Dave edged forward as if expecting the manacled man to launch an attack at any moment, and helped Hector lift the archer across the strawberry roan's saddle.

"I'm sorry, Teal, but you have to ride."

One of the Karukera islanders stepped forward. "Bajari, we take Itu Teal ta zi hospi-tahl. You take Atiao Dave to Baba Bohiti tai'bara zi Boya-moin."

Hector cocked his head to one side, trying to parse out the meaning within the islander's patois. "Baba Bohiti? Tai'bara zi boya-moin?" he finally asked.

The woman nodded.

"Lo siento, no comprende."

"Baba Bohiti is what the islanders call their head shaman," one of the other sailors replied as he backed away from Dave. "She says your friend has a blood-demon."

Hector sucked in a sharp breath, and his hands crept toward his weapons. "Dave's sick," he said. "Alcohol poisoning. He's not possessed. We're all going to the hospital."

The islander pointed at Dave. "Bajari, he dies without Baba Bohiti."

Hector cursed and turned to Teal. "Give me your weapons."

"Thou hast them already, Hector, in the bags upon the dread Feldspar's back. Madame Ivy did think it best to pack them afore we departed Blaiðwyn Hall."

Hector gave Teal a sharp nod, then glared at the four sailors. "The four of you bring Teal to the hospital. No delays, no excuses, and no side trips."

"Aye, those were the Admiral's orders regarding you and *him*," the sailor jabbed an accusatory finger at Dave, "when she sent us to collect you both from the brig. She said nothing about the girl."

Hector gathered Feldspar and Chili's reigns, then swung up onto Caballo's saddle. "I'm not going to argue with you, sailor. If Teal won't ride, he stays in your charge. Either way, I'm not waiting on you lot to keep up on foot." Without a backward glance, he and the horses followed the dim lanterns lining the path into town.

Ozera's hospital was one of the few places in the village that never slept. Hector reined in his horse at the main entrance. "Wait here," he instructed Caballo as he slid from the saddle and raced inside. Moments later, he returned with a pair of orderlies and a stretcher.

Dave was unconscious. Sweat poured from his skin, and tremors shook his body. The hospital workers rushed him inside and down a hallway, passing a desk manned by a grey-haired villager.

"What happened to him?"

"Withdrawals, I think." Seeing the desk clerk's disapproving frown, he added, "Alcohol sickness, señor."

"His name?"

"Dave Blood."

"The archer El Patrón banned from brewing poisons in the village?"

Hector nodded. "Me llamo Hector de los Santos. I need Dave kept in a secure room, preferably chained to a wall. Lady Aneirin is sending another prisoner, Deputy Gilliam of Herian Hill, who will need similar restraints. Also, there are four sailors from the *Lady Luck* bringing a young woman called Teal. She has a fractured skull, possibly cracked ribs. I need her confined as well."

"She's a prisoner, too?"

Hector nodded. "Until Padre Phaedrus can determine who and what she is. There's a strong possibility she's possessed."

The old man gulped and turned to a series of colorful cords stretching from the ceiling to a row of wall rings. He tugged the red one urgently.

Assuming the man summoned a healer, Hector stepped outside, unclipped the reins from each of his horses' bridles, and removed Caballo's saddlebags. "Take them home, Caballo, and remember to close the livery yard gate this time. Rodrigo will have your balls off if you let everyone out again." The willful Akhal-teke snorted at his human. "Fine, don't believe me, but don't come crying to me when you're gelded."

Caballo stamped, then nodded before nudging Feldspar and Chili away from the hospital.

Once the horses were out of sight, Hector returned to the hospital lobby. A moment later, a door opened at the far end of a second hall, and a lean, hawk-faced woman in clerical robes hurried forward.

"Roald, what is it?"

"Hermana Inez, Señor de los Santos has dangerous prisoners in need of healing. He said one may be possessed." The desk clerk's voice held an edge of fear.

The healer studied Hector with a raised eyebrow. "Are either of these prisoners responsible for the condition of the young elf in our critical care ward?"

"No, Hermana. They didn't harm Hummingbird." He glanced at the desk clerk, then down each of the hallways. "Is there somewhere private we can talk? There are things I need to tell you about each of your patients."

Sister Inez nodded, then led Hector to a small office with a window overlooking the hospital's front lawn. "Alright, Señor de los Santos, tell me everything you know about our newest guests."

CR⬥SO

4:00am

Hector paused under the broad limbs of a chestnut oak and stared down the hill. The cart path he was on circled an oak grove with a stone and thatch prayer chapel barely large enough to seat twenty people, thirty if they were extremely friendly with one another. Candlelight spilled from the chapel's open windows, sparkling on dewy grass, and illuminating the front stoops of six single-room pilgrim's cabins slumbering at the foot of Lumikivi Mountain.

Standing between the dwellings and the cliff's edge was a two-story cottage with shuttered windows. The bounty hunter was finally home, though it was a cold, sad homecoming. He studied each of the cabins in turn. There were no signs anyone was in residence, but Jasper told him Robert, Xandor, and August were in Ozera, so at least three of the cabins held sleeping friends.

His gaze drifted up toward the mountain's summit, Sunrise Chapel, and the blanket of stars hanging above it all. Gaia's Great Dragon constellation glared down at him. Hector sighed. He would have to face Brand and Mrs. Yves soon.

Searching for signs of danger, he made his way to the cliff, skulking from tree to tree. Keeping low and moving with the shadows, he crept to the corner of his porch and reached underneath for the hidden key.

Hector stopped inside the door at the foot of the stairs, listening. Nothing moved. Nothing breathed. He crossed to the sitting area and gently placed his saddlebags on the couch before moving to the hearth. Although he was tired, the bounty hunter had work to do before he slept.

CHAPTER 20
NIGHTMARE

August 16, 4237 K.E.

4:00am

A huge eagle with a ragged feather crown rode the night on ash-colored wings. It circled above Lumikivi Mountain, its unnaturally night-sharp vision searching for a shadow in the darkness. On its third pass, the giant raptor came to rest on the lip of a cave set high in the white cliff face. The bird's form blurred, and a man-like figure rose in its place.

Mi'dnirr held his long-fingered hands splayed to either side, feeling the cool air flow from the opening before him, whispering in and out like the breath of a sleeping child. His lips drew back in a humorless smile. Of the many things which changed when an ancient dragon trapped his essence in a dærganfae vessel, his inability to travel where there were no air currents was not among them.

His nostrils flared, drawing in the scents of moist stone and ozone. His quarry lay within the cave.

He let the current carry him inside and along a short tunnel to a broad cavern. There, a young bronze dragon sprawled on the sandy floor, his head alongside a stone plinth within a wide niche. Soft light from a fist-sized chunk of citrine bathed the dragon and the treasure it guarded: an ebony and diamond casket containing the body of Aislinn Yves.

Mi'dnirr remained near the cavern entrance for several long minutes, out of reach of the sleeping dragon's lashing tail. Shivers wracked the creature's body, and breath burst from its nostrils in small clouds as its dark talons made furrows in the sand and coins beneath it. Suffering filled the air like the heady scent of flowers in spring.

Ymara Dapniš had plans for the dragon, but the dærganfae vampire wanted something different. The creature was perfect for his purpose. Before another day dawned, he would be free of the vessel called Mi'dnirr and be Bēl Šibṭu, Bringer of Plagues, once again.

Long, pale fingers clamped on either side of the dragonling's head. The creature groaned and shifted but did not wake. Mi'dnirr dove deep into the dragon's mind, rifling its memories, feeding on its pain, and tormenting the duality struggling against itself to expel the invader.

CR&SO

4:15am

Thunder rolled across the Dreaming Grounds. The storm clouds inched closer, spilling jagged trails of lightening into the dead grass. Against the slow-moving thunderhead, winged shadows of a dragon and an eagle battled.

Fear rippled through Hummingbird. The storm, the eagle, and the dragon did not belong in the Dreaming Grounds.

The scene flickered, and Hummingbird suddenly found herself on the precipice of a tall cliff. The lead-grey storm churned overhead in a slow circle, with a tiny patch of open sky directly above her. Below, a thick band of forest separated the glowing white cliff face from a black sand beach and raging sea.

The aerial combat continued, but the figures were no longer shadows. The eagle's feathers were varying shades of grey, rendering it difficult to see against the clouds above. The dragon was both terrifying and beautiful. Light bronze scales covered its body, legs, and tail. Its wings were like sheets of bright copper.

As Hummingbird watched, hand-like foreclaws captured the eagle's talons. The bird's sharp beak drove forward and tore free a chunk of scaly flesh. It swallowed the stolen morsel and seemed to grow even as its prey shrank.

"No," Hummingbird gasped.

Movement on the beach drew her attention. A figure, tiny in the distance, raced from the tree line. Although she didn't know how, she sensed this newcomer was Aislinn's brother, Eidan.

He raised his arms, and lightning shot upward. It struck the eagle, driving it back. He sent another bolt after the first.

"*Fly.* Hide in the storm," Hummingbird urged the bronze dragon, but if it heard, it paid no heed. Its wings beat furiously, and it pursued its attacker. It reached the eagle simultaneous with the second bolt of energy. The resulting explosion sent the combatants tumbling, and the white cliff trembled.

The eagle recovered first. It wheeled in a tight circle, gaining altitude. On the second turn, it dove at its prey's back.

"Behind you!" Hummingbird shouted.

The bronze dragon rolled at the last second, and the eagle's claws plunged into its chest. In a flurry of beating wings, snapping jaws, and darting beak, the two figures plummeted from the sky.

Eidan raced back and forth on the beach, casting bolts of lightning at the eagle, but his attacks missed more often than they hit. He seemed oblivious to his own danger.

"Run!" she screamed. She watched in silent horror as the eagle and its prey crashed to the ground, and Eidan vanished beneath them.

CHAPTER 21
GHOSTS

August 16, 4237 K.E.

9:45am

Sunlight slipped through the shutter slats, illuminating saddlebags and weapons covering the couch and a low storage bench. Plaster dust coated the dining table, floor, and Hector's clothes. He wanted to open the window shutters and go outside to dust himself off, but he wasn't ready to see anyone yet.

Hector yawned and took a sip of tepid tea, wishing he had the makings for a strong cup of kahve. He hadn't slept in over twenty-four hours and felt his reserves fading.

The church bells were tolling ten when someone knocked on his door. It was a rapid series of two, then three, then two knocks followed by four long knocks. Jasper. Hector padded to the window and peered at his porch through the shutter slats. There was no one there.

The series of knocks sounded again.

Hector lifted his scimitar from the couch and worked a bright silken sword knot loose from its hilt.

'Hector, it's Jasper. Open the door.'

The voice sounded like it was in the room with him. He peered out the window again. The porch still appeared empty.

"If you're really Jasper, what's the easiest way to transport horses through a cave system?" Hector asked. The question seemed random, but only Jasper or another member of Damage, Inc. would know the answer Hector sought.

'Turn them into earthworms and pack them in a jar of dirt. Happy now?'

Hector unlocked the door and snatched it open. An invisible figure brushed past him. A moment later, Jasper appeared beside the couch. The mage looked like a caravan driver in his sturdy canvas coat covered in pockets. He had a bulging leather satchel slung over his shoulder, and a staff in one hand.

"You look like something the cat drug in," Jasper said.

"Thanks," Hector replied with a grimace. He rubbed a hand across his belly.

"Have you slept or eaten?"

The bounty hunter shook his head. "Too much to do and not enough time. As for eating, a jar of tea leaves and a thin crust of honey were the only things in the pantry. I fixed myself some, but I don't know how Aislinn and Hummingbird could stand to drink the stuff. It makes my belly ache. Did you finish the second box?"

"I did. Where's Dave?"

"Hospital. Lord Vaughn and I decided to keep him sober and confined until El Patrón and Hermano Simon can see what the mask does to him. I have to finish my decoys first," Hector replied, pointing at the hearth. "They're almost done. The last coat of turpentine is drying, then I can polish them. I was about to clean the table."

"Let me help with that, then we can eat." Jasper's magic washed over Hector and the cabin's single downstairs room, leaving everything looking freshly scrubbed. He nodded toward the plaster masks on the hearth. "Those look good. Almost the same as the real thing." Jasper unpacked four small crocks with sealed lids from his satchel. "You aren't going to let Dave see them, are you?" he added as he reached into the bag again and presented the second warded box.

"Not if I can help it," said Hector. "One is for you and whoever Phaedrus assigns to research duty. The other goes in the spare box as bait for Count Dodz."

"You really think he'll come here?"

"He left Ruthaer empty-handed. The ruby brooch Dave's wearing, the mask, and the aethereal gate are all here in Ozera. He'll come."

"Have you given the mask to Phaedrus yet?" asked Jasper.

"No. I'm supposed to meet Padré Phaedrus and Brother Simon at the hospital this afternoon. I'll turn it over to them after they see what it does to Dave."

"Does Dave know you're planning this demonstration?"

Hector nodded. "He isn't happy."

"Is he ever?"

"Only when something's on fire."

Jasper laughed and passed Hector a plate piled high with eggs, ham, and bread. "Eat. I have apples and pecans, too, if you want them."

"Did you learn anything at the Academy?"

"Nothing of any use. I mean, there are plenty of works on creating magical disguises, but nothing that would transform the wearer into a vampire or give them the kind of power we saw at Blaiðwyn Hall. All the sources agreed that a vampire is destroyed by removing its head or burning the creature to ashes. You said you did both, which means Lady D is more than a typical vampire, and aligns with the demonic magic I saw."

"She's anything but typical, considering the mask *ate* the sorceress' face, and it's actively seeking a new host." Hector tapped a finger on the table while mulling things over. Finally, he sighed. "I guess the real question is, are all vampires created the same? The treatise in Ozera's library says a vampire turns someone by feeding their cursed blood to the victim, which makes it sound like vampirism is a disease."

"That's a question I can't answer," Jasper replied, "but I'll dig through the libraries in Tydway and Pazard'zhik to find out. Were there vampires in Terra?"

Hector shook his head. "Most people believed they were nothing more than villains in stories meant to scare the audience. Our bards told a lot of contradictory tales."

"And the people who did believe vampires were real?"

"Probably wishful thinking on their part, but I'm no expert. The only encounters reported by credible witnesses occurred a few hundred years ago. There was a prince who supposedly sold his soul to the Dark One for the power to defeat his country's enemies, but I'm better than ninety percent certain that was a tale invented to scare foreigners. The rest were ancient legends and myths that varied by culture. The few I read involved demons or people offending the gods."

"Demons again," Jasper mused. "You said Consuelo trafficked with demons, and the magic on the mask is abyssal. I'll keep digging."

"Thanks, Jasper, I appreciate it. Dave does, too, even if he won't admit it."

"That's what friends are for, Hector." He stood and gathered the empty crocks and dishes into his satchel. "After I take these dishes back to my cabin, I'll head over to the library and ask Sister Georgiana for what information she can give me on demons and binding rituals."

"When I give the mask to Padré Phaedrus, I'll make sure he knows you're already helping us," said Hector.

CR୫୨

11:00am

Dressed in his best clothes, with his hair carefully combed and tied back in a queue at his nape, Hector stood on his front porch, contemplating the possibility he might die at the hands of a dragon he'd called friend and brother over the past five years. Still, he couldn't *not* pay his respects to Aislinn's family.

He followed the road from his front door past the small chapel and other cabins in the cul-de-sac. He thought of taking the shortcut through the woods behind Robert and Jasper's cabins, but he needed more time to work out what to say to Señora Yves.

At the main road, he turned right toward Ozera before taking another right onto a narrow lane. All too soon, he found himself at the Yves residence. An evergreen wreath bound in black ribbons hung on the front door.

Hector's heart thudded in his chest, and his mouth turned dry. Perhaps he should have waited for Dave to be able to come with him.

Steeling his nerve, he strode onto the porch and knocked at the door. A minute passed in silence, followed by another. He knocked again. Finally, he heard footsteps within, and the door opened to reveal an older Pandarian woman in widow's weeds. Behind her, the entry hall stretched past a set of stairs on the left, a light-filled doorway on the right, and ended at a closed door draped in black.

He gave the woman a sweeping bow. "Buenos días, señora. ¿Está la Señora Yves en casa?"

"Yes, Shayla is here. May I say who's calling?"

"Hector de los Santos, señora. I'd like to pay my respects to the family — if they'll see me."

The woman opened the door wider. "Come in. You may wait in the parlor." She pointed him to a sitting room to the left of the entrance before disappearing upstairs.

Hector crossed the small room. On either side of the hearth, narrow shelves held an assortment of items, including a stack of smooth stones, unusual seed pods, shells, and several sketches in tiny wooden frames.

"Those are things Aislinn and Brand collected for me over the years."

He turned to find Shayla Yves in the foyer doorway. Black silk ribbon wound through the flaxen braid crowning her head. Hector bowed low. "Señora, please forgive me. I should have been here sooner."

"Is what my son says true? Are you and Dave Blood to blame for Aislinn's —" Her words cut off abruptly, and she pressed her lips together in a vain attempt to stop their trembling.

"Señora, we each bear some responsibility for what happened in Ruthaer. We'd already seen the creature lurking in the quarry's tunnels that day, but there were children trapped inside. None of us were willing to abandon them, especially Aislinn, but we should have sought help from Sir Francis and Ruthaer's guardsmen."

She nodded but didn't speak.

"We did save Ruthaer, though, sort of," Hector said, flashing her a weak smile.

"That's something at least."

Hector shifted from one foot to the other, uncertain how to broach the subject of seeing Aislinn one last time. Instead, he said, "Hermana Inez said you and Eidan have been visiting Hummingbird. Thank you."

"I've asked her to stay here in Ozera with me. To take up a profession less prone to danger."

"Dave and I won't argue if she says yes, señora. Does that mean you and Brand aren't going to Revakhun Toaglen?"

"I won't be going. As for Brand... There aren't words to express the pain of losing my daughter, but I think the nature of her bond with Brand has made this infinitely harder for him. Something broke inside him when Phaedrus couldn't save her."

"I'm sorry, señora." He paused, then cleared his throat. "Would Brand... Jasper said he's... I suppose mad is too mild a word, but do you think he'd be willing to see Dave and me? We'd like to say our goodbyes to Aislinn, and there's someone I want him to meet."

Shayla closed her eyes and sighed. When she looked at Hector again, she shook her head. "I don't think so, Hector. At the end of the funeral, Eidan begged us to leave Sunrise Chapel. He didn't want us to see Brand. Phaedrus and I tried to change his mind, and Brand attacked us."

"What!"

"Lightning repeatedly struck Sunrise Chapel, driving us away from Eidan. I haven't seen Brand or Eidan since. I don't think anyone has." Shayla frowned and asked, "Who is this person you want him to meet?"

"A young woman from Ruthaer. She... well, she has a unique knowledge of dragons and dragon bonds. She says she can help."

"Do you believe her?"

"Yes, señora, I do. A lot of strange, terrifying things happened in Ruthaer. We caught glimpses of ghost armies filled with dragons and dragon-kin. If anyone can help Brand, I believe it's Teal."

⍩

3:00pm

A deep gong of doom exploded in Dave's skull, vibrating its way down his spine and through his body. Before the first round of tremors faded, the gong exploded again. And again. Cracking one eye, he squinted at his surroundings. He was in a strange bed, wearing nothing but a white sheet. Windowless white walls surrounded him, with only a brown wheel-cross and a small bedside table to break the monotony. Despite the lack of a source, light filled the room. The air rippled like heat haze, but he was soaking wet and freezing.

A woman with honey-colored hair and bright sapphire eyes leaned over him. '*Your father is here for me, Clem.*'

"Mom?" he croaked. His throat felt as if he'd swallowed handfuls of beach sand and broken shells.

She pressed her cheek to his. He felt her lips brush his ear. '*Time to die,*' she whispered before darting away through the wall.

A man he hadn't noticed before rose from a chair in the room's corner near the door. Fear coiled in Dave's belly. He rolled off the bed onto shaky legs, only to discover a chain bound his wrist to the wall. He pulled and pried at the manacle but could not break free. His trembling hands were too clumsy. Weak and out of breath, he searched for a means to escape.

"Dave, what are you doing? You need to get back in bed."

"Stay away." He retreated into the nearest corner and put his back to the wall. The trembling grew worse, and he slid down into a crouch.

"I'm here to help, son."

"Stay away!" he shouted and batted at Roger's grasping hands. A wave of dizziness washed over him, and shadows clawed at his vision. He made another feeble swing. "Take Mom and go."

Horror transformed Roger's visage, and he backed toward the door. He reached blindly for the handle, pulled open the door, and fled.

Dave remained in the corner, too tired to push himself back to his feet. He hugged his knees to his chest and stared at the door, trying to ignore the shadows in the corners of his vision.

He didn't know how long he sat on the cold tile before the door opened and another man, similar in appearance to Roger, entered the room. Dressed all in black, he had the gait of a dancer — or swordsman.

"Dave, what are you doing on the floor? Let's get you back in bed," the man said. He had the same golden-brown hair and deep blue eyes as his mother. Dave couldn't tell if it was really Robert, or a hallucination.

His mother's ghost appeared and crouched beside him. She stared at the man crossing the room for a moment before turning to Dave. Her face twisted with hate. '*I kept the wrong baby. If I'd taken Robert, I wouldn't have died, and we'd be here with your father. Happy.*'

He flinched with each word.

Calloused hands gripped his arms and lifted him back into the bed. Water splashed, and a cool cloth covered Dave's forehead.

Dave wanted to push Robert away, but found he lacked the strength. "C... c... cold," he stuttered.

"No, you're burning up," Robert replied as he wet another cloth and laid it across Dave's bare chest. "I wish Aislinn was here. She was always good at this."

"My fault..."

"What?"

"I opened... d... door for fffae."

"Dave, you're not making sense. What are you talking about?"

"Mom... sh... she shhoulda k...k... kept you."

"Mom didn't give me away, Dave. She and Dad died in the fire, remember?"

"Nnnot C...ca...Cam... Br...Brie."

"Your fever must be getting worse. I'm going to look for a healer." Robert glided across the room and out the door.

Dave struggled to stay awake. Shadowy figures flitted about the room, whispering to him.

Robert returned and slipped an arm behind Dave's back, helping him sit up. On the opposite side of the bed, a dour-faced woman with skin like aged leather offered him a cup. "Drink this. It'll help."

Dave clamped his mouth shut.

"Dave," Robert admonished, worry lines etching his face. "Don't make this a fight."

As answer, Dave clinched his fists and jutted his chin out. "Flask."

"No liquor," the woman replied. "You're dehydrated and feverish. Willow tea will help both."

"No."

"Dave, if you don't drink the tea, they'll call in Jasper to compel you. Doesn't matter to me, just thought you should know." Robert studied the fear in Dave's eyes and nodded. "Take your medicine."

Dave swallowed as he looked from one to the other. With a slight nod, he let the nurse help him drink. The warm, honey-filled tea soothed his parched throat, but didn't take away the longing for his flask. As soon as his head touched his pillow, darkness overtook him.

Dave struggled to consciousness and found Aislinn's ghost glaring at him. Beside her, an ashen-faced little girl in a torn and blood-soaked t-shirt watched him with cold, dead eyes. His first foster mother, an Irish woman with fading red hair, shimmered into being beside them.

'*I should ha' known nah to take in a sidhe-cursed creature like you,*' she said, and made a sign against evil. '*The devil take ya for the monster y'are.*'

'*You wanted to kill me from the moment we met, just like Mórai and Tilly,*' Aislinn accused. '*Are you happy now?*'

"No," Dave muttered. "Tried to protect you."

'*Liar.*'

He closed his eyes, but he could still see them there, by the bedside. "No," he groaned.

'*Murderer,*' she hissed. '*You'll kill Hummingbird, too.*'

His heart clenched in his chest. "No. I'll leave Hummingbird in Ozera."

As though summoned by his speaking her name, the crimson-haired plains elf appeared on the other side of his bed. Her bright aqua eyes studied each of the other ghosts, then turned to him. Her expression was sad as she shook her head. Her voice was whisper soft. '*These ghosts aren't real, Dave. Let them go.*'

Ice slithered through his veins, and his body's tremors grew worse. Once again, darkness closed over him. Part of him hoped he would drown and never resurface.

'*My archer, you must be swift.*' Ymara's rich, silken voice filled the room, pulling Dave from the depths.

Fire ignited in his veins, burning away the fever and chills. The ghosts of his conscience wavered, then shattered, leaving only Ymara. Strength flowed through him.

Dave rolled from the bed and landed in a wary crouch. He wrapped both hands around the chain trailing from his wrist, braced a foot against the wall, and pulled. He was only dimly aware of the deep growl vibrating in his chest. Plaster dust trickled down, and the ring bolt shifted. He adjusted his grip and heaved. The chain came free with a loud crunch and a shower of plaster chunks.

"I think we've seen enough," a voice stated.

Magic seized Dave's muscles, locking them in place. Someone behind him knocked on a wall, and Ymara screamed with rage. As if falling down a deep well, her voice faded, taking her power with it.

Although weak as a newborn kitten, Dave remained upright, held in place by magic.

Wearing homespun robes of blue, Phaedrus stepped between Dave and the broken wall. Placing his palms against Dave's temples, he grasped the archer's head and forced him to meet his gaze while he prayed.

Energy flowed from Phaedrus' hands and through Dave like cool water on a hot day, soothing his parched throat and driving away the tremors, but it did nothing for the ache in his heart.

Phaedrus offered him a kind smile. "Welcome back, Mister Blood. Feeling better?"

Dave gave a noncommittal grunt.

"I see your verbal skills are as sharp as ever." Ozera's half-elven leader patted Dave's shoulder, and his almond shaped eyes filled with concern. "Young man, the poison has been removed from your body, but I'm afraid the demons in your head will take a bit longer. You are free to go or stay as you wish, but please understand the road you are on is long. Let your friends and family be your guides."

The magic holding Dave in place receded inch by inch, until he finally was able to turn and face the room. Robert stood at the end of the bed.

Dave's stomach clenched under the sudden realization some of his fever dreams may have been real.

The door opened, and Hector entered, carrying an ornate silver box covered in arcane runes and symbols. Although Hector had not described it to him, Dave knew by the weird way it seemed to disappear at certain angles that this was the box Jasper created to contain Lady D's mask.

"Hector, I understand now why you felt the need to perform your demonstration for us," Phaedrus said. "The mask's hold is strong."

Brother Simon, leading what looked like a parade of younger healers just learning their craft, approached Phaedrus and said, "Deputy Gilliam very nearly pulled his chain from the wall. It appears the mask's influence lends him strength."

Phaedrus stared hard at Dave. "I take it, anyone pricked by its fangs becomes her thrall?"

"Sí, Patrón," said Hector, "and it compels those who touch the mask into pressing their fingers to the fang-tips, like Deputy Gilliam."

"But not you?" the second priest asked. When Hector shook his head, he demanded, "How?"

"I don't know, Hermano Simon."

"Well, the Aerarium is the best place for it while we figure out what to do with it," Brother Simon stated.

"I asked Jasper Thredd to help," said Hector. "He has contacts in both Tydway and Pazard'zhik. I'd appreciate it if you included him on your research team."

Stunned surprise covered Brother Simon's countenance. "You want me to give a mage access to Ozera's Aerarium? Preposterous!"

"Señor, I need someone I know and trust working on this. Someone who will put Dave's well-being first, and who won't become sidetracked with other, more dangerous projects."

"Simon, I think we can come to a compromise," Phaedrus said. "Magus Thredd is trustworthy. I'm willing to allow him to help, so long as he's accompanied by one of our initiates."

"Gracias, Patrón," Hector replied with a short bow and handed over the silver box. "I've tried holy water, fire, and acid, as well as attempting to crush the mask. All have failed. You'll forgive me if I hold on to the key until there's a plan. I don't want to risk any accidents." He pulled a roll of parchment from his bag and passed it over. "These are my sketches, along with an account of everything we know about both the vampire and the mask, and Jasper has the plaster model I made."

Dave raised his shackled wrist toward Phaedrus. "You said I'm free to go."

"You should probably stay another day or two," Robert replied. "At least until we're sure the withdrawal symptoms are past."

"They're nothing a good stiff drink won't fix."

Robert fixed him with a solid glare. "Dave, drinking is what put you here in the first place."

"Maybe," Dave replied, "but Hector and I both know Dodz is coming for that mask, and you'll need all the help you can get to stop him. Where are my clothes and weapons?"

"The mask will be safe in the Aerarium," stated Brother Simon. "No one can reach it there."

"Never say never, Hermano," warned Hector. "Stranger things have happened and happened to us."

"It never hurts to be prepared," Dave added. Giving Phaedrus his best smile, Dave shook his wrist so that the manacle's keyhole faced the priest. "Will you please unlock this?"

Phaedrus smiled in return, but there was a hint of amusement in his eyes when he produced a key from his robe's pocket. "Remember what I said, young man, and don't burn your bridges before you've crossed the ravine in your path."

CHAPTER 22
THIEVES

August 16, 4237 K.E.

10:00pm

The lock on Ozera's library door clicked open, and Count Dodz crept into the building's darkened interior. Neither light nor sound greeted him. For a moment, he worried he'd missed the mage working for Hector de los Santos leaving for the night, but Dodz had been vigilant. The fat man was still here, somewhere.

In just over twenty-four hours, he'd learned a great deal about the less-well-known activities and services Ozera offered to those who knew to ask. Somewhere in the library lay a room devoted to studying — and then destroying — weapons and artifacts deemed too evil or dangerous for the public. Dodz had no doubt the bounty hunter would bring the mask here. While he fervently wished to be free of Ymara, his excruciating encounter with Mi'dnirr had made it abundantly clear he was in more danger than ever.

Room by room, Dodz searched but found no one. He'd picked the locks on three different doors, including the one guarding the room beyond the basement scriptorium, but found no artifacts or weapons. Frustrated, he contemplated waylaying one of the more elderly clerics and beating the information from them, but that would generate more problems.

Dodz pondered the dilemma of where to search next. Casting a glance down to the hilt of his knife with its black diamond pommel-stone, he considered the pros and cons of using it here. Expediency won out over caution.

Taking a seat at one of the study tables, he took off a glove. Laying the knife on the table, he spent a moment quieting his mind and focusing on the information he wanted.

As he steeled his will, his hand hovered over the black diamond, then he grasped it firmly in his palm. A wave of dizziness swept through him as the spirit trapped in the stone resisted answering his question. He gritted his teeth and held on, lashing at her opposing will with his own. A whirlwind of images of the nearby Grove Cathedral and its hidden depths rewarded his efforts.

Twenty minutes later, Dodz stood in Grove Cathedral's narthex. Designed to disguise the work of mortal hands, the sanctuary before him paid homage to the Eternal Father's creation. Ancient hardwoods — chestnut, hickory, oak, and poplar — formed natural columns and living shelter. Beyond a vine-covered arch inset with glowing sconces, cunning woodcraft set a network of fan-vaults amid the trees. A soaring web of spandrels, arching ribs, and cut glass formed the ceiling. From these artificial boughs, an aged hand-carved wheel-cross hung above the altar stone. There, a tome of holy scriptures rested atop a silver cloth embroidered at its edges with deep green leaves. Along the sanctuary's perimeter, ivy and jasmine twined their way up the columns, trained by patient hands to frame carved archways and wrought iron sconces. The bubble and trickle of a hidden fount floated in the air. The sound was hypnotic.

A circular mosaic of a giant oak on a grassy hill surrounded by rich, blue sky framed by a border of golden elven runes graced the sanctuary floor's center. The leaves and bark seemed to shimmer, even in the dim light. One by one, Dodz found and touched the runes in the order he saw them in the vision forced from Aislinn Yves' spirit, releasing a pressure plate hidden in the mosaic tree's roots.

Dodz pressed the plate with the toe of his boot, and the trapdoor popped open with a soft click. The dusty scent of dry earth and stone wafted up.

Closing the trap door behind him, he descended narrow stone stairs that spiraled down in utter darkness. He crouched low and traced his fingers along the wall as he slowly wound his way around. At the bottom, the shaft opened into a natural cavern lit by glowing crystals set in carved niches on either side of three tunnel mouths.

Dodz took one of the crystals and moved on, unafraid of meeting anyone in the tunnels this time of night. His path twisted and turned as it led downward into the depths of the mountain, past grottos where strange formations grew from the living stone. Thanks to the visions gained from the black diamond, each column, curtain, and crystal growth seemed familiar. As he continued onward, he wondered what other information he might force from the half-breed woman's spirit.

The way and his rumination came to an abrupt halt before a set of heavy silver and iron bars engraved with thaumaturgic symbols blocking what looked like a monstrous, stone mouth. Under a pair of black, ovoid eyes and a misshapen nose with flaring nostrils, a pair of sharp, pointed stalactites grew from the ceiling like vicious teeth. Between the limestone shapes, ghostly light from bioluminescent fungi illuminated the throat-like walls.

Count Dodz approached the gate and studied the lock. He pulled a pair of thin wire tools from specially made pockets in the lining of his boot and went to work. It was a matter of a few minutes to open the surprisingly complex lock, and then he wove his way through the strange grotto to the short tunnel beyond. Triumph surged through his veins as he stood before a heavy oak door, the last barrier between him and the Aerarium — Ozera's secret vault.

He rubbed his hands together and reached for the brass door handle. Red light arced from the metal only to be absorbed by his gloves. Dodz gave the trap a look of contempt as he twisted the handle and pulled the door open. His smile melted before a sheer wall of blackness beyond the threshold. It radiated a complete absence of hope, threatening to drain his resolve.

Stepping back, he tried to see through the black void as his anger grew to rage. It seemed the spirit in the stone had managed to hold back information after all. That would not do. He would have to teach her to obey.

Dodz worked the glove free from his left hand with a short, sharp tug at the end of each finger and grabbed the black diamond with his bare palm.

Again, a wave of dizziness washed over him as his mind ripped through the faceted barrier and made contact with the spirit trapped in the stone. Rage fueling his intent, he pushed harder, forming a vision of his own choosing.

Dodz studied the other consciousness, visible now in the construct of his mind's eye. Aislinn was just as he remembered from Ruthaer, with her slim form sheathed in dark leather, and her red-gold hair bound back in a braid, leaving the delicate points of her ears plain for him to see.

A cruel smile crawled over his face.

She hung from a thick wooden post, her wrists shackled in irons above her head. Aislinn strained and tugged against the pole, rattling the chains that held her.

Dodz' eyes locked on hers. The pair fought to dominate each other, but Dodz had the upper hand. He was alive.

When he came within reach, Aislinn lashed out with a fierce kick. He sidestepped her attack and drove his fist into her gut. The girl grunted in pain, just as she would have in real life, and hung limp, gasping. Dodz grabbed her braid near the base of her skull and wrapped it around his fist.

He forced her head back until her spine arched. "Shlyukha, you are going to regret holding out on me," he said. His hot breath rolled across her skin.

Anger flashed in her eyes. "Nothus fellator," she spat. "When Hector and Dave come for me, you're going to regret ever being born."

Holding her by the braid, Dodz slammed the back of her head against the pole. "You are *dead*, suka fyei, and your spirit is trapped in Akkilettū's black diamond eye-stone. There will be no rescue." He smirked at the flood of fear and desperation in the girl's eyes. He gave the braid another tug, forcing an involuntary hiss of pain from her. "Everything you are, everything you know, is mine."

He could see that Aislinn wanted to spit in his face and tear out his eyes, but she couldn't. His will held her. Her fire — her strength — gave way to confusion. A single tear traced along the side of her nose as he saw the dawning recognition of her helplessness.

Count Dodz' ice blue eyes shone coldly as he brought his face close to hers. "Now tell me the rest of what you know."

CR80

11:59pm

In his cavern, Brand surfaced from pain-wracked sleep. The translucent image of a dærganfae vampire he'd seen once before through Aislinn's eyes wavered before him.

"Mi'dnirr!" he roared. Hot rage boiled in his veins, clearing away the last vestiges of sleep. He swiped at the figure with his claws, but the form shimmered and then seemed to melt like smoke in a stiff breeze. Brand searched the cavern for the vampire. His focus shifted to the stone plinth, and a groan escaped him.

Empty shadows replaced Aislinn's casket.

Electricity arced along his scales as he slithered from his bed of sand and coins to the cave mouth. His nostrils flared as he sniffed the air. Clouds gathered overhead, reflecting a flickering light from the mountaintop.

Sharp bronze talons gripping uneven rock outcrops, and with his wings folded along his spine, Brand climbed the cliff face toward Sunrise Chapel.

"Something's wrong," Eidan whispered from the corner of his mind.

Brand ignored the voice in his head and climbed higher. Scales scraping, the dragon hauled himself up the precipice until he could see into Sunrise Chapel.

A lone figure waited beside the spring pool. The scents of magic and unfamiliar stone carried on the air. Brand expected it to be Mi'dnirr, but when the dærganfae turned, he caught sight of a silken eyepatch.

"Anauriel!" Brand growled and launched himself from the cliff face in a backward dive toward the valley. He rolled as he fell so that, when he unfurled his wings, he swooped over the treetops. He rose in a spiral around Lumikivi Mountain, searching for Aislinn's casket, but didn't find it.

Scales crackling with electricity, and foreclaws extended, he plunged toward the dærganfae. At the last moment, his wings opened with a thunderous boom, and his talons snapped shut.

He caught nothing but air.

Brand landed in the center of the chapel and turned, his bronze eyes aglow. His quarry stepped into view, and a single quicksilver eye glinted in the darkness. Partially hidden behind the silken eyepatch, three long, jagged scars marred the side of his face and disappeared beneath his tunic.

"Anauriel, why did you take her?" Brand asked.

"Dragon, we must talk," Anauriel replied.

"Like we did when your brethren killed Edge and stole Aislinn from me six years ago? You only lost an eye then. This time you won't be so fortunate."

"Dragon, we don't have much time. Listen to me —"

Brand's wings flexed and electricity sparked over his scales as he spat a glob of burning plasma at the interloper.

Anauriel dove aside, rolled, and came up with his hands encased in red-hot magic. Teeth bared, he flung a ball of fire at the dragon.

Brand leapt, and the fireball passed beneath him to explode in the trees along the cliff's edge.

With a peal of thunder, the dragon unleashed another plasma ball.

Again, Anauriel evaded the attack, flung a second fiery orb, and disappeared. The thatched rain shelter exploded.

"I seek a truce, beast!" he shouted as he reappeared by the altar stone. "I need the ivory dagger retrieved from Ruthaer to stop Mi'dnirr!"

Brand took a step toward Anauriel, intending to kill him. Instead, a heavy weight slammed against his back, and sharp talons pierced the scales at the base of his right wing. A hooked beak drove into his shoulder, drawing blood the color of molten bronze.

Lines of ox-blood colored magic snapped into place all around Brand, like a corral separating him from the one-eyed fae. Despite his rage, a heavy lethargy seeped into his bones. He leapt into the air, wings beating furiously. He gained only a few feet of altitude, enough to see the lines formed some type of symbol.

Magic coiled around his legs and snatched him back to the ground. With a grunt, he stumbled and went down on his side. The giant eagle leapt from his back, shimmered, and became Mi'dnirr.

'*Brand, this trap is killing us. Let me out!*' Eidan demanded.

Brand regained his feet even as the world began to spin, faster and faster. "What have you done, vampire?"

"Submit, beast," Mi'dnirr hissed.

"Never!" Brand drew in a deep breath, intending to spit burning plasma in the vampire's face, but he didn't get the chance.

Snarling, Mi'dnirr's body blurred as he lunged forward and grasped Brand's head with clawed fingers. Blood-mist burst from his ragged black clothes and swirled in the air.

Brand shivered, and electricity crackled over his scales. Limned in white fire, Eidan's semi-transparent form struck at Mi'dnirr.

Even as the three fought, the vampire's transformation into a non-corporeal form continued. The blood-mist grew thicker around Brand, coating his wings and scales.

The lines of the sigil pulsed brighter, illuminating Anauriel's horror-struck face. "Mi'dnirr, no!" A pair of fireballs streaked from his hands, through both Mi'dnirr and Eidan's transparent forms, and exploded against the only solid object there: Brand's chest.

CHAPTER 23
FIRE IN THE NIGHT

August 17, 4237 K.E.

12:30am

Hector jerked awake, drenched in sweat and out of breath. Cursing the nightmare, he struggled upright. Pale moonlight peeked in around his bedroom curtains, but thunder rumbled in the distance. Across the room, Dave's bed lay empty. Muted voices carried through the floorboards from the living room below.

Taking a shaky breath, Hector peeled out of his damp sleep pants before drying the sweat and tears from himself with the sheet. His arms and legs felt leaden, and several long minutes passed as he struggled into dry clothes.

Downstairs, thin bars of moonlight slipped through the shutters and fell on the floor in unhelpful ribbons. Coals glowed in the hearth, turning Dave into a shadow among shadows as he paced back and forth. The silhouettes of four wine bottles stood on their coffee table.

"Dave? I thought I heard voices."

"You did," Robert replied as he sat up on the couch.

"Amigo, I thought you went home hours ago."

"I was going to, but one thing led to another..."

Dave lifted a wine bottle to his lips, took a swallow, then spit it in the fireplace with a sound of disgust. The coals flared.

"Slimy half-elf cursed me," Dave grunted and held out the bottle. "Try it."

Hector crossed the room, took the bottle to the window, and tilted it into a shaft of moonlight — Domaine Royale de les Prés — King Edmund's family estate. He took a long pull from the bottle. The Francescan Duréza lingered on his tongue, and for the briefest of moments, the dry wine took him back to Damage, Inc.'s first time in Orleans. Stifling the memories, he said, "It tastes fine."

"Fucker," Dave groused.

"What's wrong with it?" asked Hector.

"It tastes like sand! All of them."

Robert laughed. "I told you, it's Hector's blue thumb all over again. This is Phaedrus' way of making you walk the straight path."

Hector eyed his thumb suspiciously. He didn't find it funny at all. Early in his career as a bounty hunter, he had used shrunken heads to collect bounties on criminals wanted dead or alive. It had made transporting proof of death easier, and went a long way toward building Damage, Inc.'s reputation.

Except Phaedrus didn't take kindly to the practice at all. Hector had come to the priest for help — a magical trap had turned his entire left hand blue. Phaedrus removed the spell but transformed it into a curse. Hector had to give up his collection of shrunken heads, and, if he ever strayed too far down the path of morally questionable behavior, his thumb turned bright woad blue.

As if reading Hector's mind, Dave said, "Face it. We're fucked."

"Language," Robert admonished.

Dave dug into his pocket and threw a silver coin at the swordsman. "Here, you might as well start a new collection."

"I stopped by to visit Hummingbird while we were at the hospital," Hector said after a moment. "The nurse in the women's ward said they think the healing draught we gave Hummingbird was tainted." He shook his head and sighed. "I couldn't bring myself to tell them that it was my blood that poisoned her."

"What did you expect troll blood to do to her?" Dave asked.

Hector shrugged. "I'm just glad they were able to save her."

Dave paused, a new bottle poised a scant inch from his mouth. "She's not Aislinn." With a grimace, he put aside the wine and retrieved his flask.

"I didn't say she was." Hector drowned his heartache with a drink of wine. "I have to see Phaedrus tomorrow. He wants me to tell him about Ruthaer and what happened to Aislinn. While I do that, you should go to the hospital and see Hummingbird."

"Why?"

"Make her feel better. Let her know you care."

"Trying not to," Dave grunted in reply and tilted up the flask. Again, he spat out the contents.

"What? Care... or let her know?" asked Robert.

"Take your pick." Dave shook the metal canister furiously. "Work, damn you!" Frustrated, he plopped into a chair.

Hector lifted his bottle, only to find it empty. He sighed again, took a seat on the couch, picked a new bottle from the collection standing open on the coffee table, and offered it to Robert. "Happy birthday, amigo. Care to join the dark side?" he asked.

The swordsman took the offered bottle and clinked it against Hector's and then against Dave's flask. "I'm glad to be home."

A hard thump hit everyone in the chest. The whole house shook as though someone picked it up and dropped it. Outside, the staccato of multiple explosions competed with thundering roars of pain that echoed from the mountainsides and rent the night.

"What the hell!" Dave demanded, lurching to his feet.

"That sounded like Brand," said Robert.

Dave reached the door in four long strides, snatching up his sabre, quiver, and longbow along the way. He pulled open the door and stepped out into the night, with Robert right behind him. Hector stopped long enough to tug on his boots, then caught up with the two men while working loose the bright silk sword knot on his scimitar.

Lurid flames lit the night sky, casting bold shadows through the trees. The distant roar and crackle in the forest canopy was enough to strike fear through even the bravest heart. The raucous clamor of Ozera's cathedral bells called a warning. At the top of the hill, figures dashed toward the trail to Sunrise Chapel, shouting directions and carrying tools to fight the fire before it spread down the mountain and devoured their homes.

"¡Madre de Dios!" Hector exclaimed.

The three darted back inside, exchanging weapons for waterskins before charging down the porch steps and past the small chapel in the center of their cul-de-sac. Another cabin door opened, and Jasper scurried out into the chaos, juggling a long staff and pulling on his sturdy canvas jacket as he went. Without a word, they hurried after the retreating mage and quickly overtook him.

"Jasper, what happened?" Hector demanded, falling in step with his friend.

"I was hoping you could tell me," Jasper panted. He was breathing heavily though he hadn't put in any distance yet. Together, they started up the winding path leading to Sunrise Chapel.

The four pushed hard to traverse the steep trail and reach the summit. Ahead and behind them, men and women carried axes, shovels, and anything else that might help stop the fire. Along adjacent trails, bucket lines began to take shape.

As they climbed, the light grew brighter, and thick smoke spilled down through the trees. Ash floated in the air. They rounded a curve in the path and stopped, staring in dumbfounded amazement at the inferno before them.

The living trees were aflame. Thick, glowing smoke swirled in the super-heated air within the chapel grounds. The shelter crumbled and collapsed with a loud crash. Bright yellow sparks billowed upward. Dead leaves and pine needles covering the ground smoked and caught as the sparks drifted down, carrying destruction in their tiny hearts. Downhill, villagers worked furiously to contain the blaze, chopping down trees and digging trenches.

"Santa María," Hector gasped, as his hand made the sign of the cross of its own volition.

"Do you see Brand in there?" Dave shouted over the roaring fire. Steam curling up from his hair and tattooed shoulders, he took several long strides toward the inferno.

A searing wind flashed down the path, sucking away the air around them. Above their heads, a tree emitted a piercing shriek and exploded. Hector darted forward and grabbed Dave's arm, pulling the archer back seconds before a massive branch crashed down from the canopy, its insides hollowed out by fire.

A wall of hungry flames sprang up between them and the chapel grounds, marching toward them.

Forced to retreat, the two found Jasper wringing his hands, torrents of sweat darkening the neckline of his tunic and jacket. "I have to get closer!" he shouted.

Hector, Dave, and Robert stared at him like he'd lost his mind. "Are you insane?" Hector asked.

"I can do something about this fire," he told them.

Dave hesitated a moment, then pulled a glossy obsidian ring from his finger. He held it out to Jasper. "I want this back," he stated.

Jasper blinked in surprise. "Thanks. What does it do?"

Dave grunted. "Keeps you from catching on fire."

"That's handy," Jasper replied.

"Remember, it won't stop a branch from falling on your head or keep you from suffocating," Robert added.

"Don't worry, I've got this," Jasper said, as he removed one of his own rings — a silver band adorned with three kite-shaped emeralds — and traded with Dave.

The lanky archer held the ring as though it might bite him and quickly offered it to Hector, then Robert, but each shook his head. The mage, on the other hand, smiled broadly as he slipped Dave's ring on his finger. The sweat soaking his clothes and hair drifted away in steamy curls.

Without another word, Jasper hustled forward and snatched a spark from the air as it drifted past. The tiny thing rested on his palm without burning him as it died and grew cold. Five feet from the wall of flames, he raised his arms, shouted, "Svíno!" and brought his hands sweeping down and outward in a sharp gesture. Ten yards in every direction around him, the flames winked out.

Jasper looked around, his eyes wide, even as cheers broke out among the firefighters who saw what he'd done. It was obvious to Hector something unexpected had happened, but the mage moved on, getting closer to the flames before casting his spell again.

Leaving the mage to his spells, Hector, Dave, and Robert joined a line of firefighters cutting a firebreak along the downhill side of the trail.

CHAPTER 24
FIREFIGHTING

August 17, 4237 K.E.

2:00am

A black blizzard of ash swirled in the superheated air, making it almost impossible to breathe. Fire still roared in the trees, despite Jasper's magic and the efforts of the villagers. Robert wished he had something to tie over his nose and mouth — or a gas mask. Sometimes, it was the little things that made him miss Terra the most.

In the mad flurry of activity, he, Dave, and Hector had become separated. Robert found himself working near the ruins of the uppermost prayer garden, the last along the trail before reaching Sunrise Chapel, and saw Phaedrus, Brother Simon, and seven others deep in prayer as sparks and cinders rained down around them. Concerned for their safety, he'd set himself to guarding them. Now, surrounded by walls of fire, they were separated from the firefighters. He believed it was only by divine grace that they still lived.

He studied the circle of eight priests, each with their left hand on the shoulder of the person next to him or her, their right hands outstretched toward Phaedrus at the center. Their chant rose and fell while light and shadow danced across their upturned faces. Though the language of their prayer reminded Robert of Latin, it wasn't... not on Gaia, where magic held sway and the Terran science he grew up with held little merit. Magic, monsters, and miracles: three things he didn't believe in when he, Hector, and Dave entered a decommissioned Terran lighthouse and stumbled out in the world of Gaia nearly six years past. Now, like everyone else, he took magic and miracles for granted.

Sweat traced runnels in the soot coating Robert's face. He tried to ignore the heat rising through the soles of his boots. Phaedrus' earlier prayer to cool the garden's ground was wearing off fast. Whatever divine favor the clerics were calling on would need to come soon, or they'd all roast up here on the mountaintop — if they didn't succumb to the smoke first.

More sparks drifted near the clerics, and the swordsman circled from one to the next, knocking aside the tiny embers with the blade of his shovel before they could ignite clothing or scorch unprotected skin. He didn't dare let them touch the men and women, lest it disrupt their prayers.

Burning ash rained down faster as the fire drew on new fuel in its ravenous journey down the mountain. Fear gripped his heart. He barely managed to bat a flaming ember away from the group. Orange and red pinpricks of light swirled in the wake of his shovel, and a chunk of wood the size of a child's fist exploded against a jagged outcrop.

The priests' chanting grew louder and swelled to a fever pitch. With a shout, Phaedrus thrust his arms heavenward. In response, a grumble of thunder rolled over the mountain, and cool air split the churning waves of heat.

A heartbeat later, the air around the priests exploded with bright red light, sharp and painful as lightning. The concussion blasted Robert off his feet. He smacked the back of his head on bare rock when he landed several feet away. Heat from the ground scorched his clothes and skin as he rolled toward his fallen shovel.

As one, the clerics crumpled to the ground, their voices extinguished. The world seemed to stand still, then a new sound filled the night: falling rain.

CHAPTER 25
TEAL TAKES CHARGE

August 17, 4237 K.E.

4:45am

Rain descended on the mountain, drowning the fire. Although the flames resisted in places, the cooling power of water was winning. Darkness returned with steam and still more smoke, hiding the damaged forest and sanctuary. Lightning flickered in the clouds, competing with the last vestiges of the forest fire that left Sunrise Chapel a blackened expanse of ash and rock.

Out of the charred, skeletal trees, a tall, blonde-haired ranger in worn leather appeared. Dark smudges of soot made the angles of Xandor's face sharper, lending the Iron Tower ranger an air of menace. Peeking above his shoulders were the well-used, leather-bound hilts of two swords strapped across his back. He skirted the drifts of ash to join Hector and Dave at the lip of a short drop-off behind the former rain shelter.

Below, a swath of splintered and mangled trees gave them an unobstructed view of a clearing below the line of fire damage. There, Brand lay in a twisted heap. Even from a distance, Hector could tell one of Brand's forelegs was broken, possibly dislocated at the shoulder. Scorched scales and a tattered, broken wing bore mute testament to the force with which Brand was thrown from Sunrise Chapel.

"There's a path about halfway down that leads from the main trail to Brand," Xandor reported. "His wounds... I don't think they expect him to live."

"Show us," Hector demanded.

Together, they made their way down the trail. Xandor led them through a narrow opening in a smoking growth of mountain laurels and across the slopes below the fire. The path the ranger used was little more than a game trail and crossed several firebreaks, but it cut a wide circuit around the destruction to a flurry of activity.

Fat raindrops sparkled in the pale light of numerous lanterns hanging from branches. Villagers worked to erect canopies over the area while a small cluster of healers examined the young dragon.

Where they weren't singed and darkened by fire, Brand's scales reflected a deep, burnished orange color. Despite the horrific nature of his wounds, his chest rose and fell in a steady rhythm as if in a deep sleep.

"Brand!" Hector called out as he raced toward the dragon. He reached out a hand but stopped short when he saw the scorched scales across the dragon's snout, amazed that he had the strength to live. "Nunca te rindas, amigo. We're going to need your help catching whoever did this."

If Brand heard Hector's words, he gave no sign. Nearby, several clerics poured their energy into healing prayers, but they had no discernable effect.

A few minutes later, Jasper staggered through the trees, supported by a tall priest wearing sooty armor.

"We need to rest," Gideon panted, letting go of Jasper. The Francescan battle cleric stopped short when he saw the dragon. "Mon Dieu, c'est vrai!" he exclaimed. "I hoped the description I heard was an exaggeration." He found a convenient rock outcropping and sat with a sigh. The silver sun-cross emblazoned on his dark surcoat flashed in the lantern light.

Xandor scanned the clearing. "Has anyone seen Aislinn's mother? She needs to know what happened here."

"I have not seen her or Aislinn's brother since the funeral," Gideon said. "I am surprised he isn't here."

"Eidan left Ozera after the funeral," Robert answered, striding up the hill. Once he reached Hector's side, he said in a low voice, "Phaedrus and the other clerics are all safe and alive at the hospital, but they're unconscious."

"Who's in charge?" asked Hector.

"Sister Inez. She's busy organizing search parties. Seems many of the firefighters became victims."

"Anyone investigating the cause?" Hector asked.

"Lord Vaughn."

Hector knelt beside Brand's head and began whispering to the dragon in the harsh sibilant language Aislinn taught him. *"Stay with us, Brand. We'll find a way to get through this. We always do."*

"Sir?" a voice interrupted. Hector looked up to see one of the healers.

"I don't know if we can save him," the young acolyte said. "We're doing what we can for the burns, but we can't determine the extent of any internal damage." Casting a quick glance toward the broken wing, he continued, "Even if he survives, he may never fly again. We need an expert on dragon physiology. Preferably another dragon. Do you know anyone...?" The question trailed off into silence.

Hector and Dave exchanged glances.

"You really are bat-shit crazy," Dave said.

"He's all we've got," Hector replied.

"Who?" Jasper asked.

"Teal," Hector said. "He helped us in Ruthaer after Aislinn..." he stopped, unable to complete the statement.

"That teenage girl who claims she's a ghost?!" Gideon exclaimed. "I saw her at the hospital. You can't be serious."

"What choice do we have?" Hector asked. "Brand is dying. Teal can't do anything worse to him."

CR&Ð

5:30am

The rain had stopped, and dawn was just starting to lighten the horizon when Hector returned, deep in conversation with a tall, teenage girl with long, tawny braids and a freckled face. The group of healers were hard at work applying ointments and salves on the worst of the burns.

Robert watched as the girl took one look at Brand and stopped in her tracks.

"By the ancients, 'tis a miracle the child still breathes!" Teal rushed forward, pushing aside the healers. "Everyone, stop thy labors!" All around, heads turned, and people stared at the young woman in disbelief. "Prithee, let me examine his wounds afore thou dost inadvertently do him harm."

"Listen to him," Hector said. "He knows what he's doing."

"*Him*?" Robert asked. "Hector, you *do* know that's a girl, right?"

"Only on the outside," Hector responded. "Inside, he's Flight-master Tealaucan Rathaera, the last dragon-rider in existence."

Robert leaned in and whispered, "Are you sure you haven't lost your mind?"

"That's what I said," Dave added.

Teal cast a glare in Robert and Dave's direction before gently probing the dragon's ribs and legs. "We must support his wing. I need parchment and coal to sketch what needs be built." Clerics and herbalists simply stared. "Why art thou not moving!" Teal ordered.

"Now see here, young lady, Ozera has the finest healing facilities on the continent of Parlatheas!" one of the healers sputtered.

"Aye, for a human or an elf, I am sure 'tis."

"Brand has never been hurt like this before," Hector said. "Aislinn always took care of him."

Teal looked up from examining the burns on Brand's face and chest. "I am truly sorry," she said. "I shall do all I can for him." Her eyes took in each of the men standing there, and her expression hardened. "This shall take some time. Whilst I work, the lot of you go forth and seek out those behind this evil."

Dave scowled and took a step toward the girl. "We're staying."

"Dost thou know what happened here or why? Perhaps the name of the guilty?" Teal's gaze held Dave's until the archer backed away. "Get thee hence and search instead of standing about underfoot!" she demanded. Her tone left no doubt she was a person used to giving orders and being obeyed.

Robert blinked in surprise as Hector and Dave left without further argument. He cast an appraising look at the girl before following his friends. At just over five-feet-nine, Teal was uncommonly tall and held herself like nobility, with her statuesque form and military-like posture. He watched her for another minute, noting the crisp economy of motion and air of command she exuded. He still didn't understand why Hector kept referring to her as a male.

With a shake of his head, he made to follow his friends, then turned back to stare at the girl again. In the pale morning light, her eyes seemed to shine with otherworldly light, reminding him of another woman with glowing, inhuman eyes. The surge of fear in his mind almost overshadowed the sharp ache of loss in his heart. Almost, but not quite. Fists clenched against the tremor in his hands, he fled uphill to join Hector and the others.

Hector led them away from the field hospital and stopped on the path between the village and the chapel. He looked around at the small group, and said, "Someone attacked Brand.

"Jasper and Gideon, the two of you figure out how the explosions happened. I need to know if they were magical or alchemical.

"Xandor, scout around. See if you can find anything to tell us which way the pendejos who did this went.

"Robert, you and Dave come with me. We'll touch base with Lord Vaughn and offer to help canvas the village. Someone must have seen or heard something strange last night or over the past few days."

No one questioned Hector's authority or brought up the fact that Ozera was a busy place, with new people coming and going each day. Ozera also had its own police force. None of that mattered. One of their own had been attacked. Damage, Inc. would not stop until they made the culprit pay.

CHAPTER 26
SUNRISE CHAPEL

August 17, 4237 K.E.

6:05am

sh puffed into the air with each step as Jasper picked his way over fallen limbs littering the broad trail up the mountain. On either side, blackened trunks pointed skyward from the scorched earth like giant fingers of the dead on a battlefield. Soot and grime from the night's work streaked his face and clothes.

Climbing the path alongside Jasper, Gideon said, "Le dragon... He mourned Aislinn, n'est-ce pas?"

Jasper stopped and leaned on his staff, his chest heaving in the smoke-tainted air. "Yes, Brand mourned her. Their relationship was... complicated." His expression grew distant. "I won't even pretend to understand the bond that joined them, but some days it seemed like they were a single person in two bodies."

"What do you think happened?" Gideon asked.

Jasper cast an oblique look at the cleric. "It's too early to say, but that isn't what you're asking, is it? What you *really* want to know is if Brand did this in an effort to kill himself." He shook his head and sighed. "How much do you know about dragons?"

"Beyond the fact that they're intelligent, flying lizards?" Gideon asked.

"Then you don't know anything," Jasper replied. He gathered his thoughts for a moment. When he spoke again, his voice and manner became professorial. "First, and foremost, dragons are not lizards. They don't fit into any of the usual creature classifications, neither reptile, bird, fish, nor mammal, yet there is something of each in them. They can, and have, mated with humans to produce offspring."

Gideon's face twisted in disgust at the thought.

"Aislinn and Brand didn't have that kind of relationship," Jasper snapped. "He was her *brother.*"

"C'est bon.   Such a pairing would produce abominations."

Jasper shook his head. "Not really. They're humanoids, in the same way as a half-orc or an óhreint. And, just like humans, elves, and the other races, they have the capacity for both good and evil."

"You've seen such creatures?"

"Eight brothers," answered Jasper.   "They called themselves Seldaehne. Rumor was, one of their parents was a frost dragon."

"Incroyable..."

"But you wanted to know about Brand, and whether he could have caused all this," the mage said, gesturing to the devastation around them. "As a bronze dragon, he has an affinity for electricity — lightning, storms, and the like. Brand's body is naturally conductive, so he isn't harmed by it. Although he has the capacity to breathe balls of plasma and start fires, I've never known him to be destructive. So, could he have done this? Yes, but the real question is, would he? The answer to that is no. He loves Aislinn, and she loved these mountains. He would not dishonor her memory."

Gideon started up the trail again. "Then Hector is right in assuming someone attacked Brand," he mused. "Does he have such powerful enemies?"

"None that I'm aware of," Jasper replied, "but I've only known him and Aislinn about five years.

At the verge of the overlook, the magnitude of the damage brought both men to a halt. Although there was little to fuel the fire at the center of the chapel, the blackened stone had cracked in places and melted in others. The spring that fed the reflecting pool was sealed, leaving a puddle of ash-filled rainwater in its place. Even the seating within the area had been transformed into amorphous blobs of stone.

A melancholy sigh escaped Jasper. "This was one of Aislinn's favorite places," he said quietly. "She liked to sit on the edge of the cliff and watch the sun rise. She brought us up here one spring. Actually made Hector, Dave, Robert, and me get out of bed in the dark and tromp up here — *without breakfast* — to sit with her while the sun came up." A sad smile touched his face. "She didn't tell us that peregrine falcons nest on the cliff face. It was amazing to see those raptors drift up in the warming air and sail right past us without a care in the world beyond finding their breakfast." Another sigh escaped him, but this one carried more anger than sadness.

"The fire and rain together are going to make finding any evidence of an alchemical attack next to impossible. Don't get me wrong," Jasper said, seeing the defensive expression on his companion's face, "I'm thankful for the rain. It saved lives and Ozera." He stroked his beard. "I suppose if I don't find evidence of magic, we can safely assume alchemy."

"Or the influence of the Dark One," Gideon replied. "Perhaps this was an attack on Phaedrus, and the dragon was but a chance casualty. The patriarch and eight of the brethren were carried to the hospital after the rain began."

"Maybe," the mage said, but his voice was full of doubt. "Can you reopen the spring? We're going to need water before we're done, if for no other reason than to drink."

"By myself? No, I have neither the skill nor the tools." The priest watched Jasper's face fall in disappointment. He clapped a hand on the mage's shoulder and smiled. "With our Creator's help, however, all things are possible. Keep faith, mon ami." Still smiling, he strode across the open stone to the former fountain and knelt. It was nearly flat, leaving little room for the water to pool. He placed his hands on the stone and began chanting.

While Gideon prayed, Jasper inspected the cliff edge, but found nothing of interest on its chalk-white face or visible in the forest below. Sunlight reflected from the stone, leaving few shadows.

Turning his mind back to the matter at hand, Jasper faced the open chapel. He had more experience than most with fire over the course of his studies and travels. One had to become something of an expert when you traveled with a pyromaniac like Dave. Jasper had to suppress a snort of laughter. In his time, Dave had caused damage even worse than this by accident.

Closing his eyes, Jasper took a deep breath and let it out slowly, clearing his mind and centering himself. He dipped one hand into a pocket at his waist and drew out a pinch of powder. Making a series of complicated hand gestures, he threw the powder into the air. "Fanérosi!" he commanded as his eyes snapped open.

To the casual onlooker, the glow that appeared in Jasper's eyes would have been lost in the increasing sunlight. However, that glow unveiled any lingering magic in the area and helped him pinpoint its source. Faint patches of green and orange glowed amid the rain shelter ruins. To ensure the spell worked properly, Jasper studied Gideon where he knelt at the spring. Through the power of the spell, the cleric's steel armor had the distinctive azure glow of protective magic while the mace at his belt had the fierce red of battle magic. A nimbus of deep green surrounded his hands and spread over the stone.

Keeping himself aligned with the swath of destruction that led to Brand, Jasper scoured the ground inch by inch, using chalk to mark the chapel floor with symbols and notes. From time to time, he stopped to check on the cleric, but the man remained kneeling, his chanted prayer rising and falling in the hot, still air.

CHAPTER 27
A GRIEVING MOTHER

August 17, 4237 K.E.

9:00am

Sadness shrouded Ozera like a soggy blanket. Everyone was tired and irritable, but a new day had dawned, and there were tasks to be done before anyone could rest. Tattered clouds of smoke and steam draped the village in an aethereal-like veil. Voices of children floated eerily on the still air, their piping voices filled with excitement despite the horror of the night.

At the southern end of Ozera, near the trail to Sunrise Chapel, stood a unique home. Its two-story, stone walls and shallow pitched, grass-covered roof seemed to meld into the side of the mountain. In front, four pine logs stripped of bark and branches supported a single-story porch roof and its staggered rows of wooden shakes. Between the posts, rails made from smoothed deadwood bound together with wild grape vine lashings were a perfect blend of nature and home. A trellis closed off one end of the porch, supporting a mass of vines that wove their way around the eaves, trailing clouds of snowy white roses. The cut glass windows were the least natural thing about the place.

Robert thought the house odd, but, then again, he was born and raised on the coast where everyone tried to build as high above ground as they could to avoid flooding during storm season. This house was custom built for the Yves family.

He hesitated on the rose shaded porch, adjusting his collar, and brushing the soot from his black shirt and vest. Wondering if he should leave his rapier at the door or carry it in with him, he stared down at the basket hilt. Running his fingers through his light brown hair, he realized how filthy it and his boots were. Straightening his belt for the third time, he approached the door and knocked, aware that this was the most difficult thing he would do all day.

"¿Puedo ayudarlo?" a middle-aged, Espian woman asked, cracking open the door. Her terra-cotta skin and silky, silver-flecked black hair seemed out of place in the elven home.

"Señora, my name is Robert Stone," he said with a slight bow, hat in his hand. "I'm a friend of Aislinn and Brand. Is Mrs. Yves receiving visitors?"

"Come in," the lady said, opening the door wider. "One of Aislinn's other friends is with her now." She stepped back, allowing the young man to enter the modest foyer. She gestured to an arched doorway on the left. "Go ahead, I'm making tea. Would you like some?"

"Just water, thank you," Robert said with a tight-lipped smile. He wondered who else was there.

With a nod, the woman retreated down the hall to the kitchen.

Robert turned toward the open doorway and stopped, frozen by the tableau. Wearing a loosely bound cerulean shirt of fine satin, August Sabe sat with Aislinn's mother, one arm around her as she sobbed on his shoulder. Touches of soot covered their faces and clothes. Shayla looked to be in her late twenties, far too young to have raised a daughter to adulthood. Her flaxen hair was disheveled, and her pale skin blotched and swollen. Tears welled in his eyes, and Robert had to look away as the sight of the slight elven woman's suffering kindled memories of his parents' deaths.

That night flared in Robert's memory, as clear as if it happened yesterday. He was only seven and had spent the week after Halloween with his uncle, aunt, and cousins. He awoke to the sound of someone banging on the front door, and bright blue and red lights flashing outside his window.

That night, a young Robert had crept down the hallway toward the muffled sound of men's voices. Tee Middleton, his dad's partner on the police force, stood talking to Uncle Dan while Aunt Libby wept on the sofa.

Officer Middleton saw Robert, and his somber expression cracked. He knelt there in Uncle Dan's living room and held out his big hand. "Come'yuh, Bobby. I got tuh tell ya sump'n gone be hard tuh hear." Tee, a sea islander, was the only one who ever called him Bobby.

"Tee, we'll handle this," Uncle Dan said.

"Dan, please. Jes lemme do dis. Nate's been muh friend fuh a long time now. 'Sides, it's muh job."

His uncle gave Tee a single sharp nod before sitting on the sofa beside Aunt Libby and wrapping an arm around her shoulders.

"Am I in trouble, Uncle Tee?" Robert asked.

"Naw, Bobby, you ain't in no trouble. It's jes... Dey's been uh accident. Yo cuz'n Clem's been hurt, an' yo momma 'n daddy..." A fat tear had escaped Tee, and the big man sniffled. "Dey's gone tuh be wid da Lawd, Bobby."

Tee's Gullah accent always grew thick when he was upset. At first, Robert hadn't understood. When his own hot tears came, his aunt had pulled him to her in a fierce hug, rocking back and forth, and telling him that he was going to be okay. When he was older, she told him that it had been arson — his parents were murdered. The knowledge left a hole in his heart.

Now the scene repeated before him, with August and Shayla playing the parts. It was almost more than he could bear.

August took in Robert's smoke and ash-stained appearance, meeting the swordsman's sad expression with one of sympathy, and gestured for him to come closer. "Any news of what happened up there?" he asked in a rich, powerful baritone.

"I'm sorry, it's too early to know," Robert said, shaking his head. "Hector got permission to help with the investigation, though, so I expect the village will be turned upside down and shaken thoroughly to see what falls out."

"I doubt Father Phaedrus is going to be pleased with whoever agreed to let Hector help. The bounty hunter's methods leave much to be desired."

Robert hesitated before replying. "I think he'll make an exception in this case." Turning toward Shayla, he said, "They found Brand in a clearing. He's badly hurt. A team of healers is with him now."

Shayla sat up, her summer-sky eyes still brimming with tears. "He's alive? I have to go back up there. I tried to help him, but..." The urgency in her voice sent a strident chord through her normally musical tones.

"Milady Yves, rest a bit more. Give the healers time to work," August said, cupping her hand in his.

"Ms. Shayla," Robert said, kneeling in front of her, "I know this is a horrible time to ask, but can you think of anyone who might want to hurt Brand? Anyone at all?"

She shook her head slowly. "You or Hector would know the answer to that better than me. They've been with you more than me since they followed Edge that day..."

Robert could see her searching through her memories. When she spoke again, her voice was soft and distant. He leaned forward to hear her better.

"Brand wasn't big enough to carry Aislinn and get off the ground when she agreed to apprentice with Edge," Shayla said. "I made that ranger swear an oath to keep my child safe. He died trying to keep that promise."

August and Robert shared a questioning look, neither sure where Shayla's memory was taking her.

"The last time he left Ozera, Edge headed south to the Haunted Hills. Two rangers had gone missing crossing clan territories near its border." She sighed. "Even now I hear rumors about people vanishing near there, simply gone with no trace, and those who search for them disappear, too."

"Aren't the mountains south of the clans controlled by elves?" August asked.

"No. Dærganfae hold the Haunted Hills. I don't know where they came from or what dark secret they harbor within their borders, but they despise humans and elves with equal fervor.

"I begged Edge not to go into the Haunted Hills, to stay within the territories controlled by the Tanjara and Garrett clans. He promised to be careful. The day he rode out was the last time I ever saw him." Her voice faded, and she stared, unseeing, into the distance.

"What happened?" August asked. She still sat within the circle of his arm, and he gave her a gentle hug of reassurance.

"Aislinn and Brand planned to go to Ruthaer that summer. Tallinn, the Sea Ranger who keeps the lighthouse, had written to her, saying Alaric had wanted her to apprentice with him. You know how free-willed Aislinn was. She and Brand were going, whether I agreed or not." She shook her head. "I don't know how or why it happened, but they followed Edge instead. It was more than a year before I saw them again, and that was when she brought you boys here the first time." She gave Robert a half smile. "She never really told me what happened — just that they had gone into dærganfae lands after all. I don't know what they found down there. I tried to get her to tell me, but she refused to talk about what happened to Edge, beyond the fact that his killer was dead."

"Do you think Brand and Aislinn had enemies among the fae?" Robert asked.

Shayla shook her head. "Maybe. I don't know. Besides, I can't imagine anyone coming here, of all places, just to hurt him."

"I'll talk to Hector and Dave. Maybe they can think of someone."

The woman who answered the door walked in with a mug of tea and two cups of water on a wooden tray.

Shayla sniffed the tea and glared at the woman. "María, I told you I don't want to sleep. This young man brought news that Brand is alive. I have to go to him."

"Let me learn the fastest route, then I'll escort you up the mountain," August said, rising from the couch. He held her delicate fingers in his, and with a low bow, he gently brushed his lips against the back of her hand. "I will return shortly, Milady Yves."

Her soft, rose petal lips parted as she drew a surprised breath. An embarrassed flush rushed up her throat to her cheeks. Shayla bowed her head, and a fall of pale tresses hid her expression.

Straightening, August gestured for Robert to walk with him out of the room. Though both were tall, there was little similarity between the two men. August's long, wavy black hair and muscular physique seemed sculpted by the Creator, whereas Robert's lanky form and grim pallor seemed more like hardened steel forged in the fires of Hell.

"She was up on the mountain?" Robert asked when the two stood on the porch.

August nodded. "I was cutting a firebreak along the slope when I heard her scream. She found the dragon and went into hysterics. I brought her home after the rain started."

"Thank you, August. I'm sure Mrs. Yves appreciates you being here with her."

"She's Aislinn's mother," August replied. "It's my honor to serve her. Right now, though, she needs to rest. We've been trying to get her to lie down, but as you can see..."

"Good luck with that. Aislinn got her stubbornness from her mother."

August gave an amused huff. "I was beginning to suspect as much. What's the safest way to reach Brand?"

"It isn't really safe, per se, but about halfway up to Sunrise Chapel you'll find a cloth tied to a branch. A game trail cuts through a laurel grove and leads to the clearing. Watch your step, though. It's just below one of the firebreaks, so it gets rough in places."

"Where is everyone else?" August asked.

"Scattered around," he said. "That girl from Ruthaer, Teal, is with the healers. They needed someone with extensive knowledge of dragons, and Hector seemed to think she fit the bill. I'm not sure he's thinking clearly. I reminded him that we really don't know her, but Hector wouldn't listen."

August made a wry face. "Does he ever?"

"Not really. Hector assigned everyone a task, so I'm down here canvasing the village. We'll probably get together this evening to share information."

"I'm going to stay with Lady Yves as long as she needs me. Send word if I can be of assistance with the villagers.

I've seen Hector and Dave try to get information out of people. They really must work on their social skills."

Robert gave a rueful laugh. "Hector does well enough when he has a handle on his temper. Dave, on the other hand... He typically just grunts and scowls."

CHAPTER 28
HOW TO HEAL A DRAGON

August 17, 4237 K.E.

9:00am

S troking his beard, Jasper stood beside the newly restored spring and considered the chapel. He needed a sheet of parchment, a quill, and inks. Gideon had settled nearby and appeared to be deep in meditative prayer. Although he didn't want to leave without telling Gideon where he was going, Jasper certainly didn't want to disturb the cleric. Interrupting prayers was a quick way to get oneself smitten by holy retribution.

Rather than loiter about, Jasper made his way downhill to the clearing where healers and the girl, Teal, continued to tend Brand. If he was lucky, there would be someone who could fetch the parchment and inks for him.

In the light of day, the damage to the young dragon's body was ghastly. Most of the scales and skin on his chest and right side were charred and stiff despite the salves the healers liberally applied to every inch they could reach. Jasper frowned at the gaping wounds among the burns. Several wept molten bronze, making bandaging them impossible. Then there was Brand's right wing. It bore a long, jagged tear in its leathery membrane, and the main bones bore multiple fractures. Jasper shook his head and said a silent prayer to the Eternal Father.

At the edge of the shaded area, the rotund mage drew to a halt, not wanting to get in the way. An apothecary and her assistants worked at nearby tables, some grinding herbs while others extracted the sticky, gelatinous pulp of numerous cactus-like plants. He watched for a minute, lips pursed in thought, before he approached one of the tables.

"Pardon me, but how much pulp do you get from a plant that size?"

An elderly matron deftly placed the end of the plant's thick leaf on the edge of a bowl, pressed a small dowel over it, and pulled the plant through the improvised press, all in one swift motion. "Not nearly enough," she said. "We have people calling in favors to get more, but I'm afraid we're going to run out soon, what with all the others whose wounds need tending, too. To make matters worse, there's naught they can do for the poor beast's wing. He's simply too big."

Glancing at the dragon and then back at the matron, he offered, "Would it help if he was smaller?"

"You know how to shrink a dragon?" the woman asked, her expression skeptical.

Jasper nodded. "Yes, although I may have to call in a few favors of my own, and the effects would only be temporary."

"How temporary?" a young voice asked.

Jasper turned and found the tall, tawny-haired girl striding toward him. The freckles on her cheeks were a contrast to the wisdom in her eyes. He raised one eyebrow. "And you are?"

"Teal. The only person 'round with knowledge of dragon anatomy."

"Excuse me? You don't look more than thirteen — maybe twelve."

"By Xardus, not this again."

Jasper's eyes twinkled as a smile tugged at his mouth. "I'm joking. I saw you this morning, though I doubt you remember me. I'm Jasper Thredd."

Teal offered him a curt nod. "Well met, sir. I have but three questions for thee. When canst thou affect this change, how long will it last, and will he be made small enough for a company of men to carry?"

The mage blinked in surprise at her brusque attitude. "I can try tomorrow afternoon after I've had time to prepare; however, I can't guarantee the spell will work on him."

"It will work. He is too weak to resist. As is, we are having much ado with the broken bones. He needs to be amidst his hoard."

"Chica, we already told you; no one can get to his cave without wings," the matron said.

Teal huffed in exasperation. "There is a way, though thou dost not know it."

"You should ask Mrs. Yves," Jasper said. "If anyone knows a way, it will be her. For now, how about I help out with the medicinals?"

"Now you're telling me you can get your hands on ten or twenty bushels of aloe cactus?" the apothecary cried.

With a nod, Jasper said, "Possibly. If I can find him, I know someone who can probably get you the aloe." He spun and hustled back the way he came, his bulky shape at odds with the speed he crossed the uneven terrain.

The old woman watched his flab jiggle and sway for a moment before shaking her head and returning to her work.

"He did not answer my other questions," Teal muttered.

"Mages are an odd lot, especially that one," the old woman replied. "Be thankful you got any answers at all."

CR&O

9:30am

Robert approached an elderly woman feeding a flock of chickens. "Buenas días, Señora. Me llamo Robert Stone. I'm a friend of the Yves family. We're investigating the fire at Sunrise Chapel, and I'm hoping someone may have seen or heard something that will help."

The old woman sighed and made a sign against evil. "Such sacrilege. I don't think I can help you."

"Think on it, Señora. Anything, no matter how small, might be important."

The old woman nodded, and Robert turned to make his way to the next house.

"Un momento, Señor Stone. Perhaps it is nada, pero mi nieto... my grandson carried a basket of eggs and vegetables to Señora Yves for me two days ago. On his way home, he saw a strange man at the pilgrims' cottage on the cliff."

"Did he say what the stranger looked like?"

"No, just that it was a man he'd never seen before."

"Señora, would you ask your grandson to come find me or Hector de los Santos and give us a description of this man?"

"Sí, Señor Stone."

"Gracias, Señora."

Robert walked swiftly back to the main road and turned south. He passed several small shops and a meditation pool before the road branched. The right fork curved around one of Ozera's many hills and led to a series of switchbacks that eventually carried travelers to the base of the glowing white cliff of Lumikivi Mountain.

Taking the fork to his left, he meandered past tree-shrouded lanes that wound their way up the mountain to Sunrise Chapel. All around him, people moved with a purpose, and it gave him the distinct impression they were trying to stay busy. Otherwise, memories of the night's horror would catch up to them.

He strode down a lane to his right, topped a rise, and paused to study the cluster of dwellings located atop one of Lumikivi Mountain's overlooks. To the east, the mountain continued its climb, but he didn't know anyone who would try to reach the summit that way.

Robert followed the narrow cart path over a gurgling stream and around a grove of old oaks with a small prayer chapel in their midst. Moss and ivy rather than mortar seemed to hold together the stacked stones forming the building's walls. Branches wove through the roof, supporting its thatched expanse. Low steps led up to a broad, paved entry porch on the east side, and a small vestry extended out on the north. Dark bunting draped the open door and arched windows in memorial to Aislinn.

Until recently, the area had been set aside as lodging for pilgrims, but after their return from the jungles of Suthose earlier that year, Hector negotiated a long-term lease on the cottage and cabins. He claimed the largest for himself and treated the others as guest houses. Robert and Jasper each had a place of their own, as well as Hummingbird, August and the ranger, Xandor. For reasons Robert couldn't fathom, Dave refused to take the last cabin for himself, choosing instead to stay with Hector.

A pie shaped wedge of shady park spotted with archery targets and training dummies separated three of the cabins from the mountainside. Centered on the cul-de-sac, Hector and Dave's cottage perched on the overlook's edge, with less than ten feet of bare rock between their back wall and the drop-off. Hector said he chose it for the view, but everyone knew it was to keep anyone from sneaking up behind him. Although, from their rear windows, the view *was* breathtaking.

Robert circled behind the cabins, main gauche in his left hand while his right rested on the hilt of his rapier, noting that nothing looked out of place. There wasn't anything stacked under a window to lend height to a would-be thief.

When he reached Hector's cottage, he discovered the rear window was missing the sheer fabric that served as a bug screen. Stepping close, he ran his hand along the window frame and felt the tattered remains of gossamer where someone had cut it. The window was shuttered from the inside, yet Robert heard someone moving around. It was a sickening thought, but the fire could have been a diversion to keep Hector and Dave away.

Robert pushed on the window shutter. It swung open on silent hinges, telling him whoever cut out the screen came prepared. Hector always rigged hinges to give off a horrendous screech of protest. Boosting himself up and through the window, he set his feet down silently on the floor within. In the dappled light filtering in through the front shutters, he took in the forgotten wine bottles, still standing where they'd left them the night before. He eased across the room and checked the front door. It was locked. With infinite care, Robert crept to the foot of the stairs. He heard the squeal of hinges and muttering, confirming a presence above.

Easing out his rapier, Robert took the stairs one at a time, counting to four with each step. His back to the wall to allow himself the greatest view of the area above, he shifted his weight carefully in the hope a creaking floorboard wouldn't give him away to the person lurking above.

Being tall had advantages. On the fifth step, he could see over the edge of the floor. His eyes quickly scanned the room and found a rotund figure in worn, filthy boots and soot coated clothes crouched in front of Dave's footlocker, searching its contents. A wooden staff leaned against the wall within easy reach.

Eyes narrowed, Robert moved even more slowly than before as he took another cautious step upward. The stair gave off an ear-piercing shriek as he put his weight on it. The fat man leapt to his feet and whirled, magical energy crackling around his fist.

Robert instinctively leapt down the stairwell. "Don't shoot, Jasper!" he cried out.

"'Ods bodkins, Robert, you nearly scared me to death!"

Robert peeked back over the floor to see Jasper had released the energy around his fist. "What are you doing?" he asked, not yet coming up out of the stairwell. It wouldn't be easy for someone or something to impersonate Jasper, but he wasn't in a mood to get ambushed.

"I finished going over the chapel and went to check on Brand. One of the healers said they're running short of medicinal herbs." He held up a leather satchel with various leaves tooled into the wide strap. "I was getting this for them," he said.

"*Dave* has something the healers need?"

Jasper's eyes narrowed slightly. "You don't recognize it?"

Robert shook his head. "It looks familiar, but not really, no."

"It was Aislinn's," the mage said, searching his face. "It was a gift."

Jasper was testing him. Robert was sure of it. He stared at the bag, wracking his brain. He realized this was definitely the real Jasper in front of him, but now his own identity was in question. He felt the vague stirring of a memory, but it didn't seem to relate. "Why does it make me think of empty suits of armor patrolling a decrepit castle wall?" he muttered.

The mage edged closer to his staff.

"Lord Oberon," Robert said suddenly. "He gave it to her on our first trip to Orleans. I'd forgotten about the bag. It produces herbs on command, right?"

Jasper let out the breath he'd been holding and nodded in return. "That's right. Now, what brings you here?"

"One of the villagers said her grandson saw someone sneaking around here two days ago. I found where someone cut the screen out of the back window and oiled the shutter hinges. Then, I heard you in here and thought the person might have come back. The shutter was unlocked."

"So that's how you got in. I knew I locked the door behind me. Hold this for me," he said, handing him the satchel, "and I'll look everything over."

Downstairs, Robert closed and locked the window, then went out the front door to wait. A few minutes later, Jasper joined him and locked the front door.

"No one left any traces of magic behind, so whatever the burglar was after must have been easy to find," he reported. "We'll need to tell Hector and Dave. Let them see if anything was taken."

"I guess whichever of us sees them first gets to break the news."

Jasper nodded. "I'm going to put a roast on the hearth. You want to come over for supper tonight?"

"Maybe," Robert said. "I was supposed to meet with Phaedrus after vespers, but I haven't heard if he's recovered. Plus, with the fire and all, even if he is up and about..."

"Supper will be ready after the evening prayer. Come by when you're free — I'll have some set aside for you."

"All right. That sounds good. What are you up to for the rest of the day?"

"I need to take that satchel to the healers and return to Sunrise Chapel," Jasper replied. "After I start supper, I may go into the village proper. One of my old instructors from Tydway is here."

Robert looked up toward the mountain. Something bothered him about the young woman purportedly caring for Brand. "I want to check on Brand. Let me take the satchel to the healers... unless you need to speak to them."

"You can take it. I really need to get back to the chapel."

They walked together in silence for several minutes. Jasper studied his friend obliquely, noting the glints of silver in the younger man's sandy brown hair. The premature grey was even more noticeable in his short-cropped goatee and mustache, and there were visible lines around his eyes that gave his countenance a harder look. The changes to his appearance made the resemblance between Robert and Dave even more obvious than it used to be.

Jasper cleared his throat. "Robert, I want to apologize..."

The swordsman flinched and stopped to face the mage. His jaw tightened, and his bright blue eyes became guarded.

"I'm responsible for us not getting to Orleans in time to help you two years ago. I was elbows deep in an Academy project in Tydway. A day or two sooner, and we could have prevented the Sha'iry from kidnaping you."

Laying a hand on the mage's shoulder, Robert said, "Everything worked out for the best, Jasper. Neither the Dark One nor his insane brother got what they wanted. Compared to what might have happened, I didn't have it too bad."

"Still... I wish we could have spared you the experience."

"Thanks," Robert said, averting his eyes to hide the turmoil inside.

They continued onward, an awkward barrier of silence building between them. At the marker for the game trail, they paused again. "Thanks for taking that for me," Jasper said, with a gesture toward the herb bag. "Oh, I almost forgot. You'll need to show them how it works."

"I think I remember but refresh my memory. It's been a while."

"Undo this front buckle and grasp the edge of the flap like so," Jasper said as he went through the motions. "Then say the name of the herb, and a fistful of it will be inside when you open the bag. I don't know if there's a limit."

"Simple enough. I'll take care of it."

When Robert reached the semi-level area where Brand had come to rest, he stood back in the shadow of a tall buckeye, observing the healers' activity. Teal moved from person to person, guiding a hand here, helping bandage there. He wondered if he or his friends had looked that confident six years ago when they were her age. He didn't think so. Of course, he didn't feel half as confident now as she looked.

Seeing several of the healers busy with mortar and pestle at a nearby table, Robert crossed the clearing to them.

"Pardon me, Jasper asked me to bring this to you for Brand," he said, holding out the leather satchel.

"What is that mage up to now?" asked an ancient looking woman, eyeing the tall man as if he held a bag of snakes.

"Aislinn's herb bag," Robert said. "She used it mostly for teas and poultices, but I was told it can produce any plant you name. Jasper didn't know if there was a limit to how much it makes or how often. Here, I'll show you how it works. What type of plant do you need?"

The old woman thought a moment and said, "Willow." She and the herbalists sitting next to her watched in amazement as Robert demonstrated how to use the bag, repeated the herb's name, and pulled out a thick handful of fresh shaved bark — enough to make a fair bit of fever medicine.

Reaching out with a gnarled hand, the woman selected a strip and sniffed it. She took a nearby knife and cut a small piece off to chew, then nodded in satisfaction as she found the plant pure.

"Thank you," she said, taking the satchel. "I'll see that it gets returned when we're done."

Leaving the women to make medications and compounds, Robert walked over to stand beside Brand's head. The dragon had grown since he last saw him. Though still a youth by dragon standards, Brand measured sixty feet long from nose to tail-tip. Lying prone before him, the top of the dragon's brow ridge was almost even with Robert's hip. Filled with sadness, Robert sank to his knees beside the great bronze head.

"Come on, Brand. You've got to pull through," he murmured. "We need your help, and so does Shayla. Hector and Dave are at their wits' end without Aislinn, and I'm not in much better shape myself. It's been rough."

He sighed. "We — Hector, Dave, Jasper, and I — are determined to find the person who did this to you and find out why." He reached up and brushed his fingertips along the dragon's brow ridge. "It's wrong for someone to disturb the peace of the dead and the mourning, but to try to kill you and destroy so much of this mountain Aislinn loved... Someone will pay dearly, my friend."

CHAPTER 29
PHOTOGRAPHS AND MEMORIES

August 17, 4237 K.E.

1:00pm

Nestled in the far corner of the tavern, Hector finished the last of his bowl of catfish stew and reached for his mug of ale.

Dave stomped across the dining room and dropped into the chair across the table from him. A serving girl wearing a simple brown dress walked up, but he shooed her away.

"I hate this thing," Dave growled as he tugged at the neckline of the tunic Robert loaned him that morning.

"You're going to stretch that if you don't leave it alone," Hector admonished.

"It's too fucking tight," Dave grumbled.

"It isn't tight, it's unfamiliar. If you wore a shirt with any kind of regularity, you wouldn't be so sensitive."

Dave glared in response. "Going door to door was a waste of time. These people are blinded by their sense of security. Hell, they probably wouldn't notice a troll in their midst until it busted up a few shops and tried to eat someone."

Earlier, Lord Vaughn had assigned each of them a section of Ozera to talk to villagers and search for clues. So far, Hector had covered half the homes and businesses in his area. Not one person knew anything helpful.

"Maybe, but we still need to ask," Hector replied. "I've been wracking my brain trying to think of anyone we've crossed who has the means to hurt Brand like that."

"Could be someone we don't know. Who knows who he pissed off when we weren't around? It could even be someone from before we met him and Aislinn."

"If that's the case, why did they wait so long to come after him?"

Dave shrugged.

"After we split up this morning, I started thinking about something Teal told me while we were in Margate. We need to ask around to see if anyone has seen another bronze dragon in the area."

Dave tipped his head to one side and raised an eyebrow.

Hector explained, "Back in Teal's time, there were two factions among the bronze dragons: those who worshipped Xardus and could shape-change like Brand, and those who turned their backs on the deity and had only one form. He told me there was a lot of hostility between the two."

"Aislinn told us Brand's father came here. You think he tried to kill Brand?"

"It isn't outside the realm of possibility. Apparently, the bronzes who could shape-change and the Xemmassians were considered abominations by the draconic community."

"Brand and Aislinn never mentioned anything about a dragon deity. She worshipped the Eternal Father, like Phaedrus."

"In Ruthaer, you said there was probably something in Aislinn's bloodline that made Brand's mother choose Alaric to care for Brand's egg. Those same genetics are why Brand can do the things he does."

"Well, shit. I've been asking people about Dodz and dærganfae. Now, we have to add bronze dragons to the list. Why don't we add fuckin' chupacabra, while we're at it?"

"Dave..."

"I'm just saying, let's keep it simple. Dodz wants the mask, Hector. He's the kind of asshole who'd burn the mountain as a distraction."

"And the dærganfae?" Hector asked.

"They killed Aislinn's mentor, but she and Brand got away. What if they saw something back then that the fae didn't want to get out? Something the two of them didn't even realize was important. Think about it. The same thing happened to Evan Courtenay and that ivory dagger of his. The one he stole from the Haunted Hills. Don't forget, Mi'dnirr bit Aislinn in Ruthaer. She said she thought her bond with Brand surprised him. With Aislinn gone, Mi'dnirr could have come to Ozera to kill Brand."

"That's a bit of a stretch, don't you think?" asked Hector.

"No more than Brand's father trying to kill him."

"Speaking of fathers —"

Dave groaned as he pushed up from the table. "Enough, Hector."

"Sorry, amigo, but Lord Vaughn isn't going away."

"I don't want to hear or talk about him."

Hector placed a pair of silver coins on the table. "Sit down and have lunch. I'm going to check on Brand, talk to Teal, then track down Jasper."

Dave nodded. "I'll keep canvasing, then meet you at home."

"If you see Robert or Xandor, let them know supper is at our place. I need to know what they learned so I can report to Lord Vaughn tomorrow."

CRSO

4:30pm

Like everyone else, the proprietor of Glorious Gilt, Ozera's one and only tattoo parlor, knew nothing of dragons, vampires, Rhodinan counts, dærganfae, or chupacabra. Dave contemplated going back inside and making an appointment to have the bite scars on his neck and chest re-inked but decided to wait. The wound on his back where the clockwork bug in Ruthaer tagged him wasn't finished healing, and he wanted his dragon tat repaired as well.

Having had enough of people for one day and ready to rid himself of Robert's shirt, he started home. He studied each person he passed, searching for Dodz or one of the elusive fae. Instead, he came face to face with Roger Vaughn.

"Dave," the older man greeted him with a brief nod.

Dave scowled as he tried to sidestep the nobleman, but Roger moved to intercept him.

"I know you don't want to talk to me, but I have something to show you." He pointed to a tea shop with a cluster of tables and chairs on a side patio. "Will you sit with me for a few minutes? Please."

Eyeing the shop and the nobleman, Dave said, "If I do, will you leave me the hell alone?"

"Listen, son, I'm running this investigation. You and your friends are working for me. Phaedrus and eight of his highest-ranking clerics almost died last night, and your friend Brand is at the center of it."

"Talk to Hector. He's the one with all the answers."

"I intend to, but right now, I want to talk to you. It's important."

"You're as bad as Hector," Dave muttered, but followed Roger to a table at the corner of the patio overhanging a rocky creek.

Immediately, a server delivered a steaming teapot, honey, and two mugs. He opened the lid of his wooden tray and presented them with a selection of teas. Although Dave declined, Roger selected sachets of black tea for each mug.

After the server retreated, Roger sat back in his chair and said, "What have you found out?"

"Not a damn thing," Dave replied, staring anywhere but at the man across the table from him.

Roger huffed an exasperated sounding sigh. "I know you're angry with me, but we need to work together here."

"Hector's in charge. You want cooperation, cooperate with him."

"It's important to me that I have your support."

"Fuck that," Dave said with curt laugh. "You have nothing I want."

"I have people digging into Count Dodz — who he really is, who he works for, where he lives. When I know, so will you."

Dave glared at the man across the table. "What do you want?"

Roger slipped off his wife's platinum and sapphire locket. At two inches in diameter, it nearly filled his palm. He pressed a hidden catch, opened the locket, and laid it on the table so Dave could see the photos within.

"The picture of Brie and me was taken at Cam and Nate's wedding."

Dave reached for his flask, then remembered the curse Phaedrus cast on him made alcohol taste like beach sand.

"Drinking won't change facts or make this any easier," Roger said. He pulled a small leather case from a pocket inside his vest and selected a thin pick from the tools inside.

A moment later, he laid aside the crystal disc that protected the image of Brie and Dave as a toddler. "Before Lahar and her crew took Brie back to Terra, your mother and I talked about naming you after our fathers — Robert Brynmor. It wasn't until I saw your friend yesterday that I realized what Brie was trying to tell me when she said Cam and Nate adopted a baby boy named Robert. Taking into account how much she loved mysteries, puzzles, and spycraft, it occurred to me that Brie would have kept evidence close to her heart. I found this." He gently removed the photo, revealing another, with Brie holding a pair of infants.

"That doesn't prove a damn thing," Dave said. A part of him realized his fever dream had spoken the truth — Robert was his brother. Instead of making him feel relieved, he felt sick. Not only was Bryony a liar, but so were Cam and Nate. He didn't know what this would do to Robert if he found out.

Roger lifted out the second picture and turned it over. In faded blue ink, the inscription read, "Robert Brynmor Vaughn, August 17, 1974, 11:58pm and Clement Tyler Vaughn, August 18, 1974, 12:03am."

Dave swore. He wanted to rip the pictures to pieces and burn them.

"Please talk to Robert. Tell him what we've learned. Whenever you and he are ready, I'm here."

Dave glanced at the images one more time, shook his head, and shoved away from the table. Without a word or a backward glance, he left the teashop and Roger Vaughn.

CHAPTER 30
DAVE AND ROBERT

August 17, 4237 K.E.

6:00pm

Dave stalked up the path, his jaw clenched while he silently cursed his luck. He had hoped to avoid Roger Vaughn until the man gave up and left Ozera. Why Roger thought he could insert himself into his and Robert's lives baffled Dave. Three pictures and the claim he was married to Dave's long dead mother didn't give the man any right to disrupt their lives now, especially with everything that was going on. He needed to find Robert and keep him away from Roger Vaughn.

Unfortunately, Robert hadn't been in his cabin or the prayer chapel, which forced Dave to ask among the villagers until he found one who could point him in the right direction. He hated talking to people. No one could answer a simple question without telling him how sorry they felt for Aislinn's mother and asking him to let them know if she needed anything. As if their condolences or empty offers could somehow make things better. He just wanted this mess to be over. Then he could pack it away with all the other shit he'd worked hard to forget over the years.

He paused. He and Robert could both use a fresh start. Maybe they should change their names and find work in an Espian vineyard. No one would think to look for them in Oviedo or Cadiz. Or, even better, they could join the crew of a trade-ship plying the Karukera Sea. When they were kids in Terra, he and Robert had dreamed about becoming swashbucklers, like Captain Thorpe or Peter Blood in Raphael Sabatini's novels and short stories. They could sign on to fight pirates in memory of Aislinn.

A loose rock skittered off the toe of his boot, and he scooped it up, bouncing it in his hand several times before hurling it into the trees at a chattering squirrel. The stone knocked the offending rodent off its branch. Dave grunted with satisfaction and tromped on, not bothering to see if the animal was dead or merely stunned.   Either the animal would recover, or a scavenger would eat it — nothing went to waste in the forest.

Ahead, a dirty white flag fluttered in a breath of air through dry laurel leaves. Shoving the bush aside, he turned onto the narrow game trail, ignoring the branches that clawed his arms and chest in protest of his rough treatment.

Blackened leaves and scorched branches covered the path, hiding holes and washouts. A careless person could easily lose their footing and find themselves plunging down the slope in a wild and dangerous slide.

By the time he reached the clearing where Brand sprawled in a broken heap, twilight shadows filled the forest. Lanterns hung from tent poles and sat on the nearby worktables, keeping the shadows at bay.   Dave stayed outside the reach of the light, watching. Teal stood within the twisted curve of Brand's great wings talking to the healers, her hands moving over damaged skin with gentle familiarity.   Unbidden, his memory conjured an image of Aislinn, her brow furrowed in concentration as she tended Aaron Pond's arrow wound in Ruthaer.

Clamping down on his welling emotions, the bowman scanned the clearing for Robert, but he was nowhere in sight. A sense of unease snaked through Dave. An enemy powerful enough to lure Brand from his cave and do him this much harm could easily overpower a single person.

Having no desire to talk to Teal or the healers, Dave made his way around the edge of the clearing within the darker shadows.   He reached Brand's opposite side before he spotted Robert sitting at the base of an enormous pine, his hat tipped forward to hide his eyes. He slouched against the tree trunk as if sleeping, but to Dave's eye, he was far from relaxed. Lying on the ground near his right hand, the loops and whorls of his rapier hilt shown a ghostly silver in the fading light, while the blade remained safely ensconced in its scabbard.

Robert was one of the most skilled swordsmen Dave had ever met. He knew more ways to disarm an opponent than Dave knew how to kill one, and that was saying a lot. Now, however, Dave didn't know Robert's state of mind. Spending two-and-a-half years as a prisoner of Sutekh's Sha'iry was bad enough, but the bastards used magic to force Robert to serve the whims of a vicious erinyes. Robert hadn't said much about what happened before they managed to rescue him from Sutekh's minions, but then again, Dave hadn't asked. The look on Robert's face when Gideon banished the demoness back to the abyss had told Dave more than he wanted to know about how things stood between man and fiend.

Dave dropped into a crouch beside Robert and waited, watching Teal and the healers.

"Do you trust her?" Robert murmured, his eyes sliding open.

Dave snorted. "I don't trust anybody."

"Even yourself?"

"Especially myself."

"I know how you feel," Robert said with a slight nod. "Why did Hector bring her here?"

"Why does Hector do anything?" Dave shrugged. "Honestly, though? The head of the garrison in Ruthaer let his personal problems get in the way of doing his job, their priest was a complete f—" He cast a sidelong glance at Robert, who raised an eyebrow in return. "—fraud, and the villagers were ready to lynch her."

"From what little the two of you have said about what was going on there, she deserved worse."

Dave gave Robert a speculative look. "Torture doesn't make family and friends feel better or make the murdered rest any easier. It sure as hell doesn't make a killer any more dead."

Robert gave a rueful laugh. "Never thought I'd hear you advising the morally better course, or me being the bloodthirsty one. So much for penance restoring my soul."

"Is that what you've been doing these past few months with Gideon? Shit, man. There's not a priest alive that can cure what's wrong with you. Believe me, I know. Whatever happened to you — whatever that demon and her lackeys made you do — you aren't going to get over it unless you can forgive yourself. Until then, you're going to stay just as fucked up as me." There was a flash of teeth as he grinned. "Might as well curse and drink."

"Oh, yes, because *that* helps." Robert gazed over at the healers, studying Teal while the sky grew darker. "What about her? Something about her reminds me of Tisiphoni."

Dave gave Robert a sharp look and made a sign against evil. "Dangerous to say a demon's name. You should know better." Robert, however, didn't seem to notice. The archer shifted his attention to the girl among the clerics and healers. "Whoever and whatever she was, she's possessed by the ghost of a lizardman now. Hector and I saw..." He stopped, thinking how much he wanted a drink, and left the thought unfinished. "She knew things in Ruthaer. Things she couldn't have known unless she's telling the truth. Hell, I'm surprised she's still here."

Robert looked askance at Dave. "You like her?"

Dave thought for a moment. "I don't dislike her."

Stifling a laugh, Robert said, "Hector told me about Herian Hill. You should talk to her."

Dave steeled his features. "No. Its better if she hates me."

"Well, if you aren't here to make up with her, why did you come up here?"

"I was looking for you. Hector wants to have a meeting. He plans on convincing Jasper to feed us."

"That shouldn't be too difficult. Jasper invited me to supper earlier, but I have an appointment with Phaedrus first," Robert said as he climbed to his feet.

Dave shook his head. "Phaedrus isn't seeing anyone. Hector tried already. Come to supper."

"Everyone is going to be there?"

"Yeah, Hector wants us to pool our information," Dave said.

They were on the main trail down the mountain when Robert cleared his throat. "Yesterday at the hospital, before Phaedrus and Brother Simon came in, you said some things..."

Dave stopped. His jaw and fists clenched as he struggled against the pounding in his chest. "I was sick, delirious."

Robert took two more steps before he stopped and turned back, his expression grave. "I know, but I still have questions about what you meant. When Hector and I got to the hospital, Lord Vaughn was standing guard outside your room. He seemed upset and barely stayed long enough for Hector to introduce us to each other."

Dave swore. "What did he say?"

Robert shrugged. "That you were feverish and delusional."

"What about Hector?"

"Only that Lord Vaughn provided transport to Ozera. Why? What's going on?"

Dave shook his head and stared into the gathering darkness. "He claims Bryony was his wife."

"*What?* That's ridiculous."

"He gave Hector some story about spending time in Charleston before bringing her here."

"Now we know he's lying. You were born in Charleston, same as me."

"He said he sent her back to Terra to hide us from dærganfae assassins."

"You believe him?" Robert asked.

Dave shrugged. "It's a neat and tidy story that can't be proven or disproven, but it does explain how she could use magic and who those elf-looking bastards were who killed her and your parents."

"Wait. Stop. Back up. Aunt Brie used magic in Terra?"

Dave nodded. "The only time I saw her do it was against the fuckers who killed her. No one believed me at the time, except Aunt Cam and Uncle Nate, and they told me not to tell anyone else."

For once, Robert didn't admonish Dave for his vulgar language. "So, this Lord Vaughn is your father?"

"He's nothing to me."

"Dave, family is important. You're all I have in this world, but you could have more. Don't burn this bridge."

"You're telling me, if you were in my boots, you'd accept that man as your father?"

"Maybe. Does he have any proof?"

"Bryony's locket. It has a picture inside of him and her. Claims it was taken at Cam and Nate's wedding. Hector said there's a life-size painting of her in the man's house."

"Wow."

"One picture of them together doesn't mean anything. For all we know, it's fake."

"Why would he make this up?"

"I don't know. I can't figure out his angle."

"Maybe there isn't one."

"Everyone's got an angle, Robert, even you."

"I beg to differ."

"You're the first and last Boy Scout in Gaia. Your angle is trying to be Aramis and Galahad rolled into one neat package."

"I suppose that makes you Athos and Robin Hood."

Dave gave Robert a mock bow. "Touché, mon frère."

CHAPTER 31
SPELLCRAFT

August 17, 4237 K.E.

6:00pm

The sharp blade of a bone-handled knife glinted in the candlelight as Jasper chopped through carrots with the speed and precision of an expert knife wielder. Onions followed, as well as a few late summer squash, and a bevy of cherry tomatoes. He raked the pile of vegetables and juices into a cook pot containing several bits of salt pork. In the stone fireplace, a cast iron pot hung from a swing arm over glowing embers, containing a venison roast simmered in gravy laden with potatoes.

He was reaching for a loose bunch of fresh sage when he heard rough pounding on his door in a rapid one-four-two pattern. The mage sighed and wiped his hands on a nearby cloth. A harsh knock meant Hector was frustrated or angry. Knowing the Espian and the current situation, it was both.

Jasper crouched in the shadow cast by the tabletop. Leery of deception, he drew a tiny spark of magic into something akin to a colorful soap bubble that floated across the room. The rough pounding came again.

When the bubble kissed the far wall, it shimmered, releasing its energy, and Jasper's voice called out, "Come in!"

The door eased open enough to allow Hector to slip inside, then the Espian closed it tightly. His hair was still wet from a bath, and he wore what passed for casual clothes for him: leather pants and a long-sleeved cotton shirt under a leather jerkin. He looked weary, with dark circles under his eyes and a defeated air, but he didn't move from his position by the door.

His hand on the hilt of his scimitar, he squinted in the direction of the voice, seeing only darkness. Irritation flickered across his features when his stomach growled.

"State your name and where you were born," Jasper's bubble demanded, initiating their established security protocol. The request was random, but it was one that had two answers — the public one and the real one. Jasper kept his thoughts focused on the public answer in case this was a mind-reading impostor.

"Héctor Miguel Córdova y Morales de los Santos. Santiago, España, Tierra," Hector replied, his Espian accent rolling his r's. "What's the best thing to do when a giant pangolin attacks your camp?"

"Turn it into a ten-pound rabbit and make stew, of course," Jasper answered as he rose from his crouch and let the bubble go with an audible pop. Hector relaxed his grip on the hilt of his scimitar and pulled a chair over to the table, where Jasper resumed his supper preparations.

A hairy, black spider crawled across the cutting block. Jasper smashed it with a meat hammer and separated the body from the legs. When he saw Hector wince, he said, "Spiders make it spicy," and slid the gelatinous gray juices into his cook pot with the vegetables.

Hector asked, "Does Dave know you do that?"

Jasper smiled and said, "He doesn't watch me cook. He just eats what I give him." The mage dribbled a little oil into the pot and carried it to the fireplace where another swing arm awaited. "I take it you didn't learn anything?"

"No," Hector replied. "How about you?"

"It's complicated," Jasper said. "I'd rather go over everything when we're all together."

"Then pull those pots out of there and let's haul them over to my place. You know how Dave is. You can finish cooking there."

"I invited Robert and Gideon over for supper after vespers," Jasper said. "I'll leave them a note where to find us. What about August and Xandor?"

"I saw Xandor on my way back from town. He's been on the mountain all day, talking to the animals or some such thing. He went to get cleaned up and collect August."

CR**ᙚ**

7:00pm

An hour later, Jasper dipped stew and vegetables onto

plates and passed them around, along with thick slices of warm bread.

The men gathered around Hector's table waited while Gideon blessed the food, then fell to with a gusto that made Jasper beam with pride. No one spoke until the last drop of juice was sopped from their dish and Jasper was starting on his second helping.

"Did anyone find out anything useful?" Hector asked.

"Other than someone breaking in here two days ago, I got nothing," Robert responded. "Was anything taken?"

"No," Hector replied. "Nothing that we've missed, anyway, and if the hombre left anything, I haven't found it."

"It was Dodz, looking for the mask," Dave grumbled.

"I'm not saying you're wrong, but we don't have any proof he's here," said Hector.

"Who?" Xandor asked.

"Count Dodz," Hector replied, "a Rhodinan nobleman whose ship foundered near Ruthaer. He was mixed up in the troubles there, though we couldn't prove it."

"And the mask?" August prodded.

"It turns its wearer into Lady D."

"That's impossible," August protested. "You decapitated that vampire and threw her head in a lake of acid over two years ago."

"Someone retrieved her skull and made a mask." Hector nodded toward Jasper and Gideon. "Before the fire, they were working with Brother Simon to find a way to destroy it."

Gideon said, "It would help if we knew who or what supplied the knowledge and power for its construction. If we take it out of the arcaloxós, we may be able to learn more."

"No," said Hector. "It's too dangerous."

"The mask is abyssal," Jasper explained. "What we need is access to more books, and an expert or three on demonology."

"None of that helps us tonight," Hector said. "I need something tangible to tell Lord Vaughn tomorrow."

"Is there any chance Dodz is a mage or a sorcerer?" Jasper asked. When Hector shrugged, Jasper said, "Let's put him and the mask aside for a few minutes and talk about

Sunrise Chapel." He retrieved a roll of parchment from atop the storage bench in the sitting area and brought it to the table. When he unrolled it, Gideon and August studied the colors and symbols spread across the page with keen interest, while the others stared in incomprehension. Jasper stroked his beard. "I think I'd best start with a quick lesson on how magic works."

"Jasper —"

"This is important, Hector," the mage cut off the protest. "What we call magic is a cause-and-effect energy that imbues everything in existence. It's ubiquitous. Some people, through natural ability and study, can draw on that energy and redirect it to accomplish things they normally couldn't. In ancient times, the mages of Korell developed seven categories for this energy, similar to their method of classifying animals, plants, and minerals."

Jasper held up seven fingers and ticked them off as he said, "Astral, Charms, Divination, Elemental, Illusion, Protection, and Necromancy. We use the *effect* to name the seven schools. Clerical thaumaturgy, while similar, uses the *origin* to classify their magic — divine versus infernal, if you will." He cast a quick glance to Gideon, who nodded his agreement. "The Korellan system makes magic easier to teach to others, especially if someone has a predilection for one type but not another. It also defines how we approach and track that energy, because each form leaves behind a distinct residue, so to speak. The reason I asked if Dodz was a mage or a sorcerer is that I found evidence of both Gaian and abyssal magic. And before you ask, these spells weren't cast from an item like a wand or a ring. There was a mage and either a demon or one of the Sha'iry up on that mountain."

Everyone shuffled in their seats.

"Alright, Jasper, lay it out for us, but keep it simple," stated Hector.

Jasper gave a single, sharp nod. "All of the spell effects in Sunrise Chapel last night were much larger than normal — about three times the size they should have been — including mine. Someone used what's called an enischýo.

It's a spell whose sole function is to enhance all other spells cast within its area of effect. Whoever cast this one was powerful, because it encompassed all of Sunrise Chapel."

Pointing to four orange dots with dashed lines leading between them and three orange X's on his map, he explained, "These are elemental magic. Fire, to be specific. The dots are the center of the spell terminus, the circle around it the area of effect, and the X's represent their point of origin. As you can see, these two had a single point of origin, corresponding with Brand's trajectory from Sunrise Chapel to his current position. These two —" he pointed to blue dots surrounded by silver rings, "— are where Brand fought back."

He pointed at several pale-yellow circles with X's in their centers. "Here is where I fought the fire." He touched an area enclosed in indigo, with a blood-red spot within its border. "And this was the prayer garden where Phaedrus and the others called down the rain." His fingertip shifted to point at the red dot within the garden, then indicated a dozen more scattered across the chapel. "These are nodes of abyssal magic. Together, they form a rather large sigil."

"Like the one on the mask's forehead?" asked Hector.

"Similar," Gideon replied. "Sister Georgiana is searching the archives for information but, based on how it affected Phaedrus and the others, it was a trap set to weaken a person spiritually, steal their resolve."

"So, if the fire didn't kill Brand, this sigil was supposed to?" Xandor asked.

"No, I don't think so," Jasper responded. "Sister Georgiana was very clear the sigil was demonic, and we should not, under any circumstances, connect the dots on my map."

Gideon added, "A sigil that size took a while to lay out and required something or someone to trigger it. Remember, Brand was trapped inside that image." He leaned back in his chair and steepled his fingers. "We suspect the sigil opens a portal to the abyss, which means there was something on the other side that wanted to use Brand to get through. To trade places."

"And the mage?" Hector asked.

"To be honest, I'm not convinced the mage had anything to do with it," Jasper answered.

"Why not?" Hector asked.

"For one thing, it's abyssal magic, and because getting blasted down the mountainside saved Brand's life."

"That's a bit far-fetched, don't you think?" asked Xandor.

"Hear me out," said Jasper. "All four of our mystery-mage's fire spells were aimed at or across the sigil, but the first two missed Brand. This one hit the rain shelter, and this one hit these trees along the cliff edge. Only the last two hit Brand — after he was inside the trap."

"Why would someone do that?" August wondered.

"How the hell else are you going to break a sixty-foot lizard out of demonic trap?" Dave snorted.

"How can you be so callous!" August reprimanded. "Lady Shayla has suffered too much already, and yet you joke about the attack against Brand as if it were nothing."

"Leave her out of this," Dave growled, eyeing the bard suspiciously. "Besides, death is a better alternative than what the person who drew that demon sigil planned for him."

"What about Phaedrus and the others?" asked Robert. "The sigil didn't seem to weaken them or me before the explosion — which was blood red, by the way. I mean, it blew me off my feet, but I didn't lose consciousness."

"The explosion seemed like a direct clash of divine and profane forces," Jasper replied. "All of you are lucky to be alive."

"Jasper, what's this?" August asked, pointing to a dark red stain within the sigil beside two orange dots.

"We don't know." Jasper met the gaze of each of his friends at the table. "All I can tell you is the magical residue was the same as the magic imbued in the vampire mask, and whoever used it was inside the sigil with Brand."

"Fuck," Dave said.

"How's that possible?" Hector demanded. "Lady D is locked up tighter than Fort Knox."

"Fort Knox?" asked August.

"You mentioned Sha'iry," Robert said, ignoring August's question. "Could one of them have defiled Sunrise Chapel to summon a demon?"

"I don't believe so," replied Gideon with a quick shake of his head. "Not in Ozera.

"You think a demon is more plausible than a person?" August asked.

"Gentlemen, the demon is already here," Jasper said, then covered his mouth as a huge yawn overtook him. "Hector brought her here when he brought that mask."

"Perhaps we're looking at this whole thing wrong," suggested Xandor. "We've assumed that this was an attack on Brand, but what if he wasn't the intended target? He could simply have been in the wrong place at the wrong time."

"How so?" Gideon asked.

Xandor gestured toward Jasper's map. "An elaborate trap, a magical attack against Brand, and evidence two spell casters may have been involved in destroying Sunrise Chapel less than a week after Aislinn's funeral while all of Damage, Inc. are gathered here seems conspicuous. And then there's me. I've known Aislinn and Brand since I was a child, and I've made some powerful enemies in Vologda and Michurinsk."

"Your point?" Hector asked.

"That trap could have been meant for any one of us, or none at all. It could have been meant for Phaedrus."

"Possible, but not likely," Gideon stated. "If the trap were meant for Père Phaedrus or one of you, the ideal time to attack would have been during the funeral."

Hector groaned and slumped in his chair. "Amigos, we aren't any closer to a suspect than we were this morning."

"What about Mi'dnirr?" Dave growled.

"Why would Mi'dnirr be involved?" Xandor demanded.

"Who is Mi'dnirr?" Robert asked.

"A monster," Xandor replied. "Tanjaran parents use his name to scare unruly children."

"He's the fucking dærganfae vampire that bit Aislinn while we were in Ruthaer," Dave grated.

"The whole mess in Ruthaer started when Mi'dnirr killed Evan Courtenay. We don't know why, but he kept Evan's minions from killing Aislinn." Hector's jaw clenched as he fought against the memory of the quarry.

"Aislinn thought Mi'dnirr wanted that dærganfae dagger we took from Ruthaer, and I doubt the bastard has given up looking for it," added Dave.

"Bloody hell," Xandor swore. "If you have a dærganfae relic, you can be sure they're here for it."

"I turned the dagger over to Brother Simon yesterday," Hector replied. "It's out of their reach now."

"The dærganfae will slaughter anyone in their path to reclaim what they believe is theirs," warned Xandor. "You need to get that dagger out of Ozera."

"Everyone, we're getting off topic," Jasper said. "Despite the improbability of it, the evidence points to the vampire mask and its ties to the abyss. We need to find the mage who was on the mountain."

"How do you propose we do that?" Hector asked.

"Keep looking." Jasper yawned again, setting off a chain reaction around the table. "This is fun and all," he said, "but if I don't get back to my cabin, I'm going to fall asleep in this chair. I told Teal I'd temporarily shrink Brand enough for them to set his larger wing bones and for us to help move him to his caves, assuming Mrs. Yves knows a way to reach them without flying."

"She does," August supplied. "Teal asked her about it when I escorted Lady Shayla up to see Brand this morning. Lady Shayla said that, if we can bring him down to her house, she'll show us a way into Brand's caverns."

Jasper nodded and rose from the table. "I need time to prepare, but I think I'll be ready by mid-afternoon. Hector, I'll come back for my pots and dishes tomorrow. Good-night everyone."

CHAPTER 32
BLOWING OFF STEAM
August 18, 4237 K.E.

6:30am

Hector and Dave found their way to the heart of the village in search of breakfast well before the sun topped the ridgeline east of Ozera. Despite the growing light and echo of voices from their kitchens, the doors of both inns and the community dining hall remained locked, and the windows dark.

Together, the two friends trailed up one street and down another until they reached a heavily wooded park. The shadows were thicker, but they kept walking, trying to burn off some of the dangerous mix of anger and adrenaline in their systems before they questioned the innkeepers about their guests.

"Last night, why didn't you tell them?" Dave asked.

"¿De qué estás hablando?"

"Don't pull that Espian shit on me. You know damn well what I'm talking about. Why didn't you tell Robert and the others that Lady D knows every move I make? I'm the reason Aislinn is dead."

"Because it isn't true," Hector replied.

"The hell it isn't. I told you I'm cursed," Dave growled. "They at least need to know that's how Lady D and Dodz got ahead of us. That's why I know he's here, now."

"Amigo, we can't change what happened. Jasper and Gideon *will* find a way to free you of her once and for all. As for Dodz, we'll burn his bridge when we get to it."

"And beat the living shit out of him," Dave added.

Hector bent and picked up a fallen limb roughly the same heft as his scimitar. He continued along the path, slashing at trees and shrubs along the way. Dave watched him for a while, expecting Phaedrus to appear and smite the Espian for harming the plants. You could never quite tell what the holy man would do next.

After a while, the urge to spar was too much for Dave, and he drew his sabre. Hector swung at a nearby tree trunk, and found his blow deftly caught and deflected. He backed away and eyed his tall friend.

Dave could see him gauging the level of danger reflected in his expression and gestured for him to come on.

With a miniscule nod, Hector drew his scimitar, stepping forward and to the left. With his empty left hand out from his body, he held his sword in his right thirty degrees above horizontal.

They circled, each focused on the other, allowing their peripheral vision to take in their surroundings. Dave attacked first, swiping at Hector's left upper arm. Rather than jump backward out of reach, Hector dropped below the swing, rolled forward, and aimed a blow at Dave's legs.

The lanky bowman leapt up and forward, neatly rolling over Hector's back, and landed behind the Espian, where he lashed out as he turned, catching Hector across the flank with the flat of his blade.

A grunt of pain escaped the shorter man. Dave grinned wickedly. "Point," he said.

Hector frowned. Counting points meant the loser had to buy breakfast. He circled again, the tip of his weapon steady between himself and Dave. As his right foot crossed in front of his left, he suddenly changed course and sprang at Dave, raining a flurry of blows at his retreating form.

Dave parried blow after blow, then caught Hector's weapon on the back swing with his own and hit the Espian on the side of the head with his elbow. "Two."

Hector ground his teeth and punched Dave in the gut. "Point," he growled as the air whooshed from Dave's lungs. The two staggered apart to catch their breath, then came together again, trading blows with increasing intensity.

Thirty minutes later, the pair approached the Humble Servant Inn, this time sweat soaked and sporting a number of aches and bruises. The door stood open, and they heard people inside having breakfast. Hector led the way in and looked around the room. Most of the tables were empty, but the inn's guests were drifting downstairs in ones and twos.

Choosing a table near the door where they could watch the room and the stairs, Hector signaled the serving girl.

"Will it just be the two of you?" she asked, setting out silverware and tankards filled with fresh spring water. Hector waited, expecting Dave to order wine despite Phaedrus' attempt to force sobriety on the archer, but his friend surprised him by downing the water in a single, long pull. The serving girl raised an eyebrow but said nothing as Dave handed her back the tankard to refill. She eyed Dave's chest and upper arms, covered only by the knots and whorls of his tattoos. The Gael dragon on his left shoulder and upper chest glared back at her. "The master and missus require shirts, sir."

Dave stared at the girl, but neither moved nor spoke.

She fidgeted and bit her lip. She glanced at Hector, who offered no help.

"We have Turkestani kahve this morning," she finally said, "in addition to our usual tea, milk and apple cider. Oh, I almost forgot. We just received a crate of oranges from peninsular Espia, if you'd like juice."

"Juice, please," Hector replied.

In short order, she returned with their juice and two plates piled high with potato casserole, sliced apples, and ham.

Hector picked at his breakfast for a few minutes, more intent on studying faces and listening to voices. "I've been trying to remember if there are any mages who might have a grudge against Brand," he finally said.

"Any brilliant conclusions?"

"Not really.

"My vote still goes to Dodz, with Mi'dnirr and the dærganfae a close second."

Silence hung between them, hemmed in by the murmur of voices and the clatter of dishes from other tables.

"You think it was Count Dodz who broke into our cabin?" Hector asked.

Dave looked up from his breakfast, and his expression sent a chill through Hector. "Yes. We blazed a trail even that blind lighthouse keeper could have followed between Ruthaer and here."

"Watch the room. If you see Dodz, do not make a move without me."

"What are you going to do?"

"Check the inn's registry," Hector answered.

"If Dodz is here, he sure as hell wouldn't use his real name, Hector."

The bounty hunter shrugged. "Dodz probably isn't his real name, either. I just want to see if there are any names that sound Rhodinan or Detchian."

Dave rolled his eyes. "Whatever. Don't make me have to break you out of jail again."

Hector grinned. "You're the one who got arrested in Ruthaer."

A minute later, Dave heard a woman's raised voice in the lobby. Shaking his head, he dropped several coins on the table and went to see just how much trouble Hector was in now. He strode into the lobby and found the bounty hunter backed into a corner, arms raised to fend off the blows of a heavyset matron wielding a broom.

"¡Señora, por favor!" Hector exclaimed.

The woman swung the broom at his head, only to have its arc halted abruptly. She turned and was greeted by the open maw of a Gaelic dragon tattoo. Whatever she might have said died in a strangled gasp. She released the broom and backed away from the two men toward the front door so she could see them both at once.

Hector lowered his arms and met the bowman's glare. With a rueful grin, he turned back to the woman. "Señora, I beg your pardon. I was not trying to steal from you, I swear. I only wanted to look at the registration book."

"You've no business behind our desk!" the woman fumed.

"I'm looking for a man called Dodz. He's Rhodinan, average height, blonde hair, and light blue eyes. He may have been involved in starting the fire."

Her anger drained away. "My Juan is in the hospital, smoke sick, with burns up both arms." Her gaze sharpened and met each of their eyes in turn. "Who are the two of you, to be searching through my books?"

"Hector de los Santos, Señora," the bounty hunter replied with a bow. "This is Dave Blood. We're working with Lord Vaughn to catch the culprit or culprits. This man, Dodz, is one of our suspects. Please, has anyone by that name or description been here?"

The woman shook her head. "No. Not recently."

Hector's shoulders sagged.

"Wait. There was a man with pale eyes, like ice in winter, but he had dark hair. He only stayed one night, before the fire."

"What name did he give?"

"Luc Ardit. He sounded Francescan to me."

"May I see?"

The woman raised an eyebrow. "Now you ask? Where were your manners a few minutes ago?"

Dave gave an amused chuff.

The woman shook her head in exasperation and went behind the desk to retrieve the registry. Flipping quickly through the pages, she found the one she was looking for and pointed. Hector and Dave stared down at the name, then shared an uncertain glance.

"May I copy this?" When the innkeeper nodded, Hector dug out a thin piece of tracing paper and a stick of coal, sharpened to a fine point, from one of the numerous pouches on his belt. He laid it over the book and meticulously copied the name and handwriting underneath. Thanking the woman, he led Dave out into the street.

"I'm going to talk to the owner at the Oak Grove Inn. You head over to the hospital and visit Hummingbird."

Dave heaved a sigh. "Let's switch. You go see the girl, and I'll talk to the innkeeper."

"Works for me, but that means you give our report to Lord Vaughn while you're there."

The archer swore long and hard.

"Dave. Mi amigo. Go visit Hummingbird. She needs you."

"Dammit Hector, she needs to go find someone else to follow around. Sticking with us — especially me — will earn her a quick trip to dead."

"If you want her gone, grow a pair and tell her yourself. Personally, I like having her around."

"Bastard," Dave cursed.

Hector turned to his friend and gripped his shoulder. "Go. After what she's been through, she deserves that much."

CHAPTER 33
HUMMINGBIRD

August 18, 4237 K.E.

10:22am

Thirty-three years ago, when Phaedrus first arrived with his pilgrims, his mission had not been to convert the local clans, but instead to establish a haven of peace and healing. He approached the leader of the Alewen clan and gained permission to settle along the slopes of Lumikivi Mountain, provided its sacred cliffs and healing springs remained accessible to all.

With its serene landscape as a backdrop to Phaedrus' vision, Ozera grew from a tiny enclave into one of the finest places of healing throughout Parlatheas — sought out by both peasants and nobility. Over the years, the hospital had grown as well. It was an irregularly shaped stone building with slate covered hip roofs. Its numerous wings embraced a series of small courtyard gardens filled year around with flowering plants fed by fountains, tiny ponds, or narrow streams of clear mountain water.

In one of those courtyards, Hummingbird sat on a sunlit patch of grass near a flowerbed bursting with color, watching butterflies flit from blossom to blossom. She was tiny, with a childlike appearance that belied her age. Her short-cropped crimson hair stuck out in unruly spikes over her pointed ears. Red whorls and white dots across her forehead and cheeks marked her as a member of the Vaimurahvas — a tribe of empathic elves from the distant continent of Altaira. Like all patients, she wore a simple cotton tunic and pants, though the colors didn't match, and the overall affect made her look like an extension of the flowerbed.

Dave stood in the shadow of a doorway, watching his student. She never spoke, which suited him fine. He'd thought she was mute until that monster attacked them in the quarry at Ruthaer. Deep down inside, it bothered him that a single cry of pain was the only sound he'd ever heard her make.

He felt sorry for the kid. She'd been through hell. Hummingbird's people were semi-nomadic, moving with the seasons and their food sources, and were easily overrun by Flainnian mercenaries. As far as he knew, she was the only member of her village, possibly the entire tribe, to survive the attack.

The first time he saw her, she was cowering on an auction block, beaten and broken by her captors. Hector had a soft spot for elves in general, and had refused to leave the girl, so they pooled together their money — coins they couldn't afford to spend — and freed her. Dave still didn't understand why, of everyone in the world, Hummingbird had singled *him* out to teach her to fight. Either Hector or Aislinn would have been a better choice.

Dave thought of slipping away, but the girl turned and looked right at him. He suspected that she'd known he was there all along. Hummingbird gave Dave a half smile and motioned for him to join her in the sun. He hesitated, but knew Hector was right about him needing to talk to her. She was due to get out of the hospital, and he had no idea whether anyone told her about Aislinn.

Hummingbird watched him approach, her expression neutral. She took in the dark shadows underscoring his red-rimmed eyes, and how one hand hovered close to the belt pouch containing his flask. Her eyes skimmed over the stark white scars on his chest and the base of his neck. The sunlight made them glow against the black tattoo ink. Finally, her gaze settled on the ruby brooch resting in the hollow below his throat on a gold oak-leaf chain.

Dave crouched beside her. In silence, he studied her posture and expression, looking for telltale signs of lingering pain or weakness. He realized she was probably better rested than him or Hector. Then he noticed a wide strip of cloth bound around her left wrist where the Flainnian slavers had tattooed a black lotus flower, marking her as a low caste pornai.

Her eyes followed his, and she hid her wrist under her right hand. For several long minutes, she watched the activity in the flowerbed, effectively ignoring Dave. Finally, her eyes returned to his, and the shadows lurking in their whiskey-colored depths. After a few moments, her hands began to move in the precise forms of her people's silent language. "I'm fine," she signed.

"Maybe," Dave replied, also using elf signs. "You had a close call. What happened to your wrist?"

"Nothing," she signed.

"Why is it bandaged?"

She shrugged. "I don't want to see the mark of my shame anymore. This was all they had to cover it."

"You have nothing to be ashamed of," he said. "Still, if I'd known you wanted it gone when we were in Orleans, I would have taken you to the shop I use. Jacques has a girl that specializes in cover-ups. Next best thing is bracers or wrist sheaths."

"I didn't know people in this land knew what it meant when we were in Orleans." The girl looked around the courtyard, then asked, "How did I get to Ozera?"

"Tasunke and a dragon." He gave a crooked grin at the look on her face, but it soon faded. "After we got you out of the tunnels, Hector and I did what we could to patch you up." In his mind's eye, he saw her convulsing on the bare granite of the quarry floor, then the horrible stillness. "It didn't go well. Brand was coming for Aislinn. Tallinn and that winged horse of his carried you and Aislinn away from Ruthaer to meet him somewhere safer. They brought you both here." He fought the memory's pain, keeping his voice as neutral as possible despite the piercing ache within.

"How did we get past the spider?"

"Fire arrow. Blasted the shit out of that monster and caved in part of the tunnel. It's dead and buried."

"You can't kill what isn't real."

"What are you talking about? Of course, it was real." He pointed to the scar he knew lay just below her collarbone. "You and I have the scars to prove it."

The girl huffed an exasperated sounding sigh and shook her head. "I mean it wasn't really a giant bug. It was something else, something not alive." Her hands stopped moving, and her eyes dropped.

Dave struggled against the chasm yawning in his heart, all too aware that Hummingbird could sense his rage and despair. "Aislinn..." his voice cracked, and he stopped. For several long minutes he couldn't speak, only suck in one ragged breath after another.

"I know," Hummingbird signed. "Shayla has come to see me almost every day. She asked me to stay with her."

"That's good. She shouldn't be alone, and it will be safer for you."

"What about Aislinn's brother? Isn't he with their mother?"

Dave reached for his flask, thought better of it, and scratched at his beard. "I don't know that we'll see Eidan again. Especially now."

"He must come back," Hummingbird signed. "His mother is worried about him."

Dave looked around the courtyard, searching the shadows for eavesdroppers. Finding none, he leaned toward Hummingbird.

"What I'm about to tell you is a secret," he murmured. "If you stay with Shayla, you'll probably learn it anyway, but don't tell anyone. Promise?"

Wide-eyed, she nodded.

He leaned closer to whisper in her ear. "Brand *is* Eidan." When he sat back, her mouth was open in an 'O' of surprise.

"What happened on the mountaintop?" Hummingbird signed. "Shayla didn't come to see me yesterday, and the woman who brought my breakfast said there was a terrible fire. People were hurt."

Dave nodded. "Someone attacked Brand and destroyed Sunrise Chapel. He's — I don't know if he's going to survive."

"The eagle from Ruthaer," she signed. "It fought a dragon in the Dreaming Grounds."

"That was a nightmare, Hummingbird. It wasn't real."

"Someone did attack Brand. I saw it. Why not the eagle?"

"Because that eagle was Mi'dnirr," said Dave, "and he was too small to be any danger to Brand."

Hummingbird shook her head. "The eagle grew each time it swallowed a piece of Brand. It was huge."

"If Mi'dnirr could change his size like that, he would have destroyed Ruthaer and Evan Courtenay," Dave growled. "Hector and I talked things over. We think it was either Dodz or dærganfae who attacked Brand."

"We're going to look for them, then?" she signed. "The healers said I can leave when I'm ready."

"Hummingbird, about that..."

She narrowed her eyes and her spine stiffened. "I am not done learning, and *you* are the one to teach me."

He stood and glowered down at her. "Don't you get it? You can't stay with me. You'll get killed, or worse," Dave said, unconsciously touching the scars along his neck. "Stay with Shayla. Find something safe to do with your life. Barring that, find someone else to teach you to fight."

She flinched at the tone of his voice but held firm, staring up into his dark eyes. He knew she felt the torment surrounding his heart, as well as how much he cared. What she didn't understand was that he would eventually get her killed.

"There is no one else," she signed.

Dave wanted to turn his back on her. He wanted to get away from this place — from her — as fast as he could. Instead, he felt trapped by her aquamarine eyes and the shadows of pain and terror that mirrored his own. "Why?"

"Because you are the best choice."

CHAPTER 34
THEFT IN THE AERARIUM

August 18, 4237 K.E.

10:30am

A boy skidded to a stop scant inches from Hector's feet outside the Oak Grove Inn. "¡Señor Santos, ven pronto! ¡Ellos te necesitan ahora mismo!"

"¿Qué pasó, muchacho?"

The little boy shrugged and darted away toward Grove Cathedral at the center of the village with Hector trailing in his wake. Rather than the sanctuary, however, the boy led him across the street to a two-story building with narrow grisaille windows that served as Ozera's archive and library. It also housed items deemed too dangerous to be out in the world.

Xandor rounded the building's corner, studying the ground as he walked. There was a coiled tension in his stance, like a cat ready to pounce.

Cold dread swept through Hector. There could only be one reason they would be summoned to this building, and it made the destruction of Sunrise Chapel, as well as the attack on Brand, that much more sinister.

Hector and Xandor followed the boy through the heavy wooden door and into a small lobby. A wide desk curved in front of them, and arched openings offered views of book-lined shelves on either side. The librarian, a young acolyte in parchment-colored robes, stood behind the desk. The wall behind him held two nondescript closed doors, with floor-to-ceiling shelves between them.

The acolyte glanced down at the boy. "Gracias, Elisio. Back to your studies, now." After a short bow, the boy scampered through the arch on the right.

They waited while the librarian listened to the boy's fading footsteps. He finally turned back to them, a grim expression descending over him. "Good morning, gentlemen, thank you for coming so quickly."

"What happened?" Hector asked.

"Sister Georgiana will explain everything."

"How is Brother Simon?" Hector asked.

"Still recovering in the hospital, along with El Patrón and the others. Most of them are still unconscious," the young cleric replied. "Follow me, please." He motioned them to join him behind the desk, then unlocked the door in the left-hand corner. Beyond lay a short, brightly lit passage ending in a stairwell spiraling downward. At its bottom, they found themselves in a scriptorium. Orderly rows of desks filled the room, and scribes were hard at work copying tomes, overseen by a short, round cleric. Their guide gave the elder cleric a polite bow. "Armarius Lorena, these are the men Sister Georgiana requested."

"Thank you, Disculpi Humberto. Please return to your duties." The scriptorium director led Hector and Xandor to a heavy wooden door bound in black iron in a shadowy corner at the end of the hall. "The Aerarium has very limited access. Anything you see or hear within must be kept in strict confidence unless Patrón Phaedrus, Sister Georgiana, or Brother Simon give you permission to speak of it to others. Do I have your word to abide by these rules?" She held out a palm-sized wheel-cross made of pale wood inlaid with gold and silver filigree in the flat of her hand.

Xandor placed his right hand atop the holy symbol, his larger hand completely covering that of the Armarius. "I will keep the secrets of the Aerarium," he promised. An amethyst glow enveloped their hands, sealing the ranger's promise.

Armarius Lorena turned to Hector, but he kept his hands at his sides. "I cannot let you pass if you won't vow to keep the secrets within."

"I won't make a blind promise," he said. "If I learn things that directly affect my team, I will not keep it hidden."

"Place your hand upon the wheel-cross and make what vow you can in good conscience keep. If the Eternal Father deems it acceptable, I will let you pass."

Hector eyed the symbol in her hand. He flicked a glance at the cleric and Xandor before reaching up with his left hand and slipping a silver necklace out from under his collar. He grasped the gold and silver crucifix dangling there and laid his right hand over the cleric's. "I will not speak of things I learn within the Aerarium unless they directly pertain to members of my team, their wellbeing, or our ability to capture those involved in the attack on Brand and Sunrise Chapel." Silently, he added, '*Espíritu Santo, ayúdame a proteger a mi familia y nuestro hogar.*' The fine hairs on his nape stood on end as a brilliant web of gold and amethyst light encased his hands and spread up to his elbows.

Surprised wonder filled Sister Lenora's face.

After the light faded, Hector dropped his crucifix back inside his shirt and gestured toward the iron-bound door. "Sister?"

The Armarius nodded and withdrew a key from the folds of her robe. "I must lock this door behind you. Sister Georgiana will meet you inside and let you out again afterward."

Hector and Xandor nodded, and the cleric unlocked the door. They stepped into the small room and stared in wide eyed silence. Behind them, the door latch clicked, and the lock slid into place.

The room was empty. No desks or shelves, no items awaiting identification or destruction, and no other door: just four blank walls, the door they came through, and the tall, lean figure of Roger Vaughn. Hector stood in shocked silence for a moment. "Lord Vaughn, where is everything?"

"Not here, obviously," the nobleman replied.

"It can't be stolen," Xandor said. A faint hint of his Alashalian accent slipped into his words. "Nobody steals furniture."

Roger turned his attention to Hector's companion. "Xandor, I don't believe we've met; however, your reputation proceeds you."

"As does yours, Earl Wolverton."

Hector opened his mouth to tell Lord Vaughn what Jasper discovered in Sunrise Chapel, but a portion of the rear wall silently pivoted into the room, revealing Sister Georgiana on a stone balcony holding a glowing lantern. Looking worn and bleary eyed in the pale light, the middle-aged priest's disheveled appearance set the bounty hunter on edge.

She led them down a dark, spiral stair that ended at a work area with several large tables. Their guide hurried them down another stair to the main floor of the Aerarium, where she set aside her lantern.

Above them, stalactites encrusted with glowing crystals illuminated row after row of shelves filled with various sized tomes and other items. Intermixed among them were iron and glass cases. Some held what appeared to be mundane objects while others displayed weapons or more exotic items. In one hung a pair of leather pants made from a skinned corpse — including its feet and blackened toenails — and a matching shirt, with the victim's ribs sewn on the outside and scored with arcane symbols. Hector felt the faint brush of compulsion to open the case and don the disgusting garments, then the protective wards on the case flared, driving away the unwelcome desire.

In between the rows of shelving, thick bars of cold iron, silver, or other, more rare metals blocked the entrances to alcoves and small side rooms, each marked with Korellan numerals. Sister Georgiana ushered them down a broad aisle to the far side of the cavern where she entered a room whose enchanted silver gate stood wide open. A single worktable bearing a pair of open crates — one small, one large — stood in the room's center, amid a haphazard jumble of damaged books, scroll cases, and piles of straw. To Hector, it looked as though someone trashed the room in a fit of rage.

"What happened, Georgiana?" Roger asked.

"Vandalism and thievery. When I came in this morning, I found this," she said, waving a hand at the destruction. "The Aerarium is sealed, warded against all magics. No one should have been able to set foot in this place! Only four of us know the secret to gaining entrance, yet this is what I find!"

Hector crossed his arms and leaned against the doorframe while Roger and Xandor searched the debris for the crate lids. "We're not deputies, Sister, and we aren't mages. Why did you summon us?"

"Because of what was stolen," the priestess replied.

"Georgiana! This is labeled Ruthaer!" Roger pointed an accusing finger at a wood panel sprouting silver nails around its perimeter.

"Ruthaer?" Hector said, alarmed. "What was in it?"

"Hector," Xandor said, lifting the second lid from its hiding place under the table. "Look at this."

Taking his eyes from the distraught priestess, Hector crossed the small room and knelt beside the ranger. A series of crude drawings filled the space beneath a meticulously written label. One might have been a tree with vertical slashes on its trunk. Another was three ovals stacked one above the other, each smaller than the one below. The last was a deep 'V' with short slashes over the top of each leg and a diamond at the base. "What does it mean?"

"It's a message... from Aislinn," Xandor said.

"Amigo, that is not funny."

"Do I look like I'm joking?" Xandor asked. He pointed and said, "You see these symbols? Iron Tower scouts use them to leave messages for Company Commanders when troops are on the move."

"Aislinn wasn't Iron Tower," Hector replied.

"No, but Edge was, and she was his apprentice," Xandor said.

"That doesn't explain why you think the message is from a dead woman," Roger said.

The ranger turned his mismatched eyes to the nobleman. "The trail signs the Iron Tower uses are based on older symbols from the Korellan Empire. Most rangers and woodsmen across Parlatheas know and use them, regardless of nationality." He appraised each of the people surrounding him in turn. "What I'm about to tell you can't leave this room," he finally said. When they each nodded in agreement, he pointed to the V-shaped sigil. "That is a dragon-rider. Aislinn and Edge came up with it as her personal sigil for sending messages to the ranger corps — a way for command to verify the message was really from her. Every ranger who works for the Tower has one."

"So what's this message say?" Hector asked.

"It says Aislinn is trapped and in danger. That she needs help," Xandor said. "But it also means that, somehow, she knew I would be here."

Hector rose and leaned heavily on the table. "Madre de Dios," he whispered. "¿Que sigue?"

Shaking his head, Xandor turned to the priestess. "Sister Georgiana, what was in these crates?"

"This one held the Orbuculum from Ruthaer, the ivory dagger Señor Santos turned over, and a few other things we took in this past week," she answered, pointing to the larger of the two crates. "The smaller crate held the vampire mask."

Roger leaned across the table, his dark eyes intense. "Tell me you have a way to track the items," he demanded.

"I take it you haven't found the arcaloxós or the thief here in the Aerarium?" Hector asked.

"I wouldn't have sent for you if we had captured the intruder. We found the arcaloxós; however, it was empty."

Hector knelt and searched through the litter under and around the table. "When did it happen?"

"Our best guess is sometime between midnight the night of the fire and vespers this morning. Everyone was too busy to come here yesterday."

Xandor crossed his arms and narrowed his eyes at the bounty hunter. "You're taking this awfully well, Hector, considering how agitated you and Dave were last night."

Hector stood and handed the ranger a bone-colored fragment with a blood red line curving over its surfaces. "The mask wasn't stolen," Hector said softly.

"What did you say?" Sister Georgiana asked, her pale face gaining color.

"The mask wasn't stolen," Hector repeated, standing straighter.

"What is this?" Xandor asked. "It feels like some kind of pottery."

"The box I gave Hermano Simon contained a plaster copy of the mask. I couldn't risk anyone coming into contact with the real one."

"A fake!" Roger barked. "Hector, you agreed to turn it over to the church. You gave me your word it was taken care of."

"The mask is safely hidden, señor."

"Hector, what if the person who broke into your house found it?" Xandor asked. "You took a huge risk."

The bounty hunter backed away from the table. His shoulders drew back, and his chest puffed out as he glared at his accusers. "I'm the only person who knows where it is, and that's the way it's going to stay until I know for certain it can be destroyed. The fact that someone came in here and tried to steal it is all the proof I need that I made the right choice."

Sister Georgiana opened her mouth and then shut it as she took in what Hector said. The bounty hunter's paranoia had saved them from disaster.

"Xandor, how can you possibly believe that message is from Aislinn?" asked Hector.

"You don't believe it's from her?"

Hector shook his head. "How could it be? She died two weeks ago. You were here when the resurrection ritual failed and for her funeral. ¡Por amor de Dios! Jasper told me Brand bought some kind of Kemetan preservation oils and a diamond casket so he could keep her in his hoard, as though this is a fairytale! How sure are *you* that only members of the Iron Tower know these personal symbols? What if this thief managed to learn hers?"

Xandor drew a sharp breath and seemed to grow taller as his spine stiffened. "Our personal sigils are used to validate messages and keep the troops following us safe. Every ranger and officer takes an oath to keep them in the corps. "

"Yet you stood here and gave us her personal sign. How many other rangers or officers do you think have shared theirs with family or friends? Based on the information you just gave us, I know to be on the lookout for other symbols.

With what I know about Aislinn's sign and you, I might even recognize your symbol."

"Why?"

"To throw suspicion off the thief."

"No. Why aren't you willing to believe it's from her?"

The fire seemed to drain out of the Espian, and his shoulders sagged. "Because that would mean she's a ghost haunting Ozera and chose not to return to us."

"But what if she couldn't return before? What if there's hope she could be restored now?" Xandor asked.

"Amigo, if I allow myself to hope, it will be like losing her all over again when it proves false. You hope if you want, but don't you dare mention this to Dave — or her mother.

"Sister," Hector continued, "show me where you enter this place."

The priestess looked appalled. "I can't show you the secrets of the church! The location of the entrance is only for the initiated."

"Sister Georgiana," Hector said with an exasperated sigh, "look around you. Someone has already stolen church secrets. I'm not asking you to take me on a guided tour of secret passages. I just want you to show me the actual door that you come through. Maybe, between the four of us, we can figure out how your mystery visitor got inside."

"It's not as simple as picking the lock," Sister Georgiana replied. "This place is guarded."

"And yet, a thief came and went undetected," Roger pointed out.

The cleric's face twisted in a moue of displeasure at being contradicted. "Follow me," she snipped, then led them to the end of the broad aisle.

Hector moved ahead, fighting his mind's desire to analyze and pick apart the message in the records room.

Sister Georgiana climbed a wide set of stairs to a balcony and stopped several feet away from a heavy oak door set in the cavern wall. Hector strode forward, but the priestess hauled him back sharply. Like a guillotine, a black curtain of magic dropped in front of Hector and barred the door. Instantly, the three men were beset by feelings of helplessness, forcing them to retreat.   Sister Georgiana seemed unaffected.

After they took several steps backward, the black curtain vanished. "Like I said, the way is guarded."

"Then how did the thief get in?" Hector asked, flummoxed.

Sister Georgiana thought for a moment and said, "There may be a way. I watched this earlier and saw nothing, but maybe you'll see something I missed." Bowing her head, she prayed, "Pater Aeternum, ostende nobis."

The lights from the stalactites winked out, and the cavern became pitch black. The darkness was absolute until a faint blue glow illuminated the door as it opened.

Limned with a ghostly light, the image of Brother Simon stepped into the Aerarium holding a small crystal in his hand.

"Brother Simon," a faraway voice said. From a nearby alcove, the glow of another crystal marked someone else's approach. The crystal light drew closer, revealing the ghostly image of Disculpi Humberto, the acolyte manning the library's front desk. Behind him, the transparent images of Jasper and Gideon hurried to keep up.

"We really need access to more tomes on demonology," Jasper said, then stifled a yawn. "I'm certain one of them holds the key to deciphering that sigil."

"I've sent requests for information and help to abbeys in Essen, Francesca, and Zaragoza, but it will take time to receive word back from them. In the meantime, I've given you everything that's considered safe to read," the elderly priest replied.

"But none of what you gave us is helpful," Jasper said, clearly frustrated.

"I'm not willing to risk your sanity or your soul to let you read the others," Simon said with a tone of finality.

"Jasper," Gideon said, "let it go."

"Gideon, the answer is down here," Jasper said, looking around at the array of shelves and alcoves. "Somewhere."

"We may never know what that sigil means, mon ami," Gideon said. "Hector may be forced to accept the fact that the

mask cannot be destroyed and trust the Church to keep it secure."

"Anything made can be destroyed. It's a matter of finding the correct method," the mage replied. "As for Hector, you clearly don't know him that well. Trust is not in his vocabulary."

At this, Hector couldn't help but smile as he followed the ghostly images back down the aisle.

"On the contrary, I think he exhibits a great deal of trust in Dave — and in you."

"Gentlemen, it's late. Let me show you out," Brother Simon said, leading them to the far side of the cavern.

"That's it," Sister Georgiana said as the lights came back on. "He led Humberto, Gideon, and Jasper outside and closed the Aerarium about an hour before the fire erupted. No one else was here."

"What's on the other side of the door?" Xandor asked.

"An antechamber secured by a cold iron and silver barred gate. There are only two keys: one held by Phaedrus, the other shared by Brother Simon and me."

"Let's watch it again, if we can," Hector said.

Sister Georgiana nodded and repeated her earlier prayer. The lights went out and Brother Simon's image reappeared at the door.

"So you have to drop the ward to enter," Hector said.

"Yes. Currently, only four of us can dispel it," Sister Georgiana replied.

"Could someone follow you?"

"I don't see how. They'd have to be right behind us, step for step the whole way."

Hector studied the images. When they started walking back down the aisle, he pointed. "What's that?"

They stared at the blurry, distorted shadow stalking the four images. It had a human form, but something seemed to be masking it.

"Is that another person?" Sister Georgiana asked.

"Start it over again, por favor," said Hector.

Brother Simon's image flickered to life at the doorway one more time. Behind him, a distorted shadow followed on his heels. It raised an appendage as if it meant to strike, but Humberto's appearance stopped it.

"That thing was going to kill Simon!" Sister Georgiana exclaimed.

"Can you take us through the door? I want to see this antechamber," Hector said.

Going through the motions as if in a daze, Sister Georgiana raised her arms to dispel the ward. She pulled the door open and stepped into a weirdly glowing cave beyond.

Hector took out his bone tube and popped off the end cap. The beam of light played out across slick, wet rock formations and glimmered on the silver gate.

Xandor picked his way forward and knelt on the sandy floor. He scanned the room, noting each rock and impression in the sand. "Someone in boots stood before the door to the Aerarium and skirted the perimeter of the room," he announced. He followed the trail to the bars covering the alcove's entrance. "Sister Georgiana, who is the fourth person who knows how to get into the Aerarium?"

"Sister Inez. The initiates who work here with us come in the way I brought you."

"What about Aislinn? Did she know how to find the Aerarium entrance?" Xandor asked.

The senior cleric met the ranger's intense gaze, but she didn't respond. To Hector, she appeared startled by the question — or perhaps it was the color of the ranger's eyes: one snow-cloud grey, and one spring green.

"Sister Georgiana?" Xandor prodded.

The cleric shook herself. "Aislinn was... precocious. Phaedrus caught her in the catacombs once a few years after her family moved here, but she wasn't anywhere near the Aerarium entrance. That's when he arranged for her to train with Edge Garrett. We had to give her something to do."

Excitement lit Xandor's face. "Hector, she knew how to find this place. I guarantee it." He pointed to a stack of stones outside the gate. "Look familiar? *Now* are you willing to at least entertain the idea that the message is from her?"

Hector studied the stones, remembering a similar stack in Shayla's front parlor. The topmost stone bore Aislinn's dragon-rider sigil. Not sure what to make of them, he said nothing. He walked back inside the Aerarium and stared at the crystals covering the stalactites.

Roger followed his gaze. "What is it?"

"Let's go back."

After Sister Georgiana resealed the door, the four walked back into the room with the crates. Hector looked around and asked, "Did the crystals see anything happen here?"

"No, the rooms and alcoves are hidden from view."

"Well, where did these crates come from? Did the thief have to carry them in here?" Hector asked.

"They were already here, locked behind the gate," Sister Georgiana said, gesturing toward the barred door that now stood open.

Stepping back out into the aisle, Hector turned a full circle as he looked around. "How did the thief get out?"

Sister Georgiana joined him, staring intently at every shadow. "Do you think the thief's still here?"

"If it had been me," Roger said, "I would have escaped out the back door."

"How?" Hector asked.

"It's the only way out not blocked by the black veil."

"But it has other protections. Besides, it can only be opened from..." Sister Georgiana started.

All four ran back to the spiral stairs and stopped. "Pater Aeternum, ostende nobis," Sister Georgiana chanted. Like before, the lights went out, but this time there was no ghost light — just an impenetrable darkness.

Frustrated, Hector opened his mouth to tell the priestess to kill the spell. Before he could utter a word, light from a hand-held crystal flared, revealing a cold, harsh face partially obscured by the collar of a cape. Just as quickly, it vanished as the image dashed up the stairs.

"Who was that?" Xandor asked.

"Count Dodz," Hector replied.

"How did he find his way down here?" asked Xandor.

"I don't know, but that's a lot easier to believe than Aislinn's ghost wandering around leaving messages."

"Dodz has the Orbuculum and its whippoorwill stand," Roger said. "Ozera is in danger. Georgiana, what else is missing?"

"A pair of spectacles we use to identify spells and curses, and the ivory dagger Hector gave us from Ruthaer. There may be other things, but I have to finish sorting out the mess in the records room and do an inventory to be certain."

"Send me a list as soon as you know," Roger said.

"What are you going to do?" Georgiana asked.

"Find Dodz," Hector replied. "Hopefully, he hasn't already fled for parts unknown."

"Oh, he's not going anywhere," Sister Georgiana stated. She smiled at the expressions on the three men's faces. "Did you really think the black veil and an oath were the only protections in place for the Aerarium? This thief will soon find he can't pass beyond the borders of Ozera. Each day he fails to return what he stole and seek forgiveness, he will find it harder to hide his sins."

Before he could stop himself, Hector glanced at his hand, thankful that his thumb remained its natural color. "What's going to happen to him?"

Sister Georgian's smile grew wider. "I can't say for certain. Our Patrón has a rather whimsical sense of humor, and the punishment always fits the crime. I wouldn't be surprised if the word 'thief' appeared in bright bold letters across the miscreant's forehead. He may find himself too clumsy to sneak or steal. Then again, he may feel compelled to confess his crimes to every person he meets."

CHAPTER 35
DÆRGANFAE

August 18, 4237 K.E.

12:03pm

Xandor fell into step beside Hector as he stalked out of the library, his dark eyes searching the alleys and side streets for signs of Dodz. The ranger thought about their conversation over supper the previous evening. Dave had been right: it was Dodz who broke into Hector's home, looking for the mask. Xandor broke the silence. "We should talk with the constable."

"Let Lord Vaughn do it. Right now, I want to talk to the people most likely to have seen Dodz." He pushed through the crowd and stepped up onto The Humble Servant's porch. A half-dozen tables filled one end under a vine covered arbor, but only one was occupied.

The ranger paused midstep, eyes locked on the dark-haired diner in the farthest corner. When the figure blinked and turned his attention to a passerby, Xandor shivered, as if he'd just come out of icy water, and hurried inside after the Espian. "Hector, this is Ozera. Don't do anything rash. We have to operate under the assumption Dodz intends to use the things he stole."

"All the more reason to find him quickly. We have a couple of hours before Jasper wants us at the clearing to help move Brand, and I want to make the most of them."

Out of the corner of his eye, Xandor watched the lone diner leave the small sidewalk table and ghost his way up the street. He seemed to glide through the crowd as easily as a trout swimming upstream.

Fighting the urge to hunt the fae, he murmured, "Hector, we have another problem." The barkeep placed a pair of mugs in front of them, collected their coins, and walked away.

"What kind of problem?" Hector lifted his mug and took a long pull from the stout ale.

"Did you see the dark-haired male at the table outside?"

"The elf with the eye-patch? Yeah, what of it?"

"He's dærganfae."

"Are you sure?" Hector asked, glancing over Xandor's shoulder at the crowded street. "He looked like an elf to me. There are probably a score in Ozera on any given day. What makes him different?"

Xandor quirked an eyebrow. "Skin the color of day-old milk, for one thing, and jet-black hair. Didn't you see his eye — it was solid quicksilver."

Hector shook his head.

"I told you last night there'd be trouble."

Hector pursed his lips and stared at the ranger a moment. "First Aislinn and Dave, now you. Until Ruthaer, I'd never heard of them. What is everyone's problem with these dærganfae?"

"From the time we can walk, clan children are taught to avoid them and the Haunted Hills. Every story I know about dærganfae is rife with children who disappear or adults who venture too close to their land and are found dead, if they're found at all. Some say those who vanish are fed to Mi'dnirr. Aislinn never warned you about them?"

Hector cast a side-eyed glance at the ranger and took a swallow of ale. "Should she have?"

The ranger shrugged and turned his own mug in a slow circle. "How much did she tell you about Edge?"

"Very little. Just that he was killed before we met her. I didn't press for details since it seemed like a sore subject."

"He's a legend in the Iron Tower's ranger corps. A hero from the Plague Wars. He visited our village at least once a year, carrying news and patrolling the borders. From the time I could understand the stories the scops told and realized that they were about *him*, he was my hero. I was ten summers the first time he brought Aislinn with him to visit our village."

Hector crossed his arms and waited for the ranger to get to his point.

"I was almost fifteen when Edge and Aislinn passed through our village the last time, searching for the rangers, Fox and Nathair. They'd stopped by early that spring, headed for a Clan Garrett village near the border that was having trouble. The Tower received word that they never arrived. Edge said they would be back to let us know what was happening within a month. A month came and went, then two.

"The clan elders sent word east to Carolingias. Another ranger came back with the messenger, along with a score of soldiers. They followed Edge's trail west and were gone less than two weeks. That Clan Garrett village I mentioned? Everyone was gone — dead or missing. Edge, Aislinn, and Brand were gone, too. It was the dærganfae who killed Edge.

"It wasn't too much longer afterwards that my gramma sent me off to join the Iron Tower. I didn't find out until a lot later that Aislinn had been rescued from some kind of prison."

Hector downed the last of his drink and nodded. "That's where we found her. I heard you and Jasper ran into one of the Seldaehne up north."

"We did, and knowing that those monsters were working for the dærganfae makes the fae even scarier than my da's stories ever did." His expression turned cold and his voice hard. "You can bet there are more dærganfae around here, and they're up to no good."

Hector stared at Xandor, fleeting surprise quickly replaced by a scowl. "People in Rowanoake say the same about Espians, amigo. That doesn't make it true."

Xandor blinked, took a deep breath, and held it for a count of ten before exhaling sharply. "Sorry, I just don't know anyone who's had a positive experience with them. Trust me. Whatever you might prefer to think, they aren't friendly, and they can't be reasoned with."

CHAPTER 36
LET WOUNDED DRAGONS SLEEP

August 18, 4237 K.E.

4:00pm

Hummingbird stared at Brand in amazement. There was no doubt he was the dragon from her dream two mornings past. Although she'd heard Brand's name mentioned during the few weeks she'd been in Ozera after arriving on the continent of Parlatheas, she hadn't seen him. The idea that this creature could transform itself into an elf astounded her.

Before the huge skeleton in the cave in Ruthaer, she'd never imagined anything like a dragon even existed. Her people's myths and legends contained nothing this fantastic. Although Dave had told her, she hadn't been able to believe a dragon lived in Ozera.

Brand was beautiful, despite his wounds. Part of her wanted to touch him, just to be sure he was real.

She stood at the edge of the clearing, a few steps from Dave, waiting. He'd only told her they were going to move Brand, not how or where. Her eyes darted around the clearing, counting. Despite the crowd of healers and villagers milling about, she didn't think there were nearly enough people to shift him, much less lift and carry.

Jasper, wearing midnight blue robes embroidered along the hems with mysterious silver runes, circled the dragon, studying the ground. From time to time, he bent and tossed a small rock or limb from his leafy path. On his third pass around the dragon, he closed his eyes, and his arms and hands moved through a series of strange and complicated patterns. The air pressure shifted, and she could smell the metallic scent of an approaching storm.

The mage passed in front of her again, and Hummingbird felt his exhilaration and mirth rising, even though his outward demeanor remained studious. She wondered briefly what the man found so funny.

Everyone jumped when Jasper spoke. His words were incomprehensible, yet they held a hypnotic quality as he strung them together in a sing-song chant. Hummingbird became mesmerized when his steps turned into a pattern that complimented the motions of his hands. It reminded her of a dance. Motes of multi-colored light rose from the leaflitter in Jasper's wake, sparkling like gemstones in the afternoon sun.

From the corner of her eye, Hummingbird saw Dave take a half-step back and felt a sharp spike of fear. She tore her gaze away from the mage to stare wide-eyed at the archer. Outwardly, there was nothing in his expression to give away his feelings, other than his hands clenched in tight fists. She counted her breaths, expecting him to reach for his bow. Instead, he pulled out his flask and took a deep drink. It struck her as odd that he no longer carried the earthy scent of alcohol. Instead, she caught the faint fragrance of mint and green tea.

Hummingbird scanned the small group of Dave's friends around them. Hector stood on Dave's left, impressed by the show. He glanced at Dave, then flashed her a wicked grin and winked. Her eyebrows flew high, not sure how to react. Hector shook his head and turned back to Jasper's show with a silent chuckle.

Behind Hector, Xandor leaned against a tree, cleaning his nails with a jackknife. He seemed calm enough on the surface, but inside, she sensed something troubled him. He was awash with worry.

Beyond the ranger, the man introduced to her as Robert Stone stood beside another tree, his black clothes blending with the shadows. Rather than watching Jasper, he stared at the tawny haired girl called Teal, who stood among the healers. A welter of emotions churned inside Robert, dark and heavy as a thunderhead. A shiver crawled up her spine, and she turned away before losing herself in that maelstrom.

A wave of despair washed over her skin like a cold breeze foretelling a storm. It was oddly familiar. She searched those gathered, but the feeling was already gone.

White mist swirled around Brand, magnifying Jasper's sparkling lights, and a sharp clap echoed through the trees. Now sweating, Jasper moved faster through his motions, dancing at a fevered pace. He disappeared behind the dragon's wings and shouted, "Mazévo!" before falling silent.

As one, the variegated lights began to pulse like the beating of a heart. The leaves and forest litter hissed, crunched, and crackled. Slowly, with each pulse of light, the dragon shrank.

CR&O

4:10pm

Jasper heaved a sigh of relief and wiped his brow with the sleeve of his robe. Despite Teal's assurance that Brand wouldn't be able to fight the spell, he hadn't been sure. He carefully slid the wand inside a pocket in his robe before anyone noticed it.

He'd just put on a masterful performance, even if he did say so himself. No need to disillusion the crowd by revealing his trick. The lights pulsed again, and Brand grew another yard shorter.

Another pulse and his audience came into view. The looks on their faces were priceless. He sought out Dave and found him standing near Hector. He met the archer's glare and smiled. The bowman swayed back but held his ground with an effort — and a pull from his flask.

The light show continued for a quarter-hour. Brand was still over twenty feet long when he stopped shrinking, but that was a good sight more manageable than sixty. Jasper dismissed the tiny sparkles and mist with a wave of his hand.

The healers sprang into action. Several villagers set about assembling stretchers from long poles and heavy canvas while Teal and the healers set the young dragon's wing bones. They worked quickly and efficiently, fitting a specially made splint around each break.

CRSO

4:25pm

Hector knelt by Brand, speaking softly to him. The dolorous feeling swept over Hummingbird again, and she realized it came from sleeping dragon. She took a cautious step forward, then another. Before she realized it, she crouched near Hector. He radiated determination, as though he could heal Brand by force of will alone, and it seemed to push against the dragon's despair.

Hummingbird's hand hovered over Brand's head, then settled on it, soft as a butterfly.

The world shifted, and Hummingbird was falling. The wind rushed past her ears in a dull roar. The sky burned black all around her, and the smell of smoke choked her. Her descent came to a crashing halt as she plunged into a roiling sea of pain.

She struggled there for ages. Wracked with grief. Tormented by waves of agony.

Eons passed, and she came to rest on a rocky ledge. Dark, jagged rock walls surrounded a black sand beach littered with boulders. Hummingbird pushed herself up to her knees, still half in the water. A pale mountain towered in the distance, its glistening face floating in a starless sky.

She was on the beach she saw in the Dreaming Grounds, where Brand and Eidan had battled the eagle. Searching the darkness, she made out Brand's shape among the boulders at the far end of the beach, waves lapping at his tail and hindquarters.

Light flickered, drawing her attention. Midway between the rock walls and the sea, an elf child crouched with his knees against his chest on a smooth, white boulder, its surface marbled with veins of copper and verdigris. Scars and bruises mottled his naked form. He half bowed over his cupped hands, cradling something that crackled and flashed like lightning in a bottle. His bronze-skinned face and dark copper hair flickered in and out of shadow.

Hummingbird staggered to her feet and climbed the slope toward him.

"Go away." The boy's voice was a rasping growl.

She stopped and looked back the way she'd come. The dark rocks surrounding the beach disappeared under the waves. For a moment, she felt as though she was back in the dragon's tomb near Ruthaer, but the skeleton and roof were gone, replaced by a view of the trackless sea.

She turned back to the elf child. *"How did you come to be here?"* Her voice was the soft rustle of wind through tall grass.

"It's the land of the dead and dying. It's where I belong."

She looked up at the black sky where neither moon nor stars shone. Only the mountainside and the thing the child held cast any light she could see. *"Who are you?"*

For a moment, his form blurred, and she saw the hazy outline of a dragon surround him. *"Leave me alone."*

"Brand?"

He looked at her for the first time, and his eyes glowed bronze with mossy green flecks, the color negatives of Aislinn's eyes. *"My* name is Eidan.*"*

"Eidan?" Her brows drew together. Aislinn's brother was an adult. This boy had yet to reach adolescence. The light flickered again.

He saw her looking at the spark in his hands and pulled it closer to his chest. *"Mine,"* he growled.

She held up her hands. *"I promise I won't try to take it. I don't even know what it is."*

"It's all I have left of Aislinn, and now it's fading." He looked at her with haunted eyes. *"There's a hole in my heart, in my soul."*

"That's what it is to love," Hummingbird said. *"My grandmother once said we share pieces of ourselves with those we love. When they're taken away, we lose something we can never get back, but they leave their love for us in its place."*

He turned his back to her. *"I'm dying,"* he whispered.

"I felt that way, too, when I lost my family. I'm all that's left of my people." Tears coursed down her face. *"But you aren't alone. Your mother needs you. The humans in Ozera are fighting to save your life."*

"It hurts so much..."

Hummingbird's heart ached. She climbed onto the boulder beside the boy.

Her hand hovered over his head, then settled soft as a butterfly. She felt his thin arms wrap around her, and the world shifted.

CR&O

4:26pm

Hummingbird swayed. Her hand slid from the dragon's head as she crumpled towards the ground. Hector caught her and eased her down. He barely had her settled in the leaves when her eyelids fluttered open. She pushed him away as she struggled to sit up. Tears welled in her aqua-colored eyes. She didn't bother to wipe them away when they spilled out.

"Let me help you, chica. You know I won't hurt you."

Dave crouched on her other side. "Drink some water," he commanded, holding out his flask.

She took the silver container and wiped its mouth on the hem of her shirt before sniffing the contents and taking a sip. The water was cold and crisp, even though the container was not cold on the outside. She took a second, longer drink before handing it back.

"What happened?" Hector asked, handing her a handkerchief.

She smoothed the square of soft cotton across her knee and shrugged.

"You can tell us," Hector urged. "We're your friends, remember?" He slid his arm around her shoulders and gave them a gentle squeeze.

Hummingbird rolled away from him and came up with a dagger in her shaking hand.

Hector held both hands up, palms out and fingers splayed. "Whoa! Hummingbird, relax. I'll back off!"

Her lip trembled as she looked from Hector to Dave, then around the clearing, seeing the others staring at them. Slowly, she slid the knife back into her boot, drew up her knees, and curled into a ball. Her entire frame shook with silent sobs.

Hector turned beseeching eyes to Dave. "Do something."

"What? She doesn't like to be touched, and you damn well know that. You shouldn't have hugged her."

"Let me talk to her," a gentle voice said.

The two men looked up to see Aislinn's mother standing over them. With a nod, Hector rose and stepped back.

Shayla knelt and laid a hand on Hummingbird's shoulder. "Ei se mitään, Hummingbird. Let it all out."

The girl turned tear-filled eyes to the older elf, then suddenly grabbed her in a fierce hug and cried harder. Shayla petted the girl's spiky hair, crooning.

Dave rose and stalked away from the group. He came to a halt at the far edge of the clearing, back stiff as he stared, unseeing, into the forest.

"Lo siento," Hector said. "I know I should remember not to touch her, but I forget when she's obviously upset."

"Apologize to Hummingbird, not me." Dave's voice was scratchy, and he refused to look at Hector.

"Are you okay, amigo?"

"No. What the hell are we doing, letting that kid follow us around?"

Hector shoved his hands in his pockets. "We saved her life. Now we're responsible for her."

"Bullshit. We're barely responsible for ourselves."

Hector shrugged. "What are you going to do? She chose *you*, amigo. We tried to leave her in Kemet, and she managed to follow us here. She could have returned to Altaira and lived with one of the other elf tribes, but she didn't."

"Damn it, I wish you'd stop throwing that in my face. I tried to talk to her this morning. She refused to listen."

"Think of it as a way to atone for past sins," said Hector.

Dave glared at the Espian over his shoulder, then turned back to the forest.

"¿Que?"

"Just checking to see if you'd turned into Robert when I wasn't looking," Dave answered.

Hector grinned. "Come on. It looks like Mrs. Yves has Hummingbird calmed down, and I think the healers are ready to move Brand."

CHAPTER 37
BROKEN BONDS

August 18, 4237 K.E.

7:00pm

It took the rest of the afternoon to get Brand down the mountain. The light had turned deep, gloomy green by the time they finally arrived at Shayla's house and realized Brand was still too large to fit through the cellar doors.

"What can we do?" Shayla asked. "He can't stay out here like this for a month or more."

Jasper frowned at the small yard. "He can't stay here more than twelve hours. The spell I cast will only last a day. After that, he'll return to his normal size. He won't fit in this yard."

Teal asked, "Canst thou not make him smaller?"

The mage shook his head. "He's already one-third his original size. If I make him any smaller, I might hurt him... or the spell could backfire and make him twice his normal size. Neither option is good."

Hector wiped the sweat from his face and eyed the dragon. "Jasper, can I talk to you for a minute?" When the mage turned his way, one eyebrow raised, he added, "In private?"

Hummingbird watched the two men disappear around a bend in the path, then turned her attention back to Brand. She considered her vision of the boy child on his dark island. As clearly as if the tribe shaman spoke in her ear, she knew what she had to do.

Fists clenched at her side, she strode forward. Behind her, Hummingbird heard Teal warn her to stay away from Brand.

Hummingbird ignored the strange girl and knelt on the moss-covered loam beside Brand's head as she had earlier. Behind her, she heard a scuffle and the hiss of Dave's sabre leaving its scabbard. Her right hand floated above Brand's head, and for a moment fear warred with her resolve. She drew a deep breath, cleared her mind, and let her hand come to rest on Brand's psychic eye.

The world tilted, and Hummingbird landed on the sandy beach to a chorus of thunder and waves. Jagged lightning split the sky, but no rain fell. She pushed herself up onto her hands and knees, aching from head to toe. Perhaps landing in the sea again would have been a better option. She climbed to her feet and scanned the beach.

Eidan lay in the sand at the base of the boulder, curled in a tight knot. With each boom of thunder, every wave's crash, he trembled.

Hummingbird staggered uphill. The sand seemed deeper, looser. It sucked at her feet and legs, slowing her progress to an agonizing crawl. She called to the boy, but wind howled down the mountain and whistled across the jagged rocks, dashing her voice out to sea.

Boom! A blinding bolt of lightning slammed into the sand less than ten yards away. The force threw her down the beach, almost all the way back to where she started. Only then did she realize that Brand/Eidan was fighting her.

"Why?" she whispered.

"Death comes," the wind howled.

"No more death," she cried. "Not again. Please!"

Thunder shook the sky. Wave after wave scoured away the edge of the beach, slowly tugging the unconscious dragon into the sea.

Hummingbird crawled toward the boy, fear quaking in every muscle. Again, lightning struck between her and the child, turning the sand to a red-hot pool of molten glass. She peered through the fiery fumes. The spark he held in his cupped hands barely showed through his fingers.

"Eidan, let me help you," she called.

Slowly, the boy opened fever-bright eyes.

CRSO

7:05pm

Hector and Jasper stopped out of sight and earshot of

the friends, healers, and neighbors gathered in Shayla's yard. When Jasper turned to face him, Hector said, "I have an idea on how we can get Brand inside."

"I take it Dave's going to hate this idea of yours?" the mage asked with a smile.

"Probably. I was just thinking, Brand's not much bigger than that pangolin you turned into a rabbit..."

"Good gods, man! I couldn't do that to him. Besides, he would fry and eat me if he ever found out. Lord knows what he'd do to you."

"Would you keep your voice down? I'm not asking you to turn him into a rabbit! I was hoping you could turn him into Eidan."

"Oh. Why didn't you just say so?" The mage thought for a moment and shook his head. "Wish I could, but I don't have the wand I used on the pangolin anymore."

"You *lost* it?"

"Of course not. I used up its magic getting home from Trakya. Besides, it would have been risky, anyway."

"How so?"

"The casting can be... unpredictable. I've seen cases where the subject lost themselves — forgot who they were, their friends, everything — and it's permanent. Brand could become trapped in Eidan's body. Trust me, we don't want that to happen."

"Oh... Probably just as well, then. What about altering the house or maybe you can create a direct gateway?"

Jasper shrugged and, again, shook his head. "I don't have the resources on hand or the power. Best case, we might hire someone from Tydway, but it'll be expensive on such short notice."

"Money isn't an issue. Find what or who you need. I'll pay for it."

The sound of running feet brought their conversation to a halt. Xandor rounded the bend in the path and skidded to a stop. "You need to come back."

"What's wrong?" demanded Hector.

"You'd better see for yourself."

Hector bolted back down the path. The tableau that greeted him was nothing like he expected. Hummingbird knelt beside Brand, one hand on his forehead, her hair matted with sweat. Dave stood with his back to her, sabre drawn, and deadly menace on his face. Teal glared back at the archer. He held no weapon, but that didn't seem to matter to the flight-master. Robert stood between Dave and Teal with his hands outstretched, keeping the two apart. The others in the small yard stood frozen as they watched the scene play out.

"Teal, this is your last warning. Stay back," Robert said.

"What is that girl-child doing?" Teal demanded. "I saw her lay a hand 'pon Brand's head earlier, whilst we tended his wing. None of the clerics' healing worked afterward."

Robert looked over his shoulder. "Dave, what is she doing?"

The bowman growled, "She didn't say." His eyes never left Teal's.

Hector raced across the yard to stand shoulder-to-shoulder with Robert. "Everyone, calm down. Teal, back up. Hummingbird is... special. She can read emotions, sense things. She's trying to help." Giving the archer a warning glare, he said, "Dave, no one is going to touch Hummingbird. Put away the sabre."

Dave scowled at anyone he deemed too close, but his shoulders relaxed, and he slid the sword back into its scabbard with a metallic clink.

Hector studied the young elf for a moment. Every muscle in her body seemed to tremble with tension. "Let's give her time. Maybe she can reach him and tell him what we're trying to do."

"Nay," Teal said, taking a step forward, but Robert shifted to remain in his way. "She's working mischief upon him, I tell you. I shall not stand by and let her do him worse harm."

Dave growled as he gripped the hilt of his blade.

"Dave!" Hector snapped. "Focus on Hummingbird."

Dave held Hector's gaze for several long seconds before he finally let go his sabre and turned his back on Teal.

"Madre de Dios, dame fuerzas," Hector muttered, then faced Teal once again. "Teal, I know you think you're Brand's best hope, and maybe you are, but we don't have a way to fit him through the cellar doors. You heard Jasper. The spell is going to wear off, and then where will we be? Although I don't know what Hummingbird is trying to do, you have to trust me when I tell you that we can trust her."

CRSO

7:07pm

"Eidan," Hummingbird said, "your friends are trying to help you. They want to bring you home."

"I don't have any friends," the child said between sobs. "Aislinn had friends, and they took her from me."

Hummingbird felt hot tears burn down her cheeks. "Eidan, please listen. They didn't take her. They couldn't. You still have part of her right there, but it belongs in your heart. It can only survive as part of you."

The child pushed himself into a sitting position with his back against the boulder. Around them, the storm subsided into the distance. The melted sand between them cooled to smoked glass.

"How? She used to be as real as me. We were together. Now she's gone."

Hummingbird crawled to the boy and knelt in front of him. "Hold her spark in your right hand, Eidan. Concentrate. Feel your heart beating. See how the light in your hand pulses? Your heart and hers beat in time together.

"Hold the light to your heart, Eidan. Let it be part of you. You don't need to see her here to feel her love. It was her gift to you."

The boy pressed the light to his chest, and his skin glowed as the soul-spark flowed into him. The child wept, but they were no longer the bitter tears of despair. "I miss her."

Hummingbird opened her arms, and the boy leaned his head on her shoulder. She wrapped him in a tight embrace. "I miss her, too." Brushing back his hair, she said, "Eidan, I need you to do something for your mother."

"Emä?"

"Yes."

The boy yawned and said, "I'm sleepy."

"Your mother needs you to come home, Eidan. Brand is hurt and sleeping in Ozera, but he's too big. You need to go there and let Brand sleep here by the ocean. Can you do that?"

"Brand isn't in Ozera." He pointed to the dragon's broken body half submerged in the surf, then up to the cliff glowing against the skyline. "A dærganfae attacked us in Sunrise Chapel, and we fell off the mountain. Brand is dead, and soon I will be, too."

"You're right. If you give up, you will die, but everyone is fighting to save you. The thing is, this is a nightmare, Eidan. You have to want to come back to Ozera in order to wake up."

The child was silent for a time, and Hummingbird held him close. Perhaps it was too much for a child's mind to comprehend, even if the child was a dragon. Maybe she was asking the impossible of him. Finally, the boy stirred in her arms.

"You didn't tell me your name," he said.

"I'm called Hummingbird."

The boy scoffed. "That's not a real name."

"No, but it suffices. Once upon a time, I was a girl called Wind Dancer, but she's gone, along with her family. Now I have a new name and a new life."

The boy lifted his head, but stayed in the circle of her arms, studying her bright crimson hair and aquamarine eyes. One finger traced the whorls on her cheek. He gave a timid smile. "If you wear bright green clothes, you might look like a bird."

She smiled back at him, feeling a warmth in her heart that hadn't been there in a long time. She leaned forward and gently kissed his forehead.

The world shifted, and she felt herself fall.

CHAPTER 38
CHANGES

August 18, 4237 K.E.

7:10pm

Lightning streaked across the darkening sky, dragging thunder in its wake. The ground shook, and the glass in Shayla Yves' windows rattled. Out of instinct, Dave ducked and glanced up at the clear evening sky.

From the corner of his eye, Dave saw Hummingbird fall away from Brand like a cut sapling. Diving forward, the archer managed to catch her before her head struck the ground.

Lightning flashed again, and electricity crackled over Brand's hide, dancing from scale to scale and along the bones of his wings. The villagers and healers in the tree-shrouded yard fled.

Dave rolled to his feet, Hummingbird's still form cradled against him, and ran for the safety of the house. He had almost reached the porch when he heard the whisper.

'*Eidan.*'

Dave skidded to a stop and glanced around. He saw Mrs. Yves and August through the mat of rose vines but couldn't hear what they were saying. Hector and Robert were pulling Teal across the yard, each gripping an arm, their voices drowned out by the crackle and hiss of a growing cloud of electricity surrounding Brand.

He swallowed hard and looked down at the girl in his arms. Hummingbird remained unconscious.

"Get down!" Hector shouted.

Dave dropped to his knees and curled over Hummingbird, drawing her tight to his chest. Behind him, thunder exploded, and light blazed around them. The world trembled. Leaves and rose petals rained down from the porch trellis.

"Fuck this shit!" he grated between clenched teeth.

Thunder rolled up and down the mountainside for several long minutes, echoing in the distance. The light faded, taking the last vestiges of twilight with it, leaving the yard in total darkness.

Dave laid Hummingbird in the petal-covered grass, then peered through the gloom. Although he could pick out the shadows of Hector, Robert, and Teal rising from the turf, he couldn't make out Brand's shape — only a lump about the size of the shrunken dragon's head.

Hector pulled a light from his belt and shined it around the yard.

"Xardus have mercy," Teal said. "What hath the wench done?"

In the center of the stretchers they used to bring Brand down the mountain, a naked body lay curled in the fetal position. Hector's light glimmered on bright, copper colored hair.

Jasper came down the porch steps, the head of his staff glowing like a lantern. Behind him, a cleric appeared from inside the Yves residence bearing an oil lamp, followed by August and Shayla.

Jasper stopped beside Dave and cast a quizzical look at Hummingbird's still form. "Is she hurt?"

Dave shrugged and remained silent.

"You don't look so good, yourself. Maybe you should take her inside." Without waiting for a reply, Jasper continued across the lawn to join Hector and Robert.

Dave watched the small group congregate around Hector. They talked in hushed whispers, but their attention kept drifting to the unconscious boy.

Hummingbird finally stirred. He turned to see her staring up at the sky, fingers curling through the leaves and rose petals.

"How ya doing, kid?" he asked.

Her eyes darted to his, then she raised her hands and made a sign he'd never seen before.

He shook his head. "You need to learn to write. Can you sit up?" He pulled his flask and held it out to her. "Drink."

Hummingbird pushed up and sat with her back against the side of the house. She reached out for the flask, but her fingers closed over Dave's. A rush of images featuring an elf boy with copper hair flashed in his mind, and again he heard a girl's voice whisper, "Eidan."

Dave jerked his hand back as though he'd been burned. "Stay out of my head, girl." The menace in his voice promised dark and horrible consequences. "You won't like what you find."

The flask landed in the grass between them. Hummingbird matched his glare with one of her own. Her signs were sharp between them. "I am not afraid of you."

Dave blinked in surprise. He tried to remember if he'd ever seen her angry. "You should be," he growled.

"I gave you information you need," she signed.

"Without my bloody permission!" he snapped. "Don't you ever fucking do that again!"

A look of horror passed over her face, and she struggled to her feet. "I'm sorry," she signed before staggering across the yard.

Dave scrubbed a hand across his face. "Fuck," he muttered. He spied the flask still lying in the grass and scooped it up. He popped the top and took a long pull, then spit the sandy tasting contents into the grass and wiped his hand over his mouth. "Damn that half-elf's curse."

C&SO

7:20pm

Hector watched Hummingbird weave her way across the yard toward them. Dave still sat by the house, flask in hand. Hector had a fleeting moment to wonder what had passed between them before the discussion picked up again.

"That lightshow was brighter and louder than anything we've ever seen Brand produce," said Robert. "Could it have been an illusion, and someone used magic to kidnap Brand? Maybe the boy isn't real."

Jasper shook his head. "It's so far beyond the realm of mortal possibility as to be utterly impossible."

"Why — and give us the short answer," said Hector.

"The simplest reason is someone would have to know *exactly* where he is, and we've spent most of the afternoon moving him. The real, and slightly more complicated, reason is there are limits to a teleport spell. Even if every archmage at the Academy in Tydway worked in concert, I don't think they could kidnap a dragon the way you're suggesting. He simply weighs too much. No, I believe Hummingbird convinced him to change shape. What I can't figure out is how she knew he could."

"But Brand is too young to change his form," Teal argued. "'Tis a skill which doth not develop until after a Tenné reaches adulthood and completes the vaatzheymah oath with a Xemmassian partner."

"And yet he figured it out years ago," Robert replied. "He and Aislinn traveled with us for months before we discovered their secret, and that was by accident."

"Brand has always been able to change," Shayla said as she and August joined the group. Her arm twined around his, with her hand resting on his forearm as though they were entering a ballroom.

Brother Jonnas, the only healer who hadn't fled during Brand's lightning storm, knelt beside the unconscious youth, examining his bruises.

"After my husband died, I packed what belongings I could into a wagon and left Ruthaer for Ozera with Brand hidden among our things. Our second week of travel, I woke one morning to find I had a son the same size and age as Aislinn. I named him Eidan." Shayla's hand slid from the gallant's arm, their fingertips brushing as they separated, and she joined the healer beside the stretcher.

"If it really is Eidan, why does he look like a child barely into adolescence?" August asked.

"Because that is what he *is*," Teal protested, "and he shan't be mature for another ten years at the least. That elf-girl trapping him in an unfamiliar aspect does him no favors."

"Hummingbird did not do this to him," stated Hector.

"I will also vouch for the purity of Hummingbird's intent and actions," August stated. "However, this form exposes Brand's vulnerability. Can you imagine having the strength and power of a dragon but choosing to be a youth? It takes us back to a time of innocence —"

"The more important question is whether or not he's safe to touch," Robert said, cutting off August's impending speech. "If he can't hold this form and another lightning storm goes off, someone could get hurt."

"Teal, what do you think? Should we risk carrying him inside?" asked Hector.

"I don't know. 'Tis unprecedented. I never heard of a Tenné who changed shape whilst unconscious."

"Just because you never heard of a thing doesn't mean it hasn't happened," said Hector.

"Nay, but I was reared amongst a bevy of dragons, so the likelihood of my *not* hearing of such an occurrence is miniscule."

Conceding the point, Hector asked, "On the off chance that this wasn't Brand's doing, Jasper, how many people do you know who could force him to change shape?"

"Two, but neither is in Ozera at the moment," he replied. "At least, not to my knowledge."

"What about the mage who attacked him at Sunrise Chapel?" Robert asked.

Jasper thought about it for a few minutes, then shook his head. "It doesn't follow. The mage left Brand to burn. You don't try to kill a creature then turn it into a child."

"You would if, like August said, it made him more vulnerable," Robert suggested.

"So, do we move him or not?" August asked.

"August, all of you, look at him," Shayla said. "This *is* Eidan. No matter what he looked like the last time we saw him, right now he's a naked boy covered in bruises. He isn't dangerous." Her gaze drifted from person to person before settling on Hector. "Please, let me wrap him in a blanket and take him inside."

"Jasper, what do you think?" Hector asked.

"Whether outside forces caused it, or he did it himself, I think we should pick him up on that stretcher and take him to his cavern before this wears off."

"Here is the wench responsible. Ask her what happened," Teal demanded.

Hummingbird staggered to a halt by Shayla and Brother Jonnas. The girl's chest heaved as though she'd been running, and dark smudges underscored her eyes. She looked as though she might collapse at any moment.

"Hummingbird, are you alright?" Hector asked. When the girl nodded, he continued, "What happened?"

She pointed a shaking hand at the sleeping boy, then her own forehead. Her first few signs were uncertain, as though she was trying to explain something that was new to her as well.

Shayla turned to Hector. "What is she saying?"

"I'm not sure. Hummingbird, slow down. Is that Brand?"

Her head canted to one side in a half-shrug, and she waggled her hand side to side, then signed again.

"Jesu..." he paused and stared at the boy for a long time before meeting Shayla's eye. "I think she's saying she spoke to him." He looked questioningly at Hummingbird.

The girl nodded and gave him a tired smile.

Hector watched Hummingbird point to Mrs. Yves, then sign again. He glanced from the boy to Shayla. "She says Brand changed into Eidan for you."

CHAPTER 39
WATCHERS

August 18, 4237 K.E.

7:45pm

From the darkness under the trees surrounding the tiny yard, Count Dodz glared at Hector de los Santos, imagining ways to torture Ymara's location from him and the archer before killing them. After three days in Ozera, he was no closer to completing his mission of killing the bounty hunter for Boyar Zinovii Tretyakov or finding Ymara's mask.

His foray into the Aerarium had not yielded the results he expected. The bounty hunter had given the clerics a plaster mask rather than the real one. Then, after acquiring the relics from Ruthaer and exiting the Aerarium's back door into the library scriptorium, Dodz discovered he was unable to leave Ozera. The magic of his teleportation sand would not respond to any destination more than a half-mile from the village center. When he attempted to walk out of the village, he reached the same half-mile point before finding himself re-entering Ozera from its opposite side. Adding insult to injury, he'd woken that morning with angry red welts on his right arm. As the day progressed, they'd darkened to unnatural bruises that spelled the word 'THIEF' in perfect block letters.

A heavy cord of magic wound itself around Dodz, snapping him back to the present. He searched for his attacker while struggling to raise his arms. The spell tightened. Sparks burst from Dodz' gloved hands, and the spell dissipated like ice in the desert.

Leaves crunched directly behind him. Pulling a narrow blade from the sheath on his belt, he spun and hurled it in the direction of the sound. At the last second, a tall, thin figure spun aside. The blade thunked into a tree trunk.

Before Dodz could throw another knife, the unknown mage cast two heavy bolts of magic at him. He brushed aside the first bolt with his gloved hand. The second bolt, though still misdirected, exploded when it hit the ground in front of him. The concussion knocked Dodz off his feet, and he flew backward into the bushes. The sound of snapping branches echoed in the night.

Dodz rolled to his feet, took two staggering steps, and collided with a sapling. Another binding spell struck his legs and feet, tying him to the slender tree. A second spell twisted the tree's branches around his arms.

"Chto ty khochesh'?" Dodz snarled. *What do you want?*

"I want the ivory dagger stolen by the Carolingian knight from Ruthaer," the shadowy figure spat. His colorless skin seemed to glow in the darkness. "I know it is here in this village, and so does Mi'dnirr."

A frisson of fear pulsed in his veins, but Dodz stifled it. "Let go! You can't frighten me, dærganfae."

Starlight glinted in his captor's single quicksilver eye. A black patch covered his other eye, and three long scars marred half his face. "You can give me the dagger, or you can face Mi'dnirr."

"If I had anything Mi'dnirr wanted, he would have come for it himself."

The fae said nothing.

"Prayhaps we make deal, no?" Through the trees, a red light bobbled like a will-o'-the-wisp and voices floated in its wake. Sweat beaded on Dodz' forehead as he slid one gloved hand toward the Akkilettū blade on his belt. "I have the relics from Ruthaer. I will give them to you, but you must let me go."

"Where are they, human?"

Dodz licked his lips. Before he could reply, a twig snapped nearby.

For a moment, the dærganfae stood perfectly still, his attention fixed on the shadowy underbrush behind Dodz, then he took a step forward. "You have something else Mi'dnirr wants. Give me the relics and the black diamond you took from Ruthaer."

Dodz lunged and drove the Akkilettū blade under the dærganfae's ribs into his lung.

The one-eyed fae gasped and clutched at the blade piercing his chest. His face twisted with pain, he stumbled over a tree root and fell headlong in the leaflitter.

Dodz resheathed the black blade and sneered at the dærganfae sprawled at his feet. "Neither you nor Mi'dnirr will get anything from me tonight, volshebnik fyei." Light sparked off his gloves as he broke the spell holding his legs, and he slipped away into the darkness.

CHAPTER 40
NIGHT HUNTERS

August 18, 4237 K.E.

8:10pm

"Someone fell hard," Hector said, pointing to a dark patch of bare loam with his red light.

Dave shined a second, pale blue light through the underbrush and across a clearing, where it glinted off an oak bole. He retrieved a polished steel blade, forged with a full tang, and bound with a lightweight leather cord rather than a standard hilt. Its balance made it perfect for throwing.

"Who's this guy?" Robert asked.

Under the light of Jasper's staff, the wounded man's pale, translucent skin resembled bleu cheese. "Dærganfae," Dave spat.

Hector knelt beside the body. "This is the same guy Xandor and I saw in town earlier. He has a punctured lung, but he's still alive." He searched the darkness and the yard uphill. "Speaking of Xandor, where did he get off to?"

Robert shrugged. "He didn't come back after he went to fetch you and Jasper."

"Yes, he did. He was right behind me when I came into the yard," Jasper said, "but I lost track of him in the excitement." He looked toward the house, then followed the path with his eyes. "The way down to the road is right through there. Maybe Xandor saw whoever stabbed this guy and followed him."

"He should know better than to go off alone."

Jasper gave the bounty hunter a curious look. "That's what rangers are trained to do."

"We should take this guy to the hospital," Robert said.

"Brother Jonnas is inside with Mrs. Yves and the boy," Jasper said as the four hoisted the unconscious fae.

"Eidan," Dave corrected.

"Beg pardon?" Jasper replied.

"The boy. It's Eidan."

"That's what Señora Yves said, too," said Hector. "Hummingbird tried to explain, but it was some really mixed-up stuff about Brand's *spirit self.* The only part I really understood was that he changed for Aislinn's mother."

"His mind is fractured," Dave said. "It's like he has a split personality. Eidan thinks Shayla is his real mother."

Robert, Hector, and Jasper stared at Dave in mute shock. Hector managed to find his voice first. "I'd like to know how you know all that."

"No. No, you don't," Dave said.

Hector raised an eyebrow. Not getting an explanation, he asked, "What about Xandor?"

"He'll be back," Jasper replied. "Let him do the job the Iron Tower trained him for."

"What are we supposed to do in the interim?" Robert asked.

A rumbling gurgle from the direction of Jasper's stomach answered, and he gave a self-conscious smile. "I believe that's the signal for supper. Why don't we pillage Mrs. Yves' pantry? If we're lucky, Brother Jonnas can patch up this fae enough for him to answer a few questions. This may be the mage we've been looking for."

CR&SO

8:20pm

Xandor slipped through the darkness, stalking a man in an ermine cape who resembled the image of Count Dodz he'd seen in the Aerarium.

The ranger had heard the man arguing, then negotiating, with a fae for the items stolen from the Aerarium. He'd also heard them mention Mi'dnirr. Before Xandor reached their position, the man ahead of him had crashed out of the trees onto the main trail. Fleet of foot, he moved quickly despite the darkness, heading back toward the village.

The cough of a Parlathean lion slid through the trees, freezing both the ranger and his quarry midstep.

Although the typical territory of the big cats was in the grasslands west of the White River, it wasn't completely unheard of for a solitary hunter to cross the river and wander into the Alashalian Mountains to prey upon the weak. Even as his ears strained to locate the lion, Xandor kept his eyes focused on the man in front of him. In the gloom, it would be all too easy to lose him to the shadows.

After a few minutes of quiet, the man turned and glanced back toward the ranger. Xandor held his breath, trusting the trees and his mottled cloak to hide his profile. The man ahead produced a tiny light and shined it up and down the path. Finding it clear, he continued toward the heart of the village. The ranger listened to his quarry's footfall pattern, then fell into step behind him.

Just as the man disappeared around a bend in the path, another shadow slipped out of the trees on silent feet and waited for Xandor to approach.

"Greetings, San Sebek-wy," the lioness purred. Her eyes glinted in the darkness, almost level with his chest.

Xandor paused and reached an empty hand toward the lioness. "Hello, honored sister. You are far from home."

Her nose and cheek brushed along his palm and wrist. "The Akshan wished me to convey his sadness for the loss of your pride-sister."

"Thank you, Sahmaht," Xandor said, bowing his head. "Aislinn counted the Akshan as a friend. Will you honor me by joining my hunt? The man I track is stalking my pride-brothers, and I want to know why."

The lioness turned her head in the direction the man had gone and growled. "Your pride has many enemies, San Sebek-wy. This one carries the scent of fresh blood. Let us teach him not to hunt in your territory."

Xandor smiled and laid a hand on the lioness' shoulder. Together, they ghosted through the darkness, and quickly came within sight of their prey. Dodz was passing a half-circle of benches overlooking a flowerbed and would soon reach the first shops along the village's main thoroughfare.

The lion's muscles tensed. Her tail lashed side to side, and Xandor knew she wanted to charge the fleeing figure and pounce on his back. Part of him wanted to let her, but Xandor also wanted to see where the man was going.

He and Hector had spent several hours talking to the innkeepers and shop owners and getting nowhere. Now, here Dodz was within easy reach. Xandor stopped. It was still early enough for the main street to be busy. Not wanting to cause a panic, he motioned for the lioness to shadow them from side streets.

The man strolled past Buck's Brews. Light from the windows and open door revealed dark hair and tanned skin. His ermine cape, grey silk shirt, black pants, and glossy boots were the latest fashion among noblemen and looked like something August would wear. A black diamond the size of a barred owl's egg winked from the pommel of a curved dagger at the man's belt. Xandor wondered if that was the black diamond Mi'dnirr wanted and, if so, why.

The shadows swallowed his target again. They passed the Oak Grove Inn and several small shops before his quarry turned down a side street. Sahmaht chuffed, stopping the ranger at the corner of a building beside a shallow creek. At first, all Xandor could hear was the sound of water tumbling over stones. He waited. Then he heard splashing coming from the bank beside the bridge that didn't match the rhythm of the stream. The man was washing his hands.

Sahmaht's muscles tightened, and her shoulders shifted as she prepared to pounce. Xandor pressed his hand more firmly on her back to signal her to wait. The cat's ears drew back, and the tip of her tail lashed in irritation, but she remained silent.

Long minutes passed before the man finally returned to the road and crossed the bridge. He walked uphill and headed toward a cluster of cottages near the hospital. A few windows glowed, but most of them were dark. Xandor watched the man produce a key and enter one at the end of a row. Light bloomed inside, spilling out onto the narrow strip of grass between the house and the lane through slatted shutters.

In the corner of the windowsill nearest the door sat three small, stacked rocks.

The ranger and the lion shared a look.

"Sahmaht, go behind the building. If he tries to sneak out, hold him for me."

"What will you do?"

"I'm going to watch the front. I want to make sure he stays here, and that no one else comes."

"Why not catch him now?" she asked. "You could gift him to your pride brothers."

Xandor looked around. Something about the man made him uneasy. "We'll watch for a while, so we don't step in a trap. When he sleeps, we'll take him."

The lioness drifted into the darkness and disappeared behind the small house. Xandor imagined introducing Sahmaht to his friends and huffed to himself. He'd have to handle *that* carefully. Giving himself a mental shake, the ranger turned back to the task at hand. Wishing he could see more than the shadow moving across the curtain, Xandor reflected on what he and Hector saw that morning and the conversation from the night before. They needed to take Count Dodz alive.

CHAPTER 41
AISLINN'S ROOM

August 18, 4237 K.E.

8:30pm

Hummingbird followed August into the house. In his arms, the boy called Eidan was sound asleep. He seemed taller, older, than he had inside his mindscape, but still not the adult she'd met previously.

Shayla fetched an afghan made from earth-toned yarn and draped it over Eidan. "Bring him this way," she said, heading toward the stairs. "We'll put him in the spare bedroom for now."

"Shayla, I hate to say this, but we should probably take him into his cavern," August called out gently. "We don't know how long he's going to be able to hold this form."

"I agree," Brother Jonnas said.

Shayla laid her hand on the banister and shook her head. "It's all sand and cold rock, and the tunnel from here to there is too long for me to hear him if he needs me."

"I mended his broken arm, but it will be for naught if he resumes his true form inside this house," the healer argued.

Standing in the central hallway, Hummingbird looked from Shayla to August and the cleric, painfully aware that none of them knew enough sign language to understand her. She eyed the broad-shouldered warrior-poet warily. There was something in the air between him and Shayla, and it set her on her guard. She struggled with how to tell them Eidan wouldn't change into Brand any time soon, but Dave's reaction to her sharing thoughts with him caused her to hesitate. She looked at August again and shivered. She did not want to get into that man's head. It was almost more than she could bear being this close to him and his... emotions.

"Is the cellar the only way to access the cavern?" August asked, his voice quiet as he approached Shayla.

"Yes. There's a door and stairs from Aislinn's room," she said. She stopped on the first step and stared at the door at the end of the hallway. "I just... I haven't had the heart to go in there."

"You are not alone. We're here to help," August said. "Right, Hummingbird?"

Hummingbird's eyes darted up to his and back to Shayla before she nodded. The gentle affection August felt for Shayla filled the air like a warm blanket on a cold day and quieted the anxiety in the older elf. Instantly, Hummingbird's guard snapped back into place, and she stepped past August.

She gently touched Shayla's arm and pointed at the sleeping boy. She laid her first and middle fingers, splayed in a V, flat on the palm of her other hand. Again, she pointed at Eidan and laid her fingers flat on her palm. Next, she wound her thumbs together forming the shape of a bird — or a dragon — with her hands. She quickly spread her hands apart and waved them back and forth in a negative manner.

August's brow furrowed as he tried to decipher what Hummingbird was saying. "He won't turn into a dragon?" he guessed.

Hummingbird nodded, then touched her forehead and her heart. She reached up and gently brushed the boy's copper hair back from his face. In the lamp light, the dark circles under his eyes were more apparent, and a line of purple shadowed his jaw.

"Let's get him into bed, then," he replied.

Shayla took another step up the stairs, but Hummingbird stopped her with a gentle hand and pointed toward the door at the end of the hallway. Tears shimmered in Shayla's eyes. "That's Aislinn's room," she said in a broken voice.

The pain Hummingbird felt from Shayla was palpable and threatened to overwhelm her. Picturing Dave, emotionless and uncaring, she steeled herself and pointed at Eidan, then at Aislinn's room again.

"Are you sure?" Shayla asked.

Hummingbird knew what she was asking. She felt the waves of fear coming off Shayla. To open that door, for Aislinn not to be there, and to realize she was never coming back was too much for a mother. Hummingbird pointed at Eidan, then Aislinn's room, and finally laid her hand over her heart.

"You think he needs to feel close to her?" August asked.

Hummingbird nodded and gave a wan smile. She led the way down the hall, past the small music room and eat-in kitchen, to the back of the house. Behind her, she heard Shayla sobbing.

She laid a hand on the knob and took a deep breath before opening the door. Shadows filled the corners. Sheer curtains covered the windows on each side of the room but did nothing to add any light at this hour. The dim glimmer reaching the bedroom from the kitchen was barely enough for Hummingbird to find a lamp and the stub of candle inside. Holding the lamp close, she lit the wick, and the tiny flame struggled to drive away the darkness.

August walked to the heavy framed bed in the corner and stared at the pillows stacked in its center. A rag doll with red hair sprawled, face down, across the top.

"What in the world?" Shayla asked. Her eyes darted around the room. Her fear quickly turned into anger. "Someone's been in here." She stared at the four framed drawings hanging beside the window on the right-hand wall. Each was of a different tree. All four bore three vertical slashes through the trunk that dug into the wallboard beyond.

Hummingbird and August shared a wide-eyed look.

"I'll find Dave and Hector," she signed. She didn't wait for him to nod before racing out of the room.

Hummingbird snatched open the front door and darted onto the porch. She jumped over the edge, skipping the steps altogether, then slammed to a halt when she realized the yard was empty.

"What is the matter?" a voice demanded from behind her.

She whirled around into a defensive posture, a dagger in each hand, to see Teal standing at the porch rail.

"I did not mean to startle thee," Teal said. "Has something else happened?"

Hummingbird nodded and searched the yard again.

"Hector and the others are yonder in the trees," Teal said, pointing down the path toward the road. "They heard someone fighting. Look, here they come."

The small elf returned her daggers to the sheaths at her wrists and looked where the other girl pointed. The four men carried someone up the hill in their direction.

Hummingbird raced across the yard to Dave.

"What's wrong?" he asked.

"Come inside. Shayla says someone has been in Aislinn's room," Hummingbird signed.

"Can you tell if the intruder is still in the house?" Hector asked.

Hummingbird closed her eyes and searched the house. "No one else is there. Just Shayla, Eidan, August, and the healer."

"Come on, then. Show us."

CRSO

8:40pm

They found Shayla in the front room, sitting in a rocking chair holding Eidan, while Brother Jonnas murmured a healing prayer.

Looking like he was striking a pose for a painter, August stood guard at the foot of the stairs. He held his sword in front of him with both hands, the point poised just above the floor. Hector gave him a questioning look. He knew August didn't do it on purpose, but to Hector it seemed that the Rhodinan warrior would have been better off with a career as a model — or a male stripper.

August snapped to attention and reported, "I searched the house. There's no one else here, and other than Aislinn's room, I saw no sign of anything being disturbed."

"Good job," the bounty hunter replied, his tone just as serious. "Did you see any white sand?"

"No, but I wasn't looking for it. I was more concerned with Shayla's safety."

Hector nodded. "Check again."

August saluted and dashed away, but not before giving Shayla a look of assurance.

"You sure that's safe?" Dave grumbled. "You know he'll find the maid, or a Minotaur, or something."

Hector ignored Dave's comment and sent Brother Jonnas out onto the porch to tend the dærganfae before following Hummingbird down the hall to Aislinn's room.

The far wall of the spacious bedroom sparkled in the meager lamplight. Emitting a low whistle, he realized the wall was the stone face of the mountain. Cool air drifted off it, reminding him of days spent camping in the wilderness. Dave stepped into the room behind Hector and went to work lighting the fireplace.

While Dave arranged the wood, Hector got his bearings and slowly rotated widdershins. To his right, beside the bedroom door, the wall held a shelf crammed with books of various sizes and colors. Underneath lay the biggest pillow he had ever seen. Above it was another shelf that held shells, unusual rocks, and a lifelike set of stuffed animals crafted from leather. All looked untouched.

Continuing his rotation, he noted the curtained window in the far corner was closed and that there were four drawings on the wall beside it. There was a narrow, wooden door set into the face of the mountain. By the time Hector's eyes drifted to the doll laying atop three pillows stacked in the center of Aislinn's bed, each smaller than the one below, firelight flooded the room. Dave stood up with a satisfied grunt, dusting his hands off on his pants.

Hector turned back to the drawings by the window. The stacked pillows and damaged drawings reminded him of the ranger signs slashed on the crate in the Aerarium that morning.

"I remember when she drew these," he murmured, examining the damage. He lifted the framed oak drawing down, and fingered the back of the heavy parchment, then the gouges in the plaster wall. The slits were angled downward from the drawing, as though the blade was curved.

A murmur of voices in the hall preceded Jasper and Robert's arrival. The mage aimed toward the small door set into the mountain. He let out a surprised, "Oh!" when he opened it.

"Anything interesting in there?" Hector asked over his shoulder.

"Stairs. Looks like they go down to the cellar," Jasper replied. "They must connect to Brand's cave somehow." He gave his cheek a thoughtful scratch. "Teal said Aislinn would have a secret way in and out..."

"Huh. We'll check that out later," Hector said. "What did Brother Jonnas say about the fae?"

"He has him stabilized," replied Robert from the opposite side of the room. "Eliezer Vulmaro and two others who helped us carry Brand came back. They're taking the fae to the hospital. I asked them to keep him restrained until we can ask a few questions about what happened and why he was here."

"What is *that*?" Dave grated. "It looks like a Voodoo doll." He stood near the foot of Aislinn's bed staring at the pillow assembly in the center. Beside him, an open trunk spilled blankets and bed sheets onto the floor. "Do they have Voodoo here?"

"What's Voodoo?" Jasper asked. He closed the door to the stairs, joined Dave and Robert at the bedside, and studied the rag doll sprawled face-down on the pillows. "I don't mind telling you, that's more than a little weird. Is that a pin sticking out the doll's back?"

"It *is* a Voodoo doll," Dave said, his voice bordered with an edge of panic.

Hummingbird crawled onto the bed and gently lifted the doll. The top pillow clung to the doll briefly, then dropped away, revealing the long, sharp point of a black sliver that protruded from the doll's chest at an angle. With a look of wide-eyed fear, she threw the doll onto the bed and scrambled away, backing toward the door.

"Bloody sarding hell," Dave said, tugging his flask from his belt pouch as he retreated toward the fireplace.

"Language, Dave," Robert admonished.

Hector's swarthy skin paled, and he drew in a ragged breath and crossed himself. "Take it out," he gasped. "Get that damned thing out of her chest!"

"What's wrong with you three? There's nothing magical about this doll," Jasper said as he grabbed it from the bed and pulled out the thin pin. Both Hector and Dave let out an involuntary gasp. "What is this? It isn't metal." Jasper rolled it between his fingers. "It almost feels like beetle carapace."

Hector's breath hitched and caught, and his expression grew haunted.

"It's from that thrice-damned thing that killed Aislinn," Dave said. He took another long pull from his flask.

"Why would someone do this?" Robert asked, standing next to Jasper.

"Diversion, maybe," Jasper replied. "Keep those two crazies off balance," he continued, with a nod toward Hector and Dave. He dropped the black sliver into one of his pockets and laid the doll gently on the bed. "Episkeví," he murmured softly, letting a thread of magic close the holes in the doll, as though it was never damaged.

Jasper turned to the others. "We need food. I'll go see what I can put together in Shayla's kitchen while the rest of you check those stairs and make sure no one's lurking in Brand's cavern."

CHAPTER 42
DRAGON CAVERNS

August 18, 4237 K.E.

9:00pm

Hector shined his light over shallow crates of root vegetables and hanging bunches of herbs. A steep wooden stair led to a trapdoor in the wood floor above and the kitchen pantry. On the opposite side of the cellar, a ramp sloped up to the pair of wooden doors from the yard. The stone stairs from Aislinn's room came out in another corner. The rest of the room contained boxes stored on shelves.

"I don't see anything in here that looks like a hidden entrance to Brand's cave. We're going to have to ask Shayla to show us," Hector said.

Dave shook his head and sauntered over to the shelves. Slipping his fingers behind one end, he felt his way up the edge.

"What are you doing?" Robert asked.

A loud click sounded, and Dave pivoted the shelves away from the wall.

Hector arched an eyebrow. "How did you know about that, amigo?"

Dave chuffed. "Remember when you and August got yourselves poisoned outside Erinskaya three years ago? Eidan and I didn't feel like dragging your sorry butts around looking for a healer, and that Tretyakov dick put a price on our heads big enough to draw every hitman in Vologda and Zhitomir. Besides, we needed to get to Orleans."

Hector made a face. "What does that have to do with the rain in España?"

"Eidan has a magical rucksack that he uses to add things to his hoard. We dumped all our stuff inside, Xandor sent the horses cross country to Ozera, and the three of us brought you here through the bag." He grinned. "Eidan made Xandor wear a blindfold until we reached the cellar."

"But not you?"

"Nope."

"I still don't understand why Eidan looks like a little kid instead of our age like he always did before," Robert said.

"No sé, amigo," Hector replied. "Maybe it has to do with losing Aislinn."

"Do you think it was something Hummingbird did?" Robert asked.

Hector and Dave exchanged a glance and shrugged. "As far as I can tell she's empathic, but what went on today was completely new," Hector replied. "I just hope whatever happened between them doesn't end in tears."

"It would help if she talked," Robert said.

"I agree, but she hasn't said a single word since we bought her off the auction block in Tirna Flainn."

"*Bought?*" Robert choked.

"We had to," Hector protested. "Los cabrones had beaten her half to death and were trying to sell her as a sex slave. How could we leave her to a fate like that?"

"No wonder she's so skittish," Robert murmured. "It also explains why she likes Dave."

"What the hell is that supposed to mean?" the archer demanded.

"*Language,* Dave. You can count on getting a swear jar for your birthday," Robert said.

"What did you mean about Hummingbird and me?"

Robert shrugged. "Just that you're scared of women, and she's fragile. It probably gives her a sense of power."

"I'm not scared of women," Dave groused. "They're trouble, and I've got enough problems as it is. If I could make Hummingbird leave me alone, I would."

"You like her, and you know it," Hector said. "She's like the kid sister none of us ever had."

"Whatever," Dave said. "Come on, we're burning daylight."

The three friends walked in silence down a smooth tunnel. Hector's light refracted from quartz deposits and sparkled like stars.

"Do you think someone mined this, or did Brand do it?" Hector asked after a while.

"I asked Eidan the same thing," answered Dave. "He said Phaedrus found it for him when they first came to Ozera. This tunnel, and the cavern it connects to, are why Shayla's house sits where it is."

Hector turned and shined his light in Dave's face. "Who are you?"

"Dammit, Hector! You're fuckin' blinding me!" Dave snarled.

"Say it," the Espian demanded. "Say your real name and where you were born right now."

Dave glared at the shorter man. "Clement. Tyler. Charleston. Terra," he bit off each word. "Who the hell else would put up with your bullshit?"

"I had to be sure," Hector replied. "You never let on that you knew any of this, now you're suddenly a fount of information. It's suspicious." He glanced at Robert. "Speaking of Terra..."

Dave snatched the light out of Hector's hand, pushed past him, and marched down the tunnel, grumbling under his breath.

"What was that about?" Robert asked.

Hector pulled out another light. "We saw and heard things in Ruthaer that got us both thinking about home. Would you go back if you had the chance?"

Robert walked beside Hector, lost in thought, while the light that marked Dave's progress grew smaller. When it was nothing more than a pinprick in the distance, he sighed, then spoke in a soft voice. "Home... When we first arrived in Rowanoake, there wasn't a day that went by where I didn't think about it. Now... Now, I don't know that I *could* go back." He slowly shook his head. "It's not like I could show up on my uncle's doorstep with no explanation of where I've been. No one would believe the truth. They'd think I'm crazy and stick me in a padded room. Besides, all three of us have probably been declared dead. Lost at sea or something."

"It didn't seem right to not ask you, amigo. Gaia is a different world, with different rules from what we grew up with. You and I both have family back there."

"What about you? Would you go back?" Robert asked.

"I miss my family, but I like who and what I am here. Like you said, everyone there has likely finished mourning us and moved on. It would break my mother's heart all over again if she found out I was still alive and never let her know. Besides, someone has to keep Dave out of trouble."

Robert's somber expression turned skeptical. "Keep Dave out of trouble? That's not possible."

"That's exactly what Dave says about you." Hector stopped and peered down the tunnel, but Dave and the other light had moved out of sight. Hector turned to the swordsman. "How much do you know about Dave's mother?"

Robert's brow furrowed and his eyes pinched shut as he shook his head, trying to get a grip on the sudden change in topic. "What? Does this have anything to do with Earl Wolverton and the things Dave said while he was feverish?"

"It does. I haven't had another chance to ask you, and it's important. I learned some things about Bryony. Things that I don't know if Dave has ever told anyone before."

Robert ran one hand through his hair. "She and my mom were identical twins. They did everything together, even going into labor with us. Aunt Brie had talked Mom into having me at home, with a midwife. Dave and I were born about five minutes apart, on either side of midnight, in the same house. It's why my birthday was yesterday and his is today."

"What? I thought his birthday was on Halloween."

"That's what he tells everyone, but that's the day Aunt Brie died."

"Huh. I suppose, in a way, the person he is now was born that day," said Hector. "What else do you remember about her?"

Robert shrugged. "There was a picture of the four of us — both Moms, Clem, and me — when he and I were about three, I guess. It must have been right before Aunt Brie and Clem left Charleston. I found it in the bottom of a box in my parents' closet and kept it hidden in my room. It burned with everything else in the house the night my parents died.

"Aunt Libby thought something happened, some sort of falling out between Mom and Aunt Bryony, and that was why she left with Clem in the middle of the night. She and Uncle Dan didn't know we saw Aunt Brie and Clem on our annual camping trips, up until the year they died. That year, we didn't go camping." He sighed. "My aunt and uncle didn't have a very high opinion of Aunt Bryony, and generally tried to ignore Clem's existence. They didn't want me to have anything to do with him. It was the first time I openly defied them." His eyebrow rose. "What did you find out?"

Hector glanced down the tunnel again then leaned closer to Robert. "Amigo, I found out how Bryony died. It's why Dave won't stay in a cabin alone, and the reason magic freaks him out."

Robert's bright blue eyes widened. "That bad?"

"Worse," Hector replied.

"Hurry up, you two!" Dave's deep voice echoed down the tunnel.

Robert startled guiltily. "Come on. Dave can tell me about it someday when he's ready."

Hector and Robert caught up with Dave in a cavern containing a broad, shallow lake illuminated by dim crystal pendants in a rainbow of colors. Lazy fish swam among plants growing out of the sandy lakebed. A narrow shoreline curved around the water's edge to another tunnel on the far side.

"Someone's been here," Dave informed them. He pointed to tracks leading back and forth along the beach.

"Couldn't those be Aislinn and Eidan's tracks?" Robert asked.

Hector exchanged the red light in his hand for the bright white one Dave held and studied the ground. "No," he said after a few minutes. "There are only two boot patterns, but they're both too big to be Aislinn's. Look here, someone was on his knees at the water's edge." He shined his light over the mishmash of prints leading around the lake to the other tunnel mouth. "We'd have to get Xandor down here to sort them out."

"Shit," Dave muttered. "Come on. Let's see if they took anything."

They followed the tracks into a wide tunnel that opened into a series of rooms, grottos, and niches, each illuminated by a different colored crystal. In one, soft blue light shimmered over a scattering of broken coral, pearls, and multicolored shells. In another, milky white light refracted in the shards of a crystal punch bowl and a spray of uncut gemstones. Each room looked ransacked.

"Whoever it was made a mess," Robert commented as they passed yet another overturned display, "like they were looking for something in a hurry. Do you think Xandor was right, and dærganfae are looking for that ivory dagger you mentioned?"

"It's possible," Hector said, wondering when Brand had collected so many gems. "I brushed him off this morning, and I shouldn't have."

Dave stopped at a tall, empty niche. Crepuscular light emanated from a dark amethyst pendant the size of a goose egg. "Damn. Brand is going to be pissed," he said.

"Why? What was here?" Hector asked. After the pearls and gems, he expected gold, or perhaps a priceless artwork.

"A sword, a hatchet, and a skull."

"Are you serious?" Robert asked.

Dave nodded. "The sword and skull belonged to the person who killed Aislinn's mentor. She and Brand couldn't save Edge, but they killed his murderer. The hatchet was the one Aislinn buried in the guy's forehead. Brand kept trophies."

"That is disturbing on all kinds of levels," Robert replied.

"If you say so," Dave shrugged. "That sword was one of a kind, probably worth more than everything else he collected, combined."

"Really?" Hector asked. "What did it look like?"

"A huge broadsword, damn near as tall as you. Sixty inches of alien metal, black with bright red swirls and flecks, like blood spatter, about three inches wide with a full-length double fuller. Razor sharp from tip to midpoint, and then serrated from midpoint to crossguard. The hilt and guard were shaped like some kind of weird, frilled lizard. Eidan didn't tell me at the time but, considering everything we've learned in the past few weeks, it must have been a dærganfae blade."

"I think Jasper's right, and the guy we just found gut-stabbed is the one who attacked Brand," said Robert.

"Hummingbird's convinced it was that freaky-looking eagle from Ruthaer who attacked Brand," said Dave. "Told me she saw it in a dream."

Hector swore softly. "There's one thing we haven't found yet. How much farther to Brand's sleeping chamber?"

Dave tensed, then said, "Not much farther," before leading the way down the last length of tunnel. The trail ended in another cavern lit by a glowing chunk of citrine. Coins, shells, and smooth pebbles littered the soft sand floor. A warm breeze drifted in through the cavern's wide mouth, bringing the sound of insects and a lonesome owl.

To the right of the entrance, a wooden table held a single open book with a charcoal pencil lying in its gutter, and a scattering of coins across its pages. On the other side of the cavern, a low stack of square stones supported Aislinn's diamond and ebony casket. Her face pressed against the side, and both the tiny pillow and flower crown were in disarray, as if she lay in a fitful slumber.

"Poor Brand," Robert murmured. "If he'd only asked, Jasper and I would have helped him bring her here."

Hector groaned and stumbled forward to sink to his knees beside the casket. He pressed his forehead against the crystalline side near Aislinn's, murmuring a prayer in strangled Espian.

Dave stared at the glowing citrine. "That isn't where this belongs," he grumbled and plucked the crystal from the floor, then crossed to the table, illuminating the small niche above it. Inside, two signet rings shimmered. "Son of a bitch."

"What's wrong?" Robert asked softly as he crossed the room to join Dave.

"Aislinn and Eidan's rings." Dave looked down at the table and swore again while making a sign against evil.

Robert studied the book resting there. Handwriting barely recognizable as Eidan's scrawled across one of the pages. Although written like a bit of poetry, its contents were a warning:

Ogham, Tanjara, 4231

Beware, child.

Thy future is plagued by Darkness.
Danger and Death move inexorably toward you.
They will be both your undoing and your salvation.
First and last of your kind,
Two halves of a greater whole.
Key the Súmairefola longs to find,
It shall strive to own your souls.
One slain by rage in mountain naos,
One slain by hate midst sacred trees,
Spirit caught in the eye of chaos,
The kiss of Death shall set you free.

"Xandor's Tanjaran. Do you think he'd know what this is?" Robert asked.

"I think it's obvious," replied Dave. "Someone predicted Aislinn and Brand's deaths a year before we met them."

"Madre de Dios... Dave! Robert! Help me," Hector cried.

The two instinctively drew their weapons as they leapt apart and spun to see what was attacking their friend. Instead, they found him on his feet, struggling to open Aislinn's casket.

"Hector, what are you doing?" Robert demanded. "Don't open that."

"She isn't dead!" Hector exclaimed.

The swordsman resheathed his rapier. "Hector, I know you don't want her to be dead, none of us do, but Phaedrus could not save her. She's gone."

"Her breath fogged the glass," Hector insisted. "I saw it."

"Bloody Hell," Dave swore. "Don't open the casket, Hector. She's a vampire."

"Vampires don't breathe, Dave."

"Yes, they do," he insisted. "If they didn't, they wouldn't be able to talk. We're going to have to come back when it's daylight, put a stake through her heart, and cut off her head."

"Dave! We are not doing that," insisted Robert.

"You don't understand, Robert. I *have* to." Dave swallowed against the sudden lump in his throat, and his fists clenched so tight his arms shook. "After Mi'dnirr bit her, Aislinn begged me to promise we would make sure she didn't rise. Instead, I told her that cock and bull story I read in Ozera's library about how vampires are made."

"You're wrong, Dave," said Hector. "I gave her my blood, just like Hummingbird. It's working. That's why El Patrón's resurrection ritual failed — she wasn't actually dead. We have to take her to the hospital before my blood turns around and poisons her, too."

"Dammit, Hector! Would you listen to yourself? If she's alive, why couldn't Brand tell?" demanded the archer.

"I don't know," Hector shouted, "but we aren't going to cut off her head!"

Robert stepped between Hector and Dave before they came to blows. He fixed them with a stern glare. "Here's what's going to happen. None of us are opening that casket. Hector, go fetch the healer who saved Hummingbird. The two of us will stay here and keep watch. We aren't making a move until the healers determine what's happening. Now go."

CHAPTER 43
DODZ' PRISONER

August 18, 4237 K.E.

9:30pm

Dodz tossed his ruined shirt in the fireplace. After wiping away any remaining traces of dærganfae blood, he removed the wig hiding his pale blonde hair and pulled a new shirt from his bag. A mirror on the wall reflected the dark circles under his eyes, a testament to his growing anxiety. Through the theater makeup he'd used to darken his skin, he could see the word, 'LIAR,' on his forehead. The word on his right arm had settled into a deep eggplant color. On his left arm, the scars left by Ymara were pale as fresh snow. Even as he watched, a new line of red welts stretched across his stomach, spelling out the word 'MURDERER.'

He was caught between dangerous powers.

Ymara wanted a woman to wear her mask, giving the vampire a new body and the freedom to roam Gaia once again. Mi'dnirr also wanted his freedom, but that, Dodz thought, would spell the end of the world as they knew it. In Tydway, Ymara had called Mi'dnirr Bēl Šibṭu, Lord of Plagues, and spoke of releasing their siblings from the Abyss. Dodz shuddered, remembering the encounter.

The Collectors of Erinskaya wanted him to complete his contract: deliver the bounty hunter's head to Boyar Tretyakov and hand them Ruthaer's relics. He couldn't count on his employers to protect him from Ymara or Mi'dnirr. He had no doubt that, if it came to it, they would use Dodz as bait to trap the vampiric fae.

Looking at his body in the mirror, he realized he'd attracted the attention of another power. The clerics had him trapped in Ozera. Worse, they used magic to mark him with a small — but growing — list of crimes.

He paced, considering and discarding a dozen or more options, searching for a means to come away from this job with his life, his freedom, and his sanity. He could only hope Ymara, once free, would be able to save him from both Mi'dnirr and Ozera's priests, and the Collectors could save him from her.

His gaze settled on the curved knife and its black diamond lying on the cabin's single table. The gem winked at him in the candlelight, seeming to glow with an inner light which wavered, then steadied. The oily sheen on the diamond's surface did odd things with the light, and for a moment, he thought he could see the half-elf's shadow move across one of the facets. Perhaps he should have left the blade in the gut of that dærganfae mage as a gift for Mi'dnirr. He shook his head. No, that would have been a waste of a good bargaining chip.

Dodz rubbed his fingertips over the mound at the base of his thumb, thinking. He knew Hector had hidden the mask somewhere here in Ozera. It was the only piece of good luck he'd had of late. Whatever the bounty hunter and his mage had done, they'd granted him a measure of peace from the demon shlyukha, which also meant the archer was spared her savage attentions as well. Dodz stopped. The archer was the key.

Idly, he wondered if the archer and the bounty hunter would trade the mask for their half-breed woman's soul.

Dodz leaned forward and picked up the sheathed blade in his left hand and grasped the diamond with his right. A wave of dizziness swept through him as the girl's spirit fought his will, but he was ready for it and shoved her deeper into the stone.

In his mind's eye, he entered his favorite room. Aislinn hung from a thick, wooden post with her wrists shackled in irons above her head. Licking his lips, Dodz grabbed her red-gold braid and jerked her head back so he could see her face. He paused. She looked... different. The bronze flecks in her green eyes reflected the ambient light, as though they really were bits of metal.

He stepped back and studied her. Her svelte figure was still sheathed in dark leather pants and vest. Now, he noticed regularly shaped scars marred her bare arms in streaks darker than the surrounding flesh, as though scales covered her creamy elf skin. His thoughts flashed to the injured dragon and back. It seemed she and it were still connected.

He stepped forward and willed the black knife to appear in his right hand. "It's time to talk again."

With surprising strength and speed, she broke away from the post and lunged forward, bits of chain dangling from her wrists.

Count Dodz jerked to one side and swung his fist. Just as her hand closed around the knife's hilt, his knuckles connected with her cheek. Her head whipped to one side, but momentum carried her against him, and they tumbled to the glossy floor.

Dodz rolled, trying to pin the girl down, but like a serpent, she twisted and slithered her way to the top. Her free hand sought his throat. He planted his feet and bucked his hips. She pitched forward, off balance, and he wrapped an arm around her torso, knife at her back. With his other hand, he grabbed her braided hair and snatched her to one side.

She landed hard, rage bright in her eyes. He rolled up onto his knees and touched the black knife tip to her cheek, just below one eye, ceasing her struggles.

"What do you want from me?" she snarled.

"The Espian. You seem to know him rather intimately." The leer on his face made the word seem vulgar. "Tell me about him. Tell me all his secrets."

"You'll get nothing from me," Aislinn hissed. She blinked, and her pupils became vertical slits that glowed like molten bronze.

His lip curled in revulsion as he met her bizarre, reptilian gaze with eyes colder than winter. "Nothing? I think you're wrong."

CHAPTER 44
CONFESSION

August 18, 4237 K.E.

11:00pm

It had been a long day, and tomorrow would likely be just as long, but Hector couldn't quite bring himself to go upstairs to bed. Instead, he dropped into a chair and propped one foot on the low hearth. A tiny, yellow flame sprang to life among the embers. He stared into the flame, letting the day play through his mind, and tried to fit the pieces together. Count Dodz, Mi'dnirr, the attack on Brand, dærganfae in Ozera, and Aislinn's spiritless body held in a coma-like state — he felt like he was putting together one of those round puzzles with no discernible edge, and he had no idea if he had all the pieces.

At least Aislinn was under guarded care in Ozera's hospital. He had to explain about his blood and confess to Sister Inez and Brother Giovanus what he'd done to Aislinn and Hummingbird in Ozera's quarry, but it was unavoidable. After examining Aislinn for themselves, the two healers agreed Hector's assessment was correct, but they were unable to explain how no one detected signs of life before or after the ritual on Brodgar Tor.

For the time being, only Hector, Dave, Robert, and Jasper knew about this new development. They wouldn't burden Shayla with the information until the healers determined whether they could restore Aislinn's spirit to her body.

The trail signs left in the Aerarium bothered Hector. The only person who could have carved them was Count Dodz, but how had the Rhodinan known about Aislinn's personal Ranger Corp sigil? Hector was missing some vital clue — he could feel it — but reliving Aislinn's death every night in his nightmares was taking a toll.

As if sparked by Hector's thoughts of restless sleep, a massive yawn erupted from Dave. He lay sprawled on the couch with one leg across the cushions and the other foot on the floor. He gripped a half-empty wine bottle in one hand and had an unopened bottle of D'Arneau Gigondas on the coffee table. From time to time, he sniffed the bottle in his hand.

A bead of sap popped and flared in the grate, and both men jumped.

"Dodz and the damned dærganfae are here," Dave grumbled. "Probably Mi'dnirr, too. We can't catch a fucking break."

"If what Xandor said about them is true, they're the ones who robbed Brand and tried to kill him."

"What about Dodz? You know good and damn well he's the one who put together that display in Aislinn's room. We need to find him."

"We will." Hector half turned so he could see Dave. "I didn't tell you earlier... Dodz broke into the Aerarium."

Dave shifted on the couch and said, "Shit. When?"

"Don't know," Hector shrugged. "Probably the night of the fire."

Dave sat up and his dark eyes bored into Hector. "The mask?" Fear saturated his deep voice.

"Dodz didn't get it... but I bet he thought he was going to," Hector said. In a quieter voice, he continued, "He got the Orbuculum and that ivory dagger, but gracias a Dios, the mask wasn't there to steal."

Dave's eyes narrowed. "Hector, I was there when you gave the box to the priest."

"I know," Hector nodded, "but, amigo, I couldn't risk it."

"So, where is she?" Dave asked, looking about the room as if he expected the vampire to appear at any moment.

Hector didn't miss the fact that Dave referred to the mask as 'she' instead of 'it.' "I hid *it* and gave the church a duplicate."

"You know, that's why nobody trusts you."

"Yeah," Hector said with a sad smile. "I was right though, and now it works to our advantage. I have a plan to draw out Dodz."

Dave made a face and took a long swallow from the bottle in his hand. He stared at the label while he forced it down, then sat the bottle on the table. "Out with it."

"Lady D bit him. Dodz followed us here all the way from Ruthaer, just like you said he would. That means he can hear the mask calling him. It will draw him to it."

"Don't let her out of that box!" Dave jerked up from the couch and paced the room like a caged tiger, one hand grasping the brooch at his throat. "Fuck, man. I heard Ymara whispering to me even with the protection of this amulet. Have you already forgotten what happened between Ruthaer and here?" His thumb slid over the surface of the ruby, following the thin crack in one of the facets.

Hector dropped his foot from the hearth and turned to straddle his ladder-back chair. Slivers of firelight shifted and danced in the dark room. "I haven't forgotten. I also haven't forgotten it was ese pendejo who brought Lady D and that clockwork monster to Ruthaer in the first place."

"Hector, there's got to be another way." Dave leaned on the mantle and stared down into the fireplace. "You know I can't resist her. Someone will get hurt."

"I know, that's why I was thinking I'd leave you here and take the mask into the Aerarium. When Dodz shows up, I'll nab him. You'll be safe."

Dave turned and faced Hector. The flame at his back cast a dark shadow over his face, so that not even his eyes were visible. "It's not me I'm worried about."

Hector suppressed a shiver and shook his head. "So, we keep you restrained or unconscious until it's over, and the mask is locked away again."

"You're fucking insane."

"¡Dios mío! What do you want me to do?" the bounty hunter demanded. "Should I let Dodz go free? Let him keep screwing with our heads? He was in Aislinn's *room*. What if he decides to use Señora Yves or Eidan as leverage against us? Dammit, Dave, you just said we have to do something!"

The archer massaged his temples. "I know. I just wish it didn't involve freeing Lady D."

"It doesn't. I was thinking I'd just open the thing's box and let it call to Dodz. It will only be for a little while, and I promise I won't let it out of my sight."

"You're making this shit up as you go, aren't you?"

Hector shrugged. "That's how plans get made, right?"

Dave huffed and sank back onto the couch. "If you're going to pull this stunt, at least talk to Robert first." He leaned forward and grabbed the bottle from the table. "You're going to need all the help you can get."

CHAPTER 45
DREAMS OF FIRE

August 19, 4237 K.E.

6:00am

The world was on fire. A dærganfae with sharp fangs and madness burning in his silver eyes held Eidan by the throat. He struggled against the vampire but couldn't escape.

Through the shimmering air, Eidan caught sight of a second fae with only one eye — the mage Brand called Anauriel. His cruel mouth formed soundless words, and balls of angry red energy blossomed around his upraised hands. The mage hurled the spell.

The oncoming fireballs filled Eidan's vision. The vampire released him, flashed into the shape of a giant eagle, and fled.

Bronze wings curled around Eidan, and the spell slammed into Brand, blasting dragon and elf into the trees. His screams and the dragon's roar blended into an aria of agony. They skidded to a stop, Eidan trapped in Brand's embrace.

The fae mage crossed the smoldering ground, his form backlit by the blazing mountain, but Eidan could not escape.

Eidan jerked awake and groaned. He reached to wipe the sleep from his eyes and winced as his bruised muscles protested. A muffled cry from upstairs sent him kicking at the blankets twisted around him. He rolled out of bed, swaying on unsteady legs. A homespun cotton tunic hung halfway to his knees, and loose trousers cinched at the waist with a rope belt were rolled in a thick cuff around his ankles. He could remember neither donning the clothes, nor why they were too big.

His eyes drifted to the shelf of stuffed animals and odds and ends Aislinn collected in her travels, their outlines barely visible in the light of false dawn. A wave of grief washed over him. His bare feet pattered on the floorboards in his rush to escape Aislinn's bedroom, the memories, and the pain.

Eidan limped down the hall to the stairs, wracking his brain to remember what happened. Flickers of memory came to him in jagged flashes — dærganfae in Sunrise Chapel, fire, and horrible pain. Brand's broken form on a dark shore... He pushed each memory aside until the image of aquamarine eyes in an amber face framed by short, crimson colored hair rose to the fore. Hummingbird's soft voice whispered in his memory like a half-forgotten dream.

At the top of the stairs, curtains kept the living room in deep shadows. Black cloth draped the mirror over his mother's writing desk. In the back left corner of the room, her door hung open. The sound he'd been following didn't come from there, though. To his right, from the bedroom overlooking the yard where Edge taught Aislinn to throw hatchets, he heard movement. His brow drew down in confusion. Someone was in his room.

Eidan eased the door open, and his mouth fell open in surprise. The girl from his dream lay curled in a tight ball on a blanket pallet beside his narrow bed. She trembled in her sleep, and the echo of a sob reached him, even though he could see she wasn't crying. He crept toward her, wondering why she was on the floor instead of the bed. Eidan knelt, debating whether or not to wake her. She twitched, and fear contorted her features. Tears spilled from her eyes.

He brushed her cheek with the backs of his fingers. Suddenly, he could hear the crackle of flames and the clash of weapons. He twisted away, searching for the fire, and the sound vanished. Eyes wide and his heart hammering in his thin chest, Eidan turned back to the girl. Her trembling had grown worse in the moment he looked away.

"Hummingbird?" he whispered, but she didn't stir. "Hummingbird, wake up."

She couldn't hear him through her own nightmare.

Remembering how she braved the storm-tossed beach to save him from the darkness, Eidan stretched out on the blanket beside her and wrapped his hand around her clenched fist. The sounds of fighting, of children screaming, filled his ears. Darkness swept over him, and a burning village replaced the room.

Rough-looking men with swords and torches herded a group of elf children into an open patch of blackened grass. Hummingbird crouched among a group of adolescents. Iron collars and chains bound them together. Men with cudgels guarded them, lashing out at anyone who tried to resist.

"Hummingbird, you have to wake up!" Eidan pleaded. Rather than acknowledge him, she clung to the younger girl at her side.

One of the invaders wrenched a little boy away from his mother. When she dove after the child, another man drove a sword into her back. Her eyes widened, and her face contorted with pain. A scream echoed in the dream, but the dying mother never made a sound.

Raucous laughter cut through the night. The captives in the village center huddled in a tight knot, older children shielding the younger, all sporting fresh bruises. An older boy lunged at their captors. His hand clamped around the closest man's wrist, and the human crumpled to the ground with a strangled cry, his weapon falling from nerveless fingers. The man beside him stepped forward and cleaved the boy's head clean from his shoulders. Eidan tore his eyes away from the horrible scene.

Between one blink and the next, the dream shifted, and he stood in the doorway of a musty, windowless room. Hummingbird sat on a narrow cot, still clutching the younger girl. In the flicker of candlelight, the dead girl's aqua colored eyes stared in fixed horror.

Eidan rushed across the room. "Hummingbird, this isn't real," he said. She ignored him, rocking slowly. She and the other girl bore the same red whorls and white dots across their cheeks and had similar features. He realized the dead girl was Hummingbird's sister.

He reached out and gently turned Hummingbird's face toward him. "You're having a nightmare, Hummingbird. It's time to wake up."

She shook her head and closed her eyes.

Eidan climbed onto the cot and wrapped his arms around Hummingbird. He pulled her tight against his chest, but she struggled to escape. "Hummingbird," he soothed, "please wake up."

She stilled in his arms, and silence fell.

The images in his mind's eye faded. Sunlight warmed his back. Eidan found himself staring into wide, tear-filled eyes that reminded him of gemstones. Her hand clutched his.

"I'm sorry," he whispered.

"*No,* I'm *sorry,*" her voice whispered in his mind.

His dark bronze eyes widened. "How did you do that?"

She jerked her hand away and scrambled onto the cot. Back to the wall, she drew her knees to her chest.

Eidan pushed himself up onto his knees. "How did you talk in my mind?"

She flinched and leaned her forehead on her knees.

"Hummingbird, please. I'm not mad. I just want to know how you did it."

Slowly, she raised her head. Her arms unfolded from around her legs, and she made a series of gestures.

"What are you doing?" he asked.

She touched her throat and shook her head.

"Are you hurt?"

Again she shook her head, then crossed her forefingers over her lips.

"You can't talk?"

She offered him a wan smile and nodded.

"So talk in my mind," he replied. "I can't understand finger wiggles."

Tentatively, she held out her hand. Eidan climbed onto the cot and slid his palm over hers.

"*My tribe's gift was to communicate with a shared touch and to hear each other's call, no matter how far.*"

"Is that how I heard you crying from downstairs?"

"*You heard?*"

"It woke me up, and I followed the sound up here."

"But that shouldn't be possible. You aren't of my tribe. They are dead."

"All of them?" Eidan whispered. "There must be someone, somewhere."

"My sister and I were the last two. She's been gone more than two years now."

With his free hand, he brushed the tear streaks from her face. "I lost my sister, too. Have you come to live with Emä and me?"

She closed her eyes and gave a tiny, slow shake of her head. *"Only for a little while, I think. I doubt your mother wants me to stay."*

"You're here, aren't you? That means Emä likes you. Why wouldn't she want you to stay?"

"Because Aislinn died saving me."

Eidan blinked slow and hard. "How... How did it happen?" he whispered.

"There was a monster. It wasn't alive, and I couldn't sense it. We were trying to save children, and it attacked us. She pushed me out of the way, and it killed her instead." Fresh tears trailed down her cheeks. *"Seeing me hurts Shayla."*

"You don't know that it's you," he replied. "We're all sad Aislinn died, but it isn't your fault."

"But I do know, Eidan. That's the other side of my so-called gift. I can sense other people's emotions, even when I don't want it. I just have to be close, not even touching them. If I concentrate hard enough, I can block out specific things for a little while, but not before I've already felt them."

"That's amazing."

"It's horrible. Can you imagine walking through a crowd, feeling every sorrow, every pain? Sure, you could feel someone's hope and joy, but then you get blindsided by lust or rage."

"Yesterday, I was trapped inside my own head. I didn't even know it was a nightmare until you found me." He sighed. "I wish I had magic like that."

"But you're a dragon," she replied. *"That's much better."*

He snorted and shook his head. "You're funny. Do I look like a dragon?"

She eyed him critically. *"You look like an elf."*

"Of course I do. Just like my mother and sister."

"Brand —"

"Died saving me from a pair of dærganfae on the mountain," he said. He gave her a sad smile. "You know, I thought I dreamed you." Eidan touched the spot on his forehead where she kissed him in the dream. The skin tingled. He gave her hand a gentle squeeze. "Can you teach me your hand signs? Maybe we can think of something I can teach you, in exchange."

"Do you know how to read and write? Last night, Dave said I need to learn."

Eidan scowled. When he spoke, his voice came out in a growl. "You should stay away from him. Hector, too. They're dangerous."

She cocked her head to one side. *"Maybe, but they saved my life."*

"Aislinn would be alive right now if she'd stayed here and not gone off with them."

"What happened in Ruthaer wasn't their fault," Hummingbird replied.

"Everywhere they go, trouble swarms like fleas on a dog," Eidan said. "That old lady warned Aislinn and Brand..."

Hummingbird brushed a hand through his hair, pushing an unruly curl back from his eyes. *"What old lady?"*

Eidan shrugged. "Some sort of seer Aislinn met on one of her trips among the mountain clans with Edge, when she was his apprentice. She told Aislinn that danger and death were coming for her. That's Hector and Dave: Danger and Death." His jaw clenched and he closed his eyes tight. Even so, a tear escaped and trailed down his cheek.

Hummingbird drew in a startled gasp, and her fingers stiffened in his before she pulled her hand away. Sadness swirled in the air between them. His forehead dropped to his knees. Grief overwhelmed him.

Her hip brushed against his, and her arms circled his bruised ribs. He raised his head and wrapped his arms around her in turn. They sat for a long time, heads on each other's shoulders, transforming their shared grief into something resembling comfort.

CHAPTER 46
PREPARATIONS

August 19, 4237 K.E.

7:30am

The buzz of conversations and clatter of utensils on dishes flowed from open doors and windows of the Oak Grove Inn. Hector stopped in the arched doorway and scanned the dining room, searching the faces of the guests. Not finding any obvious danger, he wound his way past them to a small table in the far corner of the room beside a sunlit window.

"Buenos días, señor. May I join you?"

"Is it a good morning?" Roger asked, motioning with his half-eaten muffin to the empty chair in front of him.

"The sun is shining, and I have a plan to capture Dodz," Hector replied with a broad smile. "I'd say that qualifies as good, despite everything that's happened."

Roger took a slow sip of kahve, watching Hector over the rim of his mug.

Hector briefly relayed the previous afternoon and evening's events, starting with the dærganfae at the Humble Servant, finding the ranger signs in Aislinn's bedroom, and ending with the discovery of the theft from Brand's cavern. "What I can't figure out is why Dodz would try to make it look like Aislinn is sending us messages."

"What about the dærganfae?"

Hector shrugged. "Not sure. He was having lunch when Xandor and I saw him yesterday, then he left. He didn't appear hostile, but from what I hear that doesn't mean much. Until he regains consciousness, we won't know who he is or why he was watching us."

Roger settled back in his chair. "Queen Ambrose has a treaty with one of the fae noble houses from their home realm beyond Gaia, but the dærganfae residing in the Haunted Hills don't acknowledge it. If they are looking for the ivory dagger, it may explain why they attacked Brand and plundered his lair, but not the sigil used to harm Phaedrus and the others." He was silent for several long moments while he mulled things over. "My people in Vologda managed to dig up some information on Count Zhevon Dodz, mostly rumors."

"Is he really nobility?" asked Hector.

Lord Vaughn nodded. "He recently inherited the title when the last of his elder siblings died."

"Did he kill them himself?"

"Not that anyone can prove," said Roger. "Nor can they prove he works for the Collectors of Erinskaya, a shadow organization that runs the local Mage's Guild and Library. They send out people all over Gaia to find artifacts and other relics. My people are looking for any possible connections between them and the dærganfae."

"I doubt you'll find one. In Ruthaer, I saw fresh scars on Dodz' arms. Scratches, and at least one bite. Dave told me Lady D warned him Dodz would come for the mask. He hears her call, just like Dave."

Roger narrowed his eyes at the bounty hunter. "Is that why you lied to me, passing off your plaster model as the real mask?"

"Sí, señor. Dodz is slippery, and I feared exactly what happened."

A waitress stopped, and Hector asked for a cup of kahve. He waited in silence for her to return, taking the opportunity to scan the changing crowd.

"Tell me about this plan of yours," said Roger.

"We know Dodz wants the mask, and we know he was in the Aerarium. I believe he left himself a way to get back inside."

"I'm listening," said Roger.

"I want to take the mask — the real one — into the Aerarium and open its box. Lady D will call to Dodz. When Dodz answers, we'll capture him."

"Nothing is that simple, Hector. Believe me, all plans work great until you get punched in the face."

"You're right, it isn't. I have a couple of obstacles I'm hoping you can help with."

"Only a couple?" asked Roger.   A hint of mischief twinkled in his whiskey-colored eyes.

"First, I need you to help me convince Sister Georgiana — or Brother Simon if he's out of the hospital — to let us lay this trap."

"Who is 'us'?"

"Me, Robert, Jasper, and Gideon. Xandor, too, if I can find him."

"Not Dave?"

"No, señor, that's the other thing I need your help with. Taking Dave into the Aerarium would put the rest of the team in danger.   I intend to leave him tied up at home with Hummingbird to watch him, but she's no match for him if he were to get loose.   I need someone to back her up, so to speak."

Roger's expression sobered.   "Dave doesn't know you're here, does he?"

"No," Hector replied, shaking his head.   "When I left home, he was setting up archery targets and straw effigies. It looked like he planned to be a while."

Roger ran a hand through his hair, then said, "I'll help you on two conditions."

Hector waited.

"First: Don't kill Dodz. Bring him in for questioning. I'll speak to Brother Ignatius, let him know there's a bounty out on Dodz, one I'm backing, and that you're bringing him in tonight. Keep in mind, Ozera's gaol isn't much more than a drunk tank, so strip that bastard of anything and everything he could possibly use to escape. I want him naked."

Hector nodded. "And your second condition?"

"Introduce me to Robert."

"You met him at the hospital, señor."

"We all had other things on our minds at the time, Hector," Roger replied.   "I want a real introduction, to sit down and talk with him. Get to know him. If I wait for Dave, it may never happen."

Hector studied the nobleman. The similarities between him and Dave were uncanny, but then he remembered the painting of Bryony. "Señor, I think I know what you want to tell him. Believe me, I understand the importance of family, but do you really think it's the right thing to do? It'll destroy everything he's ever known about who he is and where he's from."

"I'm not trying to destroy anything." Roger's brow drew down, and his jaw clenched briefly. "Nate and Cam were my friends. I purposely sent my wife and unborn child... *children* to them for protection. Eventually, they would have told Robert the truth of his parentage. He deserves to know."

"Perhaps, but you don't have any proof."

Roger fingered the locket on his chest. "Yes, I do. I've had it all along."

"What kind of proof?"

"A photo of Brie and our sons, right after they were born. I found it behind the one of her and Dave."

Hector straightened in his chair. He couldn't see how the situation would turn out any way other than bad, but it was obvious Roger would approach Robert whether he agreed or not. He sighed. "Fine. I'll see what I can do."

CRLØ

8:30am

Hector found Xandor dozing against a broad oak bole in the wedge of wooded park separating their cabins from the cliff edge. The sound of metal on metal echoed as Robert and Dave sparred. Rapier and sabre flashed in the sunlight as the brothers lunged, parried, and slashed at one another, faster and faster, until Robert executed a maneuver which sent Dave's sabre flying. Hector picked up the blade on his way across the yard.

"Damn," Dave panted. "You've gotten faster."

"I've had a lot of practice." Robert's face became grim. "My 'traveling companion' from Orleans to Suthose enjoyed watching me bleed. She insisted I spar with her twice a day. By the time we reached southern Deshret, I made her work for every drop."

Dave shifted uncomfortably. He took his sword from Hector, saluted Robert, and sheathed the blade.

Robert returned the salute and sheathed his sword as well. "Let it go, Dave. None of us can change what happened. Besides, I'd rather dwell on the positive. Like how I just beat you left-handed." He brandished a sly grin that was less bravado and more a friendly challenge.

Stepping between the two duelists, Hector said, "It's definitely impressive, amigo. Why don't you both get cleaned up while I wake sleeping beauty over there? We have a lot to do today."

"We do?" asked Robert.

"He has a half-baked plan to catch Dodz," Dave grumbled. "I hope you can either talk him out of it or come up with a way to keep it from going pear-shaped."

"Stop grouching, I've got this," Hector protested. "Now, go wash."

Dave stalked away, muttering to himself.

When Hector turned to fetch Xandor, Robert grabbed his arm. "Hector, wait. Dave told me Earl Wolverton is his father."

"He did?"

"Well... he said the earl claimed Aunt Brie was his wife. I don't think Dave wants to believe him. What do you think?"

"I think..." Hector studied the man before him and chose his words carefully. "I think Dave looks a lot like Lord Vaughn, too much to just be coincidental. He wears a locket that Dave recognized as belonging to his mother, and there's a photo inside of the two of them together. Robert, he seems to be a good man, and, as far as I can tell, he sincerely wants to help Dave and heal the wounds they've both been living with for the past fifteen years."

"Is there anything we can do to help? I'd offer to sit down with Lord Vaughn, but I get the feeling Dave would go ballistic."

"You should definitely talk to Dave before you meet Lord Vaughn." Hector's eyes bored into Robert's as he said, "Dave needs you, but once you start pulling this thread, there's no turning back."

"I get it," Robert replied, stepping away. "I'll talk to Dave first."

Hector watched Robert cross the yard and disappear around the corner of his cabin. He was used to trouble, both starting and finishing it, but this was different. He didn't know how he was going to keep his promise to Lord Vaughn without pissing off Dave or hurting Robert. Putting the matter aside for the time being, Hector wandered over to the sleeping ranger, stopping well out of sword-reach.

"Xandor."

The clansman's mismatched eyes popped open, and he reached for his weapons while surveying the yard for danger. His attention settled on Hector. "Your horse is bored."

"What did Caballo do now?"

"Rodrigo didn't mention anything specific, but he insisted I take Caballo with Xerxes down into Grimshaw Valley for a run this morning. I worked off his excess energy for now, but you need to find someone to pasture him if you're going to stay here much longer. Maybe buy some breeding stock."

"Do you think any of the farmers around here would want to raise a pasture full of willful, stubborn horses that are too smart for their own good?"

Xandor laughed. "You might be surprised. The Iron Tower pays good money for Ranger Corps horses. With proper training, horses like Caballo make excellent partners."

"I'll think about it. Now, where did you disappear to last night?"

"After I fetched you and Jasper, I caught a glimpse of someone spying on Mrs. Yves' yard. Brand's lightshow started before I reached him, though. Turned out, it was Dodz and a dærganfae."

"Do you think they're working together?"

Xandor shook his head and recounted what he overheard the night before. "Dodz gut-stabbed the fae and left him for dead. Did you find the body?"

"The fae was still alive but unconscious. We delivered him to the hospital with instructions for the staff to send word when he wakes. What happened to Dodz?"

"I followed him back to one of the visitor's cabins near the hospital. I waited until the light went out, gave him enough time to fall asleep, then broke in. He wasn't there."

"Did you find a circle of white sand?"

"How did you know?"

"It's how he escaped Ruthaer."

"I watched the cabin the rest of the night but didn't see anyone. I have a friend watching it now, in case he comes back."

"Good work," said Hector. "I have a plan that will bring Dodz to us, but I need your help."

❦

11:00am

After working out the finer points of their plan to capture Dodz, Hector sent the ranger to check in with his friend, Sahmaht, and keep an eye out for the elusive Rhodinan.

"Now what?" asked Dave.

"We should check on Mrs. Yves and Eidan," replied Robert. "Someone invaded Aislinn's room and Brand's caverns. They really shouldn't stay in that house without some kind of protection."

Hector nodded. "Let's go. While we're there, we need to make sure Eidan wears his ring. It does him no good on a shelf."

"It's weird that he looks like a thirteen-year-old boy," Robert said as they walked along the forest path. "Do you think he has some form of memory loss?"

"I hope not," said Hector. "We need to know what happened in Sunrise Chapel."

A few minutes later, August Sabe answered their knock upon Shayla Yves' door. "Good morning. Jasper was just saying he thought I should go look for you three."

"How is Eidan this morning?" asked Hector.

"Surprisingly well." August pointed upstairs. "He's reading to Hummingbird in the family's drawing room. Come to the kitchen. Jasper is preparing lunch, and Teal has been sharing what she knows of bonds between dragons and riders. She seems exceptionally worried for Brand." He paused. "She speaks as if he were her kinsman."

"Teal believes he may be distantly related to Aislinn and her father," responded Hector.

"Wait. Does that mean Aislinn's part lizard?" asked Dave.

Hector shook his head in disbelief. "We already suspected Aislinn and Brand's ancestry made their bond possible. Makes sense to me that she'd have a dragon somewhere in her family tree."

Jasper appeared in the kitchen doorway. "Oh, good, you're here." He pointed at the stairway and sent a colorful bubble drifting into the space overhead.

A boy's voice said, "Look!" a moment before they heard a soft *pop*, and Jasper's disembodied voice announced "Lunch!"

"There in a minute!" Eidan called.

The men followed Jasper into the kitchen. Shayla and Teal were arranging place settings around a long, oval table with six chairs. A platter of sliced ham, a basket of warm brown bread, a pan of potatoes and onions fried in butter, and a big bowl of crisp salad filled the table's center.

Shayla took in the newcomers and said, "August, would you be kind enough to bring more chairs from the music room?"

"Of course, Milady."

"Come on, Dave, let's help him," said Robert as he followed the gallant from the kitchen.

They barely had the nine seats arranged when the sound of running feet preceded the arrival of Hummingbird and Eidan. Hector studied this younger version of his friend. Dark circles underscored Eidan's eyes, and a yellow-green bruise highlighted his jaw. His left arm rested in a sling.

The smile on the boy's face died when he spotted Hector and Dave. "What are they doing here?"

"Eidan Yves! Where are your manners?" demanded Shayla.

"They shouldn't be here, Emä."

"Young man, have you forgotten everything Phaedrus, Edge, and I taught you? Be polite to our guests," said Shayla.

Eidan scowled at the floor and mumbled, "Yes, ma'am." He chose a seat between Shayla and Hummingbird, across the table from August and Teal.

After Robert gave a brief prayer of thanks for the food and everyone's health, an uncomfortable silence settled over the table, punctuated by the clink of silverware.

Eidan shoveled food into his mouth as if he hadn't eaten in a week and didn't know when he would see another meal. When he finally stopped, he glanced at Hummingbird, then turned to Shayla. "May Hummingbird and I be excused?"

Before she could respond, Hector cleared his throat. "Eidan, a lot of people were hurt by the fire on Lumikivi Mountain, including Phaedrus. The person or people responsible could still be in Ozera. We need you would tell us what happened in Sunrise Chapel."

Shayla turned pleading eyes to the bounty hunter. "Hasn't he been through enough?" she asked. "Does he really need to relive the fire?"

"I'm afraid so, Mrs. Yves," answered Robert. "Someone — possibly the same person who attacked Brand — was in your home, in Aislinn's bedroom, and Brand's caverns. They stole some of his treasures. You and Eidan aren't safe until we capture these villains."

Fear drained the color from Shayla's cheeks. She wrapped an arm around Eidan's shoulders.

Hummingbird shifted and, to Hector's utter shock, laid her hand atop Eidan's. Their fingers twined together.

Finally, Eidan spoke. "Dærganfae were in Brand's caves. Mi'dnirr and Anauriel stole Aislinn's body."

"What!" shouted Shayla. She fixed Hector, Dave, and Robert with an angry glare. "Is it true? Is that what you found last night?"

"I told you that damned fae was here," snarled Dave.

"Not now, Dave," replied Hector. "Señora, Aislinn is not in Brand's cave. Until Eidan goes through his treasures and takes stock, we won't know the extent of the theft." He pushed his chair from the table, rose, and walked around to crouch beside the adolescent. "Amigo, what happened?"

Eidan refused to look at him.

"Answer the question, Eidan," Shayla urged.

Instead of answering Hector directly, he spoke to Shayla. "I was with Brand. Something woke him, and he saw Mi'dnirr standing over us. Aislinn was gone. Brand attacked Mi'dnirr, but he escaped. He didn't think a lone dærganfae could get far with Aislinn, so we circled the mountain, searching. A second fae was in Sunrise Chapel. He attacked us."

He shivered, and Hummingbird squeezed his hand. Giving her a wan smile, he said, "They tried to kill us both, but Brand saved me."

Hector held out one of the signet rings he retrieved from Brand's sleeping chamber. "Eidan, you need to wear this ring."

The boy shook his head. "I don't want Brand's ring."

"Please, Eidan," said Hector. "If something happens to you, it's the only way we have to find you."

"It's too big," argued the boy.

"I'll thread it on a ribbon for you," said Shayla, "and you can wear it as a necklace."

"In the meantime," said Robert, "is there anywhere the two of you can go? Somewhere safe you can stay?"

"This is our home," Shayla replied. "Where can we go that's safer than Ozera?"

"We'll protect you, Milady," vowed August.

"Yes," added Teal. "You should have at least one, preferably two, guards at all times."

Robert nodded. "That's what we think, too. However, sheltering inside a church would be best."

"He's right," said Hector. "Neither Mi'dnirr nor Lady D entered the church in Ruthaer."

"Mi'dnirr was in Sunrise Chapel," argued Dave. "That was holy ground, wasn't it?"

"It was," Jasper replied. "Gideon said someone desecrated it."

Hector paced across the kitchen and back. "How about we try something unorthodox? In Ruthaer, Aislinn used horseshoes over doors and windows to protect everyone — even public places, like the inn and the church. We can ask Gideon to bless them and the nails we use to hang them."

Shayla pulled Eidan close. "Do it."

CHAPTER 47
IN MOTION

August 19, 4237 K.E.

7:00pm

Hector cinched the last knot binding Dave's arms to those of a stout wooden chair. "Try getting out of that," he said, taking a step back and surveying his work. Earlier, they'd pushed aside the sitting room furniture to make an open space and moved the chair from the head of their dining table into the center of the room. If Dave turned over the chair, anything he could use to escape would still be out of reach.

"For the record, this plan is stupid." Dave looked from Hector to Robert as he tugged on the ropes. The chair creaked under the strain but otherwise held fast.

"We could always get Jasper to bind you," Robert offered. "He could do that trick of his with the spider webs."

"Asshole," Dave muttered.

"Mind your language," Robert replied and pointed to a new ceramic jar on the mantle. Slime-green paint declared 'Swears' on the side. "Happy belated birthday. Every curse word costs you a silver, and the jar's contents go in the offering plate on Sundays. Every solstice, the price doubles."

Dave glared at Robert but kept silent.

"Do you have a better plan?" Hector asked Dave. "We know Dodz is here, and tonight we're going to catch him."

Dave's doubtful expression plainly said he didn't believe Hector.

Hummingbird sat on the couch under the front window, watching the three friends. She snapped her fingers at them, then signed, "Why are we staying here instead of going with you?"

"It's safer this way," Hector replied. "Just keep an eye on Dave and make sure he doesn't break free."

She gave him a skeptical look, then eyed the wooden chair dubiously.

"It only has to hold him a few hours," Hector said. "If he gives you any trouble, hit him on the head with one of the cast iron skillets."

"Pòg mo thòin," Dave growled.

"Not likely," Hector replied and turned back to the girl on the couch. "I'm not joking, Hummingbird. You saw what happened in Ruthaer. Lady D is going to summon him tonight. If you even *think* he might break loose, knock him out. Don't wait. If that doesn't work, go out the window and run to the chapel. Lord Vaughn will be there, waiting."

"What the hell, Hector?" Dave shouted. "You invited him to spy on me?"

"Yes, I did," replied Hector. "He's your backup tonight."

Turning his back on Dave, he walked to the hearth, pried loose a medium-sized stone above the corner of the mantle, and sat it on the floor. A cavity held a silver box inscribed with black and red sigils, not quite ten inches to a side and four inches deep. It seemed to disappear and reappear as Hector lifted it out. Behind him, he heard Dave's sharp gasp.

Hector sat the box on the table and replaced the stone, ignoring the string of curses Dave aimed at his back. "Let's go, Robert. We have a lot to do. Hummingbird, I'm going to lock this door behind us. Keep it that way." He held the girl's gaze and pointed to the front door. "I mean it. Don't open it. Not even if Aislinn's mother is outside on fire. You hear me?"

Hummingbird squared her shoulders and nodded.

Hector twisted the key in the lock, then rattled the handle to make sure it caught. Satisfied, he dropped the key into his pocket and joined Robert at the edge of the yard.

Robert handed over the silver case. "You think this is going to work?" he asked.

Hector shrugged. "Fifty-fifty. I couldn't tell Dave that, though."

"I'm surprised he let you tie him to a chair." He eyed the box. "He must be *really* afraid of that thing."

Hector nodded. "It's *awake*. I don't know how or why it even exists, but it has a hook in Dave. He'd kill us all if the thing in this box told him to. He wouldn't have a choice."

"And we're leaving that timid little girl alone with him?" Robert asked. "She barely looks fourteen."

"You know elves don't age like we do. She could be a hundred forty for all we know," Hector replied. His face grew pensive as he thought through his plan. "It's her abilities I need tonight. If anyone can keep Dave grounded, she can.

"August and Teal are protecting Señora Yves and Eidan this evening, and I need you and Xandor in the Aerarium with me, Jasper, and Gideon." Hector glanced back at the house and sighed. "I really hope we find a way to destroy the mask. I should have done like Aislinn told me and burned the creature's head to ashes when we burned her body."

"You're questioning yourself, but did it ever occur to you that the mask was already there? If you had burnt the head, all you would have done is exposed Lady D's mask. Then what would you have done?"

"You think she may have been a mask all along?"

"It's possible, and from what you've told me, likely."

"Jasper said the mask's magic is abyssal," said Hector, "but whatever is trapped in the mask acts like a vampire: it bites people, drinks blood, creates thralls, you name it."

"Vampire or not, it's something old, that's for certain."

Hector gave Robert a quick smile and said, "I've missed these talks."

"Me, too," Robert said, then his voice trailed off. "Hector, I've been wondering... No, never mind."

"¿Qué pasa, amigo?"

Robert drew a deep breath and gathered his courage. "Phaedrus has done and can do a lot of amazing things. He's obviously in the Creator's favor."

Hector stopped and stared up at the swordsman, his face carefully devoid of emotion. From the center of the village, bells signaled the beginning of sunset worship.

"Why do you think Aislinn's spirit didn't return when Phaedrus called?"

"I don't know. At first, I thought she chose to remain with her father," Hector replied softly.

"Pardon? Did you say her father?"

"Sí. The first night Lady D and Evan's phantoms attacked us in Ruthaer, other spirits came to our rescue. She... Aislinn ended up fighting beside her father's ghost." Hector fell silent, thinking about the sadness and longing he'd seen in her eyes that morning when her father vanished in the sunrise. "Knowing what we know now, though, I think something else happened. I just can't figure out what."

The two continued on in silence, listening to the aethereal sound of evening vespers echoing through the trees.

Hector pushed open the library door and held it for his friend. Inside, a young woman wearing a library vest over a plain homespun dress looked up from sorting scrolls behind the desk.

Soft hazel eyes studied them as they crossed the foyer. She gave Robert a shy smile. "Good evening. May I help you?"

Robert gave the girl a halfhearted smile in return and avoided her eyes.

"Good evening, señorita," Hector said. "We've brought something for Brother Gideon. I believe he's waiting for us in the Aerarium with Jasper Thredd."

The girl rolled her eyes and turned to Hector. "And you are?"

"Hector de los Santos and Robert Stone."

The girl nodded and tried to catch Robert's eye again. "Let me lock the front door, then you can follow me back. Sister Lorena is waiting." She glanced at Hector, eyes sparkling with excitement. "Is it true that you have something dangerous?"

Hector gave the girl a sharp look. "Sí, señorita. Too dangerous for idle curiosity — unless you want Ozera destroyed."

The girl paled and her eyes grew wide with fear.

"That's better," Hector said. "Open the door for us, then be on your way. If you know what's good for you, you'll go home and stay inside the rest of the night."

CHAPTER 48
UNDERSTANDING

August 19, 4237 K.E.

7:15pm

Hummingbird remained on the couch for several minutes after Hector and Robert left, wondering how long they would be gone. Her eyes wandered around the room, from Dave tied to his chair, to the fire in the fireplace, to the crate shoved against the empty wine rack, to the dirty dishes stacked on the counter by the small sink.

Dave broke the silence. "Open the crate."

"I'm not helping you drink," she signed.

"Not asking you to," he said. "Some of what's inside is for you."

Puzzled, she crossed the room and examined the box. The lid fit into place but wasn't nailed down. There were markings on the outside, but she couldn't read them. She touched the crate, then drew back her hand and turned to Dave. "What is it?" she signed.

"Just open it and bring what's inside over here where I can see."

She eased the lid off and stared down at a book sitting on a bed of straw. Colorful symbols adorned its cover, similar in shape to those on the crate. Setting it aside, she found a thin plate of slate bound by a wooden frame, and a small box with a sliding lid. Inside that box, she found five white sticks as thick as her thumb. She dug through the packing straw some more and uncovered five bottles of wine resting near the bottom.

Leaving the wine, Hummingbird deposited the book, slate, and box of sticks on the floor in front of Dave. She stood with her hands on her hips, waiting for him to explain.

"I told you yesterday you need to learn to write. You can use the slate and chalk to practice."

"You're going to teach me this?" she signed.

He shrugged. "If you insist on following me around, I want you to have more than one way to communicate. Open the book."

On the first page were more symbols, and in the upper right corner was a sketch of a hummingbird. She stared at it briefly before turning the page. Each bore a pair of symbols in bright colors, with a drawing and more symbols underneath.

"The pairs at the top are the letters. The picture tells you what the word is underneath. It's a book for children, but it's a place to start," Dave explained.

She laid the book, slate, and chalk on the storage bench, then glanced around the room again. Returning to the crate, she quickly pulled out each bottle and slid them into the wine rack. From there, she moved to the kitchen area, moving dishes out of the sink.

"Don't clean! We'll get to it... eventually," Dave said. "Why don't you —"

Hummingbird waved her hand at him and pumped water into the kettle and hung it over the fire to warm. By the time it began to steam, she had the floor swept and the dishes rinsed. "Do you have any tea?" she signed.

"There's some in the pantry," he said, "but I don't know how old it is." He watched her dig through the cabinet and wondered if he'd overstepped a boundary by offering to teach her how to read. She seemed to be looking for excuses to avoid the exercise. A minute later, she emerged with a small tin and an infuser on a chain. She filled the ball and dropped it into a large clay mug before pouring the steaming water over it. The scent of peppermint filled the room.

"Hummingbird."

She glanced at him, then turned her attention to bobbing the silver ball in her mug on the hearth.

"Don't you want to learn to read?"

She shrugged. "Why do you want me to go away?" she signed.

"Hummingbird, look at me." He waited until she finally faced him. "It's not safe to be anywhere near me. Someone cursed me when I was a little boy. Every woman I've ever cared about — my mother, my aunt, the only girlfriend I ever dared have, even some of my foster parents — have all died horrible deaths. It's why Aislinn died. It's why you almost died in Ruthaer. You have to stay here and not follow me anymore."

"Nowhere is safe, Dave," she signed. "I learned that the day my family died. The men who attacked my village did horrible things to us, and there is nothing to stop people like that from coming here. Look what happened to Brand and Eidan."

"I can't protect you from the evil in the world. Hell, I can't even protect you from me."

"I don't want you to protect me!" she signed, her hands and fingers flying through each word. "I want you to teach me how to protect myself!"

"If you hang around me, you won't live long enough to get to that point. Why didn't you choose Hector or Aislinn to teach you? Or go back to Altaira and search for other members of your tribe?"

"There are no other members of my tribe. As for choosing a different teacher... Aislinn already had too many things going on in her life. From the moment we arrived here in Ozera, I could feel the strain she was under, the conflict between her loyalty to Brand and her love for you and Hector. As for Hector... He's too..." She stopped, frustration and uncertainty warring on her features. "I'm not comfortable with him. There's too much fire in his blood."

"How in the Hell am I your best alternative?"

"You don't look at me with hunger in your eyes." She drank a big gulp of tea, as though the admission made her nervous. "And you know what it is to be broken inside."

ଓଃ৪০

7:45pm

Dave wished he could get his hands on his flask, even if its contents tasted like beach sand. For several long minutes, he battled his personal demons as they tried to force their way out of the dark shadows of his mind. He sighed. He knew all too well what it meant to be an emotionally shattered child no one wanted. "Alright, I'll make a deal with you. I'll let you stay on two conditions: one, let me teach you to read and write, and two, you have to learn how to brawl."

She gave him a quizzical look, clearly not understanding the word.

"Up close, in your personal space, fighting," he clarified.

"Why that?" she signed. "I'd rather learn to shoot a bow like you."

"Because you won't always be able to keep your enemy at a distance. You're doing alright with the daggers, but you're timid. You panic every time someone touches you, and that's no good in a fight. You have to be able to think straight and be willing to do whatever it takes to win."

He saw the fear in her, and thought he'd stumbled on the one thing that she wouldn't — perhaps couldn't — do. He watched her emotions war with her need but didn't offer any reassurances. She had to overcome her own demons.

The girl stared into her cup for a long time before she finally looked at him again, resolve in her expression. "If I agree, you'll let me stay?" she asked.

"Yeah," he said, shifting in the seat, trying to get comfortable. "Now open the damn book so we can make a start before Hector opens that infernal box and takes out the mask."

Hummingbird was into her second cup of tea and had filled the slate with the first letter of the alphabet when her hand flew to her mouth. She stumbled to the water closet and barely got the door open in time to be noisily sick.

Scooting his chair around, Dave could see a fine sheen of sweat covering the back of her neck. He yanked on the ropes and cursed Hector's stupid plan.

A second flow of vomit streamed into the latrine, leaving Hummingbird on her knees, clinging to the seat, head propped precariously on one forearm.

With a click, the lock on the front door disengaged. The archer's head whipped in the direction of the sound. "Hector!

Get in here and untie me!" The door opened, but it wasn't Hector who entered the room.

"Dodz, you bastard. What are you doing here?"

The count locked the door behind him. A cruel smile covered his face as he took in the archer's situation. "Well, well, Gospodin Blood. Were you playing a game with your pornai? I must admit, this game I have not seen with clothes on. Mayhap she will teach me, da?"

Dave struggled against the ropes. He heard Hummingbird collapse on the floor. "Asshole. You poisoned the tea?"

"It was the only thing in the pantry the first time I paid a visit. It is not fatal. It will only make her weak and manageable. I hoped to catch you and the bounty hunter, but no matter." His eyes moved from the sick girl in the water closet to the balas-ruby brooch and gold chain that hung around Dave's neck. "First, I will have my charm and that pretty chain."

Dave fought to keep the necklace, attempting to bite the count's hand.

"Give me the brooch, or I will kill the pornai right now," Dodz said, placing a gloved hand on the hilt of his black blade.

"Son of a bitch," Dave hissed. Quick hands snagged the necklace clasp. Murder filled his eyes as Dave watched Dodz fasten Aislinn's necklace around his own throat and drop the brooch inside his shirt.

"I have something special for you," Dodz sneered. He pulled a paper wrapped bundle from a cloth sack and walked to the hearth. He used the poker to close the flue, laid more logs on the fire, then tossed the package on top. Smoke drifted into the room. "I think that will just about do it," Dodz said, rubbing his hands together. "It will take a while for smoke to fill the house, but do not worry, you will be dead long before your friends return."

Dave watched the count drag Hummingbird from the water closet and kneel beside her. He unstrapped her new bracers with their daggers and tossed them on the water closet floor. Licking his lips, Dodz ran a fingertip over the black flower on her wrist and traced it up her amber arm. His finger came away wet from her sweat. "Ymara has requested a host." Dodz touched his finger to his tongue. "She tastes sweet, does she not? Too bad for her."

"You fucking shit! I'll kill you!" Dave scooted the chair toward Dodz, its legs leaving scrapes on the bare wood floor. Bucking and straining, he fought against the ropes binding his arms and legs. Veins bulged along his temple and neck, and his face turned beet red as the chair creaked and groaned but held.

One by one, Dodz removed Hummingbird's boots and flung them across the room toward the fireplace and wine rack, their daggers still tucked in the lining. Eyes full of malice, Dodz peeled off her clothes — groping and touching as he went. Silver scars crisscrossed her back and legs, flashing harshly in the firelight. "Much better," he said, and lifted the young elf across his shoulder like a sack of grain. "I'll be going now. I would hate to disappoint Señor Santos. That was Ymara's mask I saw him taking to the Aerarium, no?"

With his free hand, Dodz pulled a flask from his pocket and poured a circle of white sand in the floor just behind the front door. He stepped into the circle, muttered a single word, and vanished with Hummingbird.

Dave's bellows of rage echoed through the cottage.

CRSO

9:00pm

'*Come to me. Release me.*' The words slithered into his mind, tugging on his will. Dark, whiskey-colored eyes slid open inches below a stinging cloud of smoke. His lungs burned, and he was bound to a chair that refused to break. Her strength became his strength. He arched his back, giving himself more leverage against the arm of the chair. The rope stretched and the chair cracked, but it wasn't enough — at least not yet.

'*Hurry,*' Ymara urged, '*free me from this prison.*'

His scars burned, and his body longed for the pleasure and pain she offered. "Fuck."

He felt the poison from the smoke in the fireplace working through his system, making him drowsy. A part of Dave's mind catalogued his symptoms — nausea, dizziness, erratic pulse — and compared them to the poisons he knew. He caught a sweet scent in the smoke. *Oleander.*

How long had it been since Count Dodz had vanished with Hummingbird?

With his hands and legs bound, the door and the windows might as well be on a different planet. Earlier, he'd wasted a lot of time trying to reach them. Dave scanned the room. There was nothing within reach. Hector had removed every sharp object. All that remained were Hummingbird's boots, and the daggers sheathed in their lining.

'*I'm here. Why do you not take me?*' Ymara's voice insisted. Her eyes swam in his mind, deep pools it was so easy to drown in, and he felt himself slipping.

CHAPTER 49
CAPTURING DODZ

August 19, 4237 K.E.

9:00pm

*U*sing the sight granted to him by Ymara, Dodz peered through the keyhole and into the darkness beyond. The arcaloxós rested in the exact center of a heavy oak table with a square top and solid base, as if the bounty hunter had pulled a podium from one of the chapels. Otherwise, the room was empty.

'Hurry, free me from this prison.'

He listened for the telltale signs of someone hiding nearby — breathing, the rustle of clothes, the scrape of boot on stone — but heard nothing. Dodz set to work with his lockpicks. The faint scrape and click of metal on metal pierced the air. A minute passed as he worked the tumblers, and the lock disengaged with a heavy sounding clunk. The door drifted open on silent hinges.

Dodz ghosted into the alcove, searching the corners for hidden danger. After making certain the space was empty, he stared at the silver box, poring over it, inch by inch. Similar to the one with the false mask, it bore glyphs and sigils on every surface and seemed to disappear and reappear as he turned his head. He pulled a pair of spectacles from his breast pocket and balanced them on his nose. Even with the clerics' magic eyewear, the arcaloxós refused to give up its secrets. He turned his attention to the table itself. He expected traps, but nothing presented itself.

'I'm here. Why do you not take me?'

He pursed his lips and glared around the room. It was too easy. Everything he'd learned about Hector de los Santos and Damage, Inc. indicated there should be traps and alarms, both mundane and magical, yet there was nothing. He had passed through the library to the scriptorium, entered the Aerarium, and found the room where Hector had hidden the arcaloxós without issue. Yes, a priest guarded the Aerarium's back door, and the lock barring the door to this room was complex, but none of that was a challenge. There should have been MORE.

Returning to the doorway, he scanned the empty aisle outside the room. His instincts screamed this was a trap, yet he could neither see nor hear anyone.

Dodz turned back to the ornate box on the table and crouched before the lock. The end of his lockpick glowed, and he caught the glimmer of a needle along the bottom edge of the hole. That was it, a simple poisoned needle to protect this cursed mask?

His lip curled in a sneer. The bounty hunter was not nearly as clever or talented as his half-breed shlyukha believed. It was a moment's work to trigger the mechanism and remove the needle with a pair of tweezers. A few seconds later the lock yielded, and he reached for the lid.

With a blinding flash, electricity arced off the coffer to his gloved hands. An ozone haze rose from the rocking table. The magical surge shoved him back, but the gloves did their job and absorbed the brunt of the attack.

Muttering a curse against his own impatience, he removed his spectacles and rubbed his eyes. The sudden burst of light left him half-blind, and he tried to blink away the spots dancing across his vision. It took him a few moments to realize Ymara's voice had vanished, along with his ability to see in the dark.

When his vision finally cleared, Dodz pushed the spectacles back on his face, lifted the silver lid, and illuminated the container's interior with his lockpick. His eyes widened in surprise. Affixed to the bottom was a single scrap of paper with the words "GOT YOU" in block letters.

Light flooded the room. Dodz' hand flew to the shashka at his hip as he spun on his heel.

"Uh, uh. Don't even think about it," the Espian said. Hector stood in the doorway, backlit by a lantern, holding a loaded hand crossbow aimed at Dodz' chest. "Step out and let's have a chat."

Dodz held his hands up, careful to keep the left between his heart and the Espian's crossbow. "I am quite happy to stand here and chat," he replied. He glanced around the room one more time. Ymara was here. He knew it.

Hector shrugged. "Your choice. Either I shoot you and drag you out, or you come out on your own, sit in a semi-comfortable chair, and answer some questions."

"Give me the mask. I will make you a very attractive offer."

"There's nothing you could buy or steal that I want."

"Prayhaps I have something more precious to offer," Dodz said with Cheshire cat grin. "Something only I can give you. Something you do not even know you desire, da?"

"I want información, pendejo. Now come out before I lose my patience."

CRSO

9:10pm

Count Dodz gave a mocking half bow and followed Hector through the door.

Out in the main cavern, Xandor and Robert approached the prisoner from opposite sides. Robert drew the shashka from Dodz' belt and studied the Rhodinan sabre before passing it to Hector. He stared at the prisoner, studying the color of his eyes and the shape of his features. His eyes settled on the dark purple letters covering the count's forehead.

"Odd choice for a tattoo," Robert commented.

"It is not my choice. The priests saw to it that I have nothing to hide."

"I doubt that," Robert replied. He flipped open the front of Dodz' vest, checking for inside pockets, then felt his way down each of the man's arms.

Robert and Xandor took their time, and a small pile of tools and bric-a-brac soon lay in a sack by their feet. Dodz' only weapon was the finely wrought Rhodinan sabre.

"Gloves, boots, specs, everything," said Hector. "Lord Vaughn said strip him naked."

"Now wait just a minute!" Dodz protested, but the crossbow bolt in his face didn't waiver.

After removing the count's clothes, Xandor bound his hands behind his back with a thin black cord. The ranger eyed the words on their prisoner's arms, face, and torso. "Sister Georgiana was right about the Aerarium's protections," he said to Hector. "Looks like we have a confession of crimes."

"Is he ready?"

"We need Jasper to give him and his gear a once-over to make sure we didn't miss anything," Robert said, hoisting the bulging sack.

Hector nodded. Moving to the oak table, he set aside the crossbow, removed the empty coffer, and raised a concealed panel in the tabletop. The second arcaloxós glinted in the light when he lifted it from the secret compartment, the lid already closed.

"Simple tricks are the best," mused Hector, locking the box.

"And the most risky," Robert added.

They marched Dodz, naked as the day he was born, through the Aerarium to a secluded reading room where Gideon and Jasper patiently waited. A circle of unlit candles surrounded a lonely, ladder-backed chair with a cowhide seat still bearing the animal's brown and white hair.

"There," Jasper said to Dodz, pointing. When Dodz was settled, the mage made a series of complicated gestures and muttered a string of arcane words before his hand dropped into one of his many pockets. More gestures followed, then he threw a pinch of pale powder into the air as he shouted, "Fanérosi!" His eyes blazed with golden light, and he stared at Dodz.

"There's nothing magical hidden on his person," Jasper reported. "Where are his things?"

"I have them," Robert answered, handing over the sack.

Jasper spread Dodz' belongings across a desk, checking each item against a list provided by Sister Georgiana, and set aside the sword, vest, and spectacles. He lifted a platinum bracelet bearing four charms. "This is a pretty piece of work," he said, holding it up so everyone could see. "The bracelet has some type of alteration magic, but each charm has its own, separate magic as well. I'll try to figure out what their enchantments do."

"Let me know if you do," Hector said. "We still need to recover the Orbuculum and ivory dagger." He turned to Gideon. "Let's get started."

The priest stepped forward. "Eternal Father, hear our prayer. Guide us this night in rooting out evil in its many forms. Please grant us patience. Let none here speak falsely that we do not all see the lie in the words. In nomine sancte precor, fiat voluntas tua." He raised his hands, prayer beads with a gold sun-cross twined through his fingers, and the candles around them burst into flame.

The priest nodded to Hector.

The Espian turned to Dodz. "No lies between us this night. We saw the display you left in Aislinn's bedroom. Did you do that before or after you went wandering in Brand's cave system?"

"I did no such thing, comrade."

"Don't lie to me. We saw man-sized tracks in the sand, and someone plundered his treasures."

"It was not me," Dodz replied. "I was not even aware the dragon's lair is accessible from the fyei suka's house."

Gideon leaned closer to the bounty hunter. "Hector, he's not lying."

Hector eyed the count. He seemed calm for someone who sat naked in a room full of enemies. In fact, Hector had to give the man credit. The first question resulted in him learning something rather than Hector. Score one for the count.

"Did you have a hand in the attack on Brand and desecrating the mountain?"

Dodz laughed. "You give me too much credit. None of that was my work. Ask yourself, why would I care about the dragon?"

"I have been asking that very question," Hector replied. "You know as well as I that fire was the perfect distraction."

"Too unpredictable," Count Dodz said, leaning back.

"Then who started the fire?"

The count neither flinched nor batted an eye. "I do not know. Prayhaps the fyeì I killed near your dead half-breed's home."

Even without Gideon's prayer, Hector knew the count was telling the truth — or what he believed to be true. He stepped back and forced himself to calm. The count's voice and smug look grated on Hector's every nerve. All he wanted to do was punch him in the throat. "What elf?"

"You have seen the dærganfae. They serve the *vampir*."

"Which vampire?" Xandor cut in.

"Mi'dnirr," Dodz spat. "He is your enemy, too. Ymara called him 'Lord of Plagues' and brother. Like her, he seeks freedom, but I think their ideas of such differ." Dodz looked up at Hector and gave him a wolfish smile. "Together, we could pit one against the other and be rid of them both. The enemy of my enemy, no?"

Hector grabbed hold of the chair, tipping it back on two legs. "Is that what you think this is — us working together? Ruthaer is still a fresh wound, Count, or whoever you are. Maybe we should treat you the same way you treated my friends." Hector stepped back, and the chair dropped onto its front legs with a tooth jarring thump. "By the way, that dærganfae you stabbed yesterday is not dead."

For a precious moment, Dodz' smug expression slipped, replaced by surprise.

"Talk to us about Lady D — Ymara. Did she bite you before or after you put her and that clockwork spider on your ship?"

"She did not —"

All around them, the candles flared red.

Hector backhanded the count.

"After," Dodz answered and spat blood. The circle of candles returned to their normal, golden glow.

"Where did you learn the symbols that you carved on the crate you emptied?" Xandor asked.

"What symbols?"

"The same ones you created in the windowsill of the cabin you're hiding out in, and in Aislinn's room at her mother's house."

"I do not know of what you speak," the man replied. His eyes narrowed in what looked like suspicion. Around them, the candles remained unaffected.

"Hector, look at this," Jasper called. On the table with Dodz' gear sat a footlocker.

"Where did that come from?" Robert asked.

"It was a charm on Dodz' platinum bracelet. When I removed it, the chest grew to full size." Jasper stepped back from the table and used his staff to flip open the lid. When nothing exploded, he edged closer and peered inside.

"Well, what's in there?" demanded Hector.

"The Orbuculum and its stand, a wooden box with a stag-head crest, and some potion bottles."

"Check the box for an ivory dagger," Hector said.

The mage gingerly lifted the narrow box past the orb and slid aside its lid. "Interesting."

"Jasper, everyone here knows the kinds of things you find interesting. Should we start running?" Xandor asked.

Jasper grinned at the ranger but shook his head. "Not this time." He turned the box so his companions could see its contents. Intricate carvings covered the ivory blade. "The carvings are part of a powerful abjuration spell. You said this belonged to the dærganfae?"

"That's what I was told," Hector confirmed. "Abjuration... that's related to banishing demons and such, right?"

"Usually," Jasper said. "However, it can also be used for protection — or containment."

Hector turned to their prisoner. "That dærganfae you stabbed... is this what he wanted?"

Dodz stared at him in stony silence.

"Answer the question, Dodz."

"No. Is time for you to untie me. We get down to tacks of brass."

"I have no intention of untying you," Hector said.

"You will untie me if you want your archer friend and his pornai to live. We have been talking for a while, maybe too much."

All around them, the circle of candles burned with a steady, golden glow.

CHAPTER 50
SMOKE DAMAGE

August 19, 4237 K.E.

9:10pm

𝒟ave woke slumped over on his left side, the rope digging into his right arm. Mercifully, Ymara's voice was gone, but now the smoke was thick all about him, and he had trouble breathing. He leaned his head down toward the floor as far as he could and drew in a shallow breath. Under the haze of smoke, he saw the five wine bottles in the rack, but he'd have to reach the hearth to break one. One of Hummingbird's boots lay beside the empty crate with a dagger he could use to cut himself free... if he could only reach it.

He tried his bonds, and sharp pain from bloody rope burns coursed through his arms. The feeling of nausea grew in the pit of his stomach. Grimacing, he tried again and felt the left arm of the chair give. Fresh blood trickled down the rope, making it sticky.

The dagger was so close.

Head almost to his knees, Dave jerked forward with his left arm as hard as he could while twisting with his right. The scar on his back pulled and burned, but the heavy chair rocked. He jerked his arms again, rolling with the tiny motion of the chair. For one precarious moment, the chair teetered on two legs, then crashed over sideways. Dave's head hit the floor. When his vision cleared, Hummingbird's boot was inches from his fingertips, but it may as well have been miles.

The front door crashed open, and a bright flash lit the room. Dave looked up from his struggles against the chair into a pair of quicksilver eyes.

Magic crackling around his hands, the dærganfae gestured, and the thick smoke began to churn, drawing itself up toward the ceiling, where it spun like a hurricane. He seemed to take in the room with a single glance and strode to the fireplace. Prying loose the medium-sized stone above the corner of the mantle, he let it fall to the floor with a crash, revealing the empty cavity in the chimney wall.

The dærganfae spun on his heel and glared down at Dave. "Where is the ivory dagger?"

"Go fuck yourself," Dave gasped.

In one swift motion, the dærganfae drew a long, narrow blade. Black as pitch, it glistened with red flecks like sword stolen from Brand's hoard. He pressed the tip to Dave's throat. "Worm, that blade is a talisman. Until we recover it, Mi'dnirr roams free. Tell me where you hid it, or I will end your worthless life."

Roger Vaughn charged through the open door, flinging knives as he came. Blood crusted the nobleman's temple and left ear where someone had hit him.

The dærganfae darted away from Dave, avoiding the projectiles.

Unsheathing long-bladed daggers, Roger met the dærganfae head-on with one in each hand. He caught the black sword between them and shoved the dærganfae away. The two slashed at each other as they parted, both missing their target.

Overhead, the smoke stopped churning and began to settle toward the floor once more, billowing this way and that as Roger and the fae fought.

A second fae shoved open the cliff-side window shutters and climbed inside. He was tall and thin, with the same jet-black hair and silvery almond shaped eyes as the first. In his hand, he carried a longbow.

Dave's mind reeled under an onslaught of memories from the night his mother died. Adrenaline pounding in his veins, he yanked on his restraints. Cursing, he pulled his arms toward his torso and shoved against the chair back. With a loud crack, the chair shattered.

Dave shook his hands free from the loosened rope and flung a chair arm at the fae with the bow. It struck the dining table with a loud clatter, and the fae ducked.

Caught in a wave of memories and emotion, Dave pushed up on his knees and snatched a wine bottle from the rack. He held it by the neck, waiting. The moment the fae archer crept into sight around the end of the table, he threw the bottle as hard as he could and lunged for Hummingbird's dagger.

The bottle hit the fae with a meaty thud, eliciting a snarl and what sounded like a string of curses.

Dave's heart fluttered and beat erratically. Pushing back up onto his knees, he twisted to face the fae archer. The invader had a thick arrow aimed at Roger's back, its black broadhead arrow glistening with oily residue.

"Not this time, bastard." Dave whipped the dagger at his opponent and dove toward the hearth, where Hummingbird's other boot lay.

The blade lodged itself in the fae's throat, and his body jerked as he loosed his arrow, sending it wide of its target to strike the cabin wall.

Near the front door, Roger dodged another blow, snatched a vial from his belt, and flung its contents into the fae's face.

Flesh sizzled. Screaming, the fae dropped his sword. His fingers dug at his face as he fell to his knees.

Roger drove his remaining dagger into the fae's chest, twisting it to be certain the dærganfae was dead.

Dave's stomach clenched, and he swallowed back the bile that rose in his throat. Using the dagger from Hummingbird's other boot, he cut the ropes binding his legs and stumbled to the couch, watching Roger. Despite the open door and window, smoke still hung thick in the air.

"Son, are you alright?" Roger asked. Fresh blood trailed down from his scalp, and his chest heaved from exertion.

Dave swallowed hard and nodded. "You?"

"Dizzy," Roger replied, "and my heartbeat feels wrong."

"It's the oleander in the smoke. We need to get out."

Together, they made their way to the door. Dave paused to stare at the smear of white sand. Even if he knew the word Dodz used, he couldn't make the sand work now. Muttering a curse, he pushed Roger out onto the porch and dashed upstairs to retrieve his weapons and the herb bag.

"Gimme your shirt," Dave said when he returned.

"Why?" Roger asked.

Enough light spilled from the cabin behind him for Dave to see Roger's eyes were unequally dilated. "Don't argue, old man. Give me the shirt. You have a scalp wound and poison on your skin. We need to wash it off, so you don't die."

Roger plunked down on the steps and pulled his shirt over his head. Bryony's platinum and sapphire locket hung against his chest, a shimmering reminder that this man was Dave and Robert's father.

"Where's Hummingbird?" Roger asked.

"Dodz took her."

Dave dunked the shirt in the rain barrel at the corner of the house and brought it back dripping. He wrung it out over Roger's head, then wiped his face and hands, and rinsed the shirt. The wound above Roger's temple continued to bleed. "Damn it. Hold this on your head."

Returning to the rain barrel a third time, Dave dunked his arms, head, and torso. The cool water helped clear the cobwebs from his head. Dripping wet, he tromped back to the porch steps, not nearly as steady as he wanted to be. Another wave of nausea swept over him. Roger sat slumped against the banister, his eyes closed.

"Wake up, old man! Don't you dare die."

Roger opened one bleary eye and stared at Dave. His breath came in ragged gasps.

Swearing, Dave sat on the edge of the porch and picked up the herb bag. "Belladonna," he muttered, and flipped open the bag's top. He considered Roger's symptoms and held out a single leaf. "Here. Chew this twice and swallow the juice, then spit out the leaf." He watched to make sure Roger followed his directions, then dosed himself.

"Ugh," Roger complained, "what was that?"

"Medicine to counteract the irregular heartbeat. Are you nauseous?"

"A little. Mostly tired."

"Give me a minute." Dave pulled peppermint and a piece of ginger root from the herb bag for their nausea. "Chew these," he said, offering half to Roger before stuffing his own share into his mouth. While he chewed, Dave considered his options. What they really needed was Turkestani kahve to get their blood moving, but there wasn't time for someone to brew it. Then he thought about maté and coca leaves. Both were used for tea in some places. In short order he had a handful of each. The coca leaves were smaller and less waxy. Choosing the four smallest, he gave them to Roger.

"Last thing, for now. Chew these. They'll give you energy."

Selecting several for himself, he popped them into his mouth, and chewed. At first, the pungent juices made his mouth feel warm. When he realized the inside of his mouth was going numb, he spat the mass into the grass and instructed Roger to do the same.

Five minutes passed, then ten. Finally, Dave's stomach settled. His pulse increased, energy spread through him, and his mind slowly cleared.

"I'm going to find Hummingbird. Can you walk?"

"I feel better," Roger said, but as he rose to his feet, he lost his balance, and had to grab the rail.

"Come on. Looks like you have a concussion. Let's get you to the hospital."

"What about you? You inhaled a lot more smoke than me."

"I'll live," Dave said. Climbing back onto the porch, he pulled the door closed, then stripped a red vane from one of his arrows and fed it into the lock. Hector and Robert would recognize the warning and stay out of the house if they returned before he found them.

Weapons settled in place, he and Roger staggered toward the hospital, each leaning against the other.

CHAPTER 51
BARGAINING CHIPS

August 19, 4237 K.E.

9:25pm

Hector leapt forward, the point of his dagger pressed into the tender skin under Dodz' chin, forcing the man's head back. "What have you done?"

Count Dodz bared his teeth in a silent snarl, but his ice blue eyes held a look of triumph.

"¡Asqueroso hijo de puta! What did you do to Dave and Hummingbird?" Hector shouted.

"Hector," Robert said, "you have to move the blade for him to talk."

Dodz stared at Hector, ignoring the others around them. "Untie me. Give me the mask and my possessions, or they both die."

"You're not getting the mask," Hector said. The candles that circled them held a steady golden glow.

"Let's drag him out of here and take him back to your house," Robert said. "For all we know, they're already dead. If they are, I say we kill him right then and there."

Hector turned to the swordsman in shock, unused to Robert being as bloodthirsty as Dave. After a moment, he said, "No, you and Xandor go check on them. I made a deal with Lord Vaughn. When he leaves here, Dodz goes to jail." He pulled a key from his pocket and held it out to Robert. "You'll need this. Let us know what you find."

The ranger and the swordsman raced toward the stairs at the far end of the Aerarium.

"Tick tock, bounty hunter. The lives of your friends are in your hands."

Hector leaned close to Dodz, his face eye level with the Count. "We're in Ozera — not Ruthaer, and not Erinskaya. These people won't give a damn if I kill you right here." The candleflames around them turned red.

Dodz smiled. "Lie. Prayhaps you would like to try another empty threat? We both know you need me alive. The only way to save the archer and his pornai is to do exactly as I say. You're not the one in charge here. You never were." The candlelight turned gold.

Hector turned to Gideon, doubt worming into his confidence. "Can you make him talk?" When the cleric shook his head, he turned to Jasper. "What about you? Anything to make him magically tell us everything?"

"No. I wish I did, though."

"Give me the mask and my things," Dodz said.

"Forget the mask. You aren't getting so much as a breechclout until Lord Vaughn approves it. Tell me what you did to Dave and Hummingbird," Hector demanded. "Jasper, is there any proof Dodz was in my house?"

Jasper dug through Dodz' clothing and belt pouches. Seconds ticked by. The mage let out a sharp gasp. In his hand, he held a short lock of fine, crimson hair. The expression in Jasper's eyes said it all. He sniffed the hair, eliciting a quick cough. "It smells funny, like sweat and some type of drug. Dave might know what it is, but I don't."

"Was it poison?" Hector shouted at his prisoner. "Answer me!"

"You know my demands, bounty hunter."

Hector eyed the candles, and the steady glow. He flicked the tip of his dagger across Dodz' cheek, drawing a thin line of blood from his mouth to his ear. The bounty hunter's stony exterior hid the frustrated rage building inside him. He pressed the dagger tip against Dodz' other cheek. In a tone as cold as ice, Hector said, "I heard a rumor you have a black diamond, and Mi'dnirr wants it. Why would a vampire want a gem like that?"

"I don't know what you mean." The candles turned red, and Hector slashed his blade across the Rhodinan's face, leaving a second, deeper gash.

Hector lowered his dagger, pointing it at Dodz' crotch. "Lie to me again, pendejo. I dare you."

Sweat broke out on Dodz' forehead and trickled down to mix with the blood dripping onto his bare chest. "I... I do not know what he intends to do with it." The candles faded back to normal.

"Where is the diamond now?" Hector asked.

Dodz stared at Hector with hate filled eyes and remained silent.

"Let's go." He jerked Dodz to his feet, but left his hands bound.

"Where?"

"I'm going to tie you to my horse and drag you through the streets until you tell me what I want to know."

"Hector, stop!" Gideon commanded. "Think about what you are doing. You can't torture him, no matter how much he deserves it."

"That's up to Lord Vaughn," Hector replied.

"I have a feeling Père Phaedrus will have a thing or two to say about what we do to him," Gideon replied.

Dodz' attention shifted to Gideon. "For my possessions, I will tell you why the dærganfae seek the ivory blade. For my life and freedom, I will tell the name of the man offering me a small fortune for the Espian's head in a jar of vinegar. For the mask, I will tell you the name of the poison."

"No," Hector said. "I don't care why the dærganfae want the dagger. It's enough to know that they do. As for this person you say wants me dead, he can get in line. Tell us what you did to Dave and Hummingbird right now."

One corner of Dodz' mouth curled up in a smile that never reached his eyes. "I'll give you this for free, bounty hunter. Mi'dnirr took your half-breed shlyukha in Ruthaer's graveyard." The color drained from the faces of Dodz' audience, and he laughed. "Even had the priests called her back to life, she is no longer yours.

"The time will come when you will be forced to make a painful decision, as did Sir Courtenay. Tell me, bounty hunter, who will you turn to in that darkest hour?"

Although he knew Mi'dnirr had bitten Aislinn, the words still hit Hector with the force of physical blows, and his imagination conjured an image of Aislinn as a ghūl.

"I promise you will live long enough to reach the gaol," Gideon said to Dodz. "Gallowen's judges may look on you more favorably if you cooperate."

"My life, my freedom, and the mask, priest, or you get nothing."

Hector scowled. "Come on, Dodz. I have someone I want you to meet."

Dodz glared at Hector, his jaw set.

"Hector?" Gideon asked.

The Espian rounded on the cleric and said, "We're running out of time. We want information, and Caballo has a lot of excess energy. Who knows, the count may even enjoy it." He looped a chord around Dodz' neck and jerked it tight.

"No," Gideon said, his face red. "I will not allow you —"

"Get out of my way, Gideon," Hector demanded.

Outside, Hector pulled Dodz around the library and onto a narrow path. Under a hemlock tree, Caballo stood, saddled and ready. Jasper and Gideon followed in tense silence. The buckskin stallion, for his part, snorted at the naked prisoner and gave the man a knowing look.

Hector tied the end of Dodz' leash to the saddle horn.

"Hector, you can't do this," Gideon sputtered.

Dodz' eyes darted from man to man.

Talking to Caballo, Hector said, "Sweetgum trees, rose bushes, brambles, poison ivy, sharp rocks. I want you to find as many as you can between here and the gaol. Take your time."

Caballo bobbed his head and pawed the ground, eager to start.

"You have to stop this," Dodz pleaded to Gideon, eyeing the dark path with obvious fear. Fresh blood seeped from the wounds on his face.

"It's out of our hands," Jasper replied, carrying the sack with Dodz' possessions. "Only Dave or Aislinn has ever been able to stop Hector when he gets crazy like this, and neither one of them can help you, now, Count. You should tell him what he wants to know."

Dodz swallowed.

"Time's up," Hector snapped and slapped Caballo on the rump.

The stallion reared and lunged.

Dodz stumbled after the horse, barely able to keep upright.

Caballo pushed his way into the underbrush, dragging his prisoner behind him. The bushes whipped against Dodz, leaving dark stripes on his lily-white flesh.

"Stop, beast!" Dodz shouted.

The horse neighed in response, and another limb slapped against bare skin.

Dodz hissed in pain and muttered a stream of curses in Rhodinan.

Hector, Gideon, and Jasper followed along the path, listening. Caballo circled a short spruce, dragging the Rhodinan through the prickly needles the entire way, then lunged in a different direction.

Dodz uttered a strangled cry and fell with a thud.

Hector and Gideon pushed their way through the bushes to stand beside Caballo, who looked down at his prisoner in disgust. Dodz sprawled beside the Akhal-teke, his eyes rolled back into his head.

Gideon *tsked* as he shook his head and helped Hector lift Dodz over Caballo's saddle. "I think the two of you scared him."

"That was the point," replied Hector. "El cabrón was supposed to give us answers, not pass out."

"You and Jasper, take the mask and get out of here," the priest replied. "See to Dave and Hummingbird. If Dodz talks, I'll let you know."

"Watch him," Hector replied. "He still may have a trick or two up his proverbial sleeve."

Gideon took the sack of Dodz' personal effects from Jasper and hoisted it over his shoulder. Before he turned away, he told Hector, "By the Eternal Father, Dodz will pay for his crimes. I shall see to it."

Caballo snorted and shoved the priest's shoulder with his head. Gideon eyed the horse but corrected himself, "We both will."

CHAPTER 52
RESISTANCE

August 19, 4237 K.E.

9:40pm

The heavy pounding in her head forced Hummingbird awake. Her entire body ached, and she wanted to curl up and sleep until it went away.

Dust that smelled of elderly humans and pine oil crawled in her nose, and she sneezed. Only then did she realize she was lying on the floor, naked but for the ropes binding her hands and feet. The room was dark and silent. She reached out with her sixth sense, searching, but found no one nearby.

How long had she been unconscious? The last thing she remembered was being sick and someone coming to the door, Dave's sudden rage, then... blackness.

The girl struggled to sit up with her hands tied behind her back. A tether led from her wrists to the heavy post of a bed frame. Moonlight peeked through a crack in the curtains on the far side of the room, giving her just enough light to make out furniture shapes, but no fine details.

She pulled herself up against the side of the bed. The acrid scent of unwashed human male filled her nose and she recoiled, fighting visions from her past. The stink clung to her skin, stronger than the lavender in her bath soap. She screamed but could not tell if the sound was aloud or only in her head. Fear gripped her heart. It felt like there wasn't enough air. The room spun as she writhed on hard boards, kicking and tugging on the ropes that held her down. Her head whipped side to side and tears fell, hot and heavy.

Eventually, her muscles seized up, curling her into a ball, too terrified and exhausted to move. Her body forced her to be still, but she couldn't rest. Her mind conjured images of the day her village was attacked, the elders and children who were cut down as they ran, of the sister that died in her arms.

Dave's voice cut through her panic. *'Hang in there, kid. I'm coming.'* He sounded so close.

She opened her eyes and drew a deep breath, held it for a few seconds, then let it out slowly. There was no one here, now. She needed to calm down and get out of these ropes.

Scooting until her back was against the bedpost, Hummingbird pushed up into a crouch. The tether was knotted in a groove of the post, preventing her from standing. She wriggled and twisted, contorting her thin frame until she managed to get her backside through the circle of her arms and bound wrists. The skin on her arms was raw and bruised by the time she got her legs untied.

Muscles quivering from fatigue, Hummingbird wondered what had been in that tea. She rested her head on her knees and her mind drifted.

Sudden loss of balance jerked her awake. She had no idea if she'd slept or for how long.

Twisting her wrists this way and that, she tried to stretch the rope and felt the burning warmth of blood seeping into the rough fibers. She pulled harder, desperate to be free, but the rope only dug deeper into her skin. Panic threatened to overwhelm her again, and tears stung her eyes. She angrily swiped them on her upper arms.

The tether brushed over her bare feet, and she froze in place, the obvious answer hitting her with the force of a slap. Her fingers traced the rope to the knot, tight against the bedpost. The shadows were too dark to see the path of the binding, even with her elf vision, forcing her to work slowly, by feel alone.

It felt like hours passed before she finally loosened the last twist and felt the rope come free from the bed. She stood on shaky legs and surveyed the bedroom. The night air was cool on her bare skin. She shuddered to think what happened while she was unconscious. A satchel on the bed proved to be full of fancy clothes that reeked of man sweat. She backed away and opened a cabinet. The scent of cedar and roses washed over her. A thin dress and a man's jacket hung in a narrow space beside shelves with a few tunics and a pair of pants that were too big for her. She briefly wondered what had become of the people who belonged to those clothes.

Hummingbird wanted her hands free, and she needed a knife for that. Dim light seeped through a tear in the curtain serving as a door and guided the way into the living area. A small pile of coals glowed in the hearth, illuminating a wooden bench with threadbare cushions beside a low counter. Plates and bowls rested on a shelf over the sink, and two chairs in a corner of the room flanked a table bearing a single lamp with a stub of yellow candle. The people who lived here had few possessions.

Hummingbird turned back toward the hearth, where a hint of light winked at her from the oily looking pommel stone of a curved knife resting on the mantel. Her heart lurched and relief spilled through her. The hearth stone was warm under her bare feet as she stepped up and grasped the black wire-wrapped hilt. Aislinn's gold oak-leaf necklace and Dave's brooch lay beside the weapon.

Fearful of being caught, she grabbed the jewelry and knife, then dashed back into the bedroom to crouch behind the large bed. She pressed the sheath between her knees and pulled free the black blade. An image of the creature in the quarry tunnels flashed in her mind's eye, and she nearly dropped it.

Hummingbird clamped down on her fear and turned the blade on the ropes binding her wrists together. In less than a minute, she was free.

She fastened Aislinn's necklace around her throat, then pulled a tunic and pants from the cabinet, thankful that they didn't carry the same vile scent as the bed and satchel. A length of rope served as a belt to cinch up the waistband and hang the weapon's sheath at her hip.

She spun the knife in her hand, and the pommel stone touched her palm. A wave of dizziness assaulted her, and Hummingbird felt her consciousness slip sideways.

CHAPTER 53
EMPTY NEST

August 19, 4237 K.E.

Xandor and Robert stopped at the edge of the yard and stared at the cottage. The shutters hung open, and the pungent stench of smoke hung in the air. Light spilled out the window, giving them a clear view. Dark patches of water stained the porch floor, and the doorframe was warped and splintered near the latch.

"Looks like someone left something in the keyhole."

Robert strode around the end of the porch for a closer look. "It's a red feather — Dave left that so we wouldn't go inside — and someone overturned the rain barrel."

"Maybe it was Dave and whoever left here with him," said Xandor, pointing to water stains on the porch. "Looks like one bathed and poured water over the other before they headed off toward town."

"Hummingbird and Dave?" Robert asked as Xandor knelt in the grass by the porch.

"No. Two men."

"Probably Dave and Earl Wolverton, then," replied the swordsman.

The ranger lifted a masticated wad of green leaves on the end of his dagger and gave it a tentative sniff. "Peppermint and ginger."

Robert climbed onto the porch and peered in the window. "What the... Dave managed to break free and kill two elves."

Xandor hopped the porch rail and joined him. When he saw the bodies, he tensed and let out a low growl that sounded more feline than human. "Dærganfae." The ranger spat the name like a curse. "Good riddance."

"There's white sand behind the door. Do you think they were working with Dodz?"

"I doubt it. They're probably after him, too." He pointed near the hearth. "Hummingbird left here without her boots."

Robert took in the room's disarray and the exposed hiding place above the mantle, wondering if it was Dodz or the dead fae who found it. Staring out into the surrounding darkness, he twisted his signet ring and clenched his fist on the embossment, searching for Dave. "One thing's for certain, Dodz is going to wish he used something stronger to poison Dave."

"Why didn't he kill him outright?"

"He was counting on us — specifically Hector — to trade that mask for Dave's life." Robert gave a half-hearted laugh. "He couldn't know that Dave has enough poison in him already to fill an apothecary. He's been experimenting and building up tolerances to things since we were kids."

Xandor shook his head. "Anybody ever tell you he's crazy?"

"All the time." Robert glanced at the ranger. "If Dodz or the dærganfae took Hummingbird, Dave will tear this town apart looking for her. Can you follow him in the dark?"

Xandor made a chuffing noise. An answering chuff echoed from the trees uphill. "Let me introduce you to Sahmaht."

CXEO

9:40pm

Dave stood between the two rows of dark cabins, trying to decide which one he should try first. Neither had stones stacked in the window.

He stepped up on the short stoop of the left-hand house and pressed his ear to the door. Silence greeted him. The knob turned easily in his hand, and the door swung open to reveal a single room containing a pair of beds and a square table with two chairs near the hearth. Striding across the room, he shined his lantern into every corner and under the beds. Hummingbird wasn't there.

Dave bumped against one of the chairs, snatched it up, and threw it against the wall.

In the darkness, he heard Hummingbird scream. Overwhelming fear and panic flashed through him, as if Hummingbird was projecting inside his head the same way she'd shown him what happened to Brand/Eidan.

'*Hang in there, kid, I'm coming,*' he thought. The lanky archer flew out and across the road to the other cabin. Not pausing, he aimed a sharp kick beside the knob, and the door burst open. This cabin was a mirror of the first, with only one difference: a circle of sand lay between the two beds.

Rage consumed him. Voicing an inarticulate yell, he smashed the table and chairs against the fireplace, followed by his lantern. Oil gushed from the base, igniting the broken furniture. Dave snatched the covers from the beds and piled them into the sand circle, then plucked a burning chair leg from the impromptu pyre to light the blankets.

"Come back to that, fucker."

The fire flickered and danced in tongues of orange and yellow. It reminded him of Aislinn's hair blowing in the storm winds off the Carolingian coast. Dave closed his eyes and shoved the memory deep into a crack in his heart. Tears welled, and he dashed them away, angry at his momentary weakness. He hadn't cried since Tilly died when he was twelve, and he wasn't about to start now.

His skin prickled as sweat seeped from his pores. It took him a minute to understand heat from the spreading fire was affecting him. Brow furrowed, he held up his left hand. Rather than his obsidian ring, Jasper's silver ring with its kite shaped emeralds glittered on his index finger.

Overwhelmed by a sudden wave of dizziness, Dave stumbled toward the door. Glittering blackness ate his vision. Before he could stop himself, he collided with the doorframe.

CR80

9:50pm

After Gideon and Caballo left with Dodz, Hector took a moment and used his signet ring to find Dave and Robert. They were both down in the village but not at the hospital, and not together. He frowned. Dodz must have taken Hummingbird rather than simply poisoning her, and Dave was out there searching for her.

Dave was going to kill him if Dodz hurt Hummingbird.

Hector hitched the knapsack containing the two arcaloxós higher on his shoulder and turned toward the path home. After only a few steps, he stopped and swore softly.

"What's wrong?" asked Jasper.

"Dave. He knows where I hid the mask. If I take it home and the box's wards deteriorate like you said, it will be too easy for him to get his hands on the mask and run amok."

Jasper pointed back at the library. "Take it to Sisters Lorena and Georgiana. They're still there, working on repairing the damage Dodz did to the Aerarium's back door. No one will sneak in that way again. Let them lock away the mask like you were supposed to do in the first place."

Indecision gnawed at Hector, and he shifted from one foot to the other. "We don't know that Dodz is the only person looking for the mask. What if someone else breaks into the Aerarium?"

Jasper sighed. "Hector, what Dodz did was unprecedented, and the priests are going to do everything they can to prevent it from happening again. You need to acquire a little faith and trust."

The bounty hunter made a face. "And a little pixie dust, I suppose."

"Beg pardon? What are you talking about?"

"Never mind," grumbled Hector. "Let's get this over with. I have more questions for Dodz."

Disculpi Humberto led them down to the white room behind the scriptorium, where Librarius Georgiana and Armarius Lorena worked on the Aerarium's secret door. A toolbox sat to one side, its lid open. While Lorena worked with hammer and chisel to remove the device Dodz affixed to the doorlatch, Georgiana chanted and held her wheel-cross aloft. A glowing orb of azure, amethyst, and ruby light emanated from the holy symbol, surrounding the two women and the door.

Hector and Jasper waited silently until the two clerics completed their task, then the bounty hunter stepped forward. "Hermana Georgiana, will the Aerarium be secure when you're done?"

"It will be as secure as it was before Count Dodz followed Brother Simon inside. In a few days, after El Patrón is fully recovered, we plan to add several more layers of protection to both entrances."

Hector nodded, and Jasper nudged his elbow.

When the bounty hunter neither spoke nor moved, Sister Georgiana asked, "Was there something else?"

"Come on, Hector, give her the mask," said Jasper.

Hector struggled to keep his distrust from showing in his expression as he knelt and removed the arcaloxós from his knapsack. He lifted the unlocked lid of the empty box, then handed it to Jasper. After checking that the second box containing Lady D's mask was secure, he rose to his feet, clutching it with both hands. "This isn't easy for me, Hermanas, especially after everything that's happened."

The clerics nodded their understanding. Georgiana stepped forward and gripped the other end of the arcaloxós. "We'll keep it safe."

Hector couldn't bring himself to release the box. He feared for Dave's safety and sanity. He worried about Dodz' employers in Erinskaya sending others for the mask.

Sister Georgiana did not try to pull the box from Hector's hands. Instead, she waited silently while he made his choice.

Jasper placed a hand on Hector's shoulder. "Let it go, Hector. I'll be back here tomorrow and however many more days it takes until we find a way to break Lady D's hold on Dave."

Hector reluctantly removed first one hand, then the other from the silver box. Before he could change his mind, he spun on his heel and stalked from the building.

Away from the library and on the road to the gaol, Hector finally spoke. "Jasper, what do you think of making Hummingbird an official member of Damage, Inc.?"

Jasper gave a non-committal shrug. "Have you asked Dave or Robert?" When Hector indicated he hadn't, Jasper said, "After tonight, she may not want anything to do with our lot ever again."

"That would be alright with me, if she chose a safer profession, but if she decides to stick with us, I want her to have a signet ring in case she goes missing again."

"If Dave and Robert agree, it'll take a couple of weeks to have one made," Jasper said, "but I'm amenable if they are." He paused. "Are you thinking about giving her Aislinn's ring in the interim?"

"No. Sister Inez agreed not to remove Aislinn's signet ring while they figure out why they haven't been able to revive her. With dærganfae lurking around Ozera, Mi'dnirr is probably close by. If anything happens to Aislinn, I want us to be able to find her."

"Thank the Eternal Father that Brand insisted on that diamond casket and keeping her with his hoard," Jasper

said.   He refrained from mentioning the alternative —
Aislinn's mother could have followed the elven custom of
cremation.

CHAPTER 54
UPRISING

August 19, 4237 K.E.

10:05pm

Hummingbird barely had time to register the glittering blackness of the walls and floor before someone grabbed her from behind.

"You will not use me again, asshole," a familiar voice hissed in her ear. An arm covered in warm, metallic scales snaked around her throat, cutting off her air.

Hummingbird wrapped both hands around the arm at her throat and pulled for all she was worth. "Aislinn?" she gasped aloud.

The arm dropped away, and the other presence receded. Hummingbird turned and froze. Bronze scales covered Aislinn's skin, and the brown flecks in her green eyes now had a metallic shimmer. Even her pupils were narrower, more oval. She thought of the dragon that turned into a boy, and realized, to some extent, Aislinn had become a dragon.

"Hummingbird?" The stunned look on Aislinn's face turned suspicious. "You can't be. Hummingbird doesn't talk." Her fists came up, as she backed away, leery of an attack.

"I am Hummingbird," the younger elf signed. "What is this place?"

"This is a magical trap," Aislinn responded. "If you're really Hummingbird, tell me where we stayed the night before we arrived in Ruthaer."

The girl shivered. "There was a storm," she signed. "We slept in a cave with a huge dragon skeleton. She was Brand's mother."

Aislinn sagged to her knees. As her fists unclenched, and her anger faded, so did the scales on her skin. "I was beginning to think I'd never see a friendly face again."

Hummingbird eyed the other girl. "You told me a secret the morning after the storm. What was it?"

"Hector, Dave, and Robert aren't from Gaia. They're Terrans." Aislinn smiled. "Let's sit." Her face scrunched in concentration, and the black stone around them transformed into Aislinn's bedroom.

Surprise washed through Hummingbird. "It's like the Dreaming Grounds." Her soft voice carried through the room, though her lips didn't move. She sat beside Aislinn on the giant floor cushion and reached for her hand. "I don't know an easier way to tell you this... you died."

Aislinn sighed. "Dodz told me, but I hoped he was lying."

Hummingbird shivered and drew herself into a tight ball.

"You didn't know about Dodz?" asked Aislinn as she wrapped an arm around Hummingbird's shoulders.

The plains elf shook her head. "The last thing I remember, I was drinking tea, and Dave was teaching me letters. I felt sick... then nothing. I woke up tied to a bedpost in an empty house. I don't know where it is or how I got there."

Anger clouded Aislinn's features. "Dodz must have taken you, but I don't see how, if you were with Dave."

"Dave was tied to a chair."

"*What*?"

Hummingbird quickly summarized what she knew of the mask, the attack on Sunrise Chapel, and Hector's plan to capture Dodz.

Aislinn hung her head. "Poor Brand. I wish I could see him, talk to him, again. Did they scatter my ashes from Sunrise Chapel?"

"No one burned your body," Hummingbird replied. "Brand wouldn't let them."

Aislinn tipped her head to one side. "What did they do with it?"

"I heard Brand has it in his caverns — in a diamond casket."

"Ugh... I think he listened to one too many bedtime stories when we were children." Aislinn shook her head. "So, how did you get here?"

"I found a knife with a black diamond pommel stone, like the quarry monster's eyes. When I touched the stone, it brought me here."

"The eye of chaos," murmured Aislinn. "I'm surprised Dodz left it unattended."

Hummingbird worried at one corner of her lip, then asked, "Aislinn, if Dodz has me, what did he do to Dave?"

"I don't know, but we're going to find out."

"How?" asked Hummingbird. "No one knows I'm here, and I don't know how to get back."

"Dodz is staying in or near Ozera," Aislinn replied. "I can get you home, but I need to ask you a huge favor."

"What is it?" Hummingbird asked.

"Don't tell Hector or Dave I'm in this stone. Go to Phaedrus. Ask him to find a way to free my spirit so I can pass on to the afterlife. If he can't get me out of the stone, he can lock it away in the Aerarium."

"No! Why would you ask me to do that?"

"Because if Phaedrus restores my spirit to my body, Mi'dnirr will use me against everyone I care about."

Hummingbird shook her head. "I can't — I *won't* make a promise like that. Eidan needs you. Plus, your death is slowly killing Dave and Hector. They need you, too. You and I both know they won't give up until you're safe from Mi'dnirr."

Aislinn sighed. "At least see Phaedrus first. Let him decide how to handle things. For now, let's focus on getting you back home. I know every inch of ground around Ozera, so you aren't anywhere close to lost."

"How are you going to guide me from in here? I don't want to stop and meditate at every turn. If Hector's plan didn't work, Dodz might be back any minute."

"You won't have to stop, just stay in contact with the stone. I've been practicing on Dodz, giving him suggestions to do things."

"Did you make him slash your drawings?"

"Yes, and I've made him leave messages for Xandor all over town." Aislinn gave a vicious grin. "He doesn't realize he's doing it, either."

"Let's go, then. I'm worried about Dave."

"I am, too. Alright, you said the stone's attached to a knife? Is there a sheath?"

"Yes. I'm already wearing it."

"Tuck it inside your clothes. That should hold it against your skin and keep your hands free."

Hummingbird felt a rush as her mind left the construct in the stone. When she came to herself, she breathed a deep sigh of relief — she felt Aislinn's presence the same way she could sense the presence and emotions of people nearby.

She leapt to her feet and sheathed the blade. It took time she didn't want to spend trying to position the curved knife, and nothing felt comfortable. In the end, she settled for tying it to her stomach with the blade pointed up, wrapping the rope around the sheath multiple times until the stone pressed into her navel.

Barefoot but dressed, Hummingbird raced from the bedroom and snatched open the cabin door, ready to dash out into the night. She was greeted by a shape in the doorway. The rank scent of sour olives, garlic, and sweat assailed her, and she fell back.

"Well, well. It seems I returned just in time," Dodz purred. "You must learn your place, pornai." He stepped into the room and slammed the door.

CHAPTER 55
SEARCH

August 19, 4237 K.E.

10:10pm

A light burned in the constable's office when Hector and Jasper arrived, but the door was locked. Staff in hand, Jasper walked to the building's corner and shined a light down the alley in search of another way in. Hector peered through the barred sidelights but couldn't see anyone. A game of cards lay unfinished on the desk.

Hector knocked at the door. When no one answered, he knocked again.

"Hector!"

The bounty hunter turned to see Lord Vaughn striding toward him. "Milord, I thought you were with Dave."

"He left me at the hospital a little while ago. I'd have been here sooner, but they had trouble with Deputy Gilliam earlier. It seems he escaped."

"Damn," Hector replied, "I forgot about him. He didn't show up at the Aerarium."

"Where is Dodz?"

Hector gave Roger a quick rundown of everything that happened since they captured Dodz. "I came here to force Dodz to tell me what he did with Hummingbird. Thing is, no one is answering the door."

"You told Gideon to keep a constant guard, didn't you?"

"I did," replied Hector. "I don't know where everyone is." He pounded on the door again, harder this time.

"Can I help you?" a voice asked from the street.

Hector, Roger, and Jasper turned to find a stocky man with sleepy eyes staring at them over a pair of steaming mugs.

"We're looking for the constable or Brother Ignatius. We need to speak to Brother Gideon and the prisoner he brought in a little while ago," Hector said.

"The constable and Brother Ignatius have both gone home for the night. I'm Deputy Reiner. Who are you?"

Hector gestured as he made introductions. "Earl Wolverton, Magus Thredd, and I'm Hector de los Santos."

The deputy paled, then made a quick bow to Lord Vaughn. "The prisoner's inside, Milord."

Hector stepped down from the narrow wooden stoop and approached the deputy, hands open in front of him. "Deputy, it's a matter of some urgency. A young woman's life is in danger, and Count Dodz is the only person who knows where she is."

The man nodded and sat the mugs on the porch rail to unhook a ring of keys from his belt. "Come on in. I insisted Brother Gideon take his crazy horse to the stables. It tried to come inside the office with him!"

"Then what are you doing outside, deputy?" Roger demanded. "I gave strict orders for this prisoner to be guarded at all times."

"Leyton's holding down the fort," Reiner said. He led Hector, Roger, and Jasper into the office. "Leyton, I'm back!" Reiner called. Silence greeted them.

The deputy took a gulp from his mug and grimaced as the hot cider burned his mouth. "He's downstairs with the prisoner. I'm afraid we're ill equipped to handle real villains."

"Dodz is restrained?" Hector asked.

Reiner nodded. "Of course. Brother Gideon made sure he was bound and shackled."

"Perfect. We won't be long."

The deputy eyed Hector nervously. "I should go with you. I'll have to write up a report on the interview for you to sign."

"That's fine, deputy," Hector said. "I'll sign anything you want, but the girl Dodz kidnaped comes first."

"Yes, yes, of course." Deputy Reiner unlocked a door on the back wall of the office, revealing a set of stairs down to the basement. Hector took the lead, gliding down silently, back close to the wall.

As he dropped below the level of the main floor, the open basement came into view. There were no bars, no cages, just shackles bolted around the wall above wooden benches. On the far side of the basement, wide, shallow windows looked out at ground level.

Hector stopped on the last step and visually swept the room. In one corner, a spray of glass shards led from the broken window there to a body flung carelessly in the opposite corner.   Deputy Leyton gazed sightlessly at the beams and boards above them.

CR&

10:10pm

Face twisted in a grimace of pain, Dave pressed the heal of his hand to the throbbing lump on his forehead. Although he wasn't bleeding, he'd probably have one hell of a bruise. Gripping his longbow, he made his way outside and turned in a slow circle, but his connection with Hummingbird had gone silent. He found himself staring into a pair of huge, glowing, golden eyes in the center of the road leading back toward the hospital. "Shit..." he whispered, reaching for a black arrow.

"Dave!" a voice called from the same direction.   It sounded human, but the huge glowing eyes indicated otherwise.

Raising his bow, he nocked an arrow and trained it on the human form advancing from the darkness. Passing the creature with over-sized eyes, the figure resolved itself into Robert.

"Don't shoot." He held up his hands as he approached. "Hector's plan worked. We caught Dodz in the Aerarium."

"Is he dead?" Dave growled.

"No, we saw Gideon and Caballo delivering him to the jail on the way here."

"Stop there. How do I know you're really Robert?"

"You owe your swear jar thirty-seven silver pieces for the curses you spewed at Hector this evening before we left for the library," the swordsman replied. "Xandor and I came to help you look for Hummingbird."

"Shit."

"Thirty-eight," said Robert.

The arrow lowered, but Dave still held it nocked. "Xandor, come out where I can see you!"

The ranger appeared from the shadows off to Dave's right, forcing the archer to turn his back to Robert and the thing with glowing eyes if he decided to shoot. "Put away the arrow, for now," Xandor said. "Sahmaht won't hurt you."

"What the hell is it?"

"She's a Parlathean lion. The Akshan sent her. She's here to help." The ranger made a deep purring sound, and the lioness glided into the pool of light spilling from the cabin at Dave's back.

Dark honey-colored stripes and rosettes dappled her tawny fur, like an overgrown tabby cat. From the tip of her nose to the base of her tail, Sahmaht was at least seven feet long, and four feet high at the shoulder. Dave estimated that she weighed somewhere in the neighborhood of eight-hundred pounds.

When the cat sat beside Xandor and he rested his hand on her shoulders, Dave finally slid the arrow back into the quiver at his hip. Behind him, the tiny cabin groaned, and a section of roof collapsed, shooting sparks into the air.

Robert ran forward and pulled the archer into the roadway. "Dave! Why did you set the building on fire? What if the fire spreads?"

"Dodz took Hummingbird, Robert. She's out there, right now, scared out of her mind, and I can't find her!"

"We'll find her together," Robert assured him. "We can go to the jail and beat her location out of Dodz."

Dave gave a curt nod. "Fine, but I want that cat where I can see it."

"Where's Lord Vaughn?" asked Robert.

"Dropped him off at the hospital. Someone bashed him on the head, then he got his lungs full of poisoned smoke keeping those fae bastards from killing me. Where's Hector?"

"Gideon said he and Jasper went to hide the mask."

"Just for the record," Dave said, "Hector's dumbass plan nearly got us killed."

"I know," Robert replied.

"Hummingbird may not recover from this, Robert. If Dodz hurt her —"

"We'll see that he never hurts anyone ever again. Come on. Standing around here isn't getting us any closer to finding Hummingbird, and we need to rouse the bucket brigade."

"We can do that," Xandor said. He made a low rumbling sound to the cat at his side. Suddenly, she let out a roar that rattled nearby windows. As soon as the echoes died, the ranger drew in a deep breath and bellowed, "FIRE!"

Down the street, a light flared in a window, and a door banged open. Voices shouted, and more lights appeared.

"Time to go," Xandor said.   One hand on Sahmaht's shoulder, he led Dave and Robert south into the darkness. "We can skirt around the stable yard and hop the stream."

Several minutes later, the big cat stopped. She growled at the ranger, who knelt and pulled a light from his belt pouch. He seemed to reply to the cat, and it growled again.

"Looks like Dodz had help after all. Sahmaht just caught a whiff of him and another man," Xandor said. He pointed his light northwest. "They went that way."

CHAPTER 56
REVOLT

August 19, 4237 K.E.

10:10pm

Hummingbird backed away from Dodz, hands up in front of her chest, palms toward him.

'*Don't be afraid,*' Aislinn whispered.

But she was afraid. Outside of sparring with Dave using practice blades, she'd never actually fought anyone — if you didn't count ghosts. Her eyes darted around the room. There was nowhere to run.

Her heart beat frantically, and her stomach churned.

Dodz slid the bolt on the door and leered at her. "You belong to me now, pornai."

The petite girl shook her head, desperately trying to shake away the aggression, lust, and rage-fueled vengeance assailing her as she backed across the room. He followed her, body slightly crouched, and arms held wide, ready to grab her if she tried to dart past.

'*Hummingbird, fight him,*' Aislinn urged.

She tried to focus on Aislinn's voice in her mind, but Dodz' emotions overwhelmed her. Hummingbird's back hit the wall, and she gasped.

Dodz rushed forward and grabbed her upper arms, pinning her in place. He leaned forward and breathed in the scent of her, his blood-crusted cheek skimming along hers.

The girl cringed and turned her face away. The past and present crashed together, and Hummingbird fled to a dark corner of her mind, hiding from the pain she knew would come.

CR&D

Aislinn had faced dangerous, deadly situations throughout her life. No matter how bad a situation, though, she had never despaired. She always *knew* she had help if she needed it. Brand, Hector, and Dave would always come for her. Nothing, no matter how awful, had ever taken away her last sliver of hope.

Hummingbird had lost her hope with the death of her family, and she hadn't yet learned to trust Dave or Hector.

Rage for the past pain her friend experienced and that which threatened the girl now blazed through Aislinn's spirit. She reached for Hummingbird and drew her close.

"Fight him," Aislinn demanded.

"I can't," she whispered. "He's too strong, too close."

"You have weapons, use them!"

"I can't."

"Bite, kick, use the knife!"

The girl wrapped her arms around her stomach. "I don't want to hurt anyone. Dave was right. I can't win."

"What are you talking about? Why would he tell you something like that?"

"He said I panic, and then I can't think, can't fight."

"Then stop panicking! Think! If you don't fight Dodz, he's going to take the knife back, then we'll both be alone with him. He will use us to kill Dave and Hector."

Hummingbird met Aislinn's gaze. "How am I supposed to fight him?"

CRSO

10:15pm

Hummingbird's eyes snapped back into focus, with Dodz' face mere inches from her own. He held her wrists above her head with one hand and groped her breast with the other.

She closed her eyes and whipped her head forward, smashing her forehead against his mouth and chin. She was rewarded with a surprised curse and a backhanded blow that threw her to the floor.

"Suka! You're going to regret that." He wiped blood from his chin with the back of his hand and turned to the mantle. His eyes widened. "What did you do with the Akkilettū blade, little pornai?"

Hummingbird crabbed backwards across the floor.

'Get up,' Aislinn urged.

The girl rolled just as Dodz lunged, and she felt his fingers graze over her back. She rolled again, coming up on her feet. She managed one step toward the door before his hand clamped around her ankle.   Hummingbird fell headlong, hands out to stop her crash onto the floor. A sharp tug from behind, just as she hit, shot her arms out from under her body, and her head slammed against the boards. Stars danced in her eyes.

'*Kick! Use your heel.*' Aislinn's voice was loud in her mind.

Hummingbird turned on her back so she could see the man rising onto his knees. He pulled on her ankle again, dragging her closer. Her shirt rode up over her waist, exposing the bottom edge of the black diamond. She drew up her free leg and kicked out at his waist.

Dodz twisted to the side and trapped her leg under his arm. He jerked her toward him again and pinned her thighs under his knees. When she tried to sit up, he shoved her back down with a hand in the center of her chest. He leaned on her one handed and punched her in the gut with the other. The air whooshed out of her lungs.

"This is mine," he snarled. He grasped the hilt at her waist, careful to avoid the gem on its end, and pulled the knife free of its sheath. His eyes shone with cruelty as he drug the tip across the soft skin of her belly, leaving a thin line of blood in its wake.

Despair glistened in her eyes.

He lifted the knife, letting it catch light from the coals in the hearth. The black blade absorbed the single drop of her blood on its tip. "That was almost fun," he said. "Now it's my turn to choose the game."

CHAPTER 57
HUNTERS

August 19, 4237 K.E.

10:15pm

Hector crossed to the bench below the broken window and studied the spray of glass, dirt, and grass on the floor. "He didn't go out this way," he said. "Someone came in and helped him escape." He pinched the bridge of his nose. "Dave's going to kill me."

"What happened to your thumb, Hector?" Roger asked.

The bounty hunter glanced at his hand to discover half his thumb was bright blue. "El Patrón's idea of a moral compass. Apparently, my methods in the Aerarium tonight were a bit extreme by Phaedrus' standards."

Hector saw the corner of Roger's mouth twitch before the nobleman spun on his heel and ascended the stairs. Jasper grinned.

"Come on," Hector said. "We should catch Dave and Robert outside. I'd hate for Dave to get arrested for wrecking the constable's office."

Roger sent Deputy Reiner to wake the constable and round up more guards to search the town. While they waited, Hector checked his ring to see how close Dave and Robert were getting. Instead, they were farther away.

"Milord, Dave and Robert must have found a clue to Hummingbird's location, or Xandor happened across Dodz' trail."

"Where are they?"

"Heading northwest."

"The millpond is in that direction," replied Roger. "Lead the way. They may need our help."

"Jasper, stay here and wait for Gideon, then the two of you follow us."

CR80

10:20pm

The cat led them northwest, trotting past a cluster of

farm buildings. This late, no light shone in any of the windows. Insects fell silent at their approach, resuming their songs long after the hunters had passed. All too soon, they reached the edge of the village.

The moon waxed toward full, nearing its zenith. Pale silver light slid through early autumn leaves, dancing in spots across the trail and through the thickening forest. The cat turned onto a side trail that wound uphill, and for a moment, the moon dappled her coat. A faint hint of wood smoke caught Dave's attention, but he couldn't tell if it was new or from the fire two nights before.

The sudden shriek of a screech owl sent the hunters into a mad scramble for cover and weapons before they recognized the sound. The lion gave a rumbling growl in return, and the bird fell silent.

"Is she sure he came this way?" Robert asked Xandor as they returned to the trail.

The cat looked to Xandor to translate, then cast a narrow-eyed glance at the swordsman before resuming her hunt.

"I don't think Sahmaht appreciates your doubt," Xandor replied. They hadn't traveled much farther when the cat gave a short series of sounds, then sneezed. The ranger listened to the lion, then signaled a halt. "She smells death near here." He pointed into the trees. "Through there. Recent." The ranger drew his swords. "Aduro," he murmured, and flames raced up the blades.

Dave and Robert followed the ranger and lion into the trees almost one hundred yards before they, too, smelled the coppery tang of fresh blood. The great cat led them to a body sprawled in the leaf litter. Whoever left it didn't bother digging a grave. By the light of Xandor's burning blades, they could see that it was a young man, and the blood on his shirt still wet.

"Looks like Dodz killed his partner," Xandor said. "Sahmaht says this is one of the men we've been following."

An image of Dodz attacking Hummingbird flashed before Dave's eyes, and her scream echoed in his mind. For a moment, he thought he heard Aislinn shouting for her to fight. He leaned against a nearby tree, his fists clenched. "We're wasting time."

Robert and Xandor shared a worried glance. "Are you okay to go on?" Robert asked.

"We need to get to Hummingbird. *NOW!*" Dave snarled.

"Xandor, you heard the man. We can send someone back to find this poor sod in the morning."

The ranger nodded and cut blazes on a few trees as they backtracked.

The cat led them onward. The trail split, and the cat didn't hesitate, taking the fork that led farther uphill. Five minutes later, they found themselves standing on the verge of a fifty-foot drop overlooking a dark cabin near a broad pond. The sound of water flowing over a low dam carried on the still night air.

"What the fuck, Xandor?" demanded Dave.

CHAPTER 58
WHATEVER IT TAKES TO WIN

August 19, 4237 K.E.

10:20pm

Dodz leaned forward, pressing against Hummingbird's chest, until she thought he would crush her. The tip of his nose glided over her throat to the pulse point below her ear, inhaling her fear as he went. His wet tongue slid up the line of her jaw to her chin, then he buried her mouth under his. She felt his teeth dig into her bottom lip and pull, bruising without quite breaking the skin.

Her fists beat at him, but he ignored them.

He finally pushed back onto the balls of his feet, then lunged up, dragging Hummingbird to her feet by a fistful of tunic. He pressed the black blade under her chin, the sharp point just below her ear. She tilted her head back, exposing her throat, both avoiding the blade and giving him an easier target.

She kept her eyes closed, not wanting to look into his face.

"You will only wear what I give you, pornai," he hissed in her ear. "Remove the pants, now, or we will see just how much pain you can take."

Hummingbird quivered with fear. Shaking hands fumbled with the knotted rope at her waist until it loosened, and the voluminous fabric collapsed to the floor around her feet, leaving only the tunic between her and the man who smelled and sounded too much like a Flainnian slave master. Nausea churned in her gut. She tried to think what she could do to escape, but her mind fluttered and beat in a hundred frantic directions.

Satisfied for the moment, he tugged on the tunic twisted in his fist and pulled her toward the bedroom. He drew her close against him and walked her through the curtain backwards and up against a bedpost. "Put the rope and the sheath on the bed."

Tears leaked from the corners of her eyes and dripped from her chin onto the knife and his hand. Shivering, she did as he commanded.

"Open your eyes and unbutton my shirt." She didn't move fast enough to please him, and he gave her a rough shake. "I'm going to take great pleasure in using you, girl, while Santos spends the rest of the night raging over the death of your former master."

Hummingbird's heart turned to stone in her chest, and her eyes met his. The dim light from the other room made his pale blue orbs glitter like frozen pools in midwinter, and she could feel his malicious joy.

Aislinn was right about Dodz, and Hector would be next. Suddenly, she understood what Dave had been trying to explain about fighting earlier. *Whatever it takes to win.*

One by one the buttons slid free. Swallowing back the bile rising in her throat, she let the fingers of one hand trail back up his stomach to his chest.

Dodz released the front of her tunic to grab her wrist. His eyes never left her face as he shoved her hand to the front of his pants. He didn't have to tell her what he wanted. The musky scent of his lust permeated the air.

Hummingbird tugged on the laces at Dodz' waistband, letting the pain and memories of the past well up in a bitter wave. Trembling fingers moved lower while her eyes watched his face.

His eyes slid closed.

Her hand jerked up. Although it broke the First Law of her people, she slapped her palm against his bare chest, and shoved every horrible memory, every ounce of pain into him.

Dodz screamed. The Akkilettū blade clattered to the floor and his hands grasped his temples, trying to push her from his mind. He collapsed to his knees, and Hummingbird followed him down.

Her foot bumped the dropped weapon, and she fished for it with her free hand. Her fingertips brushed the stone and, for a moment, Aislinn's thoughts touched hers. Hummingbird's concentration slipped, and Dodz fell forward, pinning her to the footboard of the bed.

His breath came in ragged gasps even as rage burned in his eyes. Shoving his hand up between them, he grabbed

Hummingbird's throat and pushed back, sitting up and locking his elbow to keep her still.

She reached out desperately, fingers of one hand scrabbling to grab the knife while the other pulled on Dodz' fingers cutting off her air.

His eyes turned to the floor, and his free hand slapped hers aside. The hand choking her jerked her away from the blade. Dodz' face twisted into a harsh snarl as he brought up the weapon. "I'm going to skin you alive," he spat, "and leave parts of you scattered for the bounty hunter to find."

Hummingbird grabbed the hand holding the knife in both of hers. Black spots danced in her vision. She struggled to push the blade away. One hand slid against the black diamond, and Aislinn's consciousness flooded into her mind, burning with rage. Images flashed from Aislinn to Hummingbird.

The girl suddenly stopped pushing against Dodz' hand. Instead, she pulled hard, using his strength against him to pull the blade past her body and under his other arm, slicing into the muscle between his elbow and wrist.

Dodz hissed in pain and jerked his arm back, trailing a stream of blood.

She drew a shuddering breath.

He rocked back on his heels and surged up, dragging the girl in his wake.

The Akkilettū blade rose between them, his fist still tight around the handle. Her hands locked around his, one over his hand and around his thumb, the other under and around the stone. Hummingbird struggled to turn the blade away.

His free hand flashed up and slammed against her ear, snapping her head forward. The point wavered.

Their bodies crashed together, and the blade sank deep into soft flesh.

CHAPTER 59
RESCUE

August 19, 4237 K.E.

10:30pm

The lion only paused a moment to make sure the three men were following her before descending narrow steps cut into the cliff face.

Robert's light swayed over the stone, adding to the bright moonlight. The pitch was steep, and there was no handrail. They moved slowly in the cat's wake, shoulders brushing stone. The cat bounded across the yard and around the cabin when they were a little more than halfway down. By the time they reached the bottom, she was back.

Sahmaht growled, and her tail lashed in anticipation. Her ears swiveled toward the cabin.

Xandor nodded to Robert and Dave. "How do you want to go in?" he asked.

Dave didn't answer. He simply stalked across the grass toward the house.

"I guess he's going for the direct approach," Robert replied, racing after Dave. He caught him just before he rounded the corner toward the house's pond side.

Longbow slung across his back, Dave unsheathed his sabre and peered around the corner at the porch. A pair of rocking chairs sat together on the near end, away from two windows and the door.

Robert waved to Xandor, who followed Sahmaht around the house in the other direction. In less than a minute, they made a full circuit.

"No other door," the ranger murmured. "One window facing the cliff, couldn't see through the curtain. I could hear movement."

"He'll have the door locked, maybe warded," Robert replied. "Windows are the best option." Shuttering the lantern, he drew his main gauche before stepping lightly up onto the wide porch and easing over to the pair of windows. Both the fixed tops and the movable bottom panels were divided into nine panes by narrow wooden lathes. He pressed the tip of his blade under the window and tried to lever it up, but the window wouldn't budge. He stepped closer to the glass, looking for the locking mechanism. A length of wood as thick as his thumb wedged into each window held them closed. Shaking his head, he turned toward the door.

"Fuck this shit!" Dave leapt onto the porch, grabbed one of the rockers, and slung it through the window in a shower of glass and splintered wood. He swept his sabre through the remaining glass shards. Not looking back, he snatched the curtain aside and stepped through the opening into darkness punctuated by the glow of coals in the fireplace.

Robert followed more cautiously. Glass crunched underfoot as he crossed to the door, slid the bolt aside, and pulled it open for the ranger.

The thud of a body landing hard vibrated the floorboards.

The bowman ran the last few steps to the curtain on the far wall and ripped it down.

In the dim light spilling around him, Dave spotted a pair of boots lying at the foot of a wide bed. He charged over and found Dodz sprawled atop Hummingbird.

With a roar that rivaled any lion's, Dave grabbed Dodz by his hair and threw the man backward. Following Dodz' trajectory, Dave extended into a full lunge, and his sabre skewered Dodz' heart before the man even hit the floor. Not satisfied, Dave repeatedly stomped and kicked the hated villain.

Lantern light bathed the room. "Dave," Robert said, warily approaching the enraged archer. "He's down, man. You got him."

Only then did Dave see Dodz' sightless stare.

"Is Hummingbird alright?" Robert asked.

Dave turned his back on Robert and the dead man. A glossy black knife lay on the floor underneath the elf-girl's limp hand. The coarse fabric of a blood-soaked tunic clung to her thin frame. His sabre dropped from nerveless fingers, and he fell to his knees beside Hummingbird. "Not again," he choked.

He stroked her hair with one hand and pressed trembling fingers to her throat, above the ugly bruises darkening her amber skin.

Her pulse beat strong under his fingers.

For a moment, Dave sat frozen, as much surprised as relieved. He grabbed the hem of the tunic and peeled the wet cloth away from her stomach, then ran a hand over her belly. Blood pooled in her navel, but he only found a long, shallow scratch.

"Dave, I think your little bird found her talons," Robert said. "Is there a blade over there?

Dave glanced over his shoulder to find the swordsman kneeling beside Dodz' body. "Yeah, a wicked looking knife."

"He's been gut-stabbed. Looks deep."

The archer turned back to the girl, laid his longbow and quiver on the bed, and scooped her up from the floor. "Stoke the fire and see if you can find her a clean blanket or some clothes."

"Where are you going?"

"To wash off that asshole's blood."

Dave almost collided with Hector and Roger on the front porch.

The bounty hunter backed away under the ferocity of Dave's glare. "Amigo, I'm sorry. How bad is she hurt?"

Dave shook his head. "She'll live, no thanks to you and your dumbass plan." He pushed past Hector and off the porch.

"Where is Dodz?" Roger called after him.

"Dead," Dave replied without looking back.

❦

10:45pm

Hummingbird drifted toward consciousness. The smell of smoke mixed with the beeswax and lemon oil Dave used on his longbow filled her nose. For a moment she thought, perhaps, she'd fallen asleep on the couch waiting for Hector to return and had a horrible nightmare. The feel of bare skin under her cheek, and arms cradling her killed that hope.

Water splashed and the person carrying her slowed his pace. The sudden chill of water around her feet and legs elicited a startled gasp, and her eyes flew open. In the moonlight, he looked like Dave, but Dodz said he was dead... Maybe she was dead, too.

"We aren't dead," Dave answered her unspoken question. He eased her onto her feet in the waist deep water.

Voices echoed across the pond, and she saw Hector on shore, along with Xandor and a huge lion. She glanced up at Dave.

"Wash the blood off. Robert's going to stoke the fire and look for a clean blanket for you to wrap up in." He backed away, giving her space, but she dove forward and wrapped her arms around his waist.

Dave froze, shocked by the sudden close contact, unsure what to do. Hot tears poured from her, and her slim frame shook. Slowly, he brushed one hand over the top of her head. When she didn't flinch or shy away, he continued to stroke her hair.

"You did good, kid," he murmured. "Dodz can't hurt you, or anyone else, again."

THE END

Author's Note:

Back in 1993, when Jason, Alan, and I were in varying stages of our university careers, we spent almost every Saturday night gathered around a battered coffee table, consuming unhealthy quantities of pizza, chips, and Mt. Dew, telling each other adventure stories and slaying imaginary monsters. At some point that summer, we realized our beloved characters had grown so powerful that the game was no longer a challenge.

Each of us wanted not only new characters, but something different from what we'd played before. We wanted them to be less perfect and more real. Men and women who struggled, not only against monsters and injustices, but in their personal lives as well.

Initially, there was no Damage, Inc. There was simply Hector (a boy who dreamed of being an infamous bounty hunter), Dave (who only spoke in growls and curses), Robert (who spent most of his time trying to keep Hector and Dave out of prison), and Jasper (a jovial fellow who engaged in creative cooking and spellcraft.) The four of them had something of a gift for mayhem, wreaking havoc everywhere they went and causing no end of problems for the city council of Rowanoake. Aislinn and Brand came into being almost a year later. Oddly enough, she, too, had a propensity for getting arrested.

The characters and their backstories have grown over the years. They've experienced both amazing and horrible things and responded in like kind. None of the characters you'll meet in the *Chronicles* are perfect, and we hope that you, dear reader, will feel that makes them all the more real.

Thank You for Reading!

We hope you've enjoyed this adventure with Damage, Inc. as much as we enjoyed bringing it to you! No author would be where they are without readers, so please accept a HUGE thank you for taking a chance on our endeavor. Whether you loved it, hated it, or landed somewhere in between, it would be of immense help to us, as well as other readers, if you would take a moment to leave a review on Amazon and/or Goodreads. Even a single sentence will mean a lot.

We love to hear from readers! Feel free to drop us a line at mcdonald.isom@gmail.com Let us know what you loved (or what you hated). If you have questions about the story, we'll do our best to answer them. For more information about cultures, countries, creatures, and races of Gaia, visit the glossary on our website, www.mcdonald-isom.com. You can also find us on Facebook, @McDonald.Isom.author.

There are more adventures yet to come!

Acknowledgements

No book is ever truly a one (or two) person accomplishment. As always, special thanks to our children, who not only put up with our storytelling obsession, but gamely participate in brainstorming sessions, offer pearls of teenage wisdom, and inspire us to always strive to be better versions of ourselves. Thank you as well to our editor, Dana Isaacson, for your questions, words of wisdom, and sage advice. Last, but certainly not least, to our beta reading team, who take time out of their busy lives to tell us what they really think.

About the Authors

Jason McDonald

An engineer by day and world builder by night, Jason is an advocate for using both sides of the brain.

With his stepfather as a guide, Jason traveled the worlds of Edgar Rice Burroughs, Robert E Howard, and JRR Tolkien at an early age. As he grew older, he discovered Dungeons and Dragons and the joys of creating his own campaigns.

During all this, Jason embarked on a career in engineering, graduating from Clemson University, and now owns a successful engineering firm. Still a practicing engineer, he continues to design a wide range of projects. His attention to detail and vivid imagination helps shape the various adventures that challenge his characters.

Stormy McDonald

Born in the midst of a thunderstorm in the darkest hours of a solstice morning, Stormy has been told she has a personality to match: full of sound and fury, and highly unpredictable. Coming from a family of storytellers — traditional, oral storytellers, that is — it's little wonder that she's driven to weave words as well.

She can't remember a time when she didn't love books — from the feel and smell of the pages, to the information they hold, to the tales that they tell — but storytelling is a labor of love, which doesn't always pay the bills. A ridiculous variety of side jobs have supported her writing habit, including waitress, security guard, library minion, salesperson, hairdresser, handyman, engineering drafter, and small business owner.